Route of S·D· [...]
from East Point to the
BATTLEFIELD
OF SEPT. 1

CHANGED
A4449880B

W9-CNY-971

McPeak

M&W.R.R.
4TH

14TH A.C.

Warren
CLE[...]

Dep[...]

JO[...]
⊕ Chu[...]

[...]LD
[...]RO

AUG. 31–SEPT. 1

1864

The Far Side

of Home

MAGGIE DAVIS

The Macmillan Company, New York

✍ Acknowledgments

The author wishes to acknowledge the generous help of the following gentlemen in preparing background material for *The Far Side of Home:* Colonel Allen P. Julian, U.S.A. ret'd., Director of the Atlanta Historical Society, and a foremost authority on Civil War military affairs; Mr. Wilbur G. Kurtz, artist, mapmaker and Civil War historian, technical advisor for the motion picture version of *Gone With the Wind;* Dr. Bell Irvin Wiley of the History Department of Emory University, author of *The Life of Johnny Reb, The Life of Billy Yank,* and *They Who Fought Here.*

Verses reproduced as chapter headings are taken from *War Songs and Poems of the Southern Confederacy,* collected by H. M. Wharton, D.D.

Newspaper excerpts are from the December issues of the *Augusta Constitutionalist,* 1863.

Second Printing

The Macmillan Company, New York
Collier-Macmillan Canada, Ltd., Toronto, Ontario

Library of Congress catalog card number: 63-14191

Printed in the United States of America

DESIGNED BY RON FARBER

CHAPTER 1

Ah me, the rain has a sadder sound
    than it ever had before,
And the wind more plaintively whistles through
    the crevices round the door.

Lately the bad thing about waking up was that he always found himself somewhere dismal. In the past two years he couldn't hardly remember a single time that he had waked up and found himself satisfied, much less even pleased, with where he was.

He could tell there was nothing in this particular time, either, that would make him hopeful it was going to be any different. Since he was sitting upright, he guessed he had slept that way all night again.

He had been sleeping with his head thrown back and his mouth open, too, he discovered, for his tongue was like a piece of flannel and his teeth, when he tried to pull his lips down over them, were as dry and numb as pebbles.

Damned if he wasn't afraid to look.

I've gone and done it again, he told himself. This time, I can't even remember where I'm supposed to be . . . or rather, I know where I'm supposed to be . . . I'm supposed to be home, and I know damned well this isn't it.

He opened his eyes, and it was so dark that he thought for a moment that something terrible had happened to his eyes. But they were all right. It was just dark as hell wherever he was, that was all. A yellow lamp burned over a door, and the wick was turned so far down the light was just a button-hole of brightness.

1

He was in a little dinky, dust-smelling railroad car that had some kind of imitation cut-velvet seats that were worn down to the threads, and tattered window shades at windows so dirty you couldn't even see out of them.

"If you boys are going to Carolina," a voice said in the back of the car, "you'd better lift yourselves up out of here and get going. This train's going out to the yards, and it's not going to wait for you, you know."

He squirmed around in his seat to see who was back there, and found it was twice as dark as sin in the back, with only another little oil lamp left burning over the rear door. He thought he saw somebody standing there in a dark suit like the conductors wore, and it seemed he was bending over one of the seats trying to rout someone out.

"If you want to go to Carolina," the voice back there said, "then you boys are on the wrong railroad. You want to get off this train and go across town and get the Carolina Railroad at the depot on Washington and Reynolds Streets. That's your connection. This is as far as the Georgia Railroad goes."

"Goddammit, conductuh," a voice cried that was still thick and glued together drunkenly, "you mean we ain't got to Greenvul yet?"

There was some sort of shuffling around back there . . . he really couldn't see on account of the lack of light, and another head came up out of the seat and looked around.

"This line don't go to Greenville, that's what I'm telling you," the conductor's voice said. "You take the Carolina Railroad at Washington and Reynolds Streets. Now, are you sober enough to get up? How's your friend over there?"

"Goddammit, conductuh, he's no friendamine, he's some goddamned cavalryman as drunk as I am. Ain't you, you sonofabitch?"

Greenville? he thought. Where the hell am I, anyway?

He bent over to the window and tried to see out, but the pane was so dirty it reflected like a black mirror.

2

He saw the specter of his own face hanging in it, and that was all.

He stared at himself. Well, he thought, he was on the wrong train. There was no place that he could think of that he was supposed to be in the middle of the night at the end of some damned railroad line where everybody had to get off because there wasn't any farther you could go.

He was, as he remembered it, supposed to be home in Jonesboro by the middle of the afternoon of some day or other. He guessed it must have been yesterday. Or at least, he told himself, he damned well hoped it was yesterday or sometime fairly recent.

It was pretty bad, alright, just as he had expected.

It seemed to him, now that he tried to buckle down and think about it, that he had been fairly drunk in the Atlanta railroad station on account of the whiskey that the bugler, Bobby Hart, and that lank devil of a Texan from Hood's brigade had insisted on buying when the train stopped at Kennesaw.

And he remembered the reason he had been so drunk was that he had somehow considered it a bounden duty to drink up most of the whiskey, as the bugler was just too confounded young to drink a whole quart of whiskey all by himself, being only fifteen years old and not half as tough and hairy as he thought he was. He remembered thinking that it was a person's duty to see that a fifteen-year-old bugler didn't start off his Christmas furlough by landing on his family waiting for him in Atlanta dead stone drunk and making a fool of himself.

But, he also remembered gloomily, it seemed to him the bugler had been dead-drunk anyway, in spite of everything he could do, by the time the train got to Atlanta. If he recollected rightly Bobby had been as stiff-legged as a stork and hiccuping a hailstorm when they turned him over to his father, with Mr. Hart calling down eternal damnation on the Texan and himself for leading his son into paths of evil, which made the Texan laugh like hell.

Well, he had been pretty sorry about the whole thing, that was the truth. Fifteen was too young to be getting poisoned up on bad whiskey. It wasn't so damned funny, and he remembered telling the Texan so.

"I ain't goin'ta get off this here train til we get to Greenvul," the drunken voice in the back yelled.

"Aw, shuddup, Tom," a new voice said.

Then somebody else evidently came in back there, for the door slammed, and still another voice started joining in.

All the racket made him jumpy.

Well, he told himself irritably, he sure as hell couldn't hang around where he was. There was a crowd collecting by the sound of it, and all of them noisy as the very devil.

He searched around in the seat and got up all his gear, the Enfield, his hat, bedroll, and the rest, and noticed with some small satisfaction that evidently he hadn't been too drunk to look after his things. There was nothing missing. He found the stub of the railroad ticket in his hatband and pulled it out and tried to read the infinitesimally small printing on the thing to find out where he was, but it was too dark to see.

"Better get that other one out up there," one of the voices said.

But he was already half out of his seat and on his way.

If he hadn't been impressed with it before, he was certainly impressed with the fact now, that all railroad stations look exactly the same at night. It was a big station, that was all he could tell, so apparently he was in a town of some size. If there was a sign telling the name of the place down on his end of the platform he missed it, and to make matters worse, he was in such a hurry to get away that he got out on the wrong side of the train, the trackside instead of the walkway. Since it was hellishly dark he thought, in the first few minutes, that he had only got out far up on the end of

4

the train where there wasn't any platform, but after he had gone a good way in that direction he realized he wasn't going to join up with the platform at all; he was going in the opposite direction out of the sheds and into the train yards.

God, he wasn't doing anything right, it looked like!

In a fit of discouragement he kept right on until he came out into the open where the sky was much lighter than he expected, rather pale in spite of drizzling rain.

What time was it, anyway? Not night. Not as dark as he thought it was at first.

Four o'clock? Five o'clock?

No, he corrected himself, it would be later than that in December. Winter light was late.

He stooped to slip his arm through the bedroll and get it on his back and admitted to himself sourly that he didn't know what time it was and, considering the circumstances, didn't know that it mattered one damn bit.

He had four dollars and thirteen cents in his jacket and a canteen full of fresh water—(he guessed it was full; he hadn't bothered to check it lately)—which he carried out of habit, and his army gear, a pass for three-weeks' Christmas leave, and he was lost, baffled, and still sleepy in some town he didn't even know the name of—out in the damned railroad yards, too; he couldn't even make the right turn into the station. He wasn't making much progress.

He felt so bad just thinking about it that for a second he thought he was going to have a sickish spell, just when he had thought they were all over with. He had had pneumonia at Dalton in November, and every once in awhile a green, queasy feeling took him by surprise. Just weakness, the surgeon had said.

Weakness or not, he could just as soon do without it.

He snatched at his jacket so as to pull it across his chest. One bout of pneumonia a winter was enough. He had nearly died at Dalton. The trouble was, the damned jacket

5

was only army shoddy, half-wool and half-cotton and not enough of either, and so loosely woven that it soaked up the cold and damp like a sponge.

He cursed the thing routinely, hardly thinking about it, and shivered.

The cold seemed to him ten times more piercing than it had any right to be. The car must have been warmer than most, to make such a difference.

But the air did look cold, in spite of the rain. Every time he breathed out a white cloud hung in front of his face and cold sparks flicked along the metal rails and the little ragged ballast stones between the ties that had flecks of mica in them. Now and then the drizzle would stir with a gust of air and clear the view ahead for a few feet. He heard an engine somewhere moving slowly, the bell ding-dinging, and he stepped off the tracks, but it didn't come his way. It gradually faded off.

It was a mournful, dismal damned place, wherever it was.

And then he came up on a switchman poking at the tracks so suddenly he nearly fell over him, the switchman all done up in a carpet-coat and a long knitted muffler wound over his head.

The switchman put down his prod and just stood there, looking at him.

"Mornin'," he said.

"Morning," he told him. "Is there a road around here?"

The switchman lifted his arm.

"Right over there. Can't miss it."

He told him thanks. For the merest, shortest moment he was tempted to ask him what city or town this was, but he changed his mind. You meet a person out stumbling around the railroad tracks in the morning, he told himself, and he asks you what town this is, when the station's probably got signs hung all over it, what would you think?

He wasn't going to be taken for a perfect fool.

Ahead in the drizzle there was a fieldstone wall and be-

6

yond that a road with high banks covered in old dead Johnson grass stalks. A big building like a warehouse ran off to the left, and right in front a line of mule wagons were trying to back up to a stone pier to unload, the Negro drivers talking and laughing and running around, some of them with lanterns held up shoulder high in the fog. All of them making as much racket as they could, having a damned good time, it sounded like. No white people in sight.

"COLE, Lor, ain' ih COLE," he heard. "Nevah seen ih this cole to be so spittin' rain!"

He almost stepped on somebody sitting on the wall, holding a lantern between his legs.

"Say boy," he said, "what town is this?"

"SAH?"

He tried to keep his voice down, so the others wouldn't hear or notice him in what was going on.

"What do you call this place?"

"SAH?"

Oh, for God's sake! He didn't know what it was going to take just to find out a simple thing like where he was.

He jumped down from the stone wall into the road and picked his way across the ruts to the far side where he could see, when he had gone midway, that there were a row of stores over a boardwalk and a light in one place with lettering on the windows that said Connally's Saloon. He went straight for it, in such a hurry he missed the first step up to the walk and nearly fell. The Enfield slid down his arm, and the bedroll came with it. He had to stop and get it all shifted back before he could go farther.

The walkway in front of the stores was covered with a tin shed roof, and the light rain dripped down and hit the outer edge of the flooring planks and dripped again into the softening earth of the road in a series of liquid drops and ricochets and then dull sounds in the last descent, a dim, depressing wintry song, cold and solitary. There wasn't much to be seen from that side of the street: the roadway

7

and the mule wagons beyond and a green lantern light hanging in the switchyards like an emerald and the vague black yawn of the railroad cavern. He heard the locomotive bell again.

He still hadn't any idea where he was.

A stray breath of wind lifted the rain and sprayed it against his face, and he smelled the scent of coal smoke and wood smoke and the fine rotten-ripe perfume of a hundred cisterns and sumps and sewers and cesspools and all sorts of wet hidden places like wood porch lattices and sour dirt under steps and crumbling board fences and lumber piles and alley trash and drains and gutterpipes and rain barrels full of black still water.

The place smelled bigger than a town; it smelled like a whole damned reeking, sprawling city.

It smelled like engine grease and whale oil from lamps and waxed wood floors and pleasant things like rose water and quinsy linament and clove balm, and other not especially pleasant or unpleasant things like leather and cotton quilts and dust and horse harness and manure and paper wet with ink and musty books and the open door, gusty smell of nigger houses and woolen clothes and grease smoking hot and boiled rice and roasted peanuts and fresh-cut pine knots and fried bacon. And more, much more, in that fine cold damp freshness, of cotton in the bale and thick mud and river bilge and wet brick and urine and fish and the heavy green weight of the river.

He used to walk along the riverbank every morning going to work, and because he was from upcountry that smell was new and rank and vivid and he knew he would never forget it as long as he lived.

By God, he told himself, he knew where he was!

All places smelled different even if they didn't look different at first, and if anybody had ever lived in Augusta, Georgia, long enough to know what it smelled like on a wet winter morning as he had, then they wouldn't forget it, even if they wanted to!

The first thing he said when he went into the saloon was, "This is Augusta, ain't it?"

And the bartender looked up from his paper spread out on the bar and said, "It ain't no place else."

There was no reason for him to feel so pleased at having figured out where he was with nothing more to go on than just the smell of the place and a half-guess, half-stab at it out of memory and hunch, but he was. He had been so low and dismal about the whole thing that it was more or less natural to swing up over something small and pretty silly like guessing where he was, and it made him feel just a whole lot better.

He pushed back his hat and put one foot up on the rail of the bar and looked into the mirror behind it and saw himself grinning from ear to ear.

You are a first-class, number-one fool, he told himself amiably.

He wasn't lost after all. He could have ended up in some totally strange place like Albany or Macon, for instance, instead of a place he had lived in once when he was apprentice printer—and when he thought about it, he was damned glad he hadn't ended up in Macon by mistake. He didn't have anything against Macon particularly, but he didn't think he would like it much, at least going about it the way he had, getting drunk and waking up on a train at the end of the line with four dollars or so between him and the world. That was a fine way to start off Christmas furlough.

But Augusta was different.

The first job he had ever had was in Augusta. Apprentice printer on *The Augusta Constitutionalist*. He had lived there a whole year before the war broke out. He had had a pretty good time in Augusta, too.

As far as he was concerned, Augusta was a pretty good place. Of course, people who lived there thought it was the damned center of the world—the whole damned world, too —and while he recollected that this attitude had annoyed

9

him before, it might have had its points, when you looked back. People in Augusta, though, were almost as bad as Charleston people about where they lived.

The city was stuck on the fall line of the Savannah River, and the division of the universe, according to Augustans, was pretty clearly laid out: going northward toward Atlanta was upcountry and going down-river to Savannah was downcountry, and that proved that Augusta was the middle of creation.

It didn't make him mad anymore; he just thought it was pretty funny, and smart, too.

"You got any beer?" he asked the bartender.

The saloon was one of those all-night railroad places, and the bartender looked like he had been born with it, white and fat with little granite eyes.

"Nope."

"Whiskey?"

"Barreled or jugged?"

Jugged whiskey was cheaper, being local run. When the bartender brought it in a tumbler it looked as thin and clear as ice water.

He had better be careful, he told himself. At least it didn't have any fuzz floating in it, and that was some comfort.

He caught his own eye in the mirror and saw himself lift the glass and the muscles of his throat working and the stuff going down with no sign of what it was doing to him.

It had taken him a long time to learn to drink corn whiskey like that, right here in Augusta. The journeyman printer on *The Augusta Constitutionalist* had taught him how in many an agonizing lesson in a bar almost like this one near the boardinghouse where some of the printers lived. In a part of town called Pinchgut.

The name of that other saloon escaped him, but he remembered it as a rare old place . . . sand on the floors, no tables to sit at, just a long bar where the customers stood up and drank until they couldn't stand up anymore and had to

10

go home—or be dragged out of the place. There was a big Gullah Negro, part Indian, that the proprietor kept around for just such work.

His friend Stokes, the journeyman printer, had drunk himself unconscious a couple of times. The Gullah Negro left you out on the sidewalk, and it was up to your friends to see that you got out of the way before the constable came by on patrol.

One time he had had to get Stokes to the boardinghouse all by himself, and Stokes must have weighed nearly 250–300 pounds.

"Come in on the train?" the bartender said.

"Yes. Just a little while ago." There was no one else in the place, but he wasn't in any mood for a lot of conversation with the bartender while the bartender washed up his glasses and wiped off the mirror.

"You been to Augusta before?"

"Yes, used to work here before the war."

That long walk to the office of the *Constitutionalist* every morning had taught him Augusta as nothing else could. Some mornings he would come down to the riverbank, cutting over from the canal, to get a look at the steamboats tied up at the docks loaded with cotton to be shipped down-river to Savannah, the niggers in their black coats and boiled white shirts shaking the dinner crumbs out of the tablecloths on the steamer deck, all of them waiters for the deluxe saloon featuring the very best cuisine overnight to Savannah —and ten times more elegant than you, white boy, their blueblack faces said, toting your sack of boardinghouse lunch on your way to work.

Yes, looking back, he could allow that Augusta was a fine place, one of the best! That was a year worth remembering, when he was seventeen, and free as a bird, with no war or worries in sight. Lord, he had had some good times! Augusta was a good town to have a good time because there was something always going on: it had people from the medical college and railroad people to liven things up, and in "The Season" which the newspapers made so much of, there were farmers and planters come to town for the horse shows and races, and performances at the Opera House. Lola Montez had been there one time. And Jenny Lind. There was baseball on the parade ground in the spring. And gambling and entertainments in the big hotels the year round.

And rain and cold in January, just like this.

And fever in the summer with the threat of the yellow plague which had nearly killed the place in the fifties.

And that hot, hot sun in July and the hot, hot nights when the sun went down. The boardinghouse room in Pinchgut was a place where you could lie on top of the sheets and try to breathe with the air like a wax layer, pressing you down.

The bartender took his rag and came down to his end of the bar and wiped all around until he got right up to his glass, then he lifted it up and wiped under it and stood there.

"Worked down here before the war?" the man said.

"On the newspaper. The *Constitutionalist*," he volunteered. "It was a pretty good job."

"Printer?"

"Apprentice." The man was worse than a barber. Talk, talk.

"The *Constitutionalist* is a good paper," the bartender said, flicking his little granite eyes up and down, as if trying to remember him. "People read that paper all over the state. You know Mr. Hammond pretty well?"

"The editor? Yes."

Not that he had known Mr. Hammond the editor more than to speak to him in the shop. An apprentice printer wasn't exactly the most important person on a newspaper.

That year of his first job he had had his picture taken in one of those new photograph places, wearing a blue striped shirt and a black broadcloth coat which he had bought secondhand in a store in Hammock Road and which turned out not to be broadcloth like the man said but some queer

12

cheap imitation of it that melted dye on his neck and around his wrists when he sweated.

The photographer had put his head into a metal bracing stand, and the clamp on the thing cut into the tender part of his neck, and pulled his head back so it was agony to sit still.

When the picture was done it showed him with his chin stuck out at a strange angle and his cheekbones gone tight, looking so pale and defiant that at first he did not recognize himself. It took him a minute to study what he had bought and paid for and decide that it was him, alright, John Alford MacLeod, apprentice printer, Augusta, Georgia, in the year 1860. Aged seventeen.

The picture looked enough like him to send home to prove to his Aunt Matt that he was well and prosperous and looking out for himself just perfectly fine, in spite of all the predictions to the contrary when he had left Jonesboro.

The damned bartender was back.

"Then you must have come in on that night train," he said, as though they had just been in the middle of a conversation.

Johnny nodded, and he saw himself in the mirror nodding back.

Well, there was one thing for sure, he thought, marveling at it, he was certainly changed from that picture of three years ago.

He leaned a little, cautiously, across the bar so that he could see his face better. Just for description's sake—if he were going to describe himself to somebody else, say—he would allow that he was not just lean, but downright skinny. Not gaunt—not yet, but skinny. Not that he had ever been heavy. All the MacLeods were what you would call spare. But some of the flesh was gone alright that he'd had at seventeen. The army and dysentery and a bout of sickness had done that.

He was getting, he thought with a certain satisfaction, to look more like the tribe of MacLeods with each passing year. Just like his brother Robert, his Uncle Trennon MacLeod, and his father's Stockbridge cousins. Like his father, too, although the only yardstick there was was the old daguerrotype stuck forever at the age of thirty-five, the year before his father had died. But they were all stony-faced Scotch Irish with a lot of straw-colored hair and too much yellow in their skin color, and a common set of small square jaw and thin lips and that stubborn look across the forehead.

He was satisfied with the look; he was more reconciled to that business about his mother's blue eyes and long eyelashes and mouth which he'd damned sure heard enough about, as he had been raised listening to his Aunt Matt tell people what a pretty mouth he had for a boy.

Godalmighty, there was nothing wrong with his mouth! If anything, his mouth had gotten pretty grim in three years of war; it was a damned grim taciturn-looking mouth, and he certainly didn't need to get excited over fool things said about it because his nose and jaw and face and all was so skinny and hard that it made up for all the rest.

God knows after three years of war he had gotten as worn down and ragged-looking as any jasper a person could find, and his beard, when he let it grow, was twice as thick as his cousin Ed Grimes'. Ed's beard never looked any more respectable than a billy goat's fringe.

Once, about a year ago, he had decided he was going to let his beard grow out until he looked as fierce and hard as that damned Texan from Hood's brigade. Or like his Uncle Haas Rainwater who had a beard three feet long and was so stern that most of the time he didn't bother to move it enough to speak. The more beard a person had, the less he had to listen about people discussing his mouth or telling him the girls sure followed after a good-looking boy like you, didn't they?

"Want another?" the bartender said.

Lord, there was somebody else he couldn't get rid of.

He didn't, but he felt like a jackass getting caught making faces at himself in the bar mirror. He had to watch out. His

14

stomach was pretty empty, and he was already getting a little tight.

"Been in the army long?" the bartender said.

"Hell, yes," he told him. "Three years. Right from the beginning."

He put the whiskey down the same way he had the first, standing stock-still before and after and never flinching, not even swallowing a second time, and the bartender watched him.

"Well, you look pretty young to be in it three years," the bartender said. "You must have joined up pretty young. You go up as drummer boy?"

"Hell, no. I went in as private, full private, went up to corporal, and got busted at Pittsburgh Landing."

"Well you can't be over nineteen, twenty," the bartender said. "When you stand right under the light you look pretty young at first. People ever tell you that?"

He didn't need to look in the mirror to see that he was getting red in the face. He hated people to say anything about his age or anything of the sort.

To do something, he looked around the room and held the empty glass up in his hand for nonchalance and then he saw the big picture that was hanging over the bar mirror.

"That's a pretty good-looking picture you got up there," he muttered.

"That's supposed to be a nymph," the bartender told him, not even turning around to look. "That means a lady fairy. That's what the drummer said what sold it to me."

Actually, he didn't like the picture one bit. The nymph, or whatever she was, lay stretched out on a couch, her backside turned outward and stacked up like white pillows, one ham on top of the other. She had little wings sprouting out of her shoulder blades and some sort of transparent mosquito netting thing draped over her. One hand had a fistful of the stuff, holding it over her head, and her elbow was moved out just enough to show one big fat white breast with a pinched nipple in profile.

15

She was so white and fat-looking her skin was just like bread dough . . . as though it would punch in and stay if you touched it. She was just about as fat as those slab-sided girls up at Memphis Bertha's in Chattanooga where the army had been last fall.

He couldn't say he had any taste for fat women left after those girls at Bertha's. They would be enough to cure anybody. Those girls at Memphis Bertha's had been fat as hogs from eating themselves to death on what the commissary officers brought them, while the rest of Bragg's army was starving to death on corn-meal and acorn flour rations.

All that seemed an awfully long time ago, he thought, as he looked at the lady fairy. But it had only been two months. He wondered what those girls looked like now, catering to the Yankees. Twice as fat, probably.

Smells , . . . lord, talk about smells! In Chattanooga it had reeked of mud and manure and fried onions and hay and smoking tallow candles and bad whiskey. All the time.

And especially, as he remembered it, the low, desolate smell of the place was worst at one o'clock in the morning when a person was staggering drunk and out of money and dreading muster at dawn, or in Memphis Bertha's where, drunk or not, you had to be careful to wash off good in the little room down the hall where the basin water was as cold as ice and a jar of soft soap on the shelf and one towel did for the whole army of Tennessee.

He had hated Chattanooga. In fact, each year he spent in the army was worse than the last. Slow death as the boys said, instead of the other kind, the quick one by bullet.

He had gone wrong too many times. At Pittsburgh Landing, when it didn't help to know there were a whole lot of others in the same sort of fix, and then getting sucked into Ed Grimes' ideas of good times at Chattanooga.

He looked up at the big fat lady fairy and thought, I've wasted my life these last three years, I swear I have.

If it hadn't been for Ed Grimes he knew he wouldn't have done a lot of things he had done the past year. Especially at

16

Chattanooga. He had been drunk too much, for one thing. And for the other, why, a person had to be drunk just to go into a place like Memphis Bertha's, and once there, well, it wasn't much. The rooms were as dark as caves and on army payday the girls were so busy they didn't even bother to get out of bed, or look to see who it was. A skinful of whiskey was the best preparation for the dirty bed sheets and the stink of all the others that had been there before you.

He glared at the picture above the bar.

One time, for some damned reason, that one girl, that Aggie or Sally or whatever her name was, singled him out. Ed Grimes had put her up to it, probably. While Ed was standing on the stairs waiting she leaned over the railing and called out, "Say, sojer, where's your friend? The yeller-headed, handsome one?"

That was all it took, to have a whore asking for you! That gave a person some reputation.

He could not hardly stand to think about it, even now.

The whole of Lowrey's brigade had been standing on those stairs at Memphis Bertha's, and afterward it was the biggest joke of the season. At muster or on parade somebody would start it up when they saw him coming, and before you knew it there was a whole chorus of "HAAAAAAAND-SOME, wooo-hoo!" until even the colonel, old Rum Tom himself, asked about it, and somebody told him about the soldier all the whores were asking for, and it gave him a laugh. The best joke ever.

After that, the colonel called him out of muster, just to look him over.

"So this is the regimental Don Juan," old Rum Tom had said.

If he could have found Ed Grimes at that time he would have killed him, cousin or no cousin, and Ed knew it, for he dodged him for nearly a month after that.

The bartender was folding up the newspapers and putting them in a neat stack down at the end of the bar.

"You ain't from the army of Virginia, then," he said.

"No, army of Tennessee."

"Well I thought so," the bartender said. "Most of the army of Virginia has taken to wearing them little forage caps. When you see a big brim hat it means the cavalry or the army of Tennessee these days."

"Guess so," he said.

"That Braxton Bragg y'all got," the bartender said. "That's a hard man to understand, I swear. One time he seems like a fine sort, and then the next thing you know the newspapers are all after him, hollering that President Davis ought to remove him, that he ain't fit for command and all that. A person can't make head nor tail of it."

"Bragg's a damned lunatic," he said, without thinking.

The bartender looked surprised, or pretended to.

"Well, I never heard him called that in so many words," he said. "But I will tell you one thing, every time there's one of his sojers in here they cuss him to hell and gone, I mean to tell you. You'd think that if Bragg was any kind of general his own men would have more to say for him than that, now wouldn't you? Or leastways, if there was any truth to what you hear, that Jeff Davis would remove him, sure enough."

"Davis is a damned lunatic, too," he told him. "They make a pair."

This time the bartender didn't bother being surprised.

"Well now, you do hear a lot of people saying that," he allowed. "Especially upcountry people. And then there's some people what think Alec Stephens ought to be running the government. But that's politics for you."

"That's right," he said. He wasn't going to argue.

"But you army of Tennessee boys got a right to feel a little sore after the whippin' y'all took up in Tennessee."

"Um," he said, looking down into the empty whiskey glass.

"Y'all just ain't got the speerit of Lee's boys."

"We ain't got General Lee, either," he said.

The bartender fell to picking his teeth.

18

"Well that's true, that's true. But a little more speerit would help."

"Um," he said.

"Maybe you do need to get rid of old Bragg," the bartender persisted.

The place was getting on his nerves.

"I guess we have," he said. "He wasn't in the retreat and he didn't show at Dalton when the army rendezvoused there."

"Well the army of Tennessee's had some bad times," the bartender said philosophically. He had found whatever it was in his teeth and was searching for it on his fingernail.

Fortunately someone came into the place at that moment, and the bartender moved away. The newcomer was a man in an army slicker. It was raining hard outside apparently, for the raincoat was draining a puddle onto the floor.

They started to talk, leaving him down at the end of the bar with his empty glass, a little raw and angry.

What you need, he told himself with fine sarcasm, is a little more speerit. And he remembered that retreat through the mountains down to Dalton and how sick he had been, burning with fever and with pains in his chest, not knowing then that he was coming down with pneumonia.

He knew he ought to get back to the railroad terminal and find out when the next train left for Atlanta, but the thought just slid through his mind without stirring up much enthusiasm. The whiskey, and what he had had in Atlanta, had taken the edge off things. And, he had to admit, he was awfully tired of doing what he ought to be doing. Just sick and fed up with it.

He reached over the counter where the bartender had stacked the newspapers and ruffled through them. He would like to take a look at the *Augusta Constitutionalist* before he went back.

The Daily Chronicle was on top of the stack and underneath this *The Georgia Agriculturist,* and under that a two-

19

day old *Chronicle* and then the *Augusta Constitutionalist.*
He pulled it out.

It looked the same. The masthead of a paper never
changes, he told himself. Well, hardly ever.

He read the left-hand column set with some sort of tran-
script of the Confederate Congress supplied by the Southern
Wire Service out of Richmond. There were two typographi-
cal errors.

That was not too bad, he thought judiciously.

NEW YORK:
> Barnum in New York is still going full blast, three giants eight feet
> high, a dwarf smaller than Tom Thumb, a double-voiced woman, six
> automatons performing on the piano and so forth.

He was glad to see Barnum was still going on, in spite of
the war and all that. New York must be a good place to be.
But dammit, what was "and so forth"? That was a poor way
to end a news item.

FROM THE COLUMBUS, GA., ENQUIRER:
> The floods of early December have damaged the cotton factories
> in Columbus. The Gerrard Railroad is much damaged by the flood
> at Uchee Creek and no mail can be sent in that direction. The river
> was high yesterday but lacked the eight or ten feet of extraordinary
> high water of the winter before last.

A LETTER PRINTED IN ATLANTA:
> I find the troops in general comfortably clothed. A few hundred,
> however, are without blankets and many are without shoes. I fear
> the quartermaster's department will not be able to furnish blankets
> soon, but we are receiving and expecting regular supplies of shoes.
> Two benevolent ladies of Columbus, Ga., Mrs. Carter and Mrs. Law,
> brought one hundred fifty blankets a few days ago, collected by
> them at that place. Might not the same be done at Atlanta?
> EDITOR'S NOTE: We submit the point wherefore may not this
> noble example be followed here?

It was the first time in a long time he had seen Mr.
Hammond's language in print. "We submit the point."
That sounded like him.

He hunted through the paper and found the editorial column.

EDITORIAL, WHAT SUBJUGATION MEANS:
Try to imagine the scenes which would take place all over this country on the first day of acknowledged subjection—that is, the day which would witness a treaty for reconstruction upon any terms whatever. From that moment, the right name of this war would be rebellion, as rebellion it would stand in history; and what is more to the purpose, as rebels its ringleaders would be punished and our soldiers disarmed. Our Confederate flag that has blazed in the front of twenty pitched battles, would be formally lowered, officially torn, trampled and abolished forever, while the accursed Stars and Stripes would be proudly hoisted in its place upon every fort and every camp, with cannon thunders and Yankee cheers. Some maimed and battle worn Confederate who should be standing by, a witness to that formality—conceive his deep wrath and despair as he gazes on the deed of shame!

There was more, but when he had got this far, he spread out the paper on the bar and leaned his elbows beside it and looked down.

It sounded just like Mr. Hammond, and it made sense, sort of, for it was just as clear as any picture what would happen. He believed it firmly.

After all, when all the fire and brimstone oratory had worn itself out—and it had pretty nearly worn itself out after three years of war—there wasn't much left in the way of argument except that the nation was not going to surrender because it could not. Not considering what was sure to happen afterward. That was just what Mr. Hammond had in mind. That was just what the editorial said.

It was just about as sensible as anything he had seen in the newspapers recently. He started to have another drink on it, but remembered his money and how low he was running, and changed his mind.

He couldn't very well leave Augusta without going to the *Augusta Constitutionalist* though, and paying his respects to Mr. Hammond. That was all there was to it.

He put down thirty cents for the whiskey and picked up his gear and hurried out.

CHAPTER 2

Oh brothers, comrades, men,
Rush to the field again;
Home, peace, love, safety, freedom are the price!
Strike while the arm can bear
Weapon and do not spare.
Ye break a felon bond in every foe that dies!

His furlough had begun December eighth and was good for twenty-one days. He wasn't late. He returned to Dalton by the Western and Atlantic Railroad on the twenty-ninth.

The rain and the sleet which had plagued Augusta during his stay had fallen as snow up in the hills, and the town of Dalton he saw, as he disembarked, was coated with a white layer which evidently had partly melted during some thaw and then frozen again so that it glittered in the sun like so much ornamental glass. It was wicked stuff underfoot. The ruts of Dalton's main street were hard as iron and saw-toothed from army traffic, and he had not gone a block from the railroad station before the leather in the soles of his shoes had taken more punishment than they had in a month. One part of his big toe, suddenly smack on the ground, rubbed raw, and in the four miles to Crow Valley where Lowrey's brigade was camped, he worked off enough skin to make it bleed. He wasn't in the best of moods to begin with and a ragged, bleeding toe didn't help his state of mind at all.

At the Mangin House in the entrance to the valley he found that Lowrey's brigade had shifted its camp, and it took him another hour of searching to find it out. The snow had altered everything; except for a litter of wood ashes dumped out and the piles of horse manure where officers' mounts had been tethered, the only evidence of the army was smoke coming up from chimneys underground. But he knew that the huts had been dug out of the ground before the snow and the glass-like fall had laid an almost perfect blanket on top. Still, he had to get right up on the doorways before he could find where they were.

At one likely hole he stuck his head through a blanket door and found the company sergeant, Peed, playing cards on a cracker box with Walt Ashford, the clerk, and Corporal Carter. He had found Company B's camp right off. He turned down Walt's offer to come in and have some stew as he was anxious to find his own quarters, and told them in answer to their questions that he had had the best leave ever, sure was a good time, and they looked like they believed him. They told him Byron and Bobby Hart were in a lean-to down the line. Four chimneys left.

A dog was prowling in the streets looking for garbage as he came along, but turned tail at the sight of him and ran off. The fourth chimney down was just as unrecognizable as the rest of the place, but he thought he remembered the log sticking up from the fence rails and canvas that he had helped Byron put up a few weeks before. He lifted the blanket flap and eased himself in, sliding downward into soft, muddy thawed ground. The place was dark and full of smoke. A regular hole.

"Byron?" he said.

Somebody sat up in a corner, and he recognized Byron, his friend, although it was pretty hard to do, Byron was so bearded and dirty. There was the bugler, Bobby Hart, squatted by the stone fireplace, chunking wood into it.

"Hullo, Johnny," Byron said sleepily. "When did you get in?"

"Just a while ago," he said. "I thought you'd hear the train."

He could not see where to put down his gear because the place was as narrow and crowded as a field rat's nest. As cold and solitary as the little town of Dalton had been coming through, with its one bank and two churches and inevitable brick houses huddled along the railroad, it seemed a paradise of space and pleasantness and comfort compared to Crow Valley. All sorts of litter, rags, and pieces of board and newspapers which Byron had collected and which he knew from years of army life were necessary covered the place; an almanac calendar was pinned to a flap of canvas in one corner, a cracker box with a panful of stew, it looked like, and a piece of corn pone sitting on it was next to a snuffed-out candle, all perched right in the middle of things where he knew sooner or later someone would knock them over—it was all the usual sort of mess, and yet suddenly it stifled him. This was enough to make him have one of those green spells, if he didn't fight it down quick.

Byron gouged at his eyes with his knuckles and yawned. Byron's condition was about as bad as the hut's. It was nearly impossible to remember how dapper Byron had once been, a perfect dandy with a little black mustache and fancy lady-sized feet that he spent all his pay having special boots made for. He wasn't wearing anything on his feet now except a pair of mudbottomed socks. His friend looked like some mangy little chipmunk dug out of hibernation, he thought wearily. He wondered how bad he looked to them, now, returning.

"Did you have a good time?" Byron said. "You look like you picked up some flesh for a change."

"Some," he told him. He wanted to talk to Byron pretty badly. A lot had happened since he had left, and it was gnawing at him from the inside. He wished Bobby would go away somewhere so that he and Byron could talk.

Byron got up and grubbed around looking for some parched corn to make coffee, and Bobby sat right there on the hearthstone with his arms wrapped around his knees.

The bugler wasn't very happy. He sniffed every few minutes, watching them with red-rimmed eyes.

"What's the matter with you?" Johnny asked him.

"Got a cold."

"When did you get back?"

"Last night."

"What did your pa do to you for being drunk the first day you got home?"

"Nothing. I put all the blame on you and that damned Texan."

"Lord they get smart fast in the army, don't they?" he said bitterly to Byron. "The next time I meet Hart's pa, he'll probably put a bullet through me."

"It'd be better than this," Byron said.

"Why, what's the matter?"

"Oh, hell, nothing, I guess. It's better'n it looks actually. It's just the same old thing, that's all. You were off on furlough when it was the worst. But things are picking up. We even had muster yesterday. The first time in a week. Somebody told the adjutant a bunch of deserters had gone off, so the colonel got everybody out for a look-see. First time he's give a damn since we got here. And today all the officers are gone up to some sort of general meeting. The new commander's come in, you know. Finally. Joe Johnston. I ain't seen him yet, but some of Weir's has. They say he's a little bitty fellow, straight as a ramrod, another one of them West Pointers. First thing he did was order some fresh beef brought in and killed."

"But you got to wash the mud and cow shit off it," Bobby croaked from the hearthstone. "Those butchers throw it down in the mud after they cut it up."

"Your mama's spoiled you," Byron told him.

"Well, you didn't have to come back," Johnny said. "You still got two, three years before you'll even be conscripted." He really wished the bugler hadn't come back; then he would have some privacy with Byron for a change.

25

"You leave me alone," Bobby shrilled. "You leave my mother out of it, too. What do y'all know about it?"

"Don't get him mad," Byron said. "Old Bobby is a good boy. We got the only bugler in the whole damned regiment who can read music, for God's sake. We had a Company A boy for regimental bugler while Bobby was home, and every call sounded like a damned sackful of cats. I couldn't even tell what he was playing when he blew for muster yesterday. Tom had to run up the line and ask what the call was for."

They sat down on Byron's blanket and drank the terrible corn-meal coffee he had fixed for them, and they warmed their hands around the tin cups and looked down at their feet in thoughtful silence.

"We're a gay crowd," Byron said finally. "It's always like this when you get back from leave, ain't it?"

But he looked at Bobby and frowned, and Johnny realized that Byron had smelled out something bothering him. It was sort of funny, but not surprising; when you lived with somebody long enough, as he had with Byron in three years of war, you could almost tell what they were thinking. You could certainly tell when they were fretting.

"Well," Byron said. "We missed you Johnny. I didn't hardly think this army would make out til you got back. Bragg was gone before you left, I guess you remember, and Hardee had command, but even so, that didn't hold it down any. You missed out the best part, I guess. Lord, I thought there was goin' to be a mutiny, I swear I did."

"I'm glad I missed it," he said.

"I heard all sorts of rumors, that Lee was going to come down and take command and that Hardee had been offered it permanently but didn't want it. It looked like nobody wanted this army after Bragg had done his worst. On top of that, the whole damned quartermaster corps went home, nearly. We couldn't get no rations, no orders, no nothin'. Old Rum Tom, Colonel Blalock, stayed down in town at the surgeon's quarters near his medicine, and half the line officers at Weir's was either drunk or gone off on leave, and ours weren't much better. And say, listen, you haven't heard what happened . . . some of those Texans from Hood's brigade got wild on account of not being able to draw anything but ear corn for more'n a week and went on a rampage and stopped the supply train before it could get into town and broke it open and stole every damned thing in it, bacon, meal, flour, the whole lot. But that was before General Johnston came. I don't think anybody's going to do a thing like that now."

There was another silence.

Johnny really didn't want to talk army politics, but there wasn't much else they could do.

"I got some stuff here," he said, pulling out his newspaper. "Bragg's gone to Richmond, to be chief of staff."

"Chief of staff of what?" Byron said, surprised.

"Of the damned army, what do you think! Over Lee and Johnston and the whole kit and caboodle."

"You wouldn't pull my leg, would you?" Byron cried.

"Well, let me read it to you, then," he said irritably. He opened the paper to the item the *Atlanta Intelligencer* had picked up from the *Richmond Examiner*:

The judicious and opportune appointment of General Bragg to the post of Commander-in-Chief of the Confederate armies will be appreciated as an illustration of that strong common sense which forms the basis of the President's character. Johnston, Lee and Beauregard learn with grateful emotions that the conqueror of Kentucky and Tennessee has been elevated to a position which his superiority deserves. This happy announcement should enliven the confidence and enthusiasm among the people like a bucket of water on a newly kindled grate.

"But we didn't conquer Kentucky and Tennessee," Bobby said, frowning.

"It just seems like Davis wants to go against the people, doesn't it?" Johnny said. "Any time there's a choice, he'll go

27

crossgrain or bust. Bragg wouldn't rate a corporal's stripes in any other army, so Davis has made him Chief of Staff."

"Goddammit, I don't believe it," Byron cried. "Why, they couldn't do that, not after what Bragg did up in Tennessee . . . well, hell, what are people going to *do* about it!"

"Nothing," he said.

"Well, you were home, you were around everybody else, I mean people outside of the army . . . don't they pay any attention to those things?"

"Well, I wasn't home exactly," he said. "That is, I wasn't home but just for a few days. Two days."

"You didn't get home? Where in thunder were you?" Byron cried.

He did not have time to answer, for at that moment he heard his cousin's voice hollering for him in the street outside, and then closer: "Hyo down there, anybody home? Byron? Is some of my relations here?"

Johnny got up, nearly knocking over the confounded cracker barrel.

"Let me go outside," he said, "you don't want him down here."

"You're damned right you'll go out," Ed shouted from the blanket door. "I can't squeeze in there with all you midgets. Byron, whyn't y'all build a place a decent-sized person could get into?"

He couldn't get to the door soon enough. There was Ed, leaning over, right in his way, waiting for him to come out, all done up in a brand new army officer's coat with braid and cape, a little short in the sleeves, as always; his cousin had arms as long as an ape's.

"You look mighty fancy," he said.

"The coat?" Ed pulled at the lapels. "Ain't it handsome, though! I won it over at the hospital in a card game. You can pick up right nice things that way, although you have to be careful, some. One of the boys got a new shell jacket and

28

sash and didn't find out it came off a typhoid case until after he'd worn it about a week. It like to have give him fits."

He turned away in a sort of horror, and Ed saw it.

"What's the matter, you got the back-from-furlough blues? Lord, I almost forgot . . . you got a right to have the lows ten times over, ain't you?"

Byron and Bobby had come out after him, and Byron looked from one to the other, puzzled.

"You feel sick?" he asked him.

"Damned right. He," he jerked his head in Ed's direction, "always makes me feel sick, doesn't he? My God, grave robbing clothes over at the hospital . . . that's a fine officer for you."

"Oh, don't take on so. A lot of the boys do that. What do you think they're going to do with all those good clothes, anyway?"

He looked back, and his cousin was standing there grinning, his haystack hair stuck up on end as though he had just gotten out of bed, and his eyes red-rimmed.

"Look at him," he told his friend. "Just look at him."

"When're you going to tell your good news?" his cousin hollered.

"He's just guying you," Byron said. "Do y'all always have to act this way?"

"Mamma wrote me all about it," Ed hooted. "You don't have to play dumb. It's no secret, is it?"

God, he had forgotten about the mail!

"What's he talking about?" Byron said.

"What? What happened?" Bobby asked.

"He got married! The sneaky sonofabitch got married, didn't you?" Ed had circled round and came up now, reaching out one of his long arms to poke him in the ribs. "Ha, ha! He's a married man now. Ain't that hell? Some sweet young thing snatched him up while he wasn't looking. Surprised everybody. Went off to Augusta and got married!"

"Ed . . . sir," Byron cried, "why don't you keep your big mouth shut?"

And to Johnny, he said, "Is that right, did you get married?"

"Who'd you get married to?" Bobby put in.

His nerves were jumping and shrieking, and he didn't think he could stand much more of it.

"Quit it, goddammit," he cried.

"Things won't be the same now, will they?" Ed went on. He was having a fine time. He winked at Byron and Bobby. "I mean, all those fool good times we used to have together. No more larking now. The next time we go to town we'll have to hog-tie old handsome Johnny and leave him behind. Don't want the girls to know what they're missing!"

"Well, congratulations," Byron said, putting himself between. "Why didn't you say something about it before?"

"Well, cheer up, goddammit," his cousin shouted. "You look like you swallowed a burr. You're set for life, don't you know it? You just come to me any time you get to feeling dismal, y'hear, and I'll put you up for leave as soon as its mortally possible . . . ."

He looked around frantically, but the only thing he could see was a water bucket lying on the ground.

"Johnny, for God's sake, . . ." Byron cried, but it was too late. Johnny brought the bucket down at his cousin's head and missed. The thing bounced off Ed's shoulder and somersaulted away.

"What'd you do that for?" Ed crowed. He threw his arms up to cover his head and danced around. "Hey, quit!" still laughing.

"I'll kill you someday, I swear I will," he shouted.

"Jesus, don't do that," Byron begged him. He had him by the sleeve, trying to hold him. Bobby Hart followed helplessly. "Not everybody knows you're cousins. Suppose somebody was to see you? We had enough officers gettin' beat on lately. The brigadier is fierce about it. You want to get put on report?"

"Court-martialed is more like it," Bobby offered.

"Aw, he just threw an old bucket at me," Ed shouted. "Don't make such a fuss. We used to scrap all the time. He's just touchy by nature. He doesn't mean a thing."

"Ah, shut your big mouth, Ed," Byron cried. "You haven't got bat brains. He ought to half-kill you, and that's the truth!"

"You come over here, and I'll knock you down and beat your skull in," he raged.

"Aw, hell," his cousin said. The grin faded, and he flapped his arms against his sides. "Simmer down. Godalmighty, I never saw anybody so bad-tempered. I didn't mean anything. I'll tell you what I'll do. I'll buy you a wedding present. How's that?"

Byron and Bobby had started shoving him back to the hut because some of the others in the company were coming into the street to see what all the fuss was about.

Once inside, Byron gave a sigh of relief.

"It was just as peaceful as it could be around here an hour ago," he said, aggrieved.

"The captain was only trying to joke," Bobby assured them. "Wasn't he?"

He sat down on the stones of the fireplace and covered his face with his hands.

"Oh, Christ," he groaned. "You don't know what I've done."

31

CHAPTER *3*

The days rolled on and the weeks became years
But our coffers were empty still,
Coin was so rare that the Treasury quaked
If a coin should drop in the till.

He wanted to talk to Byron in the worst way, but Bobby was always underfoot, sniffing and suffering with his cold, and the hut was not big enough to swing a cat in, much less try to find a place to hold a private conversation.

He just let what remained of the day slide by, and they turned in early; he lay for a long time listening to Bobby snorting and sawing with his cold before he finally dropped off to sleep.

Sometime during the night he woke with one of those violent, all-over starts that nearly threw him from his bedroll, and as he was not yet accustomed to the place and it was dark as pitch, he didn't know where in the devil he was. For a moment it was all the nights in Augusta during his leave when he would jolt from sleep and expect to find himself strange and lost again, hearing the wind lift the shingles in the eaves of the pressroom and the scurry of rats and squirrels across the loft flooring, and the cracks and whispers of nothingness that haunted old, loose-boarded buildings. At those times he would strain his eyes out of his head searching for some familiar shape to lend comfort: the composing stool, the wooden type box or the lightless circle of the lamp in the ceiling, saying over and over to himself, Augusta, this is Augusta, the pressroom, and I was here yesterday and the day before that.

Those damned days of his furlough had just gone on and on unbelievably, without sense or plan, and it was no wonder that he had to assure himself that it was all real and not a dream.

Now he was plagued by the same feeling; he had just gotten used to being in Augusta, and all that had changed. He was in some hole of a hut that was not familiar at all.

"Johnny?"

It was Byron.

He listened for the bugler, but the breathing from Bobby's corner was adenoidal and steady.

"You awake?"

"Yes," he answered.

"Wait a minute, I'll get us a light."

"You'll get Bobby up," he warned.

"Not likely. I tried to wake him up last night to turn him over and get him to quit all that snortin', but it was like proddin' a rock."

"He might be playing possum."

"Who, Bobby? You ever see him able to lie still and be quiet?"

Byron eased out of his blankets and got a tallow lamp dish down from the chimney ledge and fiddled about at the hearth trying to catch the wick at the coals. It caught, finally, shedding a yellow, smoky light in their corner. Byron sat down on the hearthstone, close enough to be able to lean toward him and whisper, hugging his knees out of the way.

"You woke me up, stirrin' around. Can't sleep?"

"No, just woke up and didn't know where I was."

"Oh, that's a rare feeling, ain't it? It makes you think you've gone crazy, to wake up in the dark and be scared. Like you'd lost the way back. Or have clean forgot where you are and can't remember for tryin'."

"Yes," he said with relief. Good old Byron knew how it was. "I can't get used to being back. It seems like I ought to

33

be still in Augusta. Or Atlanta. Or somewhere along the line. I don't know. God knows I've had a time of it."

"You don't sound very happy . . . like a happily married man, that is."

"Hell, I wouldn't say I was."

There was a silence between them then that extended itself for a good long time.

"It must have been pretty quick," Byron said. "I never heard you mention you were serious about any girl."

Quick? It had seemed like an eternity.

The whole three weeks in Augusta had seemed like an eternity at times because he had not been fit for civilized company for one thing, having house-fever pretty bad, and crowded places like a room with curtains and a fire in the grate and rugs on the floor and tables with books and dried flowers on them, and solid ceilings overhead damned near paralyzed him. After three years of sleeping in the open he could hardly bear the feel of a ceiling. The most ordinary things that people were used to suddenly became a torture: faces, eyes, polite questions that rattled like peas on a hide, doors opened and closed, having to ask for the chamber in strange houses, parties, people, girls, mothers, men who wanted to discuss the war because their sons or nephews or other relations were in the army.

"I don't know what kept me there," he said. "I guess I just didn't have sense enough to get out."

Which was not exactly the truth and he knew it. The minute he stepped through the doors of the *Augusta Constitutionalist* and told Mr. Hammond who he was, the apprentice printer from three years back, nothing would do but he must have the returned hero's welcome. It was as simple as that, and about as hard to get away from. Mr. Hammond wanted to talk to him about Bragg's army and all, and the political situation as the army saw it, and—as if this was not flattering enough—he took him home to dinner at Mrs. Akin's boardinghouse and introduced him to his daughter,

34

Miss Annabella Hammond, aged seventeen, the most beautiful girl in Augusta, Georgia.

After he met Miss Annabella Hammond two days passed like a flash, and he hardly even realized that he was spending his leave right there in Augusta, sleeping on the floor of the pressroom, washing his shirt in the washbasin, and cutting his hair with a pair of borrowed scissors, all signed, sealed, and delivered, a victim of love. It sounded terrible, but that was the way it happened. There was no sense during that time in what he was doing, and he hated the world and was in such a state some days that he could see why a person would want to blow his brains out or walk off a dock into the Savannah River just because life was not worth living, just one meaningless struggle after another. He knew he had no reason to come into Augusta like a bat out of hell to fall in love with the first girl he met, and that girl the daughter of a man he used to work for, at that.

Miss Annabella Hammond had already been interested, at the time he came upon the scene, in that damned Verlyn Patridge, a lieutenant in the Home Guard and the biggest fool and pain in the backside it had ever been anybody's misfortune to meet—a poetry reciting boob and nincompoop, a parlor lizard of the worst sort, and officer in the world's most laughable army. God, how he hated the Home Guard! It had been a situation made for trouble.

God knows he was not, and never had been, a candidate for parlor lizard or poet. He couldn't sing, couldn't play the banjo, and was no damned round dancer; yet he took a crack at everything, including the latter, knowing full well that Verlyn Patridge was bent double laughing to see him try.

Lord, it was a mixed misery, knowing he was making a fool of himself like that—and yet while he had his arms around Miss Annabella Hammond as they danced, it was worth every bit of it. He could feel her round waist swaying and moving and her soft bosom brushing up against him, and the effect was such that his hands sweated and got

35

slippery as axle grease and he was positively sick and dizzy with enchantment. She was the most beautiful girl in the world by agreement of half of Augusta—the medical college, the convalescents in the hospital, and any one you could find. The way she dressed, the way she talked, low and sweet, and the way she wore all that dark, tumbling hair, not screwed up in all the rats and buns of the fashion but loose and natural, pinned up on top of her head with all the little loose curls cascading down over her shoulders, was perfect.

Sometimes, as she talked to you, she would pull a strand of hair over her shoulder and wind it around her finger, laughing and smiling, the whole business enough to hypnotize an ordinary person, and then, suddenly, she would let that lucky little curl go, and it would bounce back to join the rest, just like a little dark, shiny, jeweled spring.

And her eyes . . . they were perfectly set, outlined by dark eyelashes like spiked stars. They looked right at you, forthright, when she asked you something, and knocked all the sense clear out of your head and brought you down to just a sheer, babbling idiot with nothing to say. The point of her chin, which he loved to watch, sort of swept back in the daintiest imaginable line to her throat—in fact, she had the most amazing, delicate daintiness he could imagine, and absolutely clear, alabaster perfect skin, everybody said so; even the other girls said that Annabella Hammond had the best complexion in the city of Augusta. It was just like fine china. And yet she wasn't any china doll; she was tall, almost as tall as he was.

For a solid week in Augusta Verlyn Patridge was right in the way, though, reading his damned poems at parties and claiming Miss Annabella Hammond for dances, and Johnny made no more impression on her than if he had been a stick of wood. He was no parlor hero, he told himself, he could not spin stories that would set the girls and their mothers to oohing and aahing, for that took some skill as well as a talent for lying, and a good memory of your own lies to back it up.

36

Some of those jaspers home on leave in Augusta or furloughed from the hospital could lie up a storm about a simple thing like staking out a horse and make it sound as though that was what had nearly won the war. They could tell about charges as grand as any in the magazines and newspapers (which was probably where they got their material), about brave bugler boys and color bearers standing out rashly before heavy fire, waving their flags, and how General D. H. Hill looked when they came up, and what they said to General Robert E. Lee. Lies, and the girls and Miss Annabella Hammond swallowed it whole.

"I'll bet you had a good time," Byron said admiringly.

He could not begin to explain to Byron that he had been to so many entertainments, theatricals, socials, church suppers, aid society raffles, hospital dances, *conversaziones,* starvation parties, and what-have-yous that it had nearly reduced him to a frenzied lunacy. Particularly with Verlyn Patridge cropping up everywhere.

"Augusta was hell on parties," he told Byron. "Pure hell. The worse the news about the war and everything, the more parties. I never saw anything like it. The newspapers said it was the same or worse in Richmond. Everybody wanting to cheer up the soldiers, I guess, and forget their own troubles. Last ditch grab. And everybody was getting married. It was a regular marrying bee. Parties and more parties."

The chaperones and mothers had not been deceived about how the boys were feeling that winter in Augusta and how quickly the fever for gay times and forgetfulness could get out of hand. More than one party he had gone to had been broken up by rowdiness, one by some of the boys insisting on square dancing. (There was a ban on square dancing in homes because of some previous incidents.) But ban or no ban, with the help of a little redeye some of the convalescents from the hospital got a little fire and ginger in them and chose up a set, camp style, boys only, mainly because the girls would not dare, singing for their own music, "Possum on a

Gum Stump," stomping and hollering and knocking things about in Mrs. Ford's dining room with the table pulled back to make enough space.

That party had shut up pretty quick, for Mr. Ford had come down to lend support to the chaperones.

There was the other time at another party when the boys home on leave got up a table of euchre and the situation got out of hand then, for someone had said he was the champion euchre player of Stuart's brigade and somebody else had to challenge him in the name of Wheeler's cavalry and a rough sort of temper got hold of things and finally the Stuart defender, who was one of the boys from the hospital, tried to hit Wheeler's cavalryman with his crutch, saying he was a damned renegade yellow dog, and it was impossible to get either of them quieted down and the cards picked up off the floor and the chairs put back on their legs before the mothers came in to shame them all, telling them they had all turned into a pack of Indians and rascals, sending everybody home without even the refreshments.

But neither one of these scrapes measured up in any respect to his own.

He had been feeling low and well aware that he ought to go to Jonesboro where he belonged and not take advantage of the Hammond's patience and hospitality any longer, but not wanting to because of Miss Annabella, although there was not any hope that he could see in the situation. The lowness of his state contributed to his fall. At least that was his excuse. There had been a party the second week for one of the girls and a boy from the hospital who were getting married, and there had been a bottle of peach brandy (or apricot brandy someone said it was, although it tasted like peach to him) being passed around on the piazza before the card playing got started. Just a few of the boys, the same ones that he was beginning to know from these affairs, standing out on the piazza taking the air, with the bottle going around. Send for Verlyn, somebody said, and someone else said old

38

Verlyn didn't drink because he was keeping himself pure for a girl.

He had had a good horse laugh at that, and the others tried to hush him, telling him he did not know how loud he was carrying on. It was true he had accounted for more drinks than anyone else by the time they returned to the house. He was still feeling low and sore-eyed about one thing and another, and it did not help him to find Miss Annabella Hammond playing cards in a foursome which included Verlyn.

It occurred to him right at that moment, with the peach or apricot brandy sliding around down inside him, that it was time to do something, to tell his own damned war stories, for instance. It seemed he was the only jasper on leave in the state of Georgia who had not had a crack at it.

Whatever it was he said as introduction, he began too loudly. He could see how heads turned to him, surprised, and how Miss Annabella Hammond looked at him over her handful of cards as though she wished he would quit and be still. But he couldn't stop. By then he was convinced that what he was saying was as interesting as anything that had been offered to that date—maybe more so—and it was no time for anybody to try and hush him up.

He was sitting on a sofa with two girls he did not know, one leg crossed over the other, one foot wagging elegantly as it did when he was feeling no pain. He was busy with his description of the first time he had heard the rebel yell. Although half the party going on in that room were not listening to what he was saying, it sounded to his own ears as though he was telling it a whole lot better than the parlor heroes had told their tales, and he felt that those people did not know what they were missing if they kept right on with what they were doing instead of listening to him. He was really warmed up.

The rebel yell, he heard himself explaining, was something like what you yell when you're running a dog in a low place where the brush is so thick you can't see but only hear the

39

dog, eeyurp, eeyurp, the old hound voice . . . and you screeching after him, urging him on.

The excitement of just talking about it raised the hair on his flesh. That was just the way he had felt about it when he had heard it the first time: it was something nearly everybody knew how to holler, if they had ever run foxhounds or rabbit dogs. The company had been assaulting a hill where Yankees were entrenched, and they all knew it would be hard going getting up that hill. His regiment, the 79th Georgia, was in the first line of attack.

They had started up, scrambling for all they were worth, like boys eager to get out front in a Fourth-of-July pig chase, running and yelling, almost forgetting it was war when the yell started up, with the feeling that what they were after was just beyond and ahead of what they could see, and by God they were coming after it, their hearts pounding, screaming their heads off.

Right at that point Lt. Verlyn Patridge had looked up from the card table in the corner and said, "Hey, theah, old boy, how about keepin' your voice down, heah?"

He was right in the middle of a word and damned sure no one was going to stop him. He couldn't take time to answer, but he felt something rising in his craw about old Verlyn and he told him silently, you better watch out, you damned militia bombproof sitting over there playing cards with my girl. . . .

So he went right on, saying it was no surprise to him that the Yankees broke and ran when they saw the 79th Georgia coming like that, screaming and hollering like lunatics let loose. Afterward, he remembered, his company had been worn out and sick with the effort, looking around in the Yankee ditches and saying to each other, by damn, we did it, as though they couldn't believe it, and some of the boys still thrashing around, knocking things down and still yelling and carrying on like they could not stop, one or two at Murfrees-

40

boro falling over in a dead faint, just passed out from all the hollering and excitement was all anyone could figure.

One of the girls sitting next to him said, "Mercy, I don't understand what you said in all that. Do you mean there's no rebel yell, you just start hollering?"

And he told her, "Well, I mean it's sort of a hunting yell. Haven't you ever heard anybody yell when they're hunting?"

The other girl next to her gave her a poke in the ribs, and they started giggling.

"No," the first girl said, looking right at him, "I certainly haven't."

"Well, you don't have to get a minute older," he told her. "I'll be glad to oblige."

"Oh don't," the other girl said quickly and gave the first girl another poke, hard. "Don't egg him on, silly!"

"Oh, you wouldn't anyway, would you?" the girl said, smiling at him. "You wouldn't dare."

"Oh yes I would," he said, and he got up and in a fit of something or other—defiance and peach brandy and misery —decided to stand on the sofa, maybe to give what he was going to do a good start, blast it into the far corners of the house, and particularly over into that alcove where all the card playing was going on, and where they should have been paying attention to him, but weren't.

A girl by the piano stood up, sort of scared, when she saw him step onto the sofa. He put his hands around his mouth, wobbling a little on the cushions, seeing all the faces turned up to him.

He let loose with a roar.

"Don't! Hush!" the girl by the piano cried, but the girl on the sofa beside him was laughing, although her friend reached over to grab him by the trouser leg to make him come down.

"That's enough!"

"Why ma'am," he told her, kneading his feet among the

41

sofa tufts to try and stay upright, "that wasn't the rebel yell, that was just to get my voice loosened up."

He opened his mouth again but before he could do anything Verlyn Patridge slapped his cards down on the table and jumped up and said, "You heard Miss Dorothy, didn't you? Don't make that racket in the house!"

He kept his mouth open, looking Lt. Verlyn Patridge right in the eye, and let out the loudest screech he had bet any of them had ever heard, the window panes keening and all the china in the cupboards rattling. The girls put their hands over their ears and squealed. Except Miss Annabella Hammond. Her eyes were like wide, dark stars.

"Eeeeeeeeeeyyyyyyyyyyyyuuuuuuuuuuuuuiiiiiiiiiieeeeeeee!"

It was a pretty good imitation considering the time and place.

But before he could get it out to the last thin, dribbled howl, Lt. Patridge dashed over and yanked him by the front of his jacket, trying to snatch him down from the sofa.

He lost his balance and started falling, and this made him mad as fire. He wasn't going to let any damned militia bombproof manhandle him and then let him off scot-free!

He came down, but when he did so he rammed old Verlyn in the chest with his fist. But old Verlyn had hold of the front of his jacket, yanking and jerking him about. He heard the last button go, and bobble off across the floor. His last damned CS jacket button.

It drove him crazy. He charged old Verlyn and tried to get at him where he could land a blow, but the fool kept hold of him as though he did not want to fight. He could see old Verlyn's face in front of his own, white and cold and pinch-nosed mad. That made him ten times wilder, and still Verlyn would not back off and let him get to it. He had managed to block him from the very first charge.

He should have known better, but he was surprised, that was all, to think of old Verlyn being smart enough to have a trick like that. He certainly didn't look as though he knew his way around a scrap.

What happened came quick enough; he saw it just a split second before it landed, and there wasn't a thing he could do about it. He took old Verlyn's fist on the side of his head and went down as though he had been poleaxed, right on top of the girls' feet at the sofa. Both girls. They drew up their skirts and squealed as though they had just seen a mouse.

It was pandemonium clear through. Miss Dorothy went crying for her mother, and Miss Annabella Hammond flew up and pushed old Verlyn on the chest and he heard her cry, "You fool, he's been sick! He just had pneumonia!"

His head was resting on some girl's skirt and she was trying to jerk it out from under him, and Miss Annabella Hammond was kneeling on the floor beside him trying to get her hands around his neck. His nose was bleeding, and Miss Annabella was holding his head up and patting at it with a handkerchief, saying over and over, "Oh, dear Lord, are you hurt? Did he hurt you?"

Dizzy as he was, even down on the floor like that, he knew a bear cat was loose. The girls were hollering, and some of the boys were shouting and laughing, not taking it half as seriously as the girls; someone tripped over him, and there was so much milling around that shoes and boots and skirts would have drowned him if it hadn't been for Miss Annabella Hammond holding his head up. He heard one of the boys from the hospital threatening to take a poke at old Verlyn.

"You just try it, y'heah?" old Verlyn told him, still sounding mad. And then somebody else, in the low and anxious tone that people use when there is something going on, "Aw, quit it, can't you? Don't you see they're only fighting over a girl?"

The other voice, almost lost in the clatter of voices, but sounding as though it was full of peach brandy also, "Well to HELL with it, let go of me . . . I can stand up by myself . . ." and more voices shushing him: "Don't cuss, you're only making it worse." "Keep your voice down, don't you know where you are?"

"Well, why AIN'T he in the army?" the voice persisted. "HELL, I mean the REAL army. Give me one good reason a big live sonofabitch can't do some REAL fightin' for a change. . . ."

And it was this voice which Miss Dorothy's mother heard when she came in.

He had to get up, for everyone was leaving, but it was hard work. People were stepping on him, forgetting him in the general hoorah. He had to hold onto the side of his head with his hand for it felt as though it was going to fall off. Miss Annabella Hammond was right there, trying to hold him up and not let him fall when the voice of judgment saw him. When he tried to get a word in edgeways and apologize, Miss Dorothy's mother just held up her hand and closed her eyes, stop, and he knew it was no use.

Well to hell with it.

"I bet your goose was cooked," Byron said, grinning.

"I guess it was," he agreed. " 'Cause then I got married."

44

CHAPTER 4

The forest was robbed of its treasures
  The house was a mass of green
  As I reveled in Christmas pleasures
  At the dawn of Aurora's sheen.

His eye was still pretty black and blue from the row with
Verlyn Patridge, and his nose had a hump on it, but somebody got the bright idea of borrowing some rice powder
from the bridesmaids to cover it up. The powder left the
bruised parts a sort of unearthly gray, but at least it made
him presentable, and worst come to worst, some credit had
to be given for effort. His shirt had been washed and ironed
by one of the Negro maids at Mrs. Akin's boardinghouse,
and his pants had been whipped and brushed by Mrs. Akins
herself to get the mud out. His boots had been cobbled and
blackened with stove paint, and everything about him
showed the results of being sorted, picked, cleaned, and
renovated to within an inch of it's life. He was shined like
brass, stamped and certified, and for the last two days, only
partly sober. He had had enough to drink, especially since
his series of discussions with Mr. Phineas T. Hammond on
the subject of marriage and being able to provide for Miss
Annabella Hammond, to dim all pain. He existed in a nice,
twilight world of pleasant mayhem.

Of course he wanted to get married, he kept telling himself. Who wouldn't want to get married after all the trouble
he had been through?

He was just steady enough to stand upright in front of
Mrs. Akin's front parlor mantelpiece, planted before a gar-

land of paper flowers stuck in magnolia leaves, and because he was not entirely sober he entertained himself by composing a song which ran: Here comes the bridegroom with his nails pared clean and his belly button turning green and his father-in-law looking mean and damned guests numbering one hundred and thirteen . . . . All sorts of nonsense. There was no end to it.

He just stood there nodding and smiling to himself until two of the groomsmen took him out into the hall for another bracer and decided by the glassy look of his eyes that he had had enough.

"I can't believe I'm getting married," he told them, so full of goodwill that he could not stop smiling and laughing. "By God, you know, I can't believe I'm getting married. You boys don't know it, but when I came down here I didn't even know I was going to get married, didn't even THINK about getting married at all, and by God, if I had—that is, if I'd known I was going to get married or even that I wanted to I would have said that there wasn't enough damned *time* for anybody to get married. Not in three-week's leave. Now, nobody'd think a person could get married that fast, start from scratch and all and declare yourself and have to fight through her pa's objections and all that, with a sweet, beautiful girl you hardly know."

"Well, don't keep talking about it, hear?" one of the boys warned him. "Your father-in-law still don't look too confoundedly happy."

"I KNOW THAT," he said. "I know THAT, don't I? My God, I came this—this—" he tried to snap his fingers but missed, "this close to not getting married."

"You're a lucky devil and no mistake," someone agreed. "Half the Home Guard is going to blow its brains out in the morning."

"The Home Guard ain't got no damned brains."

"Well, hell, how about all the boys at the hospital?"

Someone had caught his hand and was trying to do something with it, put gloves on it. Somebody's gloves borrowed for the occasion that were about three sizes too small for his hands, as swollen and chapped as they were.

"What are you trying to do with my hands?" he said. "You're going to break my damned fingers with those damned things!"

"Aw hush, can't you? Don't you want to look nice?" This was the cavalryman from the hospital who was going to act as best man. "We got to get these things on you. Hi, can't you hold his arm? He keeps bending his wrists just like they were made of India rubber."

They perspired and struggled, working over his hands while he, remote from it all, looked around him and up at the ceiling of the hall in Mrs. Akin's boardinghouse where someone had tied a piece of mistletoe to the hanging lamp.

"Hey, it's Christmas!" he exclaimed.

"You better pull your fool head back," they told him, "or you'll fall over."

"It sure did get to be Christmas in a hurry this year," he marveled. "It's too damned hot for Christmas, you know that? I'm awful hot. I'm sweating like a horse. Ain't it awfully hot to be Christmas to y'all?"

"Well, you got to give us credit," the best man said. "He looks pretty good. That short jacket don't look too bad, after all, once it's all slicked up. It looks a lot better'n' the longcoat by far. And old Johnny is right good-lookin' once you get him organized. A little woolly around the edges, but downright handsome." He nudged him with his elbow. "You ought to have a houseful of handsome younguns a couple of years from now."

He found himself laughing agreeably when they all laughed.

"Got to live long enough," he said.

"Hell, what's going to happen? Ain't nobody going to burn down the damned hotel or raid the train!"

"The only thing you got to watch out for is you're drunk as

47

a pig already. You know what'll happen—or won't happen—
if you get limbered up."

"You got to sober up some before tonight, boy."

"You're a lucky devil," somebody said wistfully.

"I know." He wanted to be careful not to brag, but he
didn't want to leave them unimpressed with his luck, either.
"I KNOW, alright. I know how lucky I am. You don't have to
tell me."

"Well, you've got to have your head screwed on tight.
Don't get sick or fall or nothing like that. We'll all get the
blame."

"Yes, and sober up by tonight!"

"I AM going to sober up, dammit!"

"You don't want to make a botch of things with a sweet,
beautiful girl like that."

"Listen here," he said, squinting around at them and seeing their faces mostly as a blur, "you don't have to give me
any advice. I know what's what. You just leave that to me,
y'hear? Never mind about all that."

"I wish I was in your boots."

"Who the HELL said that?" he wanted to know.

"Never mind," they soothed him. "Just stand up straight
and don't get sick and pay attention to what you're doing."

"Jack," they told the best man, "sort of prod him if he gets
to leaning like he did before."

He fell asleep almost at once on the train and when he
finally woke it was somewhere past midnight, he was sure.

He was on the Atlanta train, going northward this time
from Augusta and he had a pretty fair idea of what he was
doing. Which was, he told himself, nothing short of a miracle.

The oil lamps in the car were shaking, spattering a restless
light back and forth over the seats. He looked down and
there she was, her head fallen against his arm, fast asleep.
Her gloved hand was resting palm up, against his leg.

It was a queer feeling, alright, he discovered, to wake up

48

and find the pressure of Miss Annabella Hammond's body against his, and to see this female hatted head against his arm and her hand lying open on his leg, right in public.

Married.

It was suddenly a damned strange, unfamiliar word, final and depressing. And he had a feeling that everyone was looking at him.

Which was stupid; there was no one looking. Everybody was asleep. The whole car was asleep. He was the only one awake. In the seat across the aisle he saw two men asleep with their hats held in their laps and down a little further a poor jasper of a soldier was managing to keep his feet and sleep standing up, holding onto the back of a chair seat, hatbrim over his face, swaying with the movement of the train.

Yet this girl resting against him was a stranger. He couldn't see her face, only the front of her bonnet with the blue curled feather on the brim and the points of the blue ribbon sticking up. The overlap of her skirt rested against his boots.

He was going on his honeymoon with Miss Annabella Hammond and then afterward to Jonesboro.

Lord, the whole thing was fantastic! What had he been doing these past few days? What in the devil had he been thinking about all that time?

Married!

No need to panic, he told himself. What in the devil was there to panic about?

But he was almost suffocating, weirdly strangling for air, in just those few seconds of thinking about it. One thought after another came crowding in: he remembered his Aunt Matt and Uncle Trennon at home, and that they were probably still wondering where he was.

Oh Lord!

His aunt and uncle were not much family—thank God he was not long on family like some boys were—but he knew also there were certain formalities you had to observe, like

49

letting kinfolks know where you were and where you were going and what you were doing—or what you had done. He hadn't observed a damned formality or whatever they were. Such as letting his uncle or his aunt know he had got married in Augusta. And a person ought to let his folks know where he is for nearly three weeks. What in hell had he been thinking of?

And his brother Robert, too, in Virginia. He didn't think Robert would care much one way or the other, as brothers got married without getting too excited about it, but he at least needed to write Robert a letter to let him know about it.

How had he managed, he asked himself, to stay in such a stew for so long that he hadn't let a single person know where he was, or what he was planning to do?

Hell, he answered himself violently, I didn't know myself what I was planning to do!

Well, there was one argument for it, he guessed. Everybody was getting married, it seemed like. That was the God's truth. Augusta had been full of soldiers and girls getting married the whole time he was there. When a person didn't know which days were going to be his last, he had to take advantage of whatever happiness he could get. He had heard the boys say that over and over, at Augusta and elsewhere.

Besides, he told himself, you were drunk.

Not the whole damned time, he protested. I was this morning and a little yesterday, but not hardly much before that. You can't blame it on that this time.

Oh, to hell with it!

He stirred a little, to get more comfortable, taking care not to disturb her.

There was one thing about her, he observed. She slept just like a log. They were both worn out from all the marrying business they had been through. They hadn't been married eight hours, he guessed, and he knew this about her already—that she slept like a log.

It was sort of funny, the way she slept so heavily and steadily. That was a lot of sleeping for someone who looked so delicate and fragile. He smiled a little to himself and moved her gently so that there wouldn't be so much weight against his arm.

The night train from Augusta drew into the Atlanta terminal at four A.M. Something about the railroad station, perhaps remembering how sick and drunk and miserable he had been there coming down, put him in a bad and dismal mood. He had also developed a whopper of a headache from the dosing at the wedding, and the only thing to do about it was take time to go to the men's toilet in the station and have another drink from the bottle the groomsmen had given him as a final present. It helped the infernal pounding in his head.

He had planned, vaguely, to stay at some nice hotel in Atlanta as for instance the National, but the city proved to be as crowded as Dalton or Chattanooga; everything was full up. An hour of walking and checking, loaded down with his gun and gear and her portmanteau only proved that there was no room available at the Atlanta, the Planter's, the Tennessee House, the Washington, or the Trout House, much less the National.

Miss Annabella Hammond (he had not got out of the habit of thinking of her by that name yet) didn't say much during all this. She followed along, only yawning a little now and then as though she wasn't fully awake, and didn't care.

It had begun to rain. Atlanta was as alive and open at four o'clock in the morning as though it was that time in the afternoon. The streets were jammed with wheeled traffic, horses and people, and a lot of travelers, apparently, for

51

nearly every other person, it looked like, was carrying traveling gear like themselves.

East of Five Points a man pointed out a drummer's hotel that might let them have a room, he said, and sure enough, when they investigated, the night clerk in the place agreed to let them have a room. The regular tenant of the room was out of town and would be back in a few days, but the clerk would double-let it on condition they not disturb any of his belongings.

Be out by ten in the morning, the night clerk cautioned, and remember, don't move anything around.

Johnny signed the register, bad-tempered and impatient, his headache raising hell.

The room was a dismal place. It turned out to be as cold as the bowels of Hades, and there was no light at all except the one candle on the candlestand. Not even a lamp. The furniture in the place consisted of a bed, a clothes press, and one chair. From somewhere outside the window rain water growled down a spout and the noises of the roadway seeped in: moving wagons, shouts, and the engines in the railroad yards a block away.

He bent to look at the dark hole of the fireplace.

"No wood," he said.

Well, at least that spared him the trouble of trying to make a fire, although he admitted a fire would have made things a lot cosier.

Never mind, he told himself suddenly, with a burst of enthusiasm. They would be plenty warm once they got to bed.

The thought made him feel a whole lot better at once. What he needed, if he could manage it, was another drink to put a fine edge on things and drive off the dismals.

Goddammit, after all, he was on his honeymoon!

They needed a window open in this place, that was all, to bring some fresh air and life into the place. Even as cold as it was.

52

"You cold?" he asked Miss Annabella Hammond huskily, and discovered that she was still sitting on the bed, wearing her coat and bonnet and gloves, just as she had been when they had come in.

She nodded. She looked cold and dull and sleepy as though she couldn't help it. She yawned.

It was real. She was real. And there they were, married! Suddenly he was so damned excited it threatened to cut loose and racket around the room like a shout. It was all he could do to stand still and try and look calm and sensible.

"We'd better take off our wet stuff," he said.

She sat there, looking at him, sleepy still, but now a little more alert.

"Can't sit around in wet clothes," he told her.

She nodded thoughtfully and reached up to pull at the ribbons of her hat, to untie them.

While she was doing this a fever of hurry took hold of him, and he put his bedroll in the corner, resting his Enfield against it, bustling about. When he got through there was still plenty of time, so he started unbuttoning his collar and getting his jacket off to hang on the back of the chair. He kept on going and took his shirt off, remembering the damned bottle of whiskey just in time, catching it as it started to slip out of his belt. He stuck it against his side and his arm and took it over to the corner and tucked it into the folds of the bedroll blanket.

When he had finished he found she had done no more than take off her bonnet and drop the coat from her shoulders.

"Annabella?"

Lord, he found the word almost choked him! He was going to have to find something shorter than that.

She lifted her eyes and looked at him for just a second.

"Ah," he said stupidly, for he had lost track of what he was going to say just looking at her. "Ah." He wanted to take her in his arms and kiss her breathless for looking so sweet and sleepy and adorable. Yet he couldn't move, couldn't hardly speak.

"Ah . . . hadn't you better let me hang up your coat?" he managed finally.

God, knows, he thought, what went through a girl's head at times like this. He had heard some pretty awful tales about how girls acted sometimes, not being able to help making a fuss, breaking down and demanding to be taken home and other godawful things. He was in no condition to take her home. That was out of the question. They were going to have to make out, that was all there was to it. She had been so sweet and eager and loving before, he could not exactly understand why she was so quiet now.

He put his hands up to unbutton his shirt and found that it was gone. Jumped the gun. There he was half-naked, and she had not even got her coat all the way off!

"Well," he said, and went over to the bed and sat down beside her. She did not move. "Not scared, are you?" He was talking to the side of her face, her cool proud nose, her sleepy mouth, her dark cloud of hair.

"No," she said, her lips moving slightly. But he could see that she was. He was so close he could see every detail of her face and dress as though he had never seen them before: the collar and pin at her throat, and her hair lifted up in a roll that was smooth and stylish, but which he didn't much care for; it made her look older than she was, with gold eardrops swinging from the lobes of her ears. He was damned if he could believe that he was so close and she was so real and sweet and tempting. The crawling in the roots of his belly reminded him that she was.

"Well," he said, suddenly inspired, looking at the line of her hair and a little tumble of curls escaping. "I'll, ah, help you off with your shoes."

"No," she said, startled, and moved her feet.

"I can help you off with your shoes," he told her. "Everybody helps people off with their shoes when they're married.

54

There's nothing wrong with that." But she was terrified, he could see that.

"Besides," he blurted out, "we haven't got all night. Ten o'clock! Godalmighty!"

It wasn't what he meant to say, but at least it was the truth. His head was still pounding, and he knew it was useless for him to strain for diplomacy. Everything, he told himself, was going to be alright when he could put his arms around her and kiss her.

He got down on one knee and took her foot and started to unbutton her shoes. She just sat before him, looking as though she was thinking of something which had no relation to what he was doing. He knew she was cold, for her foot in his hand was cold and her shoes were wet. She was just cold and worn out. When he lifted her foot to take off her shoe, her skirt moved, and he saw part of her ankle.

She tried to pull her foot away then, but he leaned against her knees and put his arms around her waist and drew her close. She was so sweet and beautiful and cold, so wrapped up in her confounded clothes—the most beautiful girl he had ever seen.

"P-please," she said in a rush, "don't."

He would have made progress at once except that there were so many clothes enveloping him, and as soon as he put his arms around her and started to search for catches and hooks, she stiffened right up.

Finally, after a good bit of scratching around he heard her say something like: "Ihavebuttonsonthebackofmydress."

"What?"

She stared in anguish at the far wall.

"Ihavebuttonsonthebackofmydress. Ican'treachthem."

The buttons on the back of her dress.

"Ohyes," she said, still running her words together like beads. "Ihave to havesomebody to helpme do it. I can't doitmyself."

"Well, don't worry about a thing," he told her.

She turned her back to him, and there were the buttons, running from back to waist. A mess of little buttons, he couldn't begin to guess how many. He started unbuttoning. His fingers were not used to such close, finicky work, and he did not make out very well. The buttons escaped him everytime, and he chased them, trying as best he could to punch them back through the buttonholes. The light was bad. His head hurt. He couldn't half see what he was doing.

He wondered who had buttoned her up to begin with, if the business was all that difficult, and imagined the girls, those bridesmaids who had gone upstairs with her at the boardinghouse, doing some such thing.

He could just picture what it must have been like to have a bunch of girls in one room like that helping a new bride to get dressed, giggling and carrying on. He could just picture her standing in her shift with her bosom all uncovered and her shoulders bare, while those girls were telling her about how she would soon be alone with her husband, and what would happen—he wouldn't put it past a lot of girls like that to tell her a lot of things that weren't so, and give her a bad time about it. That would be enough to make her nervous and frightened and uncertain.

She was unbuttoned all the way down the back of the dress with her skin showing white and pure as silk, her head bent forward to keep her hair out of the way, her hands clasped in her lap.

He just put his mouth down on the bare strip of her skin where the dress parted and kissed it.

She gave a jump, and started grabbing at her clothes and struggling, sudden and timid and jittery.

"Anna," he said. She was trying to lift up the front part of the dress where he was trying to pull it down, but he had most of it by then and his hands brushed whatever it was she had on underneath. He felt the stiffness of the corset thing and then his hands were full of the soft firm shape of

56

her breasts, covered with cotton cloth, shrinking away from him.

"Wait . . . wait, . . ." she was crying. He had her by the arm and then the wrist, trying to keep hold of her, and he saw her eyes, wide and glimmering, and her mouth open oh! as they seesawed around on the edge of the bed, their feet braced.

He managed to kiss her somehow, and his mouth was shaking so it was rougher than he meant it to be and this didn't help; he could feel her lips protesting under his and her arms pushing against him, but all tangled up in the dress top and not very effective.

Those confounded damned clothes!

He had expected—had hoped—he more or less knew, that as damnably pretty, downright beautiful as she was, that she would be just as lovely underneath all the damned clothes that were in the way. But he was still shaken, in spite of what he expected, to see that she really had the most beautiful skin he had ever seen. She was just as soft and round and smooth as satin . . . he kept thinking of ivory silk . . . silk as her skin. His hands tried to touch her again before she could move off, and he felt a straining cotton-cloth softness and her arms where they were bare as she did all sorts of struggling things with the sleeves of the dress.

His hands were trembling, and he couldn't be of much help, and more or less accidentally he got his hand into the top of the shift and then touched her breast and tried to keep it there.

"Ouch!" she cried.

"I'm sorry, I didn't mean to hurt you, it's alright," he told her in a burst. "Excuse me." He kissed her again, making a poor job of it, hitting her somewhere in the corner of her lips, and then he tried to kiss her throat and she pulled away, and then the top of the cotton shift where he found, unexpectedly, there was a ribbon or something of the sort.

"Wait . . . wait, . . ." she kept saying. But he had managed to get their bodies back against the bedspread and had his leg over hers, trying to hold her still a little, and he got the broken strap out of the way and some of the endless layers of the embroidered stuff, while she was still flailing around trying to get the sleeve pulled over her hand where the button would not come loose, as though this had to be done before anything else.

Her hair had come down from all the sleek moorings and spread over one shoulder and she was telling him to stop, wait, in a queer, compressed little whisper.

He knew it was wrong and yet he couldn't stop. The closer he got to her the worse effect she had on him—or the best effect—he was damned if he knew how you ought to look at these things. The dress top was pulled away and he had gotten her partly out of the corset thing, and her hands were busy trying to push him off and cover herself at the same time. There was a flurry of hands, his pulling and hers grabbing.

"Anna, darling, let me . . . ."

He got one of her hands away and tried to kiss all that creamy swelling roundness of her breasts but when his lips touched her, she jerked upright, looking terrified, as though that particular thing had never occurred to her. Never.

"No, don't!"

Well, my God, what was he going to do? Should he have explained, or something?

The light was what was doing it, he decided. Just get rid of the damned light and everything would be alright. He let her go so quickly she dropped back on the bed and the mattress bounced.

"Wait a minute," he said.

He charged away from the bed and made for the candle-stand, nearly overturning the thing. The candlestick and candle came apart in his hands, and he caught both pieces just in time. He snuffed out the candle with his fingers and

58

didn't even try to fit the pieces back together again; he put them back on the table and they rolled off the edge and he heard them drop on the floor in the darkness.

Well, to hell with it; he didn't have time to look for candles and junk.

He groped his way back to the bed and felt around with his hands until he felt something soft and ruffled. The edge of her skirt. Down under it, she was all wound in a knot, her knees drawn up.

"Anna, please darling, I love you, I'm just trying to make love to you," he told the darkness hurriedly.

He found her arms and pulled her to him, trying to get them down from where she had them locked over her breasts.

"Please, please," she whispered.

"Well, alright, I won't bother you, . . ." her elbow hit him in the chest. "Please Anna, sugar, let me do it . . . stop squirming, will you? I want to love you, love you, . . ." he said into a mouthful of her hair. He was damned near shaking himself to death, he was so excited, and he couldn't take time to calm her. If she'd just be still he was sure he could pet her and kiss her and show her that they didn't have to wrestle all over the bed. She had really hit him a lick with her elbow, though. Now she was trying to keep it out of his way, and he felt the brush of her flesh and the little sharp bones of the corset.

It was worse when he tried to pull up her never-ending skirt and petticoats because she kept trying to pull them down, but finally he got them wadded up and located the kneepants or whatever they were and struggled with them. The kneepants gave way, and his hand slipped between her thighs. She quit trying to haul up the kneepants and grabbed his wrist.

"Don't . . . don't, . . ." she cried. "What are you trying to do? Stop!"

Lord, this was a battle royal! Didn't she know? Did some-

59

body expect him to tell her? He was desperate and half-crazy with excitement.

"Nothing . . . ." It was a stupid thing to say and he knew it, but just the feel of her warm, soft flesh rattled him and the squirming made it worse. If she would just relax a little bit, put her arms around him or say something besides don't and stop, he maybe could manage to be a little calmer himself. But she wouldn't.

He felt her thighs clamp against his fingers. They set in, grimly, to struggle.

"Anna, Anna, listen, Anna, sugar, I'm not going to hurt you . . . what do you think I'm trying to do anyway? I'm only trying to make love to you . . . quit it, can't you? Dammit . . . I'm not going to do anything, . . ." but his fingers pressed forward and touched her, intruding, and the effect was like a thunderclap: she gave a jump and came right up at him, trying to sit up, her eyes, in the faint light, wide and wild.

"No, you can't . . . ."

Her hand was locked around his wrist, trying to pull him away.

"No, no!" If anybody could shriek in a whisper, she could. It was as much as he could do to hold on, his fingers caught.

"You're alright, you're alright, see," he tried to persuade her hoarsely. "Oh God, how I love you, want you, . . . you've got to let me, dammit . . . put your knees down . . . ."

But she got his hand away, finally. It drove her wild to have him touch her like that.

In a sort of nightmare flash he knew she didn't have any idea of what was supposed to happen.

He didn't want to believe that. He was damned if he was going to believe that. Besides, she'd love him, trust him, in just a minute. She had to learn sooner or later. It wasn't all that bad.

"Put your knees down, can't you?" he cried.

But she wouldn't. She still had her skirt or petticoats rolled up between them. He was shivering and shaking like a wild man and not able to get those damned infernal clothes out of there, but after some interminable juggling around he managed to get his hands underneath her so that he could hold her tightly and make her give a little and get her knees moved out of his way.

"I can't . . . I can't," she cried.

"Hold still, yes, you can. . . ."

His weight had pushed one of her legs down and he held it there maneuvering furiously, but when she felt him press against her she jumped again, and he nearly lost his grip on her.

Her eyes kept getting wider and wider and her back stiffened under his hands and her fingers clawed at him, but her head was jammed against the headboard and she couldn't get away.

"Oh no, . . ." she whispered, unbelieving.

Lord, if there was a time when he wanted to kiss her and soothe her and say something, anything, this was the moment, and yet he was afraid to let her go, excited and sweating and shaking enough for both of them.

Besides, he didn't know what the devil he could say. He couldn't think, he was all tied up in knots; it was no time for him to make a speech.

It was all going to be over in a second, anyway.

He watched her face and when she opened her mouth to screech he put his lips over hers to smother it. Nothing happened except that she tried to get up again and banged her head. Her fingernails scratched him. Then suddenly her body arched up at him and the tight, resisting flesh split and parted and it was done, her hands tearing at his hair, trying to pull him off, making strangled noises under his mouth and her legs kicking.

He felt as if he was going to explode, bedeviled and

61

harrassed; he couldn't pay attention to her and to himself at the same time.

She wrenched her mouth away, and it was all he could do to catch her and clap his hands over her lips.

"Sugar, for God's sake, don't yell!"

It was muffled, his hand clamping down, but still loud enough, it sounded to him, to wake the whole damned hotel.

"Wait a minute, wait a minute, can't you?" he cried.

But she kept right on.

No, no, stop it, she was telling him, I can't stand it! She was shaking her head back and forth and pulling at his hair.

"Jesus, don't do that!" She was squirming and lunging around trying to get rid of him, crying oh, oh, and he felt the sweat popping out on his face.

He gave up, God, there was just so much he could stand! When he moved, she didn't expect that, either and it drove her crazy. She kept kicking and squirming, and he lost his head. He was past caring, past thinking about anything except that he would apologize later, but he couldn't stop. And just vaguely he guessed he was being rough as the devil . . . she clawed at him and he heard her head hit the bed several times and each time she yelped.

Then he fell against her and put his mouth on her cheek and then on her neck and kissed her hair and it was all over.

There was a dead quiet second—just a split second of nothing at all, and then she pitched away from him, half dragging him with her, scrabbling for the bedcover, winding it around her as though she was going to lock herself up so that he could never touch her again. Then she put her face down in the bed and started sobbing, just squalling.

"Anna," he said.

But she wouldn't speak to him.

CHAPTER 5

We loved each other then, Lorena,
More than we ever dared tell,
And what we might have been, Lorena,
Had our loving but prospered well!

He couldn't sleep, and she wouldn't sleep, going off into
fresh spasms of weeping every time he even mentioned her
name, so by the first light of day he was glad to get out of
the place, pay their bill, and look somewhere else for breakfast, and this in itself was lucky, for they were so early the
dining room of the Atlanta Hotel had only a handful of
people. The Negro headwaiter escorted them to a choice
table by the window where they could watch the Atlanta
Hotel's celebrated view of the railroad station and the
locomotives pulling into the yards and the travelers coming
straight from the depot by way of a private boardwalk.

He personally couldn't take much interest in the scene.
He was so dog-tired and sleepless his hands shook, and his
nerves flinched every time there was even the most ordinary
sort of racket of dishes and silverware in the place. After
the first cup of coffee, real blockade coffee and a gift from
heaven, he managed to settle down somewhat and observe
Anna eating her breakfast and dividing her attention between it and the view through the window glass.

At least they had accomplished the fine honeymoon
breakfast, he thought. And he was impressed at once with
the ability of human beings, female human beings at any
rate, to look smooth and easy in spite of hell. For she was as
much in possession of herself, he thought resentfully, as if

she'd had a good night's sleep in her own bed in Augusta. She was so damned good-looking that a table of officers kept eyeing her, watching her eat as he was watching her, thinking, no doubt as he was thinking, that she was the perfect picture of the cool, fashionable beauty with her long straight nose and lowered eyes and sweet, demure mouth. She was eating fried eggs and biscuit, lifting her fork to her mouth as steadily and daintily as though she hadn't ever turned her hand to anything more exciting than breakfast in her life. But she hadn't had time to do her hair up in all those slick buns and rats of the day before; instead, a loose mass of black curls pushed out from under her bonnet in back and in front curled up against her cheeks. She looked adorable, and he hated himself for thinking anything about her other than how much he loved her.

God, what a confounded mess, he thought dismally.

Their conversation wobbled in fits and starts about nothing much. He suspected the only reason she was talking to him at all was because they were in a public place, a dining room with officers and headwaiters and everybody looking on. So they talked about the trains coming and going in the terminal and what a big town Atlanta was, and the number of soldiers getting off the trains which he told her were probably furloughed troops from the army of Tennessee at Dalton, and the fact that they certainly were lucky to get into a nice hotel like the Atlanta for breakfast, and she did not need any more milk for her coffee nor sugar, either, thank you.

He was discovering for the first time that they really did not have much to say to each other. He couldn't understand it. Conversation had never seemed such a desert before, filled with the sands of long-drawn-out silences, then the sudden bursts when they both tried to say something at the same time.

She was not the same girl. He could swear it.

To see her sitting across the table in her blue bonnet

and blue dress and gold eardrops shaking in her ears, no one would ever suspect what had gone on a few hours before.

He suddenly felt pretty violent about it all. No wonder there was so damned much confusion in the world, he told himself. This girl, Anna, his beautiful lovely wife, was sitting there all wrapped up in clothes from her neck to her shoe tops, only speaking to him because it was the polite thing to do, to pretend that everything was perfectly fine for total strangers looking on, just as though she was never made for anything else and damned well better not be used for anything else except society and polite sham and all that—love and weddings be damned! And God help the poor jasper who loved her fit to kill and just wanted to touch her and kiss her and caress all that silk-smooth skin and make love to her without her clothes on in spite of damned people and damned society and damned convention and damned weddings and damned rules about not telling a beautiful lovely girl what to expect!

He got so worked up about it that his hand shook and he spilled nearly half a cupful of coffee into his lap. He didn't get up, but he grabbed a napkin and started wiping away for dear life, scalded as the very devil, and she shot him a quick, scared look.

He glared back at her.

Hell, what did she care whether it got boiled off or not! He'd be better off in this life as a damned eunuch or whatever they were, the way things were going.

"Did you burn yourself?" she said, low, wide-eyed.

He couldn't trust himself to speak.

For some reason, he was suddenly mad as hell at her. There was just no sense or reason to it, that was what infuriated him. She had put pretty nearly all her clothes on under the cover of the damned hotel bedspread when a person would think there wasn't any need for modesty by then. But he had had to get up and fetch her ruffled kneepants and the corset thing that were scattered around on the floor and hand them to her, while she bent up under the covers and managed to get them on without showing herself. The only thing she had asked him to do was lace her up the back when she put on the corset thing and help her with the buttons of that infernal blue dress. If he had any friends in creation they were corset strings and buttons. You couldn't be too damned proper while all that was going on.

The waiter came and gave him another cup of coffee, and he threw sugar and cream into it, knowing that he was upsetting her. He stirred it as hard as he could, watching it slosh into the saucer.

The whole damned thing was a lot of foolishness. He knew damned well what she looked like without her clothes on. Too damned well for his own good.

God, he was a fool! He had gone off just like a firecracker, worse than any beginner on his first time. And now she wouldn't talk to him nor even pretend that he was anywhere around, unless she had corset strings that needed to be tied or needed table conversation because other people were looking.

She lifted her cup to her lips and sipped it and looked out the window, and he watched her, fidgeting, not able to eat. His nerves were in worse shape than when he had come down from Dalton.

His life was a confounded shambles.

Then she looked at him, not expecting to find him watching her, and in that quick look her eyes were startled and deep as storm clouds.

Lord, he thought, suffering, if just once he could be able to know what she was thinking about when she looked at him like that!

Then he looked away, and she looked away, quickly, and the waiter came up with their bill.

66

There was an hour wait on the train to Jonesboro, and while they sat in the car he tried to keep the conversation going so as not to have it freeze again into one of those unendurable silences. His head felt as though it was going to blow off, a result of the whiskey of the day before and no sleep, he reckoned. In fact, he felt as nervous and dragged-out as though he had not had any sleep in months. Being in the damned train made it worse; he had gotten to hate trains with a passion. It seemed to him that he had been riding trains forever.

The engine for the Jonesboro-Griffin-Macon train was the regular single, the little *Montgomery Pharr* that had been his uncle's regular run before the war, and he felt as though he knew every driver, wheel, and coupling by heart. The coaches were a hodgepodge, though, most of them taken off the Chattanooga line, which was now in enemy hands. The car in which they were sitting was an old excursion coach: it had a view of Lookout Mountain painted over the rear door. In no time the place filled up, all the seats taken, and then people began to put their luggage in the aisle to sit on. There were a lot of farmers in black wool hats and soldiers and businessmen and several women with children and an artillery captain just a few seats down with a party of four or five really flashy-looking women. The captain and his females started having a rare old time the minute they came aboard, passing the bottle around. Every now and then one of the girls would laugh and let out a squawk calculated to lift the roof. The women were full of "yew don't say's" which told right off that they were from somewhere up in the hills. One of them let out a screech that made him wonder what in the devil they were doing up there, anyway.

Anna would have none of it. She was looking out the window, whether there was anything to see out there or not. A woman across the aisle whipped out a little black Bible and started reading it for dear life.

Well hell, it was only a bunch of whores. They weren't going to do anything right out in public.

The back of Anna's bonnet moved between him and the window. He wondered if she ever sat around reading the Bible. Not that he objected to reading the Bible, he was all for it in its proper time and place, but he wondered suddenly if she would snatch up a Bible right in a train like that, like the woman across the aisle, to keep from paying attention to something like the other thing going on up there.

For a moment he was attacked by a despair so great he was certain he was going to have to jump up and walk around, do something.

They couldn't live together for the rest of their lives the way things were. Godalmighty!

He saw himself getting up from the seat and making a dash for the door. Gone forever. Just like a newspaper item: "Soldier deserts his wife in the Atlanta carshed. There one minute, and gone the next, seventeen-year-old bride testifies. No reason can be found for the incident; the young couple had only been married a day or two."

He broke out in a cold sweat, never moving, and in the next second the train gave a head-shaking lurch and started on its way out of the Atlanta terminal, to his great relief.

There was one thing about coming down from Atlanta for the first time: until you got past the city limits it was a pretty interesting place to watch. Downtown the regular traffic still rolled over the tracks, and there was always some hairbreadth chase by some fool in a wagon or carriage to see if he could beat the locomotive to the crossing. The trains moved right between brick buildings and stores and past the North Georgia Bank and Trust Company where you could see right into the windows and watch the clerks already at work for the day on their high stools. Then the railroad line passed into a vacant part of town where there was only a scattering of lumberyards and such, and then beyond that came the big gray bulk of the rolling mills and factories and then shanty town with its nigger shacks and the mule barns and auctions and then, abruptly, into a section where the train passed near the backs of fairly nice-looking houses and intersecting tree-lined yards where there were chicken coops and sheds for cows. Then on to the outskirts, the powder mill, the cavalry camp, a farm, and then another farm and finally just fields and farms, and that was all there was to see. The landscape settled down to a monotony of pine forests and wind-swept winter ridges and the gullies of the Piedmont, the trackbed taking the highest ridge on to the south.

"Pretty usual sort of scenery," he said to Anna.

The back of the bonnet nodded.

The double-track line split at the village of East Point, just outside of Atlanta, into the single-track line of the Macon Railroad, going due south, and the Columbus line, which made for Alabama. The place had a big switching yard. He knew it well. His Uncle Trennon used to take him there when he was a child, because that was the switching-over point for a lot of the trains and their crews. He started to say something to Anna about it, but he guessed, in a second thought, that she was probably not very much interested in trains and switchyards and things like that.

After they had passed the East Point yards the solid pine forests opened up a bit, and a house came by as everything is seen from a train when it is picking up speed—sort of a wink-of-the-eye—house and wash flapping on the line. Then, as he knew, just around the bend there was a big house in the popular Greek revival style but with sort of upcountry modifications: the pillars were square and rough-hewn, and the upper gallery was off-center as though the builders never had managed to get it right.

He started to speak to Anna and tell her that the house

belonged to his cousin Cass Allen, but before he could open his mouth a skyrocket of shrieks from the front of the car distracted him. Everybody craned to look.

It was those damned women with the artilleryman.

One of the girls had her leg propped up on the chair arm and her skirt pulled back so that you could see six inches of pea-green stocking. She was wagging her foot up and down. God, yellow shoes with patent-leather toes. That was a taste for glory!

He looked around to see if the conductor was coming, but the conductor wasn't in their car. If his Uncle Trennon had been aboard those girls would have found themselves hiking along the tracks in double time. His Uncle Trennon had strict Presbyterian ideas about train manners, or any kind of manners, for that matter. His uncle was hell on such things.

From where he was sitting Johnny could see the girl fairly well, a redhead with common features: big, pushed-out mouth, little eyes, potato nose, and thick bumpy skin with lots of powder on it to cover the freckles. But sort of fun. He knew the type. Anything would go with a big old girl like that, one of those rawboned, ass-slapping girls, all shove and tumble. Just like that girl, Aggie, up at Memphis Bertha's. They were a caution.

The memory of the night he and Byron and Ed had gotten so drunk at Bertha's popped into his head. He had never been so confounded drunk since. They had got loud and boisterous as the devil, and Byron got the notion that he was big and strong enough to break a chair down by running and jumping in it, buck naked, and no amount of argument could get the idea out of his head. That was the trouble with Byron when he was drunk; he was harder to handle than ten men his size, or bigger.

But old Aggie hadn't liked Byron's didos a bit and got mad and fought with him, standing up and trading punches because she was from way up in the mountains and that

70

was the way a lot of those girls up there had to be to get along at all. And she sure could drink. She had beat them all at that game.

When they finally got old Aggie to bed, Byron, little Byron with that damned dapper mustache and cardsharp hands and lady-sized feet, walked over and surveyed her with her knees drawn up and her speckled, spavined breasts and all that sagging muscular nakedness and cried, "My sweet Aunt Mary, I'd just as soon screw an old horse!" And she had raised up, trying to focus her eyes and bellowed, "Don't you call me no names, you sonofabitch!" to which Byron had yelled, "HORSE, damn you, HORSE!" and they had fallen all over each other laughing fit to kill.

In spite of his misery he started to laugh and then caught it up short and looked around. But no one was paying any attention to him at all.

The railroad tracks came straight down the middle of Jonesboro. In fact, what one could see on either side of the railroad was about all there was to the place: livery stables and saloons and the cotton gin and the depot and the courthouse like a two-story brick box. On either side of the tracks, above and below downtown or whatever the business part of Jonesboro was usually called, were houses with wide porches and stands of elm and oak in the yards, everything now shut up against the howling northwest winter wind.

He had his arms full with his rifle and gear and her portmanteau, and he knew he would have to manage the lot the mile or more to his house, as no one was expecting them and therefore no wagon would be waiting for them.

"I can carry my own case," she said timidly, but he shook his head.

The main road out of town, going west, intersected at the railroad, and his Aunt Mildred Grimes' house stood on the corner. He was in a hurry to get past for fear his Aunt Mildred or her sister, his Aunt Rose Nell, should come darting out to intercept them and be the first to hear the news. They were like that. Beyond his Aunt Mildred's house was the Negro cabin with white smoke blowing from the chimney, and two of Clem, the cook's, children sitting on the steps.

Bright as the sun was, the wind tore down the road like a fury. Anna pulled up the collar of her coat, trying to hold it against her mouth.

"You don't have to walk," he told her. "You could wait in the depot. I'll go home and bring back the wagon for you."

"No," she said, into the coat collar.

"No, I'll get it for you. It's too cold to make you walk all the way."

He started to offer to leave her at his Aunt Mildred Grimes' house, but he hated to do so; he didn't want his Aunt Mildred and his Aunt Rose Nell digging away at him with forks right off. Not this day.

They were both so cold they couldn't stand still while they argued it out. They had to jig first on one foot and then the other, their lips almost too stiff to say anything. The wind was cutting through his useless jacket like a knife, and her face was white as chalk, yet the tip of her nose was red.

"Anna," he burst out, "listen, God, whatever I've done, I'm sorry."

But her eyes slid away from him.

"Please don't let's stand here," she told him. "I'm freezing."

Beyond his Aunt Mill's house the road passed between cow pastures and slave cabins and the casual jumble of most southern towns: back yards, coach houses, nigger shacks, hogpens, and turnip patches, and the Hanes' board-fenced garden with a forest of dead bamboo canes and a flagstone piazza and a statue of a granite Psyche forever bending to mourn her toenails a few feet from the washline and rain barrel.

The road opened out on furrowed fields, the cornstalks

72

already topped for winter fodder and the naked spears leaning together. Wind pushed against them in a solid sheet as they came down the hill, and at the bottom, some distance away, they could see the black stream of the Flint through the iron-work thickets. On the far side of the river, on a ridge as high as Jonesboro's, stood a house.

"That's the place," he said to Anna.

They could not make out more than the outline of it through the empty tree branches, but it was straight-up-and-down, steep gabled roof with chimneys running up the sides. A clump of sheds lay behind in a pinewoods at the rear.

He had to stop, to shift her case from his right hand to his left, to ease his aching fingers.

"All that land," he said on impulse, "is ours, going down to the river over on the other side and then back away, west. Hannaford's gin is the boundary. A hundred and fifty acres." A burst of fondness for the subject made him go on. She might really be interested, he thought. "That chimney, can you see? That was the first place Granpa built, a log cabin, when he got this parcel of land from the government. He was in the Delaware regiment in the Revolution, and Congress gave it to him as a bonus when the Creeks and Cherokees were thrown out up here."

She seemed to be paying attention.

"Granpa was going to give up the cabin and move to higher ground anyway on account of the fever from the bottom land, but the cabin burned down one night. So then he built the house you see up there. When the stages started coming through and then the railroad was built, people started planting cotton and importing niggers and made good money. We, . . . Granpa and then my pa, wouldn't hold niggers. The Presbyterians around here were generally against it. Still are, some of them. So Granpa put his money into the house."

"Oh," she said.

They started on down the hill and crossed the wooden span at the river and beyond it the burying ground with its casual headstones, some already fallen, the old glass pitchers and vases which had once held flowers glinting in the sun. The names on the stones were the same over and over again: MacLeod, Thames, MacLeod, Hannaford, Huie, MacLeod. All county people, nearly all Presbyterians, with a sprinkling of Baptists and Methodists.

As they got up close the house seemed to rise from the red clay banks on ankles of rock pillars. A few althea and Cape jessamine bushes had been planted to hide the ugly underbelly where the chickens and dogs roosted, but in the winter they were bare and leafless. A fringe of tall crepe myrtle bushes, almost the size of trees, which his Aunt Matt had planted years ago, lined the short driveway. There was red clay everywhere, rain and wind scoured, hard and dry as stone.

The dogs came roaring out from under the house as they approached, only to fawn and squirm along on their bellies when they found out who it was. Johnny held them off as best he could, his hands full.

The door to the house opened, and a woman came out on the porch, flinging a shawl over her shoulders. Her hair was coal black, and she was stout and she had a small mouth and thick white skin and black eyes.

"Hi, Matt," he said into the wind. "I got married. This is my wife."

CHAPTER *6*

🎵🎵 *The morning star is paling*
  The campfires flicker low
  Our steeds are madly neighing
  For the bugler bids us go.

He felt that he could tell Byron just so much and then no more, for while there was no better person to sympathize with him at times than his friend, this particular predicament was sort of out of Byron's field. At least that was the way he felt about it. There was also no small amount of pride involved, too. God knows if anybody thought there was anything funny in it—his problem, that is—he would be driven to half-kill them. He remembered how sore he had been about that "handsome" business in Chattanooga.

The only person he could think of who might understand was Tom Norse. Tom was a married man of two-years' experience or so, and if he could ever bring himself to broach the subject Tom might shed some light or hope on things. But Tom was not back from his leave.

There were only a few more furloughers to come in, for most of the company had returned to camp by the end of January. There was some slight comfort in finding out that something or other had happened to nearly every member. At least he was not the only one. Babb Burnside had got religion at the Mount Zion Church in the south part of the county and had brought back a Bible which he set up every night and read by firelight. Lt. Ed Grimes, having plenty of money, had taken one week of his time to frolic in Atlanta on the way back, and Ed had regaled the officer's messes

75

of Weir's and Lowrey's brigades with recollections of the marvelous theatricals he had seen in the city, the best political gossip from the Trout House Bar, and all the tent and side shows, including one performance by a girl with a bottle which was, Ed said, the damnedest thing he had ever witnessed, and which he would go back and pay a hundred dollars Confederate to see again. Will Dixon had married Miss Mattie Moore of Lovejoy's Station, and Walt Ashford took his three weeks to become engaged to Mitchell Fitzgerald's sister Caroline. Walt bought a copper plate in Atlanta with her name engraved on it, and had it bolted to the stock of his rifle.

But still Tom Norse did not come.

When he finally got around to it, his cousin told him that he had paid a call to Johnny's house with his mother and his Aunt Rose Nell, and that the Grimeses had stayed to dinner.

"We got the bride a present of sorts," Ed told him. "Mamma got it, a thingamajig, a linen chest I think they said it was. Had brass scrolls and stuff all over the sides. Mamma ordered it from Atlanta."

"How's everything getting along?" he said, with caution.

"You mean Miss Anna?" Ed asked.

He felt himself turning red. What the devil was this "Miss Anna" business!

"Oh, Miss Anna's fine, fine," Ed said airily. "Well, I tell you, actually, they say the traffic on that road's picked up a hundred percent since you brought Miss Anna out to stay at your house. All she's got to do is sit on the porch . . . say, do you remember old Mr. Charlie Tucker, the one that's ninety or something? Well, he got his nigger to harness up his buggy and take him out to see. The damned old buggy's about as ready to fall to pieces as he is! Aunt Matt said Mr. Charlie was so red in the face by the time he got there she had to make him stay the whole afternoon just to keep him alive long enough to get back home. And he kept raving about how sweet and pretty your little bride was, and made her sit and let him pat her on the hand. . . ."

"You go to hell," he told him fiercely.

"Well, godalmighty," Ed said, making his eyes bug out and raising his eyebrows, "what did I say now? You're not jealous of a poor old ninety- or a hundred-year-old man like poor old Mr. Charlie Tucker, are you?"

"All I did was ask how everybody was getting along," he ground out, "and you start babbling like a damned idiot. I don't want to hear all that trash! I just asked you how everybody was getting along."

"Well, hell, I was telling you, wasn't I? The only thing I heard around home was your Uncle Trennon likes Miss Anna a lot, and she gets along fine with your Aunt Matt, and Mamma thinks she's sweet and pretty enough to eat, and somebody said her daddy had written her to say he was lonesome for her in Augusta and anytime she got homesick she could come on back for a visit. How's that?"

He left Ed abruptly and spent the rest of the afternoon sitting on a stump in the upper brigade area composing a letter which begged Anna to stay where she was, at least until he could get another furlough. He didn't want her to go back to Augusta with no more settled between them than there was.

Which sounded, he told himself, as though there was something settled. Which there wasn't. Nothing at all.

In fact, if he had to come right down and admit it, he guessed after their stay in Jonesboro, things were worse than ever.

While they had been home his Aunt Matt managed to be always around somewhere so that they had to act like guests in a hotel or tea-party acquaintances most of the time, and when they were alone upstairs in the privacy of what used to be his old room and Robert's, Anna just stayed out of his reach. Just like that. That first day, anyway.

The few times he had tried to touch her hair or kiss her or fool around in any way, she just sort of glided off.

And that first night at home they had almost come to out-and-out war before she would face up to the fact that they had to sleep together in the same bed because he damned well wasn't going to sleep on the floor or sitting up in a chair.

The plain truth of it was she couldn't stand to have him touch her at all. It was his own fault because of what had happened in Atlanta. But God knows he had tried to back up and straighten out things, and she wouldn't let him. She wouldn't even let him mention it to her, and when he tried to sweet-talk or kiss her she jumped out of his way as though she expected him to throw her down and take her right off the bat. Not even giving him half a chance. He hated for her to do that way. He loved her, he wanted to have a chance to pet her and talk to her. Sometimes he felt as if he would give anything just to stand and hold her hand, for God's sake! It nearly killed him to see her skittering out of his way as if he was some kind of ogre.

That first night at home he left her alone, let her sleep way over on her side of the bed as she wanted to, but the second night he was as restless as a cat and knew he couldn't put up with much more of that, not within two or three feet of her all night long, anyway, and so he insisted. He insisted like hell for three hours and then it could not have been any worse, they way she acted, than if he had made an appointment to torture her. God, he might just as well have brought a rack and chains, or something! It was all such a struggle that she was wet with perspiration and shaking all over before they were through, and instead of letting it go, he lost his temper and held her down and forced her a second time, and for once she was so worn out it wasn't like some damned pitched battle, and that was a help. But something happened even then, and she yelped

78

and scratched him, and he was sure his Aunt Matt had heard her, all the way downstairs.

"What did you want to go and do that for?" he almost hollered. She wasn't even looking at him. She was shivering, and her hair was all wild and tangled and for all he knew she didn't even realize who he was, but he could feel her trying to get rid of him—he could feel it, that was the damnable thing—and he knew she wouldn't give up. He had her, he was holding her down, and they had gone far enough so that there was nothing to fight about and yet she was still resisting, and what she was doing was just wrecking him; he had got to the place where he didn't know whether there was any love in him for anybody or whether he was some damned monster, sure enough. His mind kept churning around in circles, trying to think of a solution, and all he could come up with was to leave her strictly alone. Forever. For maybe fifty years. People stayed married that long.

Godalmighty, all this to face, when he didn't have but two days of his leave left!

Nor could he talk to her about it. They had gotten to the place where they couldn't talk about much of anything, more like actors in a dumb show than anything else.

Well, he told himself in despair, that's why there are whore houses. That's pretty damned well why. And then he thought, I'll be damned if I will! I hate whore houses, I'll never go back to one again, they're for people like Ed Grimes who don't give a damn. But I love somebody and I'm not going to be driven into any damned whore house, not if it *takes* fifty years!

But he let her go.

For a minute he thought about trying, just one more time, to say something to her. But she popped right up, sitting up, not bothering to cover herself, all white and shining with the dark shadow of her hair hanging loose on her shoulders, and looked around the room as though she was thinking of running off. She actually put her feet over the side of the bed. And he had some crazy thought then that she might sure enough get up and start running around, or—oh God! —looking for his Aunt Matt, so he went after her and pulled her back and started kissing her and telling her to be reasonable, that God, what was he going to do with her? and she kept fending him off. That made him keep right on. He put his arm around her neck and drew her down and really wasn't going to do anything at first, but the whole damned business was telling on him; he knew he was being goaded into doing everything wrong and, hell, he might as well make the most of it! Even when he knew he didn't have any right to act that way with her. It was all the worse because he loved her and wanted her to look at him, for God's sake, and quit acting like he was some sort of lunatic!

Which he went right ahead and proved.

No one in their right mind would say that he wasn't more than half-crazy then, a damned lunatic sure enough. He wouldn't let her protest nor put a stop to a damned thing. Not that she really tried to. She was too damned busy.

That surely couldn't be called anything settled between them, not at all, unless it was that he was a whole hell of a lot stronger than she was, and didn't have any damned sense.

And then, because he was hell-bent for disaster and didn't care, he had the same bright idea the next morning when he didn't let her get more than half-dressed. Daylight, too. One busted button on a petticoat and a whole bucketful of tears. He had bruised her mouth because it swelled up like she had run into a whole hive full of bees. The first thing his Aunt Matt asked her when they came down to breakfast was what had happened to her mouth. As if she didn't know.

Lord, he was in a mess! If there was any hope at all, he'd better get right home and see what he could do to fix up things, to keep her from going home to Augusta.

He thought of a dozen reasons for applying for emergency furlough, none of them good enough, and all of them subject

80

to Ed Grimes' approval, and he had vowed that he was not going to raise his cousin's curiosity about his private affairs any more than he had to.

God knows, he told himself gloomily, how much his family and relations already knew or suspected. His Aunt Mill and Aunt Rose Nell could not be beat for offhand speculation, and his Aunt Matt was a hawk for anything she suspected of being secret or hidden. Especially about marriages. He remembered the gossip from years back concerning a new minister's wife who went home to her folks after two months, leaving behind the gospel truth of the matter which was (told in whispers) that he was too LARGE for her. The damnable part of this was, as he knew, that this was probably right, but he could never feature the minister's wife telling it to any of the women in the church, nor was there any other way to reach this conclusion unless she had—or unless there had been a witness on the spot.

But his Aunt Mill, Ed Grimes' mother, knew all about it, and so did his Aunt Rose Nell, and so did Matt and the women of the Presbyterian Church and then just about every other denomination, Methodist, Baptist, and even the Catholic Fitzgeralds. After that came all their husbands and all the white population of Jonesboro above the age of ten and eventually the colored portion which never missed out on anything secret and worth telling. The whole damned town knew, including those who had to sit every Sunday morning like himself and try and keep their attention on the sermon the poor bastard was preaching and not get to thinking about the difficulties he must have gone through, while not knowing that everyone else knew, too.

It did not give him one particle of hope for the privacy of his own marital problems.

He had to go home, that was all, he decided. Letters were no good. He had to think of some way to get home.

But the matter was settled for him, although the first letter he wrote home was not the one he had planned.

My dear wife,

I am pretty well at Dalton and hope you are the same. Give my regards to Aunt Matt.

Then, because he was in haste, he got right to the news.

If you will notice my new address it is 2nd Georgia Sharpshooters and my commanding officer is Captain Rufus Stonecypher. This is how this all came about. We got a shipment of British made Whitworth rifles delivered in camp which came through the blockade. They are fine made, none better. Each brigade was ordered up for competition for the guns and out of our regiment, the 79th Georgia, Joe Fain and I were chosen and two others from Weir's and so forth down the line. We shot for the guns and I was brigade winner. I get the new Whitworth as my regular arms and also a transfer into this company of Sharpshooters where I understand we will be trained and might be attached to other divisions as needed. There was some pretty keen shooting for the Whitworths and some of the best I have ever seen. One boy was a fine shot but plagued by bad luck. His finger slipped on the trigger as we came up to the final shoot off but it was on the last round of fire. It was just bad luck as he was leading up to that time. Except for that he would have won. His name is Merriman and he is from Decatur where his father is a doctor. This new order is due to the new general, Joe Johnston and his reorganization of the army. General Pat Cleburne, division commander who is British Army trained although an Irishman, is setting up a school for staff officers in a hut here and the quartermasters have been put to work for a change. We have just been issued shoes of untanned leather for those who are still barefoot and although they curl up pretty bad they are better than nothing. Some of the boys have been experimenting with bark juice and other things to tan them.

Well I will not tire you further with army news except to tell you that the new commander, Johnston, has said that he will feed and clothe us if it is humanly possible and has already begun to carry out that plan and the army's spirits have revived as never before. Those who went home in December saying that they were going to stay and not come back are already returning and although the news from Richmond is not any better and the country's situation not much changed in other ways this army is saying that it can win this year with Joe Johnston at the head and this is the biggest step forward yet. This Army is as good as any army of Northern Virginia if Jeff Davis will just give it a chance and the people and the state governments pay some attention to it. Longstreet said as much last fall when he brought his corps down to lend aid in Tennessee. And with Lee and Johnston the Yanks will have a hard time to lick us. Johnston is small in stature but straight as a hickory due to his West Point training and he has a small chin whisker. He is about fifty years old and in clothes is a regular dandy. He has the finest uniform the army has seen for some time with every button and frog that regulations require and then some. He has a bright new sash, gauntlets and silver spurs. But his talents match his turnout as the boys say, for he has stopped desertions and done better generally up here.

He tried to get back to the subject for he was running out of paper.

I still have my request in for a leave and I have not given up hope. I must see you again to straighten out any difficulty between us and for this reason I hope you will not move your address but stay right where you are for it is more convenient for me to get a pass home than it is to try to get to Augusta. It would make me feel easier to know you are not planning going anywhere until I can see you and speak to you about these things again. God knows I have nothing but love and respect in my heart for you and miss you like the very devil and wish you could find it in yours to feel the same.

He almost broke down writing the last part of this and he was in a low and dismal state for the few days following. He did not expect a reply too soon and so was amazed and overjoyed to get her letter within a week.

My dear husband,
I am not going home right now as father has written me that the situation in Augusta is in a most unsettled state and they have had some riots and disturbances with the negroes sent upriver from the coast and one thing and another. And also paper is hard to get and Papa has found it necessary to move to the shop so as to be with the equipment and look after it. Mr. Ramsey the printer has gone off to join the Georgia Militia. I too would like to see you once more before the army moves from winter quarters but I wish to assure you with the greatest sincerity that I have nothing but the greatest love and respect for you and feel that faith can overcome our difficulties such as they may be.
I am glad to hear about the Whitworth gun and I hope this reaches you at your new address.
I remain your dutiful wife,
Annabella MacLeod.

CHAPTER 7

ఴఴArise, arise! with arm of might,
Sons of our sunny home!
Gird on the sword for the sacred fight,
For the battle hour hath come!

The spring was wet. In March and April it rained nearly every day in north Georgia, and the farmers complained that there would be no crop if the ground did not dry out enough to plow.

But when the army broke winter camp at Dalton and marched in the first week of May to defend Resaca from General Sherman down the railroad line, the fields in the limestone valley had been plowed and dragged in some manner, full of clods but ready, and by the time the battle of Resaca had been fought and the army withdrawn to Kingston further down the line, the corn stood like green sprigs, fleurs-de-lis in emerald as far as the eye could follow against the rich red-brown earth. At Allatoona on the rail line below Kingston the corn was high enough for the cavalry horses to graze on it, trampling it to death, and by then the army had reached close enough to the city of Atlanta for the newspapers there to report the sound of guns when the wind was right.

The Federal armies under William Tecumseh Sherman had by the middle and end of May driven the army of Tennessee a hundred miles southward into the state of Georgia; Dalton was in occupied territory. But General Joseph E. Johnston was a master of Fabian retreats, and the withdrawals were well ordered, wagons and supply trains kept up with the marching columns, and there was little straggling.

When the army withdrew to an area around Kennesaw Mountain the spring corn was waist-high and the wheat ripening in golden fields.

Here, the army rumor said, Joe Johnston was going to make Billy Sherman look like a woolly jackass, for the Federal one hundred thousand was no match for the Reb forty thousand; the flanking actions of the spring had proved it where Sherman had lost dearly, and Kennesaw was to be the trap. It had to be, for Atlanta was beyond the river and the whole state of Georgia was clamoring for action. Stand and fight.

The army entrenched and lines formed at Pine and Lost Mountains, those cones sticking up in the valley floor with Kennesaw as the apex, the latter being an observation tower dropped down from heaven.

On the three hills Joe Johnston controlled the railroad running through a gap in Big and Little Kennesaw to the town of Marietta and the bridge across the Chattahoochee River. The river was at their back, and they were on the mountains. Sherman could not be such a fool as to fail to see the place had teeth in it.

The night Cleburne's division moved in it was pouring rain, a sort of tropical downpour without thunder or lightning. A regular cloudburst the boys in the 1st Tennessee called it, in which a person could get caught with his mouth open and drown.

Johnny had salvaged a piece of oil cloth from the Federal wagons at Kingston and carried the Whitworth wrapped in it. The rest of him dripped and gushed like a mountain stream.

Kennesaw was invisible until they had moved into the railroad cut, but they heard that they were going into position somewhere on the top of the mountain and the boys were already complaining that they were not going to climb any damned hill in a rain so thick they could not see down to their own feet. The water had accumulated in the ditches and in the road proper ankle-deep, and line officers waded slowly up and down the columns trying to catch up with the rumors. Beyond the 1st Tennessee was the 6th and 7th, although they were also rain-hidden.

In the midst of the 1st Tennessee Johnny could not make out much of what was going on except for the occasional shadow of a tree and now and then clumps of pioneers working to open the ditches by the side of the road. There was a watery glitter of lanterns, and the muffled bang of axes and splitting trees and the cursing, strangling commotion connected with moving the artillery. There had been a lot of guns bogged down all the way in from Pine Mountain, the brass barrels of the Napoleons picking up the light like stranded treasure.

Within the space of a few feet the black side of Kennesaw showed itself, rising sheer as a wall. There was no time to gawk; he was still fairly new to the 1st Tennessee and feared to drop back for any reason in the rain and the dark to get separated. He was concentrating so much on keeping up that he missed the hail when it came up for him.

"Come up," the corporal shouted to him, "come up here, MacLeod, there's a shirttail captain out here wants you!"

He knew at once who it was. There could be no one else in the whole army who would pick such a night to go visiting except his cousin Ed Grimes.

When he stepped out of the column he had only the yells to guide him up toward the 7th. And there was Ed Grimes pulled off to the side of the road on a farm horse with feet as big as buckets.

His cousin dismounted when he saw him, going to the top of his boots in the mud and nearly losing his balance. But he grabbed him in a grip like a vise.

"Hi, Johnny, what you been doin', you old rascal?"

His cousin's greeting was so enthusiastic that he felt irritated and tried to push him off.

"We're goin' to camp," he shouted over the rain.

86

But Ed would not let go of him.

"Hold on, can't you? Y'all're goin' to have to pull up. There's a big gun turned over right up ahead."

"Alright, I can hear you," he said irritably.

"They're pullin' up right now. See? What'd I tell you? I knew you was right behind us. The 79th has had these mountain hoppers steppin' on our heels for the last ten miles, and I knew you was with the 1st Tennessee so when we stopped I came back to see you. Damned if we don't miss havin' you around. Byron is about wasted away with lonesomeness and keeps talkin' about transferrin' to the hospital corps or some such thing."

The column had come to a halt just as Ed had predicted, and the 7th Tennessee was dropping out to take what rest they could in spite of their colonel who, riding back to dress up the line was roaring, "You men go back into ranks thar!"

"How you been doin'?" his cousin asked him. "You heard from your wife?"

"No, dammit," he said bitterly. "It's this changing around that does it. My letters must be up somewhere. I went to the chaplain of the 1st day before yesterday, and he hadn't even seen any letters for me. Told me to try the 1st Georgia Sharpshooters. But they didn't have any. I'm half out of my mind." He put his pride in his pocket. "What does your mamma write you?"

"Oh, I get a line or so pretty regular, but no packages any more since we've been in the field. I swear I could use some pickles and light bread."

"Anna, . . ." he persisted. "What does your mother say about Matt, and Anna?"

"Aw, nothing much. Lessee, she told Mamma something about liking it out there pretty fine. She'n Matt were fixin' a garden the last I heard."

"A what?" he shouted. He watched his cousin's lips so as not to mistake it.

"A GARDEN. You know, vegetables and that sort of stuff."

87

His cousin had not changed much. He was still as ugly as ever, and he was thinner, so much so that his flesh was pulled tight in his face, making his nose and teeth seem more prominent than ever.

"You know what the grapevine says," Ed went on. "That Storr or French wants to put the artillery on top of old Kennessaw. What do you think of that, now?"

"What do I think of what?" he said, bemused.

"Ain't that HELL now? From what I heard, French is goin' to do it, too, if he has to unhitch them horses and put the boys in the traces. He might. I heard some of the boys in Bate's say they already been up to the top, and it's so steep up there you can spit over the side without hittin' the trees."

"Yes," he said, not much interested.

"Well, it sounded pretty wild to me, too, but everybody in Bate's acts like they're all fired up over it. Those guns'd get good range. I wouldn't put it past that crazy General French nohow. Say, you got any tobacco?"

He shook his head.

"That's too bad. I'm so short I'll even chew."

"Ed," he said suddenly. Now it was he who put his hand out to hold on. "Listen Ed, you don't have any letters for me, do you?"

His cousin was surprised.

"Why, you don't think I'd stand here and jaw along if I did, do you?"

"What else did your mother say about Anna? Did she say anything else? Just tell me. It doesn't have to be anything important or big. Just anything. I haven't had a letter in a month or more."

His cousin thought, making an obvious effort.

"Well, week before last Mamma said she had seen Matt and your wife and everything was fine. I don't see why you ain't gettin' your letters."

"What else did she say, dammit? I mean, is she still at home with Matt, not planning to go off?"

His cousin shrugged.

"Damned if I know. I guess not."

Someone with a lantern passed them, and he got a brief glimpse of the light as it splashed into their faces. His cousin's pale amber eyes were as blank as a cat's, his hair plastered down on his brow. The rain hissed and steamed around them in a moment's silence.

"Well, you ain't been sick any, lately?" his cousin said awkwardly.

"Hell no, I know better than that. I don't want to have you messing with me again."

Ed laughed.

"Well, quit frettin' then. That's my motto. Think of somethin' else. Say, were you in the fightin' up at Dallas? Kee-rist, you should have seen it. We spent a whole day and night puttin' up breastworks and we really knocked hell out of those Yanks. Right in the middle of the fight there come up this big thunderstorm, damnedest storm I ever saw in my life, with lightnin' playin' all over the ground hittin' the trees, and runnin' along. Would you believe it, there was some boys killed by that lightnin' instead of gettin' shot?"

"Ed." He was determined to have one more crack at it. "Wh...."

"Where you goin' now? You goin' to stay with these Tennessee boys?"

"I don't know," he said hurriedly. "The way I am now, sharpshooter, the general takes me out and moves me from one place to another especially if there's something going on." He did not want to go into his duties of the present in any detail. His cousin would be fascinated and would not let him say what he wanted. "Ed, don't you remember anything about Anna that your mother wrote about? Think, for God's sake."

"Well, I TOLD you about the garden."

"Speak up, for God's sake, where I can hear you. You holler everything else!"

"GARDEN," his cousin complied. "Her pa sent her a

package of clothes from Augusta because Daddy took them out in the gig." He was inspired. "Your Uncle Trennon was home for a week laid up. He was walkin' the tracks ahead of the locomotive down near Barnesville and fell into a bridge across the Yellow River and took all the skin off one leg. Went right through the ties." He moved suddenly. "Say, what time is it?"

"I don't know," he said. "About three or four o'clock."

"Well, I guess I got to go on," Ed said. He gestured toward the horse. "I finally got mounted, but I don't know that it ain't more trouble than its worth. I ain't no great shakes at ridin', and this thing's as mean as a sore-backed hound. Come lookin' for the company when we get dug in. Even if they put you on the mountain you'll know where Lowrey's is." He slapped convulsively at his neck, spraying water. "There they go again, goddammit. I have been so damned lousy since I left Kingston I can't hardly stand it, and what the lice haven't et, the chiggers have. I had every one of them graybacks boiled out of my clothes a month ago, too."

The 7th Tennessee was getting up from the mud and re-forming their column.

"Here we go," Ed said. "I got to move this horseflesh somehow. Somebody over at Weir's said it rode just like a camel because they rode a camel once out in Arizona. You always got to find somebody that's smart, don't you?"

The horse reluctantly accepted its passenger, and his cousin moved off, still hollering something incoherent as he passed from sight.

The attempt to put French's artillery on top of Kennesaw failed, but the lower abutment of Little Kennesaw was thought to be possible as an emplacement; Major Storr's battery had to move the guns by building a corduroy road through the mire of the railroad cut. The day was clear and hot, the air drier, and the ground was firm enough to raise the cannons to where they were needed.

There were two thousand men digging trenches on the

slopes of Little Kennesaw, and two thousand more on the peak watching the artillery attempting to get the guns up on the mountain without horses. General French was in command, and General Joe Johnston had ridden back from Pine Mountain to watch.

Johnny and the 1st Tennessee were halfway up Kennesaw, with a good view of what was going on.

"They'll never make hit," the corporal of the Rock City guards said.

They had been detailed to dig breastworks, but the show was too good to miss.

The horses had been taken from the traces of the caissons, and the artillerymen themselves were hitched up, eighteen or more men from each battery to a gun. But the caissons had to be abandoned so that the wheels would not slip on the steeper parts of the slope. The artillerymen spent all the morning working the thing out, with many failures.

One of the guns went up, worming its way up a path axed through the trees and underbrush. The ground was still soft from the rain and tore open under the weight of the gun, showing red clay like an open wound. The men strained with agonizing slowness, having to stop now and then to be replaced. Those who came away, staggering and heaving, laid themselves down under the trees. Those that came into the traces were bent forward, their hands almost touching the ground.

"They ain't goin' to make hit," the corporal said. He stuck his shovel into the dirt and used its handle as an armrest as he watched. "They might git one'r two up, but not enough to do any good."

"Lordee, look at'em pull."

The 1st Tennessee was full of admiration.

One of the guns came slithering down sideways, artillerymen scrambling to escape. It struck a tree and went over a high fall, bouncing like a toy and rammed a bunch of pines, which piled like jackstraws under the impact.

They let out their breath.

"Jesus!"

"Is anybody hurt? Can you see?"

"There's one lyin' down. But he's gettin' up now."

"Hell, they got to make it. That's French, the general hisself standing right under."

"Lord God, wouldn't you just hate to drop one of them damned Parrotts on a general?"

"You wouldn't catch me with them crazy bastards."

"Aw, them artillerymen is crazy anyhow. They cain't hear worth a toot after they been around them guns for a while. All of them is deaf as posts. You just try talkin' to them and see."

"Well, if they get them guns up thar," the corporal said, "Hit's goin' to take all day."

"You know," one of the Tennesseeans said to Johnny, "ef they was to drop one of them guns all the way down the mountain hit would break them all to pieces, wouldn't hit? I mean, you take a piece of arn as big as that, hit'll break ef you drop it that far, don't you think that's so? That's a high place up thar, just you look."

It was high, all right, almost as high as the crest of Big Kennesaw where they had first tried to place the guns. The whole mountain ran two and a half miles in length and seven hundred feet high at the peak, the rolling plain visible from the crest for fifty miles or more depending upon the weather. Allatoona to the north, where the army had battled last, was visible on one side, and turning to face the south, the Chattahoochee River and the rooftops of the houses in Atlanta could be seen. It was as though where they had been a month ago and where they were now and where they would go if they were unlucky enough to be forced back, the past, present, and the possible future, were all spread out for them to observe and take stock.

It was as hot as June ever gets, which is to say that it was sometimes hotter than July or August, and the days were

92

filled with thundershowers. Toward the end of June, as the army held the mountain and the newspapers proclaimed a stalemate and Sherman's onslaught stopped, there came a dry spell and the temperatures rose. The enemy was in sight, drawn upon the plain, and anyone willing to eye above the earthworks could see them out there building all sorts of military works: abatis, gun emplacements, chevaux-de-frise . . . the "frizzy horses" of the webfoot, rifle pits, forever digging.

And they dug with them, to keep them company, the lines shifting and extending from Pine Mountain and Lost Mountain and then back, like arms embracing the railroad.

Polk was out on Pine Mountain and on the 14th of June the grapevine heard that the general was in trouble. The artillery began working both sides from dawn to dark, boom, boom whurroom, boom, all day. A skirmish line of sharpshooters was called up to go out to Pine Mountain, and Johnny was detached from the 1st Tennessee to go with them. He went all the way out on the last line of sentries and could see lots of activity across the way, the Yankee generals riding around performing the duties of generals, looking things over and estimating the situation.

General Polk was out on Pine Mountain with some of his staff and General Johnston, walking along an exposed position where a battery of Union cannon were trying to get the range. The Bishop-General strolled away, his hands behind his back, lost in thought and a cannonball went through his body.

The pressure had begun. With Polk's death the order came to pull back, abandon the outposts, withdraw from Pine and Lost Mountains.

On his way in Johnny detoured through the depot in the pass in the direction of Weir's brigade. It was the first time he had been off the mountain in two weeks, and he had a mind to look up the 79th and Company B to see how they were getting along. He went down in the direction of Big Shanty where part of Cleburne's division was camped.

"Where's the 79th Georgia?" he asked a picket.

The soldier was a dried-up little sand-hiller with a Carolina accent.

"Ah don't know whyah anybody is at," he said. He leaned his elbow on his rifle barrel, his yellow eyes curious. "Say, whut you got, one of them shyarpshooter guns theah?"

He did not have time to stop and talk. He did not like low country boys as a rule; they were about as low-down and ignorant as people could get, most of them.

Just beyond the Carolina picket were the colors of the Orphan Brigade, and the Kentucky boys were camped in a ditch near the railroad tracks. Some switchmen's shacks and other buildings were beyond. All the trees in this part of the mountain had been cut down and the logs used for revetments, and more dirt was still being thrown up. He heard the click of shovels against stone in the earth and he saw curlicues of smoke from half a dozen cookfires.

A sergeant in the Orphan Brigade told him the 79th Georgia was somewhere in the cut. He wanted to know about General Polk. Was he dead or just wounded, or was it all rumor?

"Dead as a doornail," Johnny told him. "I was out there when it happened, although I didn't see. Took a cannonball right through the chest. I heard somebody say General Johnston was right there when it happened and he damn near cried like a baby."

The sergeant cursed.

He could not help but like the Kentucky boys, he told himself. They were about as bad off as anybody, not having been able to get home to see their folks since the beginning of the war, nor get mail, but that did not stop them. They were full of fire.

The thought of mail prodded him. He was pretty desperate himself.

94

He found the 79th encamped down near the sheds, but Ed Grimes was not around. Byron NeSmith hollered at him from where he was holding a frying pan over a cookfire.

"Come here! Oh Johnny, damned if it ain't you. Where have you been?"

The rest of them, Clay Foster and Walt Ashford and even Peed, stonelike and silent as ever, gathered around.

"Where's Ed?" he said. "I'll go see him and find out if he's heard from home and then I'll come back and eat with you. I haven't had anything hot to eat for two days. Been out on the picket lines doing sharpshooter duty."

"Hell yes, you can eat with me," Byron said eagerly. "Bobby's over at brigade headquarters but I'll send up."

He was faintly surprised to see the boys in the company had the same, strained, unearthly look he had noticed in Ed some time back and it bothered him. Somehow, he felt, they ought not to change.

"Where the hell IS Ed?" he said.

He noticed Peed turned and went off. But he was used to Peed. Walt Ashford, however, took him by the arm and drew him to one side.

"Listen, Johnny, seeing as you're relations, try and do something with him, hear? Honestly, half the time Ed, the captain, isn't around camp and the new Lieutenant, Boyd, has to make up for him. If Colonel Blalock wasn't as bad I guess something would have happened to him by now."

Byron was acting as though he wanted Walt to shut up and be still.

"Aw, Ed's a good boy, a good officer in a fight," Byron said anxiously.

"He's not a good officer other times," Walt insisted.

"Well, hell," Johnny told Walt impatiently, "I'm not his keeper. He's got more rank than any of us, let him take care of himself. Where is he?"

Byron pointed down the railroad cut.

"Over by the railroad sheds. And listen," he told him as he started off, "you watch yourself."

95

CHAPTER *8*

South Mountain towering on our right
Far off the river lay,
And over on the wooded height
We held their lines at bay.

He went down in the direction Byron had pointed out and before he got into the railroad cut he saw Ed Grimes strolling along, his hands in his pockets. His cousin looked up and saw him almost at the same time.

"Johnny!" he cried, starting to come up to him. "Where you been?"

He waited until they were closer together before answering. Ed had on a new hat, the gilt acorns on the brim glinting brightly in the hot sun, and a new pair of trousers. He looked better than he had seen him in a year and a half as far as dress was concerned, but up close he was as thin as a skeleton and heavily sunburned.

"I've been all over," he said slowly. "Up on the mountain with the 1st Tennessee and out on picket duty yesterday with Polk's corps."

"I heard General Polk was dead. Yesterday? The day before? I lose track of time back here. It's hot as hell-fire, ain't it? These high banks cut the breeze. We like to fry when the sun is straight up. Well, you look good. Burned black as a nigger."

"So're you."

"Except here," Ed said, fingering his nose. "It don't do nothing but blister." He grinned. "That's a pretty thing, that gun. Shorter than a Enfield, ain't it?"

96

"Yes," he said.

"C'mon," his cousin told him, taking him by the arm. "I've got somethin' I want to show you."

"Ed." He did not want to be pulled along to see something, whatever it was. "Ed, I haven't got any mail yet. I don't know what's gone wrong with my confounded mail. I've been up to see the regimental adjutant and the division commander and the chaplains and I can't find where I've had any mail at all. I thought your mamma, Aunt Mill, might have sent a letter for me. Did you tell her I haven't heard from home?"

"No." His cousin shook his head. "Damn, I forgot to do that. But I didn't know you wanted me to. God, I've been so busy what with one thing and another I haven't had a chance to think about it, that's the gospel truth. I thought you'd have got some by now. That's pretty poor goin', not to hear from your folks. Your wife, anyway. They still writin' you, you think?"

"Hell, I wish I knew," he burst out. "Matt'd write, anyway. It must be going someplace else. I don't even know if they've been getting my letters. Maybe they think I'm not writing them for some reason. Maybe they think I'm dead."

"Well, I don't want them to think you're dead. Jesus Christ. I'll write Mamma first off and let her know."

"If I thought somebody was stealing my mail," he said. "I'd kill him, I swear I would."

"Well, don't fret about it. Cheer up. They can't get into any trouble. I got something that'll take your mind off your worries anyway. You didn't know that, did you?"

"What?" he said suspiciously.

His cousin laughed again and put his arm across his shoulders confidentially.

"Listen. Listen. I got myself a treat down here. Did you know that? They got this uniform factory up at Roswell north of here and got these girls makin' uniforms for the soldiers, and well, since the fightin's so close and all, some of the girls have been comin' down here to watch. And they had to have a place to sit in between times and well, you just wait and see."

"What're you talking about?" he cried. "For God's sake, will you slow down or make some sense or something?"

It was all about factory girls from Roswell, that much he could make out.

"Well, hell, makin' shirts is pretty tiresome, any fool could see that. These girls have got to have a chance to see the fightin' and cheer things up some. Marietta's full of them. You ain't been back to town? Hell, it's a sight! Now these girls I know been stayin' back to town but its too far to walk out and back all day and so lately they've been comin' out to the sheds here."

"You don't mean you've got a whore house going on somewhere around here? Right HERE?"

"Godalmighty, do you have to yell it out like that? Do you know what'd happen to me if somebody was to hear?"

As well as he knew his cousin, this beat it all. He started to laugh in spite of himself.

"Ah, . . . I don't believe it. God, . . . when I get through this war, if I ever do . . . I'm going to tell how you. . . ."

He had a good laugh, the best in months, the tears trickling down his face, and he could not remember how low and dispirited he had been a few minutes before.

"I don't see anything so funny," his cousin said.

"No, you wouldn't, damn you." He started coughing as he always did when he laughed too much. "Who comes down? How much you charge?"

His cousin looked hurt.

"You don't have to put it like that. I don't have a damned thing to do with it."

"Mmfh," he said. "It's all for fun, then."

"Well, it depends. Well, it sort of depends on how much you're carryin'. Hell, I leave that up to them."

"I haven't got any money."

"Aw, come on now."

"I'm married," he said. "You know that."

His cousin smiled his silly smile.

"Aw, that don't make no difference, does it? Not now, anyway. Everybody's married."

He frowned.

"They ain't so bad," his cousin allowed. "They're mostly amateurs, you know what I mean. Three of them. Pretty young, too. You ain't carryin' a little snuff or somethin' like that, are you?"

"I got half a plug of tobacco."

"Naw, they don't want that. No money, sure enough?"

"I sent most of it home last time."

"No combs, earbobs, stuff like that?"

"What would I be carrying that trash around for?"

"I was just askin'. Well, come on down and meet the girls anyway."

"No," he said.

"Come on, dammit. Don't just stand there lookin' sour. What's got into you? You can't be miserable all the time."

"I'm not miserable," he said. He felt he was being badgered. "I'm fine.

"Then come on."

Ed was dragging him by the arm.

"Time was," his cousin told him, "when you were good for any kind of frolic."

"Only what you got me into," he said.

He allowed himself to be pulled along. He was curious, he told himself.

"You're going to get your fool self court-martialed."

"No, I ain't. You don't know who all's been down here."

"I can bet," he said.

It was just as Ed had said, three girls, but he could not tell all at once what they were like, coming from the bright sunshine of the outdoors into the purple gloom of the old cotton shed. The place smelled of lint and damp clay and spiders and dust; he could not see the limits of the walls, and he shook his head to try and clear his eyes of the bright green sunspots.

The girls had evidently been sitting around on some empty cracker boxes which had been provided for them, and they got up when he came in. As his eyes adjusted to the dimness inside he could make out that they were plain country girls, poor white or worse. One of the girls had a harelip and the other two looked as though they might be sisters. Somehow they had acquired new dresses of loud print cotton cloth, about the ugliest clothes he had ever seen.

"Who's thet?" one of them asked.

"It's me, girls," Ed said. "And this here's my cousin, ain't he a cutter?" He grabbed Johnny's hat before he knew what was going on and managed to rub his fingers through his hair. "Look at that natural curly hair, girls. Where you seen a good-lookin' boy like that around here?"

"Goddammit, Ed, keep your hands off me," he protested, but it was too late. The girls had gathered around to look him over, and the one with the harelip was smiling encouragingly.

But the youngest one wasn't bad-looking, he found. He was surprised that he was that much interested.

Damn Ed, he thought.

"Where you from?" one of the girls asked him.

"Oh, Jonesboro." It wasn't a good idea to spill too much about himself, he knew, but he could not think of anything right then but the truth.

"Whar's thet?"

"Down below Atlanta."

"Oh."

They stared at him some more.

"Say," one of the girls said to Ed, "I thought you said you was goin' to bring some likker down."

"Couldn't get none."

100

"You said you was goin' to bring down some likker from the surgeons. Thet's whut you said."

"Well, I brought *him*. How about that? Won't he do?"

There was a deep silence while they thought this over.

"You mean he ain't got no money."

"I got some," Johnny said. "I ain't asking for anything free."

It was a slip; he felt he had committed himself. He blushed and could feel his face turning hot.

"Wal, don't let it fuss you," the youngest one said unexpectedly. She moved in front of him, arms folded, looking him over.

"I won't," he told her.

She swayed back on her heels, surveying him, making up her mind. "I knowed a boy looked like you onct," she said cautiously.

He was on familiar ground.

"I'll bet you were sweethearts." She was a lot more attractive than the other two, pale, blond, with a sharp, skinny nose.

"Might, 'ner might not," she said archly.

He halfheartedly moved to put his hand around her waist but she wriggled away.

"Quit. You're mighty smart, ain't you?" But she was still cutting her eyes at him.

It was hot and dark inside the shed, and he could just make out how damp her hair was and the little beads of sweat on her upper lip. Something about her face, hot and shining, reminded him vaguely of something. She was younger than he had first thought. In fact, he hated to make a guess as to how young she might be. Thirteen, maybe, he thought, and felt uneasy.

"Well," the harelipped one said. "You figger you took the prize right off."

"That your choice?" Ed asked him.

The answer stuck somewhere in his throat.

"Listen, Ed. . . ."

They were all looking at him, watching him.

"Sure," he said finally. He did not give a damn what they thought.

"C'mon girls," Ed said to the other two. He was all business, pushing them ahead of him to the door. "Y'all just step outside here for awhile."

He did not exactly see how it had all happened, but he had agreed. No one had made him do it.

They went out and left him alone with the girl, alone in the shed with the door closed.

She stood watching him. She could, he told himself angrily, damned near watch a hole through a board. She stood with her head thrust forward, shoulders slumped, hips jutted out forward in the regular white cracker slouch. He had seen a thousand women just like her in his lifetime, arms folded, resting on their bellies, peering out of cabins and lean-to sheds all the years of the war, all the miles of overland marches. They were probably the most unappetizing women in creation. Yet some of those clayhoppers hung ten or twelve or more children on them in a lifetime and thought nothing of it.

And here he was, ready and willing, like a damned fool.

She stood without turning herself away from him, no pretense at modesty, unbuttoning her dress. At least, she unbottoned the dress as far as it would go in front, down to the waist. When she saw his eyes following her, she pushed the front of her dress open carelessly. She did not have much of a bosom, being too skinny, but she took her elbows with both hands, hugging herself, and the pressure of her arms squeezed the white freckled skin into some fullness with a deep, teasing crease in between, the pale, pointed tips of her breasts sticking out.

He felt his flesh crawl. It was something to see, after all, this little skinny girl making a show of herself in that way, knowing tricks to make those little pointed tits stick out, hugging herself and eyeing him as if she dared him

102

to do something about it. He found his face turning warm
again.

He put his hands out and caught her and felt the brush
of her bare skin. It was about as much as he could stand.
He pulled her awkwardly down with him, and they sat on
the floor while he tried to push away her dress. She was
squeezing and hugging and twisting all over him and seemed
to know what she was doing. If he had any reluctance it had
long since faded.

Amateurs, hell. Ed didn't know how far off he was.

He was pretty excited and anxious, but she kept pulling
away, teasing him. He didn't like that much. In fact, it was
all a little too certain and planned for his taste. And once
she got him hot and cross-eyed and riled, she put her knee
up against him and said, "Hold on a minute."

"What's the matter?"

He tried to push her knee out of the way but it wouldn't
budge. Then she got her thumb somehow just where it
would hurt the most and held him off. He tried to get her
hand out of there but she just bored in harder.

"For God's sake!" He had to back off a little.

Her mouth was open and she was breathing hard, all her
little yellow teeth right in his face.

"You know what," she told him.

He knew what, all right. It was a damned poor time for
him to try and scratch around in his shirt for some of the
bills he had put away for safekeeping. Sweat dripped off
his face, and there was not much he could do about it
under the circumstances; he tried nudging it away with his
shoulder, It was hot enough to kill inside the place, and
the condition he was in was not calculated to help him any.

"Well, let go of me a minute," he told her. "I'm not going
to do anything with you hanging onto me like that. You
trying to bore a hole in my vitals with your damned thumb?"

He held the money up to the faint light coming through
the shed's dirt-encrusted windows and counted off a bill, a

103

dollar and a half in shinplasters, Confederate, and put them into her outstretched hand.

"Paper money's more," she said.

"The hell it is. That's all I've got."

She thought it over.

"Well, I guess it's all right. Seein's it's you."

He wished she would close her mouth and quit breathing right in his face. He didn't care for the looks of her teeth and her face wasn't all that pretty. Ed Grimes might think these girls would be a big treat because there wasn't anything else to be had, but he sort of felt differently about it. He. . . .

He thought of Anna, and it was like a drop of ice stabbing him.

It was clear as day, suddenly, what a damned fool he was to let Ed Grimes get him into something like this, with a cracker girl about thirteen years old with pale fuzzy hair all over her legs like a coat of fur, and mean, low-down manners, and nose and teeth just like a wicked little possum cornered in a log.

"C'mon," she was saying, while his thoughts marched by accusingly. She gave a wriggle and suddenly tried to run her hand up under his shirt against the bare skin of his back, her fingernails scraping.

He jumped as though he had been shot. It must have been unexpected for she jumped, too, and gave a little squawk.

Quickly he got his knees under him and moved away from her, untangling himself from the folds of her skirt as best he could, and as he did so, pulling some of that Godawful purple and green drapery down so that he would not subject himself to the sight of any exposed parts of her. He did not want to see her at all. She could cover up her scrawny chest with the naked pointed tits sticking out as far as he cared. There was nothing attractive about her at all.

"What stung YOU?" she said.

"Nothing." He could not even look in her direction. "I tell

104

you what," he offered, "you keep what I gave you and we'll call it even."

It took a moment for this to sink in.

"Call it even for whut?" She pulled herself to her elbow and stared at him as though this had never happened to her before. "Even for whut? You ain't done nothin' yet."

"Never mind," he said, trying to get his shirt tail stuffed in as quickly as he could, so as to get out of there. "You just keep it."

"Well for God's sake almighty." She raised her voice, and he half suspected she was trying to stampede him. "Whuts the matter? It ain't like you can't. Look at you . . . you ain't got no trouble with that big old pecker half as big. . . ."

He winced. He hated to hear any woman, any female, with words like that rolling out of her mouth. He had to get out of there, that's all there was to it.

He charged for the door, almost falling over something, a rope or something he did not see clearly in his hurry, and when he got the door open there were Ed Grimes and the other girls standing right outside where they had probably had their ears to the latch, listening to everything.

"Get out of my way," he yelled. He wasn't going to spare a breath on any of them. He wouldn't have gotten himself into this sort of fix if it hadn't been for Ed pushing him right along.

"What's the matter?" he heard Ed shouting.

He lifted his feet so fast it could have been called running; he did not want to break into an out-and-out run in front of them, but he didn't want to be followed, either. Next to that girl back there in the cotton shed, Ed was the last person in the world he wanted to have anything to do with, ever.

He was going so fast and so blindly that when he came to the edge of the bank above the railroad ditch he stepped into thin air without thinking and came down on the seat of his britches all the way to the bottom. As soon as he could get his feet under him he started running, all out, back in the direction of the mountain. He didn't hear any of the others following him.

Which was fine with him. He was never going back there, no matter how long the army stayed, no matter how long the siege of Kennesaw held out. He turned around once, still running, to see if he had gotten away from the sheds, and the curve of the banks swept them from sight.

There were some soldiers camped right along the edge of the gully above him, cooking lunch, and they hollered to him, but he didn't stop or answer.

Now that he was down in the railroad bed, sheltered by the high clay banks, the heat was bright torment. The cut was ten, twelve feet deep or more going through the pass between Kennesaw and the shoulder of the escarpment, and the depression shut out all the air except what was trapped in it, under the beating sun. Above his head the strip of sky was flocked with June clouds, high, white roiling tops and undersides blue with rain water, white clouds floating calmly and slowly in the bright blue sky and the sun an invisible hot ball. The world was stifling.

He had to slow down. He could not run much longer with the sun on him, and a pain had caught him on both sides of his thighs. That damned girl had damned near ruined him.

He knew he had to sit down a minute and catch his breath and give himself a chance to settle. He stepped across the ties and eased himself down onto a rail and bent double, his head in his arms, resting on his drawn-up knees.

For a minute he was so dizzy he thought he was going to be sick.

He deserved to be sick, he told himself; it was his own damned fault. His and Ed Grimes' and that damned little old girl's.

An inertia of despair fell on him. He could not think. The iron rails bounced the sun off them like sparks in a furnace, and everything near him was parched and lifeless; even the

106

wire grass that grew up between the ties looked burnt and
dead. Gravel washed out of the red ground by the last rain
spewed dryly down the slope of the banks and into the
drain ditch alongside the rails. Everything was spattered
with oil from the passing engines. All around the red clay
and iron rails and the sun and heat hammered at each other
in pitiless combat.

The ever-present bump-bump of the cannons on the
mountainside kept up their serenade, jarring the rails under
him. He clasped his hands over the back of his head to pro-
tect it from the sun and looked down between his knees at his
bare feet resting in the red dirt.

Oh God. Anna.

She was always so soft and so sweet and clean and perfect, every inch of her, so cool and elusive. He could remember what she looked like innumerable times, as though he
carried portraits of her in his head, all different: the blue
dress of the train trip and before that, at the parties in
Augusta, in a dress pink and shoulder bare and ruffled,
dancing in somebody's arms, hair flying, curls, ribbons,
flowers, bouncing skirts lifting at the ankles and belling out
and her waist encircled by some lucky bastard's arm. The
waltz, the schottische, the promenade. She had gotten married because all her friends were doing it, and she did not
want to get left out, being married to a genuine, one-hun-
dred-percent-hero of the war, a private in Company B, 79th
Georgia, Lowrey's brigade, John Alford MacLeod, printer
by trade.

He remembered briefly, hectically, how she had looked
in the darkness, white and blurred and helpless. What had
happened, then?

He remembered distinctly how she looked in the mornings
when she had just washed and what she put on her face
afterward, quickly, furtively, as though she did not want
him to see. Powder, for God's sake. It was no crime. And
what she looked like with her hair taken down, ready to

brush it, one palm against the flowing mass, her elbow working, brush, brush, brush, the strands of her hair following the brush electrically when she lifted it up. And her tongue against her lips, absorbed.

Oh, hell, hell, why does it have to be so hard to love someone, when it ought to be the easiest thing on earth?

Why the devil was it what you wanted the most always escaped you somehow?

Anna.

He had even said her name aloud. He heard the word himself, and it struck him that he had been talking out loud all along, sitting there pouring out his troubles and going on about how she looked and how he felt about her, for anyone to hear.

Except that there was no one down there in that beating, sunbright hell. He had it all to himself.

He heard the whistle of a train coming, and the rails shook underneath his rear. The sun poured on the back of his neck so hot it felt like a fire burn.

Why didn't she write? Confound it, why didn't she write?

Reluctantly, he got up and moved.

CHAPTER 9

*"Rifleman, shoot me a fancy shot,
   Straight at the heart of yon prowling vedette;
   Ring me a ball on the glittering spot
   That shines on his breast like an amulet."*

The army of Tennessee had pulled back to Kennesaw, abandoning Pine and Lost Mountains, and the opinion was that the defense of the sector was strong, that Sherman would not be fool enough to come up in assault. The artillery was working well, laying down a cover of fire between Kennesaw and the connecting ridge of Brush Mountain, and the concussion and racket of the guns kept up through the day and into the night, sometimes far into the night, using the flash of the opposing cannon for range. The warm June nights were drenched with the smell of black powder and mixed with the moths and lightning bugs which hung around campfires and beat at the lanterns.

For a while the month was an artilleryman's war, like a rock fight between boys, long distance, sending cannonballs and shells into the enemy lines, and having them returned in kind, especially the confounded Long Johns which announced their coming, arching through the air end-over-end . . . szzzzzzzzzz . . . the cry going up along the lines: "Look out! Heads up yonder!" and then CUURROOM when they landed. Every so often Johnny would see the staff generals, Hardee, Hood, Walker, Cleburne, and the rest come out to view the damage and take a look around with their field glasses while they stood there talking about it.

Kennesaw was dug with trenches from top to bottom like

the stalls in a penny gallery of a theater, the sunburned faces of the army looking out from the gashes. No one liked digging, but the army of Tennessee had dug up the mountain as they had dug up everything south of Dalton. Earthworks were the mark of Joe Johnston's army. He believed in entrenching as Braxton Bragg never had, for he knew that a soldier could be as brave behind a headlog and a pile of red dirt as he could exposed to fire. He had stopped the Yankee General Sherman with his hundred thousand odd and more at Kennesaw for a month, and the northern newspapers and the Yankee congress were complaining that the war was a stalemate, and that Grant and Sherman both were finding the South too dogged to defeat.

It was not hard to get the news from northern papers; there was a lot of trading going on, back and forth between the lines. When the pickets got to hollering across they would call out: "Y'all learned digging from us, you Yankee counter-jumpers march with a shovel in one hand and a gun in the other, don't you?"

And the enemy would return: "Aw, you Rebs carry your own earthworks right along. You don't have to dig, you just unpack and set 'em up."

And once some fool hollered: "Oh, 's that so? Well by God, we're short over here, throw us one of them shovels you'uns got."

And the Yanks had thrown a shovel over the lines, and they had used it, and then had thrown it back when they were through.

But no stalemate could last. Sherman could not sit forever on the plain in front of the mountain, for beyond it was the river and then the city of Atlanta. The fight was like that over a woman, one man trying to get at her, the other saying, "You shan't," and blocking his way.

On the 19th of June Johnny watched the Yankees moving troops below, marching and countermarching endlessly.

110

Then a few pickets were pushed forward toward their lines.

The weather was dry and hot, not a cloud in the sky for upward of a week, terrible sort of weather to be marching and digging as the Yankees were doing, trying to run new earthworks in the red clay which was the color of brick and sun-baked about as hard. He could see the Yankees sweating in their dark blue wool uniforms; every so often one or two would fall out from the sun and a litter would be sent out for them. Or a detail would come out if there were enough of them, and just stack them up under a tree in the shade. Their officers were out morning to dark, scanning the mountain with glasses.

Sharpshooters had been called out of their divisions for extra duty, and Johnny went up to take a position on the skirmish line near the outermost pickets in the Thomas sector. He could see dirt popping near the group of officers at each shot he put down on them, but he could not do much good at that distance. One officer in particular had a red beard like Sherman's and walked about under fire as cool as ice, ignoring it. Johnny knew damned well he heard the whine of the minie balls as they passed him; he was close enough for that, anyway.

He made himself a sharpshooter's hole in a pine tree, his feet braced on a limb, his back against the trunk, but the group of Federal officers were a little too far, and he could not get in any closer because of their pickets.

In a few minutes one of them had called up a rifleman to answer. The officers stood watching and talking about it as the Yank sharpshooter felt out his shots. He was good. Johnny had to admit. He had a good eye, or was using one of those telescopic sights, or both. The bullets began to hit close enough in the pine tree for him to feel the wind.

He got down out of the tree in a hurry, carrying the Whitworth in his elbow by its sling, his feet feeling for the next limb under him. Down in a hurry was all he could think of, the Yankee following him all the way, nearly dusting his britches for him.

He picked out another pine along to the left where someone had used it before; there was a board nailed for a footrest along one of the limbs halfway up. But the sharpshooter found him again. He did not even have time to answer with a few shots; the jasper seemed to have him right in his sights.

He spent almost an hour going from tree to tree along that line and trying not to be driven off from the group of Yankee staffers out there in full view, but each time their rifleman found him. He was getting tired of climbing up and down, that was the God's truth.

He finally got into a clump of rocks on a shoulder of a small hill, but by then he could not see much of anything. He had been driven off for fair. The Yankee had done his work well.

He stayed out until his relief came up at sundown, not a sharpshooter but a regular picket from the 22nd Mississippi. He was sore and hungry and not sure by then why he had been brought out to begin with. There had not been much of a chance against the other, whoever he was, with those damned telescopic sights. Unless it had been Sherman or Thomas out there and headquarters had been up for a try at it.

It gave him a certain belated satisfaction to think that perhaps someone knew him at army headquarters and knew that he had the Whitworth and thought he could make it hot for the Yankee generals if he had a chance.

But he was sick and tired of climbing up and down the mountain every time he went out. It was a long way back to rejoin the 1st Tennessee. They were over on an abutment of Little Kennesaw, and it was a hard climb to get to them, through blackberries and creeper vines and scrub pine thickets. Up on the mountain, water was as scarce as hen's teeth, and you had to work to keep your canteen full, and

112

most of the time you sat out in the hot sun behind a headlog, baking and burning.

Fruitless or not, his journey had given him a break from that, at least.

The part of the mountain where the 1st Tennessee was entrenched faced a regiment of Illinois troops of Thomas's corps. There had been some friendly hollering back and forth when they first moved in down below, but it had died out after an exchange about Georgia girls and the country-side not being fit for a pig to forage in, and other things of that sort. Now, when anyone showed a head or an arm, it sent a wasp's nest of bullets flying.

To the left of where he was stationed the 27th Tennessee had fortified their extended lines. Some of the 27th were mountain boys from around Knoxville, and they didn't think much of Kennesaw, stuck out by itself on the plain north of Atlanta. They had made up a song about Kennesaw Mountain in which it was described as a pimple on Governor Joe Brown's ass and other things. The song had numberless stanzas, all pretty funny, and it was getting longer every day. The 27th Tennessee had been on the mountain, in that one spot, for almost a month.

As the days wore on it seemed to him that he could almost see the lines being pressured, the Yankee pickets moving in, a little closer all the time. Hood had been pushed into the railroad cut by the sheds to defend the right flank. Ed Grimes was probably getting a chance to do something other than look after his girls. He wondered where the company and the 79th Georgia were positioned and what had become of the shirt girls from Roswell, anyway. That littlest girl, she would make out all right. He had never seen a girl like that, to be so young.

The day came at last, June 27th, a hundred degrees in the sun at its zenith. Johnny had been trying to sleep, his head pressed against the logs of the breastworks, but he could not mistake that sound; the wood chopping of the past month was nothing like it. There was a preliminary bombardment and then a roar, a blast that shook the mountain to its roots.

Jolted awake, he put the Whitworth into the firing chink and tried to sight something.

"HERE THEY COME."

It ran all along the mountain from mouth to mouth.

"Attack. They're attacking us."

He felt the first fine fright like ice crystals falling on his flesh and he knew from other times in battle that it was only fear. It was the same each time, and it passed.

"They're coming at us, boys," the lieutenant told them, crawling along the trench. "Aim low, keep a cool fire. Those Yanks are going to get their reward."

If the Yankees had any doubts about a straight-on frontal assault against that fortified mountain they did not show it. They charged with a roar in a double-, triple-deep line, all yelling their peculiar sound: hurrrraaaaaaah, hurrrrahhhh, hurrrraaaaaah.

He worked to load, fire, reload, tearing the edges of the paper cartridges with his teeth, emptying the powder down the gun barrel, ramming the ball home. The barrel of the Whitworth was getting red-hot. It was right in the sunshine, and he could not tell which was burning it more, sun or powder charges. But it was hot enough to sear his hands at the reload.

The sun was fierce. It opened full upon him at about the same time as the first attack, and increased in power as the day went on. His head began to ache, a bad sign for so early.

He worked the Whitworth like a maniac, loading, ramming, taking aim as fast as he could go.

Take a bead, the inner voice said to him, don't get excited —the same thoughts which he told himself every time. He tried to pick out officers, color bearers, . . . the right targets for a sharpshooter's gun. The sound of the Whitworth as he fired was lost. It might have been a silent, smoking gun for

114

all he heard of it. His face was crusted with spilled black powder from the cartridges but all of the 1st Tennessee about him had the same look of battle . . . black-masked from nose to chin. Sweat cut rivers through it, showing the white skin underneath.

One of the Tennessee boys near him clapped his shoulder and dropped his gun into the bottom of the trench.

"Ah, Georgia . . . Christ, I'm hit! Can you see where I'm hit?"

He could hardly take time to move his eyes away from the firing hole.

"In the shoulder, it looks like." He had to shout to be heard.

"I know that. I mean, can you see where I'm bleedin'?" The Tennessean looked at his hand. "I ain't bleedin' anywheres I can see."

He pulled the Whitworth down to reload and took a good look at him. He seemed to be alright.

"You better get down. You'll get hit."

A bullet dug into the headlogs as the words were out of his mouth, and ricocheted between them. The Tennessean ducked, and then slid to the bottom of the trench.

"Now I'm bleedin'," he complained. His hand was red. "It's comin' out from under my shirttail."

He did not have time to fuss with him. The Yanks were coming out of their lines in full force. Their advance had been hidden at first by a thicket of pine trees stretching all along their works, but now they were in the open. Just below the 1st Tennessee a wheat field of about six or seven acres stood, still unharvested, the full heads not yet ripe, some golden and some still green, a flecked, shimmering surface in the hot sunlight. The Federal charge was coming right through some mountain farmer's wheat field slope.

Johnny saw them, a double line, soldierly and neat in their blue jackets, although he knew it must have been like hellfire inside those blue woolen uniforms, breasting through

115

the wheat in June sunshine. The sky was a painted brittle blue with artificial white clouds in it, the sun glaring in the heavy-headed green and yellow grain. The field rippled as a blast of cannonfire sucked over it, making the blue lines appear to break a little, dropping down here and there in the wheat.

It was not exactly calm where he was, either, for heavy fire was tearing into the galleries along the mountain and the 1st Tennessee was answering with red spouts of the rifle mouths and a drifting black fog. Storr's batteries had the range on the Illinois troops, plowing grape and canister into them. Johnny could see potholes appear in the midst of the wheat and men flying up into the air to lie brokenly where they fell.

The cadence of fire picked up; it was like a steam loco-motive being fired for all hell and gone, faster and faster, more wood, more water, boilers sizzing and groaning and faster yet, more and more . . . louder and louder . . . a solid roar of rifle fire, and the big guns which had been at it since first light were shaking the ground, jumping up and down on the mountain.

But still they came on.

It was a show, a spectacle, if a person could take time out to watch it. A godawful thing to throw troops in like that against a mountain entrenched and fortified with a whole army. They kept coming in a frontal assault intended to drive right through, another line of shouting, roaring, hur-rahing men across the wheat field.

"Who ordered that charge?"

Was it Thomas? That was part of Thomas's corps down there.

"Well, if it was Thomas ordered up that charge they ought to take him off the field and shoot him, I tell you that."

"He must have lost his fool mind, that general."

It almost looked as though the Illinois men were going to make it, coming on so doggedly like that.

116

"God, how many jaspers are there in Illinois, anyway?"

The Yankees had their big guns working . . . at least they were giving their troops some support . . . and the cannonfire was raising hell on Little Kennesaw, digging it up and moving it around just like the Yankees were bent and determined to whittle it down to a little mound between them and the Chattahoochee River.

The 1st Tennessee and Company A of the Rock City guards were stuck out on a little angle, a cattycorner of breastworks that made an outpost separated from the rest of the line. The bushes and trees that had partly shaded them from the sun were gone, blasted away, and out there they felt themselves almost alone.

Still another charge from the Illinois entrenchments, and the bluecoats came up out of the field where they had been hugging the ground and rushed—the regimental color bearer of the Stars and Stripes going all the way, scratching the last few feet with one hand, hardly a soul following him, and jumped onto the headlogs of the 1st Tennessee, looking right down into all the faces turned up to him, yelling and hurrahing all by himself. He looked sort of surprised to see them all in there, and they were no less surprised to find him where he was with his flag and no weapon at all, just staff and standard drooping in the windless air. He took a ball in the head immediately and went over backward, still hanging onto his flag.

"Don't go out!" the captain shouted, but none of them were fools enough to try. Another line was forming, right at their angle, trying to break it.

Johnny could hardly bear to watch the Yanks plowing across the wheat field below. The grain was all trampled and a dull red color like mud was sprayed on the gold and green, but still they came on, stumbling over their own wounded and dead to assault the impregnable mountain.

They were out of ammunition in the angle. It was over a hundred in the shade, someone hollered down to them. Only there was no shade, only the mist of gunpowder with the dead eye of the sun boring through.

The ammunition was rolled down to them from the lines above, some of the boxes breaking open as they bounced.

"Watch out below!"

He could not keep his face to the firing chink for very long, for the air coming through it was like the blast from the open door of a stove. The skin of his face had begun to crack like a side of meat roasting, and he could see, when he took time to look, that the concussion from the cannonfire was giving some of the boys nosebleed. He felt something dripping into his own mouth but could not stop long enough to see if it was sweat or whether his own nose was bleeding also. He put his hand up. It was red.

It was blood all right, and it was all over his hand, sticky as glue where the sun was drying it.

There were enough dead from the 1st Tennessee in the ditch to hamper them. The sergeant was propping up the dead at the back of the trench to give them more room underfoot. But they were not having as much trouble as the Yankee boys in the wheat field. If the Yankee charge was slowing the least bit, it was because the blue lines could not come forward over their own dead. The wheat field was a cemetery of unburied dead, four or five deep in some spots, and they were slipping and stumbling. The whole line was crawling over a field paved with dead men.

Some of the Tennesseans tried to keep track of how many times they had beaten back the men from Illinois. Was it four or five? More than that.

Now the charge had begun to slow; the Yankees were fortifying a line right under the hill, right under the angle, about thirty yards away. The 1st Tennessee took a cautious breath.

"Did you ever see those damned Yanks come on like that?"

"Who's in command over there? Is it Hooker?"

"That old fool Hooker'd do something like that."

118

"Or Logan. Old Blackjack."

"It's Thomas."

"I can't believe it. Not old Slow-Trot Thomas."

"Well, it took murder in *somebody's* heart to keep ordering them forward, over and over again."

"When it wasn't no use."

He sat down behind the headlogs and bent over and vomited. They were all vomiting and retching because they were sun-struck and exhausted and sick as horses. The water in the canteens was so hot it was undrinkable and to try only made them sicker. Some of the boys were pouring it on their heads, dashing it into their faces to try and break the grip of the sun.

And the guns pounded. He felt as though his head was going to break in halves and fall apart. His nose was bleeding alright. As soon as the blood would try to thicken up a little, the batteries would lay it on fresh and it would start all over again. It was bright red blood in quick-running drops, all down the front of his shirt, and he wondered if anybody had ever bled to death from a nosebleed. It looked to him as though he was losing an awful lot of blood.

The sergeant and some of the others were working again, trying to put the wounded in the bottom of the ditch and make them more comfortable, but it was worse down there than on top. There was almost no air in the bottom, and they suffered from that as much as from their wounds.

Cartridges were being passed out, and he reached to take a handful and then had a funny sensation: once he had bent over he could not seem to get his head straightened up.

He felt, oddly enough, that he was going to have to hold his head that way, bent over permanently, because it would not budge an inch. He struggled with it, and the more he tried to force it to return to its natural position the more he could see it was no good. His head would not follow him. The sunshine was getting green; not a cool, shady green, but a bilious, hot green, a film over everything. His damned

119

head would not straighten up. It was a hellish feeling to be so helpless about your own head.

He had to grab something; he was losing his balance. He took a firm grip on the Whitworth with both hands because it was the only thing to hang onto, to keep from drowning in all the greenish green.

It was getting dark, but he did not mind that so much as long as it kept some of the sun off him. He could hear the boys of the 1st Tennessee talking right beside him but it was as though he was not in the same part of the world they were, and they could not reach him or help him. He could still feel the guns banging and rattling and the earth shaking under his heels, but it was dark, nice dark, and out of the darkness came someone he knew. Beautiful Anna, Anna, a dream of everything that was soft and lovely and still, coming toward him in a nightgown that showed her white arms and her hair falling in a dark cloud, and she was so beautiful he could hardly believe that she was there.

"Anna," he whispered to her. "Here I am. Don't you see me?"

She was carrying a pitcher of lemonade with sweat beads of cold on the side of it and the slices of lemon were floating and hitting the sides of the glass. She was bringing him a glass of cold lemonade because he was dying of thirst. He loved her. His heart leaped against his ribs and hurt him when he thought of how much he loved her, trying to help him like that, coming all the way into the middle of what was going on, just to help him.

"Here boy," some damned interfering voice said to him. It was the captain's voice. "Let go of that confounded gun or point it the other way. I'm only trying to help you." The captain's voice was husky and tired, and he was pouring something onto his face.

"Quit!" He felt like he was drowning. He was strangling and not able to get his breath under the stuff. "God, quit it, can't you? That water's hot as hell!"

120

He could see the captain's face, it was right in his own, and the captain was squatting beside him. He seemed to have fallen back into the ditch, and his neck had gotten unparalyzed somehow. The water from the captain's canteen was all over him.

"What?" he asked him. They had to shout.

"Touch of sun."

"No, not that." He tried to get up. "Had pneumonia last winter. Got a relapse, I guess."

The captain burst out laughing. The guns were so loud he could not hear him laughing hardly at all, but he could see him laughing, his grinned face drawn up and his teeth uncommonly white in the mask.

"You waited a long time for a relapse," the captain shouted. "Keep your head down till you feel better."

"Yes sir." He did not mind saying sir to him because this captain was a damned good officer. Not like Ed Grimes.

He put his hat on. If he could keep his hair from drying out right away perhaps his brain would stay cooler. Things were still sort of green, but he wasn't going to have any damned sunstroke if he could help it.

Then he remembered Anna. Well, that showed how much things had changed. It was Anna, and she had been there, really there, when he needed her, and that was what counted. It was what she would have done. Lemonade! God, he hadn't had any lemonade since before the war. And she had shown up just in time, had known just what to bring him.

He knew as he stood there that they were going to have to work things out somehow. He could not live without her, that was all.

It was only three o'clock by the sun. It was as though the damned day would never end. It went on and on.

But it was always like that, he remembered. He had felt the same way at Chickamauga. The day would never end. The last charge had been in the dark so deep they could not even see where they were going. Cleburne's division had caught hell.

His knees were shaking, and he leaned against the breastworks. If he took things slowly for a moment it would settle down. If the rest of them could do it . . . the 1st Tennessee and the rest, then he could, too. He knew he was damned well equal to what the rest could do.

The commander himself, Joe Johnston, had come out on the mountain above them to look down and order up a support for them, but the 1st Tennessee would not have it. They did not need any support, not after this. They had held the dead angle all day against the Illinois boys and they did not need relief, hell no! They yelled their answer back up the slope.

"Go back, go back!" they yelled to the 6th and 9th getting ready to come down to them.

And the general nodded, alright.

If it hadn't been for the heat they would have cheered him.

He kept firing his Whitworth although there were times when he had to stop and lean for a moment against the wall. His hands were so swelled and sunburned they were clumsy; it was like trying to reload with mittens on that hurt.

He noticed the woods down in front had caught fire from the shelling. It wasn't near the angle but off to the left, and yet he could see it plainly from where he was. The Federal wounded were lying in the woods, and they began to scream when the fire got to them. It was terrible to watch, worse than anything else going on. The blaze was a forest fire in some places, the flames going up through the vines into the tops of the trees, in the pines particularly, through all the crowns of rosinous needles.

It was hot enough in the sun but now it seemed to him he could feel a new heat from the fire, and he could certainly smell the wood smoke even through the powder smoke of battle. It was horrible to see the forest fire inching along and swallowing up the wounded down there. Their cries were

122

faint and small, like animals caught up and protesting shrilly. He thought he felt a wind, a fire draft. It must have been that, because there had been no wind, no real wind, all day. When the fire breeze was blowing up to them he could almost make out what the wounded were yelling, help, and calling for their friends to come and get them out. And for their mothers.

The 1st Tennessee could not load and fire for watching what was going on down below in the woods, and some of them stopped firing altogether and started shouting and cussing.

The corporal in his part of the Rock City guards hollered down to the left where Cheatham's corps was entrenched: "Do somethin', can't you?" as if there was something that they could do.

The rest of them took it up, even hollering down to the rifle pits under them where the Yankees were lying, "Hey, y'all, get them damned wounded of yourn afore they burn up!"

They took it up, shouting, "Get them out of there, get them out!" shouting down toward the enemy lines, while some of the wounded in the woods were dragging themselves along to get out of the fire, skipping and hopping about, their hair burning, their clothes flaming, trying to get out of the woods.

The batteries were still laying it down pretty heavily all along the field. Up where the big guns were, they did not care what was happening. But on the angle and in the rifle pits the fire had slowed. Everyone was looking over to the left, as far over as the 27th Tennessee, and they could see the heads of the Yanks looking up also.

THE ARKANSAS BOYS ARE GOING TO LET THEM OUT.

The grapevine began with the news somewhere down near the 27th, and it swept back to them. Firing had quit altogether down at the woods, and the rumor had it that a captain of one of the Arkansas Companies down there was going to let the Yankees get their wounded out of the fire. A Captain Miller.

It was true. It was happening. They could see it for themselves.

Something was happening, anyway, Johnny saw, for the Yankees were coming out of their pits and running into the woods, getting their wounded out. And no one was firing on them. A truce, that was what it was. There was still a lot of cannonfire, but they were having their own sort of truce down in that part of the lines.

It was so damned satisfying to him for a moment to know that somebody had sense enough to do a thing like that.

But down where they were, in front of the dead angle, the Yankees were not lifting their fire a bit. The bullets were kicking up the dirt all along the tops of the headlogs.

Well, they didn't have to worry, he thought, because no one was going to interfere. If it had been some of them down in the burning woods they sure as hell would have wanted someone to call a truce so that their friends could carry them out.

The day finally ended. It got dark.

It does end, he told himself, in spite of the fact that you think it never will.

The sun had gone out, extinguished as abruptly as a burned-out lamp, and that was the most blessed relief of all. No more sun to burn his face and the back of his neck. The darkness might not be one whit cooler . . . not in June after a day as hot as this one had been . . . but the very darkness, blackness, was soothing if nothing else.

Water and whiskey were dropped down to the angle from above, compliments of the general, and a commendation for a job well done.

The angle managed a cheer for Joe Johnston finally, a

feeble, rasping sort of clamor, and hoped that he heard it, wherever he was.

The captain of the Rock City guards doled out the whiskey where he was, a pint all around, and some of the boys' stomachs were so weakened it nearly took them off their feet.

Johnny squatted down in the bottom of the trench, and one of the Tennesseans named MacAllister took his trick at the firing hole.

He put his head in his arms. Now was the time to rest, he told himself, but he found that he couldn't. The trench was full of the stink of vomit and urine, and there was no place to lie down or sit down or find a spot underfoot. He had to try and rest, anyhow, in some sort of position; the muscles of his arms were jumping wildly, and his legs had just about got so they would not hold him up.

He tried to force himself to think of something restful and relief-bringing and thought of Anna, but she would not return to him as she had in the afternoon. With a pitcher of lemonade.

There was something absurd about his dreaming of her and yet it was not; it hurt him to think about any part of it, because it still seemed the nicest thing a person could have done. It showed how sweet and helpful she could be, wanted to be, if things could just be solved between them somehow.

Inside him he groaned.

Oh Lord, he wanted to be with her, see her, so bad he couldn't stand to think about it. Why in the goddamned hell didn't she write?

He held his face back to get away from the miasma of the bottom of the ditch and rested it against the clay behind him, and moved his heels so that they braced his body, not comfortably, but solidly. He looked up and saw MacAllister standing with his face to the firing chink and beyond the shadow of MacAllister's head, the black sky. It was a clear, beautiful June night, and Georgia was under the veil of the

Milky Way, a smear of a million stars over that side of the mountain.

And a bird was singing.

That just goes to show you, he told himself, how crazy the world could be. Here was a bird that had come through the day's battle and was down there somewhere in the dark singing as though nothing had happened at all. A mockingbird. He knew that familiar June-night cheerip, cheerip, churdle, churdle, that went on without stopping, liquid and content and absorbed, with the fathomless stars of the Milky Way caressing the song.

He put his head back as far as it would go, pressing his shoulders and straining his neck, getting more of the night air as his face was drawn up to it.

How lovely and cool and peaceful that bird's song was, and how still everything else!

He held his head like that and looked upward into the darkness for such a long time that it felt as though he must have a touch of dizziness; he had a feeling of being turned around, so that it was like staring down, not up, into a pool of water that reflected the stars and not the sky itself. And he felt as though he might easily defy gravity and fall into the sky, round and round into the stars and the night and away from all the earth-bound stink and exhaustion which held him, into something vast and cool and pleasant, descending into the band of stars spread over the sky with the mockingbird's song pouring into it.

It was a feeling so sharp and clear that he could not pass it off as dizziness or a dream of hallucination; the stillness was the cause of it. It was never as quiet as this, a deep, furry stillness so a person could think, and feel, for a change.

He was not even tired. He sat and listened and looked down-up into the stars, and his brain felt so fine and clear for a moment that he could think big sweeping thoughts that were right there on the edge of his mind . . . of stars and night and men and even God . . . it seemed he could know

126

almost anything worth knowing if he just tried. He did not want to let the moment go to waste, sinking deep into the dark pool. He could know anything that might need knowing, know anything that was important, even if it was not long remembered, but seized and clear right then, at the moment of thinking it—that fortunate moment.

He was a little dizzy, not quite recovered from the terrible day on the mountain, but this was not a dream nor anything clouded like that: it was crystal-clear, star-brilliant, and he was able to grasp that it would never return, ever again, . . . in a whole lifetime.

And now, he thought, here comes the breeze.

The breeze had finally come along the old scarred mountain and it hissed in the tops of the pine trees and ran along the woods on the slopes and the mockingbird felt it, it shook the branch and moved his feathers, for he stopped. But the stars were still the same, for they were not bothered by the things that occur on the earth; they were numberless, whirling about overhead.

Now here came the breeze through the trench, passing over all of them lying there or standing at the headlogs and oh God, but it was welcome and cool! Everything was quiet, everyone was turning his face up to the breeze, and the bird was not singing now, but the fine marvelous moment continued without him, still and unbroken. No one spoke. They turned their faces up to the sky, everyone reaching up to the sky, and this was right, for all who were under it must feel its presence and turn their heads upward and look out in this moment. This was the time for all of them, shadows of men up and down the mountain in the night, to hold their heads up to the coolness and space.

For look at us, they seemed to say, we feel it, there is not a man under this sky who is not aware of it—and one can tell by this quiet which lies over us all and turns us to statues.

God, and the others down there, the enemy, quiet as any! They must have been thinking the same things, holding still, listening, for it was the same breeze which touched them and the same night which covered them.

CURRRROOOOOOM!

Not once, but three times, one right after the other, with bright red flashes that lit up their faces and turned them to demons.

"Goddammit, you sonofabitch, be quiet up THERE!"

"What the hell!"

They were cursing their batteries at the tops of their lungs, telling them to go to hell, be quiet, stop all the confounded racket.

"Aw, they don't know what the hell they're shootin' at. Whut's there to shoot at, for God's sake?"

There was nothing to shoot at.

BOOOOM, CURRROOOM, BOOOOM!

Now the Union batteries had opened up.

WHOOOOOM, WHOOOOM, WHOOOM!

Twelve-pound Parrotts.

He was in such a fit of fury that if he had had the chance he felt he could have committed murder among the artillery. He got to his feet.

Sometimes he was so damned sick and tired of war that he could quit. Desert. Go home.

A whispering started, the grapevine at work.

WHAT DO YOU HEAR?

The sergeant came crawling along the trench.

"What kin you hear? What's goin' on?"

They listened.

"Can't hear a damned thing. Not with this racket. They expect us to hear anything with all this?"

"Somebody said we was movin' out, somethin' goin' on down the left in front of the 27th."

The wind was fairly soughing on the mountain like a windstorm. The night was alive and moving and not a thing to be seen.

"Oh goddamn, it was nice and quiet for a while."

"Kin you hear them goin' out for their wounded in front of us?"

"The wounded's still there as far as I kin tell."

They stood at the headlogs, straining their eyes down the slope toward the enemy. With the next flash of fire from above they saw the trees with red tops and the shadowless drop of the sides of the mountain. Nothing there.

The captain came sliding over the embankment behind them.

"Sergeant?"

"Yes sir, right here." The sergeant had a voice like old leather rubbing together.

"We think they are going to try and flank us again. Sherman's going to try for the river. If we move out, we'll follow the 27th."

He went down the angle with the sergeant, crawling along, whispering.

"Oh damn, it's the same thing over and over again," Mac-Allister said in the dark. "Fight and retreat, fight and retreat."

CHAPTER 10

Never, while such as ye are in the breach,
   Oh brothers, sons and southrons, never! never!
Shall the foul enemy our city reach!

Coming down from Kennesaw on a back road glimmering with dawn as all the Tennesseans of the Rock City company sleep-walked around him, Johnny told himself that he was going to put up for leave just as soon as the army came to earth again. Next to him in the column MacAllister was button-eyed awake and wanted to argue about the retreat when, as he said, success had been so near at hand on the mountain. It was a crying shame, he said.

He could not be bothered with arguing. He was beaten down and almost senseless with fatigue for one thing, after the sun and fury of the battle up there, and the army's movements were just not so important at that hour. Johnston would take care of things. There was no confusion or disorder in the pull-out of the kind that breeds disaster; the general had things under control and he knew what he was doing. Flanked was flanked, that was all there was to it. His own mind was occupied with other things, such as how every step now brought him closer to the city and the railroad and home and Anna.

Atlanta was not such a bad idea. The city was a fort—the army engineers had seen to that—and the place was as good as any for the kind of war Joe Johnston fought. The general meant to make Sherman bleed the farther he got from his supply base at Chattanooga, and Atlanta was as good a stop as Kennesaw had been. He couldn't get excited over it like

MacAllister. There was no reason to get all stirred up just because the war had pushed close enough to make the city feel it.

The hell with it, he thought wearily. They were all feeling the war now, every part and parcel of the country, and it was a waste of time to howl. All he, Johnny MacLeod, wanted was the chance to get home. Just for one day. The war could take care of itself for that long. He had to have his own damned life straightened out and know that there was some future to it, that was all.

This, he admitted to himself, was something new, for up until this time everything connected with his own personal self had been tied in with the war, even what had happened at Augusta. If he hadn't been so sick and dismal at Christmas he might not have gotten on the wrong train in the first place, and once started, might never have gotten married. And might never have made such a mess of it, caught in that terrible, lonely trap of trying to love someone and finding it damned near impossible. Oh Lord, it made him sweat to think about it!

But now he was finding himself thinking of the future as though there was no question as to whether it would or would not be available. It damned well better had be, he told himself. He had to have some sort of future, pretty quick, too, just to get things straightened out.

The army fell back to a place called Nickajack Creek with its back to the river, waiting for a stand, but this did not come. Instead, old Slow-Trot Thomas, the Virginian-turned-Yankee general came up and halted, and Sherman himself came out to look things over. The next thing they heard was that Federal General Schofield had leaped the river northward at Soap Creek and got on the far bank of the Chattahoochee with nothing between him and Atlanta, nine miles away.

131

The army left Nickajack in a hurry and scrambled across the river to put itself in between.

The country north of Atlanta was rough but beautiful, the last of the Appalachian ridge country breaking into high folds of earth and steep pocket valleys, covered with a dense forest of hardwoods, maples, oaks, hickory, the dells thick with willow and dogwood and wild cherry trees. Underneath the forest covering the light was cool and green and the ground laid out with delicate deep-woods flowers, lilies and jack-in-the-pulpits and pale white Indian pipes, crimson fungi growing in dead logs and lichen making little hammocks in the damp places. But where the sun broke through clearly, blankets of oxeye daisies sprang up, and everywhere —in the woods and along the roadbanks and in the blackberry briars and persimmon brush—the masking veils of honeysuckle stretched to form green walls of yellowed, fading trumpet flowers whose perfume breathed the familiar, nostalgic, throat-clutching smell of heat and summer. Honeysuckle . . . the air was overlaid with it, and the thoughts it roused were enough to make any one dream of home. But the army set to work excavating through the earth, throwing up the wood's dirt and leaves, chopping down the trees and clearing out for the business of battle. For a battle was coming. The skirmish fire was heavy enough at any time for a decent beginning encounter, and the Federal artillery was in force; every now and then some great arm of an oak would come splintering down from the fire of the Parrotts across the creek.

But the 1st Tennessee was entrenched and that was all Johnny wanted. He took out one of Anna's letters and ripped the envelope flat and rubbed out the writing on it with his fingers and spit.

"I'm putting up for leave," he told the corporal. "I'm not but thirty miles or so from home and it ought not to be so damned hard to get a day's pass."

"I wouldn't do it," the corporal told him. "Nobody in this

132

army's got time to fuss with no furlough right now. There's two, three divisions tryin' to get across the river and a dog-fight comin' up along this here creek soon's they kin get here. Captain's busy, so's the sergeant. You better wait."

But he would not listen.

"I'm going home," he said. "If I can get there, I don't see why I can't get a pass. There's nobody in the regiment that can get home like I can. Nobody's using up passes."

The corporal looked sour.

"If I was you, Georgia, I wouldn't use that excuse, not ef you hope to get anywheres. It don't pay to rub it in."

But the corporal took the leave request and read it, anyway.

"I don't see no reason for it, myself. Hellsafire, everybody in this army wants to get home. You got to have a sick pass or invalid pass or somethin' right now. You ain't goin' to get nowheres with it. That's the gospel truth."

"I tell you," Johnny cried, "I'm not thirty miles away from home up here. Can't you see that? I don't know what's going on at home, I didn't get a letter all last month, I don't know if they're sick or dead. You can spare me for twenty-four hours, for God's sake!"

The corporal shrugged and passed him on to Morfit, the sergeant, who was busy with a detail digging rifle pits and had no time to fool with requests for leave written on envelopes.

"Whut the hell is this?" he asked, squinting at the paper. "You ain't got a prayer."

"Put your mark on it," Johnny told him desperately. "That's all I'm asking you. My wife, my folks . . . they're probably sick. . . ."

"They're allus sick," the sergeant grunted. "Whut's that word thar?" He pointed.

"Permission. Grant permission."

"Can't hardly read yore writin'. You got a turrible hand. I thought you was schooled, some."

133

He thought he was going to give it back, but instead he took out a pencil from his jacket and put a small Jas. Morfit in the corner and handed it over.

Johnny looked for the captain, White, for about an hour and at last found him standing in a patch of Jimson weeds in an open space, looking across the creek with his field glasses. This, he told himself, was the man he relied on, who had been so friendly and honest with him at Kennesaw. A short man, slender and neat, with the small face and over-hanging brow of the earnest and studious. White, he had heard, was a schoolmaster by trade, but a damned good soldier now. The best. A Joe Johnston type of soldier. Human.

He came up full of hope.

"What's this?" The captain seemed busy and distracted. He took the paper and read every word as though now once his attention was diverted, he would give the thing every opportunity to prove that it was worth the interruption. He shook his head. "No. Denied."

"Sir!" The captain didn't understand why he had put it up, that was all, nor why, being an outsider in the company, a Georgian almost home, the circumstances were different. "Sir, I'm not but. . . ."

"No use," the other man said, and put his glasses up to his eyes.

Dammit, they were all alike, from Blalock of the 79th on down; they couldn't resist putting their foot on your neck just for the fun of it. His opinion of White reversed itself abruptly. Well, he wasn't going to be put off.

"Captain, my folks, my wife, might be refugeed, sick, any damned thing . . . I only live about thirty miles from here. I haven't had any mail, I don't know what's going on down there. . . ."

"Report to Morfit and tell him I want two more pits out to the right of where he's working. One for you and one for Sims," White told him, without putting aside the glasses.

He stood for a moment in desperate silence.

134

"White," he said, and he did not care what came of it. "You've got to listen to me for a minute. All you Tennesseans don't need passes . . . couldn't use them even if they'd been issued this year . . . and nobody's put up for them, I know what I'm talking about. Because nobody can get back through the lines to go home. But I want a damned pass, I've got to have it, because I CAN. It's not like there've been too many passes issued and no more's allowed, for God's sake!"

White put down his glasses and stood looking down at his feet for a moment as if trying to give himself time to think.

"MacLeod," he said, "you don't have to remind me of the situation of the 1st Tennessee. I'd like to tell you something. I've had any number up to me in the past few weeks that swore just what you're swearing now, and which you say is impossible . . . that they can get back through the lines to Tennessee to see their people. I've had routes proposed to me that would make a four-state tour of the South look as uncomplicated as a Sunday walk. But what they're trying to tell me, and what you're trying to tell me, is that getting home is more important to you right now than anything concerning this campaign, and I'm telling you it is not, and it had better not be, or sir, I will have you up in a barrel shirt and chains until your opinions have improved!"

"You wouldn't talk like that if you had folk just thirty miles, . . ." he cried.

"Thirty miles be damned, sir," the captain told him. "I don't care if it is three hundred. The dangerous thing about it, MacLeod, is that you think you can get there, and you have no business thinking that. What is important right now . . . and should be eminently so to you . . . is that this part of the Federal 16th Corps should not cross that creek. This is not your war, sir, but the army's and the army's it will be until such time as it is seen fit to disband it. Otherwise I should think it fair to give each man jack of this company an opportunity to get home no matter what his chances are." He gave him his paper without looking, still holding the glasses to his eyes. "I'll keep it in mind," the captain said, and his voice was rather flat. "I'll give you every chance I can."

He flung himself away, sick with disappointment. Whatever feeling of admiration he had had for White was gone, he was just another tin martinet, that was plain! And he could see that the sharpshooter badge had had its price. He was going to be tied and bound by the 1st Tennessee and White as he had never been with Ed Grimes. His cousin was not much . . . White probably had it all over him as an officer . . . but Ed was Ed, and Company B was what it was—all the boys from Jonesboro. Once he was on this side of the river he knew Ed would find someway to get him home, overnight perhaps, but home. And Ed would be halfway human with his company. Ed would let the thing go. And Blalock, he did not care. Old Rum Tom did not care about anything.

And Ed, confound it, was about the only person who would understand without having to have it spelled out why it was so important for him to get home to Jonesboro.

He felt like damning White and all Tennesseans to eternity; without giving him any consideration White had flung him out again into the world of chance. Now, if he caught a ball in these woods or mortar fire found him, his whole life would end, still hanging fire, nothing solved. Never even having been home to see his wife!

The woods along Peachtree Creek were beautiful, and the army rested more comfortably than it had in weeks. The blackberries were ripe and plentiful, and beef—tough and stringy, but beef nevertheless—was coming out from the abattoirs in the city, and the wounded did not have too far to be carried to the hospitals there, but nothing went right; in the company of the Rock City guards Morfit, the sergeant, was injured by shell blast and the next day MacAllister was

136

shot through the hand reaching over a tree stump to get his hat. Dysentery, probably from the fresh beef, went through the regiment, and green-bottle flies came in by droves.

Johnny, put on sharpshooter duty in a water oak overlooking the stream was nicked in the left ear by a ricochet, a wound that bled and festered but which was not as troublesome by far as the flies that gathered to it. He got a bandage from the surgeon and wore it, but it was hot and uncomfortable, yet he could not take the wrappings off until a scab of some sort had formed. A rash from the heat broke out under the bandage and spread down his neck. Most of the time the ear and the skin around it felt as though it was on fire, and he clawed at it without thinking and sometimes, in a frenzy, he could not stand some particular upsurge of burning and itching and clapped his hand against it hard enough to make his ear pop and, of course, setting it to bleeding again. He was bad-tempered and knew it and got careless enough to sit and brood when he was supposed to be on duty, and, once, when the corporal came out to check and found him sitting in a tree doing nothing, he put him on report.

"It won't take much of this, MacLeod," White told him, and he knew that the man was down on him permanently. Loss of the badge was the next step, there were too many waiting for it for him to keep it long without recommendation.

Nothing was right.

At night crowds of Negroes beat the woods looking for a way to cross over into the promised land of Sherman's territory across the creek, and the pickets at the river said it was twice as bad down there at the bridges, Negroes trying to get across by night to head out toward Kennesaw and northward, and white refugees by day making southward for Atlanta and the railroads, a regular stream of humanity coming and going by the hour.

Every train that backed out to Vining's station at the end of the rail line from Atlanta dumped a load of visitors for

137

Johnston's headquarters: legislators come up from the state capitol at Milledgeville, the mayor and council from the city, wives and women of all descriptions out to take supper in the officers' tents, and finally—the ultimate in the unexpected guest—Braxton Bragg himself, the big bird of ill omen whose explanation was, the army heard, that his stop at Peachtree Creek was nothing official or important; he was just passing through on his way to inspect the department of Mississippi.

But no one was fooled. Something was up. The Atlanta papers had been hollering to high heaven about the Federal armies coming across the Chattahoochee River, and Johnston was no favorite either in the city of Atlanta or in the governor's office. Sherman was nine miles from the city—that was all anyone could see. Even the Yankees were taken with it. The newspapers that came across the lines were full of Sherman's capture of the city, premature but certain.

Then, in the second week of July, Johnny had a visitor. He ran all the way up from the 1st Tennessee's entrenchments along the creek to find his Uncle Trennon sitting on a felled log in front of brigade headquarters. There was no one else with him.

He didn't know exactly what he had expected, but his first feeling was one of terrible disappointment to find his Uncle Trennon standing there.

"What's wrong," he blurted out, without thinking.

His uncle looked startled.

"Nothing's wrong, John, everything's fine. I just came out to see if you were alright."

"Oh that," he said. "Yes, I'm alright."

It was a rotten way to begin. His uncle knew he was disappointed somehow and felt uncomfortable about it. Then to make matters worse, his uncle tried to give him a parcel he had brought from home, and Johnny seized it so clumsily the thing was knocked from his hands. When it hit the ground it broke open. The newspaper came apart and there was a

138

slab of bacon and a broken jar of sorghum syrup. They both knelt down to do something about it.

"Watch out. John," his uncle cautioned him, "that's glass, and sharp."

"Yes sir, I see it."

They finally got the mess picked up, and Johnny pitched it into a ravine behind one of the big oak trees. The afternoon was hot and sticky and there was no water nearby, and the flies picked up the scent of the sorghum. They sat down on a log. His uncle took off his glasses and breathed on them and polished them with his handkerchief and seemed as dry and aloof as if he had been readying one of his schedules and Johnny was just a ticket holder waiting to get his attention. Damn his uncle, anyway, he thought, he had railroad stuck out all over him, it had marked him for life, he was the Atlanta and Macon's damned best conductor and a piss-poor human being.

No, he didn't mean that, he thought hastily. He didn't know what got into him lately, he was so irritable all the time. He had no right to be short with his uncle; this was only his way. His uncle would polish his glasses to hell and back to keep anybody from seeing that he was excited or upset.

"How's everybody at home?" Johnny asked him.

"Fine. Fine."

"Doing all right?"

"Fine. Fine."

But his uncle brought out a bundle of letters, his letters, four from Anna and one from his Aunt Matt. He tore Anna's open and read them at once, in such a tear that he could not half concentrate on what they said and had to go back over them again and again.

"Uncle, what the devil have you been carrying these things around for? Lord, if you people back home knew I've been scouring the army for my confounded mail . . . I thought everybody was dead or sick or gone off somewhere! I've even been up to ask for leave and got turned down. The rest of the

139

time I've been spending out here sitting around, worrying myself sick!"

His uncle put his glasses back on and tilted back his head, to look at him through them.

"Is that your ear bound up, John? Have you been hit?"

But he was reading again, only to find that Anna's letters were the same as always, faintly impersonal, lots of news about nothing.

She had been to church to hear the Rev. Samuel Godwin of the First Methodist Church in Atlanta preach on something or other . . . he skipped over the description. They had been making lint bandages. He skipped over that. The weather was hot in Jonesboro. They could hear the guns from Kennesaw. A cavalry patrol had stopped at the house. He kept skipping down the pages. The things he wanted to read were sparse and limited. One letter said that she thought of him every day and mentioned him in her prayers and hoped he was safe from harm in this terrible war. Another said that she prayed for him daily . . . same thing. All ended, your loving wife, Annabella MacLeod.

He did not open his aunt's letter. It could wait.

"Well, what in the name of satan WERE you carrying this stuff around for," he cried, exasperated. "Has the damned mail broken down completely?"

His uncle didn't like that at all.

"Here now," he said. "There's no need to shout, John. I've tried to get these letters to you the best I could, but my runs have not been regular this month, and traffic is in an uproar because of the activity of the army up this way. I had to wait. And my instructions were that I was duty-bound not to hand your mail over to the postal clerks. Something you wrote your aunt a few months ago, I thought."

So that was it . . . some damned foolish mix-up which had kept him from getting his mail! If he had meant anything, he had meant for them not to try to send him any food

140

parcels because of the postal clerks' thieving ways. He meant packages, not letters!

"Well, tell me about your wound," his uncle said.

"My ear. It's nothing. I only wear the bandage to keep the flies off it."

He tried to express his thanks for the food.

"Don't thank me, thank your aunt. That syrup was quite an achievement, I hear."

They both looked at the ground.

"Well, don't tell her about it."

"I won't . . . if she doesn't ask me," his uncle said.

His uncle kept looking at his bandage, and he was miserable, knowing what a stir the news would cause at home. He had half a mind to take the wrappings off and show his uncle that it was nothing, just the top of his ear, more of a nuisance than anything else, but he was not sure he could get it wrapped up again right if he did.

His uncle looked tired. His face was speckled with fine red and purple dots that came from heat and the exertion of walking out from Vining's station at what was now the end of the railroad line. His uncle, he realized suddenly, was getting old. He must be fifty or more. The dark blue coat of the Macon and Atlanta uniform was edged with red dust from the road, and his uncle's gold spectacles still had little knots of red dirt in the hinges in spite of all his cleaning.

Those spectacles with their little square rims gave his memory a rather painful jolt. He could see his uncle seated in the dining room rocker on a summer's evening with the newspaper drawn across his chest, the spectacles pushed up and his head bent forward, holding the old oil lamp high in one hand so that it would shed its light across the pages, and all the while rocking for dear life, the oil sloshing back and forth in the glass base of the lamp, and the myriad leaf hoppers and moths that came in through the open windows to whirl around batting against the glass and settling on the rocker arms and on the table. He remembered the sound of

141

the chair rockers bumping against the wooden floor. It took his uncle a long time to read the paper. He read every little item, a habit picked up from long hours on the train.

"I'm glad you came out to see me," he told his uncle huskily. He really meant it. For a moment his eyes fogged, and he looked off into the woods until they cleared. "I guess you see I'm alright."

"Yes, I'm glad to see that." His Uncle Trennon put his hands down with a clap on his knees and looked about. "Well, I expect it's time for me to start back again."

They shook hands, standing up.

"Take care of your head, boy."

"Ear."

"I'll come out again."

"Yes sir," he said. "That'll be fine."

In the afternoon Johnny was ordered out on the last line of pickets in what was getting to be his regular station, right down near the creek where he could see the water all through the long afternoon heat, but couldn't go down to get a drink. Not unless he wanted a bullet in him.

That day the shouting started upon the far side. Sometimes there was a lot of hollering back and forth, sometimes there wasn't. It all depended on who was on picket duty over there. It had been the 22nd Wisconsin for over a week, but sometimes they changed unexpectedly. You could never tell what the shouting was for. Sometimes it was just to talk, and sometimes it was so as to locate you by the sound of your voice. Especially if there were sharpshooters on the line.

But this afternoon whoever it was hollering over there kept on and on, using that name which gave him a spooky, restless feeling when he heard it, as if they knew him or were finding him out, regardless, no matter how securely he was hidden by vines and tree limbs, although the name was only the same name the Yanks used for all of them:

"Johnnnny, oh Johhhhnny, oh Johnny Reb!"

142

On and on.

Finally he sang out.

"What do you want?"

"You're whipped, ain't you, Johnny?"

"Go to the devil." It did not deserve an answer, but he gave it. The same old thing. Some pickets liked to pump up their courage with lots of gabble.

"Ohhhhh Johnnny. Johnnny Reb."

Whoever it was calling on that other picket line, he had a husky, urgent sort of voice.

I'd like to get a look at him, he thought.

But he did not dare show his head, not after what had been happening for the last few nights.

"WHAT?"

"That you, reb?"

"Yes."

"Joe Johnston's been relieved. You heard that yet?"

"What?"

"General Joe Johnston is relieved of command, and they've put Hood in his place."

"You're a liar."

He didn't believe it, and the other did not call again.

But it was true.

CHAPTER *11*

Oh, sing of the glorious southland,
The pride of the golden sun!
The fairest land of the flowers
The eye e'er looked upon!

Hood for God's sake! No one south of Richmond, certainly no one in the army of Tennessee put any confidence in Hood!

The word of the change of command ran like wildfire through the woods along Peachtree Creek, and at first no one believed it. They thought of it as another one of those self-starting rumors that sprang up to relieve the heat and monotony of fighting.

But it was more than a rumor, apparently, for some of the corps staffers seemed to know something was up, and a few of the brigades called officers' meetings which ran on far into the small hours. The news was like a wave which began in front, out on the picket lines and washed to the rear and then back again with increasing force and fury; a roadful of supporting troops, it was said, sat down and cried over the removal of General Joe and the goddamned army and the goddamned government in Richmond or whatever was responsible. There was a lot of talk of mutiny, just as there had been the year before at Dalton. Along the creek the line officers went the rounds telling their men to keep cool, be calm, it would probably turn out to be a tempest in a teapot.

Would to God it had been! Johnny told himself. The trouble was, the Yanks knew all about it before they did, and when news came over the lines that way it was pretty nearly always true. He had never seen it to fail.

144

By the 18th of July it was official: Johnston had received a telegram of the most abrupt and insulting sort from Davis in Richmond, and it was all over. Whatever had gone on those past few days, Braxton Bragg's visit played some part in it the army knew. No one could forget how much the army had hated Bragg, nor how Bragg had done his best to ruin his men in Tennessee; the army believed in its hate and Braxton Bragg's pestilential talents as it believed in the rising and setting of the sun.

But to remove Joe Johnston on the eve of battle, right before Atlanta, and replace him with a subordinate, a junior in his own command—that damned prophet of hell and glory—John B. Hood!

The thought of it made Johnny sick. He could not even talk about it, did not want to discuss it endlessly as it seemed the rest of the army was bent on doing—talking and arguing from daylight to dusk. But he was not surprised to hear, as soon as the official word was out, that old General Hardee, who knew Hood as well as anyone as he had had to put up with Hood's didos in staff all that spring, had sent in his resignation, saying that in his opinion Hood was not fit to take Johnston's place. General Stewart put it more strongly: he said the war in Georgia was as good as lost.

Desertions started up again, and patrols had to be put out all along the roads leading southward into Atlanta. Later on, the army heard that Hardee was reconsidering his resignation in view of the effect upon the troops, but he had made his point.

Even, Johnny thought, if a person could take Johnston's dismissal and suffer with it through the long run of things, it was still too damned much to have to swallow the prospect of serving under Hood! Every person in the army knew that Hood was hard to get along with, that he didn't support the general's tactics but promoted his own ideas in army politics until Hardee and Stewart and some of the others put him down as an ambitious fool. And some of the staff had even come to the conclusion that Hood was some sort of spy for Bragg and Davis . . . which was enough to ruin any man with the army of Tennessee!

There was a look to Hood, Johnny thought, that made a person want to give him the benefit of the gossip. God knows he had the same sort of unfinished, born-again appearance of the Braxton Bragg school of generalship. A drinker, as some of his old troops said, or at any rate a prime candidate for certain glory by hook or by crook.

Hood was supposed to be about thirty-two or thirty-three, but most of the time one would swear he wasn't a day under sixty, which was due, probably, to the bad state of his health. Hood had lost a leg at Chickamauga and had crippled his arm at Gettysburg enough to make it almost useless. He could not ride a horse unless strapped to the saddle, and the sight of Hood riding along with his long yellow beard hanging on his chest and his fierce, hurried eyes, was a dismal and depressing thing, not calculated to inspire. The man was a cripple, when all was said and done, and it had changed him. Some of the meanest, most peculiar people Johnny had ever known were cripples, and after one look at Hood there was nothing there to make you feel he was any different.

As if all the furor over the command was not enough to keep a person bothered and upset, Johnny's ear began to give him trouble. The nick was only a minor sort of nuisance, but it had been a mistake to keep the bandage over it so long; on the morning of the 19th the inflammation had caused a swelling in his neck which some of the boys in the Rock City company noticed and commented on. Then the corporal made it his business.

"I expect I better put somebody else out on picket. That looks right ugly. Your whole neck's swole up on one side. You might have septic poisoning started in that thing. How come you didn't speak up at muster this mornin' about that ear?"

"It didn't feel bad this morning," he said peevishly. The

146

corporal, who was small and bandy-legged and swarthy like a lot of the Tennesseans, got on his nerves pretty bad sometimes; lately anything or anybody from Tennessee could make him realize how sick and tired he was of the word, and there were days when he longed to hear a Georgia voice or even, when he gave it any thought, a voice from Texas, Louisiana, South Carolina, or anything but goddammed Tennessee.

But the corporal kept at him to take off the bandage and let him have a look at the ear, and the more the corporal insisted, the more Johnny knew he wasn't going to do any such thing. It was too damned much bother in the first place, and in the second, it was his own ear, not the corporal's, and there wasn't anything that was going to come from having everybody crowd around to get a look. The whole business made him uneasy. A special sort of dread made him want to leave well enough alone. He did not want to fool with it, look at it, or have the Tennesseans look at it, feel it, or fuss with it in any way. He knew it was flaring up somehow. His jaw was rising up as though he had a toothache, and there was enough stiffness in the whole left side of his face and neck to keep him from moving his head. He had been careful about loading and firing the Whitworth all morning because the jar of the recoil ran along his collarbone and gave him fits.

The corporal would not leave him alone about it, and they got to arguing and after a while Captain White came down to see what it was all about. The captain listened to the corporal's description of the dangers of septic poisoning as though he had heard about everything in this world the past few days and was more or less getting used to it.

Johnny found that the captain's patient, weary attitude annoyed him about as bad as everything else. The captain looked him over as coolly as though he had been a lost article which had been brought up for his inspection, raising his eyebrows a little.

147

"Alright," White said. "Take off the headrag and let's see that ear."

"It's alright," Johnny said. "I don't want to fool with it. It's not important."

"I said take it off. I'll be the judge of what's important or not."

All right then, goddammit, if that's the way it's going to be, he thought savagely, and he jerked the bandage as though he did not care whether the ear came off with it or not. Which was exactly the way it felt. He almost hollered. He put his finger up and touched it, and it was just like a hard, hot blossom of flesh at the side of his head.

"That thing's swole up big as a pertater," the corporal volunteered with satisfaction. "That poison's run down into the neck, too, sure as God made little apples."

Captain White looked hard at it.

"Well," he said, "a case of blood poisoning will get you to the hospital, MacLeod. It'll get you a pass without any trouble at all."

It took a full solid minute for the sense of it to get through to him, and his first thought was that Captain White did not know how it sounded, that the man was not capable of anything so mean and suspicious and low. Then he knew for damned sure the captain knew exactly what he had said. There was no mistaking the look on his face. He really had it in for him. Goddamn him, he thought he would let the ear go till it was bad enough to get him a pass back to the hospital, and from there he could try a quick jump for home on the railroad or on foot. A regular low-down yellowhammer trick.

It made him mad as fire right off, and twice as mad somehow to think that the idea hadn't occurred to him, not once, and if it had he didn't know himself what he would have done right then to get a chance at a pass and maybe French leave. And it made it worse to know that White would credit him with something of the sort at first clip.

148

"Well," Johnny said, and he was so mad he could hardly talk, "I'll tell you right now, I don't need to go to the hospital that bad. I can get somebody . . . MacAllister or somebody, to lance it for me. I'll get it fixed, don't either of you worry about that. I'll take care of the whole confounded business myself."

"I won't give you permission to doctor it yourself," said Captain White. "The hospital is the place for anything that's begun to mortify like that."

The only thing he could think of right then was how mad he was and what a damned fool the captain was. He was sure showing himself as a short-tempered, low-minded ass. And once he had thought he was the best officer ever, glad to serve under him, the direct opposite of Ed Grimes in every respect.

"You listen here, White," he heard himself saying, almost not believing he could hear his own words, "I'll tell you something. When I want to go off I'll get a pass from you or take French leave but by God I don't need a low-down flicker trick like a running sore or chopping off my damned fingers or whatever it is you've dealt with around here before with this troop of razorbacks you officer!"

He could have said more, but even as mad as he was, he knew he had said about enough to fix him up for good as far as White and maybe the 1st Tennessee was concerned. But to his surprise the captain just stood there for a minute, thinking it over and looking tired, about as weary as a man can get and not drop right down in his tracks, and as though the biggest part of it had come over him all of a sudden.

"I know exactly how you feel," the captain said finally, and Johnny thought he was being sarcastic, but it was not that. "I know exactly how you feel, Mr. MacLeod, and I sympathize with you, but I expect you do not appreciate this in the slightest degree. In fact, I can't see much that you do appreciate or have thrown your heartfelt support toward up

149

here and I'm beginning to feel you, and it, may go to the devil so far as I am concerned."

"I don't see any heartfelt support around this man's army," Johnny answered. "I don't see any heartfelt support in any damned part of this war, do you? If you do, you just say so and I'll go look where it's at, because I want to see some of it, by God. I think it'll restore my faith in the whole world."

White looked at him for a moment as if considering whether it was worth the bother to answer.

"Good lord man," he said, "what do you expect? You youngsters, . . . " but he cut it off and cleared his throat and looked away, "expect more than you will get, which is the pity of it." Then he said, "Either report to the hospital or the corporal here will put you under arrest for insubordination, it makes no difference to me."

"I need a pass to go to the hospital," he muttered.

He was for damned sure never able to understand what White was going to do nor, half the time, what he was talking about. He just wished to hell he could get away from him.

When he had got his pass he put Peachtree Creek behind him and took the main road into Atlanta. He asked for a lift a dozen times or more from the supply wagons going that way, but there was always some reason why the driver would not pick him up, and one or two were so overloaded and their horses so poor he could see some excuse for it. One wagon had plenty of room, being occupied by four dog robbers from the hospital corps laying back like kings on a pile of croker sacks, but they would not let him in. Instead, they sat and watched him trudge along behind, eating dirt, for more than a mile, while they made all kinds of comments that apparently passed for wit among their kind. If it had not been that he was half-stupid with the fever in his ear which started a throbbing at any but the slowest, most careful movements, he would have been tempted to jump in that

150

wagon and clean out the whole nest of them. They were a sickly, whining, sniggering lot, these greaselickers; he could not stand the sight of them even when he was feeling at his best. Somebody had to work behind the lines, he knew, but there was always a certain sort to be found carrying pots and sweeping up and making themselves important, while keeping out of harm's way.

He was damned glad after a while that they did not give him a ride. He would rather be seen with a load of decent, hard-working niggers anyday than low-account whites. He thought that White would really appreciate those wagon dogs riding back into Atlanta. It would give him something to sermonize on for sure.

After a while the corporal's septic poisoning felt like it had not only inflamed his ear and neck but his brain as well. It was stupor rather than dizziness; he could walk and keep going, but he could not think. The heat and the smoking clouds of dust stirred up by the road traffic were fair to kill him if infection didn't. There might have been more miserable days in his life, but he was damned if he could recollect them.

He remembered that he sat down by the side of the road often, and once he thought of fixing his corn-meal rations but was not hungry enough to bother. Just past twilight he left the road to fall out to sleep in someone's front yard where two big magnolia trees overhung the sky, the white blossoms like moons against the darkness, suspended above his head in black leaves, and the grass unkempt and knee-deep, as soft as any bed.

In the morning he found the yard as crowded as a hotel with all sorts of stragglers, mostly boys like himself going into the city to look for a hospital. The old man who lived on the place, and he was so old his walnut hands shook in one continuous never-ending palsy, came out as soon as it was light to pass out buttermilk and corn meal all around. The old gentleman was a nice, courtly soul, and he reminded him in some small way of his Uncle Trennon. The old man was the only one left on the place. The rest of the family had either gone off to the army or the militia, or refugeed to Macon. There was not enough breakfast for everybody, and to lessen the strain on the old man's hospitality he slipped off as easy as he could.

A little after noon, with the heat pouring out of a clear, gray-white, motionless sky, he began to hear the first sound of a big fight behind him, in the direction of the creek. Not long after, ambulances racketed past, mostly with high-rankers sitting on their slats, and then wagons with the ordinary, everyday webfeet of the army bringing in their wounds. The news was that Hood had been lucky as the devil; somehow Sherman had got two corps straddling their positions with a gap between big enough to run a whole division through. Sherman had bungled that for sure. Hardee had been sent to split the thing wider and catch Thomas who was on the left, and crush him.

Crush him. That was the way everybody said it because it was the way they had heard the orders read. Crush him. It sounded like Hood, who would think it was possible to catch old Slow-Trot Thomas and squash him like a bug. Anybody who had ever faced Thomas would know that was not the word to use. Most of the wounded coming down the road from Peachtree Creek were from Walker's division, Georgia troops, and they had seen how hard it was to crush Thomas. They had gotten caught in the grape and canister from Thomas' artillery, in headlong assault. Not once, but over and over again, assault after assault.

"There won't be enough of that there division," one of their sergeants said, "to muster a regiment atter today. Except in the graveyard. After all that, after all that assault and charge and assault somebody said old Hood was not satisfied, that he had damned well told somebody that Hardee's corps wouldn't do no more than skirmish with the enemy and that he thought some of us had laid down ruther than charge breastworks." The sergeant's face wrinkled up in agony. "I tell you, if anybody in Stewart's division laid down on the field back there it was because they was dead."

The day was so infernally hot it was enough to make a person sick on heat alone; he was not hungry, only thirsty: he could not seem to get enough water down inside him to satisfy. After a while the water he was carrying got so warm he could not force it down unless he went so long just the wetness was sufficient. It took a long time to get close enough to the city to meet the first houses that were set together with yards and fences, almost twilight in fact, and the people had been standing out on the road the best part of the afternoon watching anxiously, some of them looking for relatives among the wounded coming in. It had not rained for a day or two, and the dust rose easily like an orange-tinted cloud sifting over the bushes and the trees, and each time a wagon or ambulance passed a perfect storm of it rose that clogged the nose and throat and blotted out the view so that those who were in it were half-blinded. It was a relief to hit that part of town where there were cobblestones or wooden blocks for paving.

The city looked to be full-up with wounded, or at least not able to handle the stream of casualties that were coming in. Most of the ambulances and wagons were in such a hurry they just dropped their cargoes in streets and yards, so that they could be turned back for another trip out to the battle, and the people of Atlanta were taking over the burden as best they could, either taking some of the wounded into their houses or carrying them off to the hospitals and theaters and churches in buggies or whatever could be found to roll. In spite of all the commotion there were still a lot of bystanders aimlessly milling around, it looked like to him, and gangs of Negroes, pickaninnies, children, and just plain riffraff looking on. The coming darkness did not help matters, either. God

153

knows how much was being overlooked or lost in the shuffle. The mess of an actual field of battle was bad enough, but there was something downright nerve-racking in all this, trying to do something about the bleeding stream just pouring in without any even halfway decent attempt by the army, only frantic, ordinary people hurrying and falling all over themselves to get something done in a mess that anybody could see was going to be too big to handle.

Two old ladies in black bonnets, sweating and trembling with excitement, were standing at the corner of Baker and Peachtree ladling out water from a bucket which a Negro boy kept filled from their house. There was a crowd of groaning wounded around them, but Johnny managed to get a dipperful and the water was cool and went down and felt like it would rest easy. It made him feel better.

The strangest thing about it was that, in spite of the fact it was almost dark, women were out on the streets everywhere, women who probably had not been out alone without their menfolk in their lives, young women, old women, middling sorts of women, rushing around, hauling things, carrying lanterns, cracker women barefooted with the snuff working under their lip and by God, if he was not mistaken, some who looked as though they had given up their business hours to help give a hand, feathers, paint, and all. Down where the gas lamps were burning in the area around the stores and the hotels, there was a woman so young and handsome she stood out even in that bedlam, bossing what must have been a pick-up assortment of convalescents from the hospital, four or five men in uniforms or what passed for uniforms these days, hobbling around, following her orders.

He almost tripped over the curbing at Five Points watching her. She was working like a demon, getting the wounded into litters, and she had on a nice frock with a big apron in front of it that did not half keep it from being ruined by blood and water. Her hairnet was torn, and a long, quivering rope of roan-colored hair hung down her back, and when she

154

lifted her arm to point out here, here, there were wet circles of sweat almost down to her waist. She was as young and pretty as Anna almost, and half-crazy with determination.

In spite of the night Atlanta was as hot as a closed box; there was not a breath of air. Where torches had been set out for more light in the streets the flames were almost as steady as though they had been painted. He tried to stop a drover and ask him where the hospitals were, but the man shook him off. None of the wounded still on their feet knew. Down there, somebody said, but down there was anywhere.

Aw, to hell with it. The damned confusion was more than he could take, anyway. He groped off down a side street, and it was quieter away from the middle of town. He sat down on a hitching post under a tree and put his head in his hands. His ear did not hurt. It just throbbed and pounded like some giant fist on that side of his face. A row of houses had their lamps lit, and some children were playing out in the yard. Now and then he could see them scampering across the grass and he could hear them yelling. And once, when the artillery northward at the fighting made a bright red flash in the sky he could see their faces and bare feet and arms flailing. The next moment it was dark again, and there was only their summer voices shrilling on.

He propped his elbows on his knees, bent over, and he guessed he slept.

News was cheap. He did not have to look for a newspaper to find out what was going on, because everyone went around with the question on their lips: What is going on now, have you heard? with a thousand piecemeal answers for the gathering. When anybody asked him, he told them he didn't know, and they looked like he was crazy and he couldn't understand it, until he realized that he was about the only bandaged soldier . . . oh, he guessed there were a few about . . . who had left the creek before the fighting started. But it did not take him long to become like all the rest; he just wanted to know how to get to the hospital and to find out what was happening. He found some Tennesseans who said that the 1st had been supporting them and hadn't done much fighting yet, but that their regiment, the 154th had sure caught hell out at the creek. No one that he could find had heard anything about the 79th Georgia.

The 21st of July was as hot as the 20th had been. A thunderstorm came up to the south, but it did not rain in town, which might have been just as well, with all the casualties still lying in the streets. The Opera House was being used as a hospital, but wounded were lying all in front of the place waiting to be moved in, and the only reason they were not being put in the alley at the side was that the surgeons were using it as a dump for the sawed-off limbs. They were operating in the office and throwing them out the window.

Lord, he stumbled off as fast as he could go. The flies. The flies! He felt as though a cloud of them was following him. He got sick and dizzy and found a place to grab, the tail gate of a wagon parked in front of the hardware store on Marietta, and two women came up to him and looked him over and offered to take him off with them and nurse him. To their house. They might have been perfectly alright, he couldn't tell, but one of them was rawboned as a horse and couldn't talk right, and he couldn't judge what he might be getting into. He told them he would rather go to a hospital, if that was agreeable to them, and they told him where Ward's hospital was.

"Nobody wants to go there, mostly," the rawboned one told him.

Well, he could not say that he was eager for it, either, but his orders had been to go to a hospital and get his ear looked after. If he had had a single relative in Atlanta it would have been different.

When he found Ward's hospital he heard that the fighting was moving off eastward to Decatur and that Federal cavalry were already in town out there. Old Hood was still bound and determined to pry Sherman loose and knock him good, send him back to Tennessee, although it did not look as though Hood's plans were working up to scratch. Still, you couldn't tell. The boys who had been out at the creek said Sherman was hurt aplenty. The trouble was, when you looked around, a person couldn't help but wonder who had got hurt the worst. Atlanta looked like it had half the army in it, all busted and bleeding. And while they were still rolling in from the fight at Peachtree Creek they started coming in from out near Decatur. To add to it all, the city was beginning to get a little shelling, and the excitement and hollering over that were not helping a bit. The quartermaster's mule corral across from Trinity Methodist Church got a hit, and the mules broke out of the stockade and thundered through town. He could not find foot room on the steps of Ward's so he ran across the street and got on the far side of a shade tree and pulled a boy from a Carolina outfit with a bad leg after him until the stampede was over. Only a few Negroes went after to chase the mules. Everybody was busy.

That was the 21st. That night he slept on the front porch of a house that had been closed up, and he ran a fever and got up late. The artillery, twice as loud as before, was pounding out in Decatur. He tried Ward's hospital again and got inside by afternoon and was told to sit on a chair in the hall and wait, but when a surgeon finally got around to looking at him, he pulled off his bandage, looked at the ear but did not touch it and threw the bandage over on a pile and told him to come back after dark, and he would do something for him then. He was gone before Johnny could say another word.

The incident was both pitiful and funny, when you looked at it. He had got his bandage lifted, to be washed and used on somebody else, he guessed, and he had gotten shoved out on the street as either not sick enough to worry about, or so bad off it didn't make any difference.

God, he didn't care, that was the truth! If his fever didn't

157

quit and the side of his head let up, it would be a damned relief to die!

He got the notion he was going to go down to the railroad depot to see what could be done about getting home to Jonesboro, but the idea was a mistake, for when he got within a few blocks of the place he could see all the wounded laid out, paving the ground with their bodies. Atlanta was full, more than full, with no place else to put them, and now was trying to ship the rest of the army's casualties down the line to Griffin and Macon. It was godawful. He had never seen a sight like it, not even at Chickamauga.

Before he could turn and get out of there one of the bodies lying in the street grabbed his foot and held it.

"MacLeod," it cried, "for God's sake stop a minute."

He bent over, half-dreading to see who was calling his name, and it was MacAllister of the Rock City guards, his whole side torn open and not even a blanket to cover him.

"I'm lying here all by myself," MacAllister said through his sunburned lips, "I'm fixing to die here all by myself. Can't you stop a minute? You got any water?"

There was still water in his canteen, and he lifted MacAllister's head and gave him some of it.

He squatted down by MacAllister for the better part of an hour in that blazing sun, trying to do as he wanted him to, and keep him company until he died, but at the last he got to wishing that MacAllister would die and let him go, it was almost more than he could stand. It wasn't doing any good, MacAllister wasn't even sure of who he was at the last and kept thinking he was his father or one of his brothers.

Finally when he did die some jasper lying just a few feet away wanted him to stay with him, too, but he had had enough. He got out of there and walked until he had got as far away from the sound of the place as you could get in Atlanta and looked for a saloon that a person could manage to squeeze into. But the saloons were doing as big a business as the hospitals.

158

There was a Negro woman with a barrel of whiskey set on a table right in the street selling it by the cupful. He still had enough shinplasters to pay for one and when that was down he got his pen and the last of his paper out of his jacket and traded them off for a second. The second was better. It was pure poison. He lay down on the steps of the Planters and Factors Bank and passed out.

When he woke he expected it was still the same day. It still looked like the same day at any rate, and the guns out at Decatur were still beating on the drum of the sky. When he sat up he discovered that his ear was flowing like a stream, blood and muck all over his neck and down his back, and a blanket of flies after him. Goddamned flies, all the flies in the state of Georgia had come into Atlanta, and he had seen where they had been and what they had been doing. Not on him, if he could help it. He got off his shirt and wrapped it around his head like a turban and got up and found that he was not dizzy and not stupefied for a change. Something had happened, with or without the hospital or the surgeons. Well, good enough, he was through with the place, ready or not.

A bunch of militia came scurrying along, headed east along the railroad tracks. At least he guessed they were militia, they all had weapons of some sort, although they looked just like any crowd picked up off the streets, herded together to go somewhere, most of the older men already red-faced and heat-struck.

He started after them. No one with any sense would relish being out with Hood in whatever was going on, but there was only one place to be if you couldn't manage to get home, and that was where the fighting was.

CHAPTER 12

Thick as the leaves of the forest in summer
Her brave sons will rise on each plain,
And then will strike, until each comer
Lies dead on the fine soil he would stain.

When his ear had finally healed the place where all the trouble had started was only a flattened, shiny-pink stretch about an inch long, as though somebody at one time or other had decided to trim off the top with a knife. You couldn't tell by looking at it that it had once been swollen to damned near the size of an orange. The ear looked pretty fair, if a little lopsided, and most of the time his hair came down far enough to hide it from sight. As wounds went, it ought to have been as nice as a man could get except for the inflammation which had set in and which he now guessed had been blood poisoning, to have made him so sick. And the row the whole affair had caused with Captain White and the trip to Atlanta, he also allowed, he would just as soon have missed; every once in awhile he would dream of MacAllister and the terrible sun and madhouse of that day in July, and how grateful MacAllister had been for his keeping him company until he died, and it would give him the low dismals all over again just thinking about it. If anybody ever died anywhere near him again he was going to make sure he was not going to have to sit with them until it was over. There was something in him, he had just discovered, that had a perfect horror of keeping a deathwatch.

It scared him, too, to think that he had suffered so much with MacAllister that at the last he had been raging inwardly and praying for him to die, and that it seemed MacAllister could not get it over fast enough.

It might be his ear had got better just out of pure fright.

At any rate, the whole business had whipped some of the restlessness out of him for the time being. He didn't have enough energy to fret a lot. It seemed that home was awfully far off in actual distance and otherwise, and once or twice he thought about going off to see where the 79th Georgia was positioned, and what Ed Grimes and Byron were doing, and what news they had from Jonesboro, but he was still a little sore and irritable about what had happened with those girls out at Kennesaw.

That was the whole trouble with having anything to do with his cousin, he told himself; he always got involved in some scrape with Ed that turned out to be mortifying as the very devil. Why, the drunkest he had been in his whole life had been Ed's doing. The only times he had ever been to a whore house Ed had guyed him into it and then ragged him about it later. The only time he had ever been on a regular free-for-all, too, was at one of Ed's parties up in Tennessee. They had torn up the whole damned hotel in Munceyburg.

If he went to see Ed he knew the first thing Ed would say to him would be something like: My godalmighty, you mean to tell me you spent three whole days in Atlanta and didn't manage to get home once? Not once?

And then Ed would probably tell him that he had been home half-a-dozen times himself, and that all the other boys in Company B had, too.

Johnny didn't want to hear anything like that. It would be too much right now in view of his trouble with Captain White. And yet he was so damned glad, he remembered, to get away from Ed back in the spring and be assigned to the 1st Tennessee that he had thought himself the luckiest jasper alive.

Which proved something—but he was damned if he knew what.

161

The first days of August were miserably hot. In one of those turnabouts of weather that were more like the weather of the coastal lowlands than the climate of the Piedmont spurs, the days were drenched with moisture and unbearably humid. By afternoon the clouds had collected in towering white pipes in the sky, thousands of feet up—hundreds of thousands of feet up, it looked to anyone lying out in the Atlanta trenches—and then it wouldn't be long before the towering castles and turrets and thunderheads rolled together and turned black, cracking with lightning. The storms would bring the usual monotonous scramble for cover along the earthworks, with a person spending an hour or more huddled under a board or a piece of canvas, or whatever could be snatched up for protection. Or sometimes one had to just lie out in the open, cursing the torrents of rain and the wind that snapped off pine branches and sent them hurtling around like shells, until the storm drizzled off and the oncoming night was not only dark, but cool, for a change.

Then the humid weather blew away one morning on a wind from the west, and it was hot and dry, dry as bones. The breeze rattled the stiff leaves in the hardwoods and wrung the last drop of water out of the air so that one couldn't even remember the spongelike weather of just a few days past. Lips parched and the linings of nose and throat dried out as thick and hard as leather.

The dry wind was followed by a series of days when the weather was so quiet the sun roasted in the sky like pork on a spit and the army lay in the entrenchments and looked out over the fields and pine groves to see the heat waves rising, making the already wilting weeds tremble like plants underwater.

There was no fighting to speak of; the savage weather seemed to bring things to a halt, although the army knew this was not the real reason—fighting always went on, regardless. But the violent switchings of climate came at an

162

opportune time, just to show that there was more than war to make life hell.

The Yankee General Sherman had dug his lines almost three-quarters of the way around the city: part of his army was well entrenched at Peachtree Creek and a portion of the lines extended eastward to Decatur where the big battle of July 22nd had taken place, and also southwestward where there had been some fighting on the 29th. The war was almost quiet, subdued by the weather or some other thing—for the army of Tennessee was holding Atlanta within a ring and Sherman was outside. Only the Yankee siege guns kept up a clamor. The big cannons had been brought down from Chattanooga at the end of July to bombard the city, beat it into submission as the northern newspapers put it, and a banner of black smoke hung over Atlanta by day, and a smell of burning by night.

In spite of the siege of early August there seemed to be an astonishing amount of life left in the city. People were pouring in and pouring out of the place by foot or wagon or railroad, coming into Atlanta to sell supplies to the army or visit the hospitals, or going out of Atlanta to refugee southward to Griffin or Macon or Columbus. The joke was, the army said, that as soon as Atlanta emptied out, it filled right back up; with all the coming and going Billy Sherman ought to put the Yankee army in civilian clothes and send them in that way. The Yankee army could come right in as refugees and occupy the place before anybody'd notice the difference.

The railroads, Johnny had to admit, were certainly working like the devil under all the traffic, passenger and freight. In spite of war, and the bad condition of the rolling stock the two remaining lines out of the city to Columbus and Macon were operating more or less regularly, and where the 1st Tennessee was stationed south of the yards in East Point, the shriek of whistles and the clang of engines could be heard without a stop, straight around the clock. Johnny's Uncle Trennon had been to see him several times during his layovers there, and had brought him food and letters from Jonesboro. In that respect, being garrisoned in the Atlanta lines was the most satisfactory arrangement in months—if it hadn't been for Johnny's difficulties with the 1st Tennessee, and the captain of the Rock City guards in particular.

If he had expected any sort of comment from White when he returned from Atlanta and the hospital, it wasn't forthcoming. In fact, he had not even found the 1st Tennessee until late in the afternoon of the 23rd of July, and by that time they were bivouacked out in a pine grove between Atlanta and Decatur on what had been the Atlanta-Augusta rail line. White was having his hands full gathering in his company. The 1st had been in the worst part of it at Decatur and had suffered heavily.

"You all through?" was all White had time to say to him.

"Yes," he answered. If White was surprised to see him come back at all he never showed it, and it was some time later that Johnny thought to tell him about MacAllister's death. Even then White did not have much to say. He just wrote the facts down on the report, and Johnny supposed he got around to writing MacAllister's folks about it. That was the usual procedure, and he would say this much for White —the man never failed to do any part of his job.

When the 1st moved into the ditches at East Point to guard the railroad yards, some of the Tennesseans picked up their mail from home, which caused a great stir. Most of the boys' relatives were in Yankee-occupied territory, and their mail from up there was scarce.

White's wife was dead. No one knew any of the details, only that she had taken sick suddenly and had died, and that White's two little girls were being taken care of by neighbors.

White said nothing about it. He had made a little board shelter that was both his quarters and company office down at the lower end of the Rock City's entrenchment, and during the first weeks of August he spent a good bit of time down there, his knees drawn up to support a board for his papers, his face in shadow, supposedly working on reports, but most of the time with his pen in hand, forgetting to write, and his eyes looking across the slopes toward the trees where the pickets kept up their skirmish fire. He would stare at whatever he was staring at, so still and silent it was enough to make a person wonder how long he could sit like that and be lost in whatever he was thinking, without getting restless or needing to stir around.

Dammit, why didn't he go home?

He ought to go home to look after his little girls, even if it was too late to do anything about his wife.

God, he ought to go home! It wasn't human, Johnny knew; White could get home if he wanted to. He could take the railroad to Montgomery, Alabama, and then get a horse and go north into Tennessee, taking a little care for Federal cavalry and garrisons.

But outside of his board-office hole, the captain remained as dry and duty-minded as always, less patient and a whole hell of a lot more sarcastic.

The fact that White would not go home bothered Johnny intolerably. He knew that White didn't have any more hope for Hood's army than the rest of them did, and yet the man stayed. It was a suffering sore just to have to watch White when he went down to his hole to sit and pretend to be writing reports. A fat lot of good any reports were doing. The war was a stalemate, the newspapers said. The Atlanta Intelligencer reported that Grant could not whip Lee in Virginia and that Sherman was buffaloed and discouraged from knocking his head against the gates of Atlanta.

Not that Johnny really believed this. The war was a stalemate, he could allow; the papers were right about that much. But it was this way: the army did not trust Hood, and Hood did not trust his army. That was the real stalemate, and William T. Sherman did not have a blessed thing to do with it.

165

As for Hood, he was out somewhere near the battlefield at Ezra Church, brooding, rumor had it. And drinking, too. If you could believe the rumor. At any rate, that sort of thing was nothing new. The army had got used to that with Braxton Bragg.

Just when Hood seemed to have sunk from sight, his headquarters issued new orders. The cavalry was going off, more than half if it. Forrest was to go to Mississippi, and Wheeler to Tennessee, both to operate on Sherman's long railroad supply lines extending down from Kentucky and Tennessee.

It was the first news of any real importance on the grapevine in some time, and the details sounded as though they had been thrown in for ornament. The added story was that this idea was not purely Hood's, but advisement and master planning from Jeff Davis up in Richmond. Aided, of course, by that lunatic, the commander of the armies, Braxton Bragg.

And listen to this, the grapevine said. The cavalry is going off to raise hell in Tennessee and Mississippi, and Hood is going to do without it here in Georgia by using cannonfire as feelers. To keep Sherman in sight.

"Use what?" the corporal of the Rock City guards said in amazement.

"The cannon will act as feelers," one of the Tennesseans told him. "That's what the orders said."

"Lord God," was all the corporal could manage.

Part of Wheeler's cavalry passed by the 1st Tennessee's encampment in East Point, and as the 1st Tennessee cavalry and the 9th Battalion were from the same part of Tennessee as the Rock City guards, there was a big reunion. The captain himself left his hut long enough to come up to the road and hold a conversation with a major, a friend of his, in the 9th.

"Goodbye, boys, goodbye," the Rock City boys cried.

"Goodbye, Sam."

"Goodbye, Whit."

"Goodbye, Tom."

It was, Johnny thought with disgust, a regular blowout, all the Tennesseans making a big fuss and some of the brothers, split-up, blubbering at each other.

"This is a damn-fool stunt," one of the cavalrymen burst out. "If y'all stay here with Sam Hood and we'uns go off, we're as good as licked. Y'all remember I said it!"

"That's enough," the cavalry major told him.

Johnny did not stay to watch the end of it. He noticed White didn't either. The captain went down to his hole and stayed there and didn't bother to pick up his pen and act like he was going to do something busy. He just sat there, bent over, with his arms wrapped around his head. White wouldn't break down, Johnny thought—White was too stiff and proper for that. He couldn't imagine White doing anything of the sort. The man would rather die, he guessed, than show anything.

But he couldn't stand to watch him, doubled up down there, as if he was in pain.

It wasn't too long after the departure of the cavalry that the old restlessness returned. With the exception of the endless pounding of the siege guns, things were dull. The coming and going of the trains, so close by in the East Point Yards became temptation enough and to spare. A half-hour's ride would put a person in Jonesboro.

The second Sunday in August, after a visit from his Uncle Trennon, Johnny strolled up to the yards to see him depart on the Macon train.

Although the whole jaunt didn't take more than an hour, it was a mistake, for the yards were out of bounds for that part of Hardee's corps not actually stationed in them. The first sergeant of the Rock City guards, Heffernan, was close on Johnny's trail when he doubled back, and they almost ran into each other.

167

"Where you been, MacLeod?" Heffernan wanted to know.

"I've been up to see my uncle off on the train."

"Hell, you know you're supposed to stay away from them damned trains, ain't you been told that before?" The Tennessean was hot and mad, having dog-trotted all the way down the main street of East Point in the Sunday afternoon heat to catch him.

"Not in so many words, no," Johnny said stubbornly.

"What'n th'hell do you mean, 'Not in so many words,' dammit! If these yards was ON to everybody in the whole damned division, they'd be OFF to you, don't you know that? The whole brigade knows you got the hankers to go home. You think its a damned secret?"

Johnny was having it spelled right out for him, word for word, as he knew Heffernan had had it from White.

"My uncle works on the goddamned railroad," he found himself yelling at the sergeant. "What the hell's wrong with walking a damned mile to see your relations off, for God's sake?"

"Alright," the first sergeant said to him, suddenly brisk and businesslike. "I ain't goin' to argue with you. If you're so hell-bent to travel, we kin see you get to travel, some. But you ain't goin' to like it."

There were all sorts of special details along the right flank of Hood's army: press gangs of field Negroes from the farms nearby which were working on the railroad trackbeds, conscripting parties and the like, but the worst details of all were the patrols which scoured the woods between the Federal and Confederate lines in an area where both parties hid out. Quail hunting, it was called. The idea was to flush as many deserters from Hood's army as one could find, without being shot by either picket line.

Johnny went quail hunting on that detail at once, riding muleback with a tough little corporal from the 28th Alabama, who had been stationed the year before at Andersonville

168

prison, and five others. For a week they spent their time cutting out stragglers and yellowbacks from the brush.

It was a hellish experience for Johnny. Up close, he got a good look at the sort of men who had staked everything to get out of army service for one reason or another. Some of the deserters between those lines were living in trees, like monkeys, only coming down at night to forage. One wildcat had a woman living with him in an abandoned springhouse. One poor jasper, when they picked him up, had been living on sassafras roots and berries, and kept telling them he was John the Baptist. He wasn't fooling, either—he was just crazy as a loon.

God knows, Johnny thought, after the weeks he had been living in the woods, damned if he didn't look like John the Baptist, almost naked, bearded, and skinny as a rail. He sang hymns all the way back to camp, telling them that he prayed for their souls and hoped they'd be spared so that they could follow the way of Jesus Christ, and be ready for the Coming.

It gave Johnny the cold chills, but the damned mean little corporal from Alabama thought it was funny as hell.

A couple of deserters they picked up were dog-sick with dysentery and pleaded that they had only hid out so as not to be sent to the Atlanta hospitals where, as everybody knew, a person had a better than fifty-fifty chance of never getting out.

The detail also found three razorbacks from North Carolina happy as larks, making moonshine not a stone's throw from the Chattahoochee River and a big emplacement of Yankee artillery.

The detail corporal insisted they leave the still just as it was and not bust it up, and Johnny suspected the corporal would make his own arranagements about it later. Whiskey selling to both armies was a right prosperous business.

Of all the deserters they picked up that week, four were officers, and except for one, a thin, nervous fellow with a Charleston accent, they all came peaceably, with a sort of hangdog despair. The Charlestonian, who gave them a merry chase through a pinewoods where the mules were more a hindrance than anything else, tried to put his pistol in his mouth and pull the trigger when they finally cornered him, but the little corporal hurried up and knocked it out of his hand.

"Now lieutenant," the corporal said, "you don't want to do nothing rash. Think of your folks back home for a minute. You wouldn't want them to know you blowed your brains out over nothing like a little thing such as dee-serting the army, would you?"

The Carolinian gave them all a wild look, as if seeking some kind of support.

"The damned thing misfired," he kept saying. "The damned thing misfired."

"Aw, now, don't tell me that," the corporal said gently. "It didn't misfire. You jest didn't try hard enough."

If White and Heffernan had put him to that sort of work, Johnny thought, to teach him a lesson of sorts, then they were bound to be disappointed with what he had learned. The only thing he was convinced of, after a few days of the quail-hunting detail, was that people could make damned fools of themselves . . . like trying to hide out between the lines of two armies, for instance, . . . and that the little corporal from Alabama was the first person he would elect to shoot in the back if the opportunity ever opened up.

But he did not have the chance to consider anything like that, for, apparently on White's request, Johnny was shifted over to another detail made up of boys from the 1st Tennessee regiment, all sharpshooters, and all working as scouts.

Moving closer to a state of grace, he thought wryly. He could almost see White figuring that by now he'd had enough of a dose of the deserter detail, but still was not ready yet to be allowed back in the company.

The new detail of scouts was a little smaller than the

170

quail-hunting detail had been, and not mounted, but the four men in the group were good sorts and they knew their business. They were all crack shots, and nearly all carried the Whitworths brought in through the blockade the winter before, although none of them had competed for the guns directly. The original owners were all dead or disabled. Except Johnny.

"You made out pretty good," one of them commented, grinning. "You had a right smart of picket duty, too, didn't you?"

"Same as the rest," he said, uneasily, not wanting to talk about it.

"You got a good mark on you then," the other continued. "I've knowed some people like that. Seems like a bullet can't touch them."

"Well, I've been hit, alright," he said irritably. "I'm not that goddamned lucky. And I won't get any luckier with you bragging on it, for God's sake!"

"Don't spook. I didn't mean nothin'."

But he was already spooked. It didn't take much to put his nerves on edge anymore.

Each morning before daylight the scout detail was put on the railroad, sometimes in just the wood car behind an engine, and run down the line toward the next town, which was Fairburn, to come in contact with the ever-shifting right flank of the Yankee General Howard's corps. The scouts would deploy as skirmishers and run from tree to tree until the bullets began to pop. The Yankees usually slipped a little more to the south everyday, and with the cavalry gone, it was hard work just feeling them out. Johnny supposed there was some use in all this, but every scout detail working that line usually lost pretty heavily in dead and wounded.

He had just been out for two trips and was coming back on his third—in fact, had just reported in, dog-tired, when he heard that Sherman's cavalry had come through Fairburn at the Columbus railroad (while he had been out chasing through the pine trees somewhere nearby, he thought disgustedly) and had gone east, down the Fairburn road into Jonesboro, tearing up the Macon railroad there and cutting the telegraph lines. Hood had been cut off in Atlanta, almost encircled, although the cavalry couldn't hold. The engineers had already been sent south to Jonesboro to see what could be done to repair the railroad beds and restring the lines.

The Federal cavalry had gone on, rumor having it that they were going to make a try for the prison camp at Andersonville.

Johnny didn't care about that part of it—Andersonville be damned! But the Fairburn road ran right by his house and Matt and Anna were right in the way.

"Corporal," he said, and it didn't take any effort to make his voice sound calm because he was about as cold, dead calm as he could have wished for right then, and was going to be that way until he got home. "I've got to go down the line and find my company, the Jonesboro company in the 79th Georgia. My cousin's captain. He'd know if there was any news from my folks. They were right in the middle of that raid."

"Ah," the corporal said, squinting his eyes, thinking about it.

"Dammit, corporal," he said, putting a little pressure behind it, "I just came in from scout detail, didn't I? I'm due for about ten-hours' sleep! Now if you ain't fixing to put me on picket then for God's sake let me go find out what's happened to my folks!"

"Well, don't you be gone more'n an hour," the corporal said finally. "If you do, I'll come lookin' for you."

The hell you will, he told himself.

"I'll be back," he promised.

CHAPTER *13*

And the Georgian listened sadly
As the other tried to speak,
While the tears were dropping softly
O'er the pallor of his cheek:
"How she used to stand and listen
Looking o'er the field for me,
Waiting till she saw me coming,
Neath the shadowy old plum tree."

The first hour or so at home was just pure bedlam. After all the trouble of trying to get out of East Point without getting picked up either by the provost guards or the train patrols, he had looked forward to the comparative peace of home, but his Aunt Matt seized on him the first moment he put his foot in his own yard, and staged a hell-roaring roundabout that was like something out of a bad day in his childhood.

Instead of receiving the hero's welcome, he was told to stand right where he was! or, move over there, quick! and submit to all sorts of inspections of his ear, which everyone had heard about, and finally give up his clothes in the best interests of health and hygiene—all of which he realized was probably necessary, but humiliating as the very devil, especially with Anna looking on. At least he guessed she was still looking on. He couldn't tell much with his Aunt Matt driving him ahead of her like a herd of cows.

There was no explaining to his Aunt Matt that, left to himself, he could very well manage to shuck his clothes, grease

173

his hair for lice, and take a bath. He had managed to look after himself through four years of war and, barring pneumonia at Dalton and a sore ear, he had done a pretty good job of it.

Instead, he had to hand over his shirt and britches and sit on the back porch steps wrapped in a sheet from upstairs while his Uncle Trennon and his Aunt Matt figured out the best way to fumigate his clothes.

"Over a fire," he tried to tell them. "You don't get rid of those things until they get suffocated by the smoke and come out, and then you flick them in the flames. You can tell when you've got one of them, though, because they pop."

But they wouldn't listen. His Aunt Matt gave him a look as though graybacks were something he had invented all by himself to make life nasty.

"I'd think a person would keep hisself clean enough not to bring home a whole load of varmits," she sniffed.

She was bound and determined to have enough water to scrub down an elephant, too, with both the washpot and the wooden tub brought out, one for soap and one for rinse water. What particularly irritated him was that he was not allowed to lend a hand even to draw the wash water for fear of damaging the precious sheet which his Aunt Matt said was the only one of four left in the house. So he had to watch his uncle fetching for him and then, when Matt called his uncle off to fry graybacks, Anna.

He sat on the steps during all of this, suffering the tortures of the damned as he watched his own wife carrying water for his bath, a bucketful at a time, sweet beautiful Anna with one arm thrown out to balance herself, weighted down by a brimful bucket of water in the other hand, just like some damned camp washerwoman. You could tell she was not used to heavy work like that. She acted like she would never get the hang of it, either, no matter how hard she tried; she spilled more than she got, and he was damned if he had ever intended to see her doing work of that sort. Yet

174

he was reminded of that day in Atlanta when MacAllister died, of the woman he had seen bossing the soldiers handling the wounded, how sweat-stained and disheveled she had been, in such terrible shape for such a pretty woman, and yet how forgetful she had been of it all. Just like Anna, now, hurrying along, spilling water on her feet and not even noticing it because she was so busy doing what Matt had told her to do.

His Aunt Matt had no damned business giving orders to his wife, he didn't care what it was for!

As if he had conjured her up just thinking about her, Matt came and stood in front of him, hands on hips, making another inspection so as to be sure she hadn't missed anything.

"You wash your hair good, then grease it."

"Yes'm." She had put herself right where he couldn't see Anna.

"Where's your shoes?"

"Worn out."

"What, worn out? Them good shoes I sent you last April?"

"For God's sake, Matt," he told her, "how long do you think shoes'll last? Dalton to Kennesaw's a damned long way. I've been walking on skin ever since and glad to have skin to walk on. And it don't bother me one bit . . . except to hear people fussing at me about it."

"Don't cuss at me, young man!"

"I wasn't cussing. Godalmighty, it just slips out. Where do you think I've been the last six months, anyway?"

"It ain't fit for a young girl to hear."

If she meant Anna, she had heard worse, and from his own lips, unfortunately. But he guessed Matt was right. But the way she had put it, a young girl, as though they were discussing a stranger!

"Just give me time to practice up," he muttered. "I can't do things right until I get used to it awhile. I just got home, you know. Where's Anna gone now?"

"She's busy," his aunt said. "Don't you worry her, now.

175

We got more to do than we can take care of. You just watch yourself and don't let none of them bugs hop off you onto anything around here."

"Good lord," he told her, "what do you think they are—jack rabbits?"

He didn't half get a chance to say anything to his uncle, either, for every time he got near him his Aunt Matt found something for him to do. Finally, restlessly, he got up against orders and walked down the yard a bit, by the side of the house, looking at the damage. The yard was still full of litter, mostly broken things from the house that Matt and Anna had not had time to pick up. It made him a little sick to think what must have gone on with the Yankees tearing things up just for the pure hell of it.

God, the things he had thought of when he first heard about the raid—and the way he had felt all the way down, expecting the worst! Reality was bad enough, but not as bad as what his imagination had pictured.

The biggest relief which neither he nor his Uncle Trennon could let themselves show was to find that nothing had happened to either Matt or Anna, other than their being scared to death.

There was so much relief in it he hadn't actually got his wind back. He wished that he had never seen that girl in Tennessee hanging on the rail fence of that place to keep from falling down, crying and hollering, spraddle-legged, clawing at the fence logs like a treed cat, and half out of her head. Walt Ashford and Byron, who had been first in the column and so first to come up, had been so frozen stock-still at the sight of her they could not do a thing. It was Tom Morse who ran up and shook out his bedroll blanket so that he could put it around her. That awful spraddle-legged way she held herself and the clawing and insane screaming about what had been done to her—as if she was past caring what they heard and God, some of it was bad, sure enough—was enough to make the whole company want to take a pile of

176

blankets and bury her from sight, just so they wouldn't have to look at her or listen to her, either. It was more than a person could bear. He never knew if she was ruined for life or what, none of them knew enough about such things to say one way of the other—there was just no telling about a young girl like that. She was about fourteen or fifteen. And bloody as a butchered shoat. That was cavalry. A couple of them had turned back and came to pay their respects after they saw she was all alone in the place.

Just remembering made him feel sick again, and he took a detour down past the crepe myrtle bushes not to stay out of Matt's way but to give himself a chance to move around some and work off his nerves.

Down in the knee-high grass, which needed scything badly, he found one of his Granpa's books, *The History of Dunbar County*. He had no idea where *that* was, or what the book was about.

His uncle came after him with a cup of soap.

"Don't spill it," his uncle said, handing it to him. Then, because his uncle could see something was bothering him: "When you get cleaned up and have something to eat this, ah, clutter won't bother you so much."

"It isn't the mess," he told him. "I was just thinking about what could have happened."

"Well, you get the preliminaries over with, and you'll feel better about that, too," his uncle said hurriedly, jumping right over the subject.

He sighed.

"I know, Uncle. Where's Anna?"

"Um," his uncle said, "she was here a moment ago."

That was the trouble, Johnny thought. It almost looked as if Anna was deliberately staying out of his way, and he hated to think what things were going to be like if she started off acting like that. He tried to remember exactly how things had been when he left. Pretty bad. Pretty damned bad, and as far as he could see, time hadn't done much to straighten things out. Things didn't just straighten themselves out being left alone. Every now and then one of her letters had sounded as though the situation might be better, but he couldn't really tell.

Well, at least he was home. It had taken the whole Yankee cavalry to do it, but he was there, and that, at least, gave him a chance.

He went back toward the yard looking for her but she was nowhere to be found, and so he sat down on the back porch steps again, holding the cupful of soap carefully.

Time had done something to her, at any rate, for Anna looked different, he had to admit. She . . . well, she sort of looked different in some sort of way. Her hair was different, just pulled back and not as fancy as she used to wear it, or as he remembered her wearing it, but it was still a thick mass of curls that rolled up into waves and ringlets as though it wanted to be loose and carefree and not proper and all smoothed down. It was pulled over her ears and hanging down her back, with just a hairpin or clasp or something underneath at the nape of her neck to hold it up there a little, for coolness.

And her skin was sunburned. He knew it wasn't fashionable, and it wasn't tactful to say anything about it, probably, considering how white her skin had been before and what a fuss had been made over her complexion in Augusta, but the golden-tan color of her face and arms didn't hurt Anna's looks at all as far as he could see. That pale, perfect skin was no longer pale, but it was still perfect, smooth as polished gold and made her eyes look even darker and bigger in her face. It was pretty fascinating, that sunburn, especially that triangle where women left their dresses open at the throat when the weather got hot. Anna's was buttoned down low, and the weather was damnably hot, and pretty fine viewing, too. She had on an old dress that had washed away to no-color-much and a straw sun hat Matt kept around in the kitchen for garden work. Her dress was hiked up on

178

one hip, tucked under the belt so that he could see she was wearing some old shoes, flat slippers, that her heels kept coming out of. Shoes were hard to get, and Johnny guessed she had to wear old shoes at home and all that, and these would have looked terrible except that it was funny to see Anna's feet hurrying along in the old shoes and her bare heels feeling for the backs and half the time not finding them.

All in all, she was so slapdash and loosened up and lovely and adorable that it made him nervous to think about it. After all, he was right out in the open with only Matt's sheet wrapped around him for decency.

Dammit, there was just no way of telling what the situation might be now.

She picked that time to go through the house on some errand and come out on the back porch right behind him. He heard her coming and got up in haste, churning around in the sheet. She was holding a washrag in her hand, a washrag for him. He took it from her and could not, at the moment, passing the confounded washrag like that, think of anything to say. She was so close, right up on him, and lovely. Surprise at how really beautiful she was right up so close to him almost paralyzed him . . . and her eyes were right in his eyes, clear and dark with long thick lashes and the most delicate eyelids, looking right at him, down into him, saying nothing.

"Well," he heard himself say, "you ah, got sunburned, didn't you?"

Her hand went up to her face instantly.

"Where?"

"I mean, not today. Not red, or anything. Just brown. You look like you've been out in the sun a lot."

"I have," she said.

She still looked as though she couldn't think of anything to say, distant and polite, sort of, waiting for him to begin. But she was standing so close that if it hadn't been for the

179

infernal sheet he could have put his hands out and caught her, just to feel her against him once more. It was more than he could stand, to think about it.

"It's not bad," he said. "Just sort of sunburned."

"I know," she murmured. "I hate to wear hats and it doesn't do much good anyway. It looks awful."

The triangle of her throat and breast drew his eyes. Lord, he did not even remember what she looked like without all that stuff, dress and all. He didn't even remember what his own wife looked like without her clothes. Not a bit. Just sort of dimly, and that was no help. He could not even feature himself alone with her now even though they were married, that is to say, married—dammit—in bed. He knew that they were, and that all this had happened once, but he couldn't believe it in this strange, still conversation which was taking place in the hot sunshine on the back porch steps of his own house.

"You look fine," he told her. "Just sort of different." He had an inspiration: "I guess I look pretty different, too."

"No," she whispered.

Her voice was low, and she seemed now to be occupied by some sort of daydream. She was not looking at him, but off somewhere, vaguely.

"Not different," she said. "Well, perhaps . . . some. You've been outdoors a lot, haven't you?" She seemed to be listening to her own voice. "You're sunburned, too," she said in that same distant, dreamy way.

He wished he had never brought up the subject. How long could they stand there talking about how sunburned they were?

"I missed you," he croaked. "Did you miss me, at all?"

"Yes."

No more than that. It could have been an offhand politness.

"Well," he said, "you don't act much like it."

Then she looked up at him, and the dreamy vagueness

disappeared. She looked at him—really looked at him—and the light from her eyes was darkly dazzling.

"Oh yes, I did," she said, running her words together, quick, frightened. And she fled.

For the first few moments as he sat in the water of the washpot he was not listening to any of the orders Matt was relaying to him over the top of the privet bush because he was thinking only of what had occurred and what he had said and what Anna had said, trying to find some encouraging particle of hope in any part of it. It was not bad at all. Yes, she had said. It made him crazily cheerful all of a sudden, and he washed down and hooed and hollered enough to make his Aunt Matt pretty disgusted with him and try to make him hush and finally go off because, as she said, she couldn't stand all that tomfool whooping.

When he had got through his sanitary chores to everybody's satisfaction and had his britches back, freshly washed and still wet but drying on him nicely in the heat, he tried to follow her around in the kitchen but Matt would not have it.

"Go along, talk to your uncle."

Hell, he didn't have anything to say to his uncle! Talking to his uncle was about as easy as tying a cat's tail through a knothole and always had been.

"You don't need Anna back here. There's nothing here for her to do. Why don't you let her come and walk around the yard or something? She can show me what the Yankees tore up."

"You can see what the Yankees tore up right out the window," Matt said.

Anna wouldn't look at him now. While he had been busy with his bath in the yard she had changed her dress and put the garden hat aside. She was wearing a yellow-flowered dress, not particularly new-looking, but awfully pretty, he thought, low-cut, so much so that it even showed a strip of white skin there, and it had ruffles at the elbows. The yellow flowers stretched tightly across her back as she bent to get a dish out of the safe, and he saw that she was sweating, for the cloth stuck to her a little between the shoulders and when she stood up it made a ridge there. He wanted to touch it, or touch her hair that had been pulled back and up off her neck with a ribbon.

"You don't have to fix up a big dinner," he said. "I'm not hungry." He tried to be convincing. "I had rations while I was, uh, at East Point. Bread, corn bread, that is, and bacon. I've still got some made up. I can eat later on."

"No you won't, neither," Matt said. "You go out and set with your uncle and leave that girl alone. You're goin' to worry her to death."

His aunt was padding around the kitchen as important as a pig in a cornbin, making it plain to him that Anna was going to do as she was told and no sass about it. Trying to squeeze him out. It made him pretty sore, but he knew from past experience that there was no fighting Matt. Not head on, anyway.

He went into the dining room and wandered around, surveying the damage. The house had been pretty well ripped up in spite of the way Anna and Matt had tried to straighten up and carry things back where they belonged. They couldn't hide what had been done.

Goddamned calvary! They had a talent for raising hell. Both sides. He wouldn't credit the Yanks anymore than their own; he had seen both sides at work, and it amounted to the same thing. Give a man, a boy, a strawfoot, a horse and it would make a hell roarer out of him every time.

He started opening drawers in the old oak sideboard, and there was nothing in them—ransacked, everything gone. One drawer was broken. When he pulled it out, it just went to pieces, the side falling off and dropping to the floor. There was red yard dirt all over it, and he knew it had been carried outside and left somewhere, like *The History of Dunbar County*. It just didn't make sense!

Matt heard the noise and came through the kitchen doorway across the long passage to the dining room.

"What are you doin' in there? You stay out of that! You're just makin' things worse!"

"I don't see what there is to make worse," he told her. "What'd they do, carry off every last scrap of stuff whether it was worth anything or not? What happened out here, anyway?"

Suddenly, he was scared. Things looked right enough on the surface, broken up but still not bad enough for any great worry, except that now he was discovering somebody, his aunt, maybe, had hidden things, trying to smooth them over. There was no telling what sort of havoc had gone on here that no one was going to talk about! He began to pull out all the drawers and drop them on the floor, making enough racket to bring his Uncle Trennon in from the porch.

"What the devil was in this chest, anyway?" he demanded. "Tablecloths, napkins, stuff like that? You mean that's all? You mean they tore up stuff like that? What else did those sonsofabitches do?"

His uncle stood in the hall and coughed.

"You see this?" he said, speaking to him, and leaving Matt and Anna out of it. He gave the pile of drawers a shove with his foot. "Have you taken a good look out here . . . upstairs and seen what else there is nobody wants you to know?"

"I have," his uncle said. "There was no one upstairs but the ladies. They didn't go up there."

Johnny snatched up a plate from the table.

"Half this stuff's not ours, it belong to the Grimeses. I know Aunt Mill's stuff when I see it!"

"That's right," Matt said. "We had to have somethin' to eat on. As soon as Anna and me could get to town, we bor-

183

rowed them. Borrowed's as good as bought when you're wantin'."

"Oh for God's sake!" Matt's saws had a way of annoying the hell out of him. "Well, what happened to our stuff?"

"Broke," his aunt said. "It got broke. After we eat I'll tell you all about it. When you quit yellin'."

His uncle looked at Johnny and shrugged slightly.

Damn him, he thought, his Uncle Trennon would not back him up an inch where Matt was concerned.

"Now you can pick up them drawers and put them back just like they was," Matt ordered. "That there was a lot of foolishness and you know it. Don't you try it again."

When it was ready, they sat down to eat midday dinner as though there was nothing more important than this and the fact that Christian, civilized conduct over a tabletop was the number-one duty of life. Which, of course, was the rule of all Matt's mealtimes. And especially since he had said sonsofbitches right out loud after being warned about no cussing. There was nothing like being home, war or no war, he told himself irritably.

His uncle laid the Bible out beside his plate. All as usual. When he was at home his uncle's place was at the end of the table with his back to the dining room window, and now the afternoon sunshine glared through the part of the yard that was not shaded by high bushes, and outlined him in a bright yellow light. A fly buzzed across the table, and Matt swatted at it quickly, from long years of habit.

"Oh Lord, make us truly thankful . . . ."

His uncle's eyes were closed. After the blessing he usually read a verse. Every meal except breakfast, when he was home.

Johnny studied the table. There was corn bread and corn on the cob, but no butter because the cow was gone since the raid. There was bacon in gray squares with one streak of dark red running through the fat, as bad as army issue. His

184

uncle, he thought, must have brought it out from town. There was a pot of turnip greens, probably salvaged from the garden. The blue stone pitcher of buttermilk (he had seen a crock of milk donated by his Aunt Mildred Grimes in the kitchen) cast a glowing reflection on the tabletop, like a bright shadow.

He was so tired he caught himself growing sleepy and vague, a victim of that long, peaceful pause.

Now the verse. His uncle was turning the leaves of the Bible and adjusting his glasses on his nose.

" 'Our days are as grass, as a flower of the field so does man flourisheth; for the winds passeth over it and is gone, and the place shall know it no more.' "

He looked at Anna, and she was sitting with her eyes open, looking down at the plate.

"With this in mind, and knowing our ultimate rest is in Thee, oh Lord, we ask it in Jesus' name."

"Amen," they all muttered.

Well, that was over.

"Everything looks mighty good," he said dutifully.

He would never understand why people picked mealtime as the proper time for conversation. That was the way he had found it everywhere, not only at home but everyplace else, so he should have been warned that they would begin to discuss the raid while he was trying to fill up on home-cooked food for the first time in months. Naturally, his stomach tied up in knots right off the bat.

His Aunt Matt, from the way she told it (and she told most of it) had heard everything first because she was such a light sleeper anything would wake her, etc., etc. He had heard all that before.

As it was, she said, the noise was enough to wake the dead, anyway.

Anna had come through the connecting doors upstairs,

185

. . . they had been sleeping up there, hot as it was, just for caution's sake . . . to see what it was all about.

The racket, as it turned out, was a train whistle. It went on and on like a scared shriek from someplace in Jonesboro, and after a few minutes the dogs came out from under the house howling for it to stop, and then ran down to the road. About that time the horses were coming.

There was only one thing to do, his Aunt Matt said, when things started out that way in the middle of the night: Get your clothes on. No matter what happened, you didn't want to get caught in your shift.

But they had trouble finding the flint to get a light and once they had the candle lit they didn't know but what they'd better put it out. In case somebody wanted to shoot at it.

His uncle hadn't been there. He'd been in Atlanta getting ready for the Macon run.

Matt went on and on about the next thing they heard was some sort of strange exploding thing, right up in the yard, and from what she said about it, he guessed it must have been a cavalry mortar.

"A what?" Matt said, pausing.

"A field piece of some sort," he said. "I don't know. I wasn't here. But they must have run it up in the yard from what you say, to have been so close."

It was close, alright, Matt said. All those noises sounded like they were going to come right through the window. We never could tell whether anybody actually shot at us or not. I mean aimed one of those things at the house.

Only once, in the beginning, Matt had stuck her head out of the window to yell at the dogs, but they were gone. Which was too bad. Both of them had been found later, down on the road. Shot dead.

The moon had been up that night, a nice white moon, and the view from the upstairs window was almost as clear as

186

daylight, everything black and white like a marble garden all the way down to the river.

Then there was a bursting flower of sound and an orange light, and the curtains at the window blew inside and also a whole shower of leaves.

It's a wonder the windows didn't break, Matt said.

There was no time to do a whole lot of hollering. They had to get on their clothes and move things against the doors upstairs and get shut up tight.

They threw the bolts on the doors and moved all the furniture to block them, even the heavy wardrobe in Matt's room which afterward they knew was too much to budge. Only they did it, anyway.

Like a pair of lunatics, Matt said, both of them barefooted, dragging furniture around. When they stopped long enough they could hear all the hoorah outside, shouts, horses, and gunfire.

Finally, when they had done all they could do, Anna slid down, panting, her back to the wall, and Matt flopped on the bed, to wait. It was hot as fire up there in those bedrooms and an awful lot of dust was coming in through the windows to make it worse. But by then they were afraid to get up and go anywhere near them.

After a while, an hour, half-hour, or a few minutes—they couldn't exactly remember—they heard feet on the front porch and then around at the back at the kitchen door and they could hear the voices calling to each other and the doorknobs being worked and then the smash of glass. Around at the front, anyway. Then there were footsteps in the house right under them, following the long hall from front to back, and the doors opening and more footsteps going through.

Right under where they were someone pulled up the dining room window and hollered for someone in the yard, and the voice was so sharp and strange they never did make out what the hollering was about: "Sam something" and "bring in something" were all they could make out. There was still the bright, intermittent flash of the orange thing lighting up the trees outside the window, but it was moving off. They were going toward town.

But underneath in the kitchen there were enough noises to make the house shake, with crockery breaking and boots bumping on the floor and the cow mooing out at the barn and the chickens and those strange, hard-edged voices:

"It's too goddamned dark in here. Don't those damned Rebs have a light around someplace?"

"Sergeant, there's somebody upstairs."

Then, Matt said, their ears strained out sideway, listening.

"The door's locked. Want me to rout them out?"

"Women."

Bang! went the downstairs door leading to the stair well.

"It's locked, alright."

"Leave that alone. I want that door left alone."

So there was no more of that, to their great relief.

It was probably just as well they couldn't see, Matt said, for right about that time the furniture was being tossed about willy-nilly and some of it thrown out into the yard and the chests and drawers were being turned inside out, and there was a mob in the kitchen looking for food. Not to eat it, they found out later, but just to spoil it. A lot of food was just thrown out, or dirt put into it.

And after a while, an hour, a half-hour, or perhaps a few minutes, it was hard to tell, they went away.

When light came Matt and Anna could see the fires burning in Jonesboro across the river. At first they thought it was stores and homes burning, but it was actually the bonfires which the Federal cavalry made of torn-up railroad ties. The rails had been prized up out of their beds and heated in the bonfires, and the Yankees had brought great hooks to bend them around the telegraph poles when they were hot and soft. The train which had been caught in town was broken up—the cars unhitched and set afire and the engine

188

wrecked with sledge hammers. The same thing had been done over at Fairburn on the other railroad.

When Matt and Anna got to town the next day there was only a smoking pile of timber where the depot had been, and the elms standing nearby were frizzled with the flames. The imprints of a thousand horses' hooves were in the dust, and fly-cloaked piles of horse manure, fodder scattered, and some Yankee's coffee can perched, forgotten, on the gatepost of Dr. Burnside's house.

Lord what a mess! Matt said: you should have seen it! Jonesboro looked like it had been hit by a cyclone.

Well, he told himself silently, he had seen plenty of towns like it after a cavalry raid. He could imagine.

"It's not safe out here anymore," he said.

He could see his aunt stiffen at once.

"I mean it," he insisted. "Sherman aims to cut these rail lines one way or another, that's plain. He wants to bottle Hood up in Atlanta. The war is coming on down this way, even if Hood and some of the others don't have sense enough to see it. I've been on scout detail these last few days and I know what I'm talking about." He looked to his uncle for some help. "Uncle Trennon knows what I'm saying is right."

But his uncle said nothing.

"I'd let General Hood do the worrying, if I was you," Matt said. "He ought to know what he's about."

That just plain baffled him. He sat there for a moment, suffering with something near to fury because he knew they didn't understand and never would—not being in the army or even near it—and that just because Hood was a general his aunt and probably his uncle thought he was nearer to God. Which couldn't be any further from the truth if a person tried.

"Hood's a little rash at times," his uncle said. "The railroads have their problems with him. But when you talk of not staying in a place, there's the problem of refugeeing and all the misery that brings. People leave their homes and rush

189

off and then sometimes find themselves in a worse fix than ever. Sometimes right in the path of war, whereas if they'd stayed at home they might have avoided it."

"Uncle, for God's sake, would you say you'd let them stay out here like they were the other night, all by themselves?"

"The only place I got to refugee," Matt put in, "is down to Fayetteville to all them Trammell cousins, and I don't know that I've come to that yet. I'd rather live with the Yankees."

Oh, for God's sake!

"Fayetteville's not far enough even to think about," he told his aunt. "If Sherman was to make a big enough swing southward, Griffin, maybe Macon wouldn't be far enough. But if you stay here you might end up behind Yankee lines. What that damned cavalry did out here last week won't amount to a hill of beans compared to a real army occupation. You don't know the trash that moves in with an army —any army, and God knows the Yankee army is bad enough! Christ! Sherman's even got nigger troops in uniform!"

The words came crashing down into the midst of them, and everybody sat perfectly still, not moving.

He realized he had done the worst possible thing. You couldn't mention things like that.

"Alright then," he said. "I'll put Anna on the train to Augusta then. I'll take her over to Madison or wherever the line picks up, and put her on the train myself."

Anna did not look at him, and his aunt was sitting there with her face like a thundercloud.

"I don't know how even that could be managed," his uncle put in. "I don't know whether the trains are coming out of Madison since the raid or not. There certainly isn't a stage to connect with the rail line anymore."

"Young girls don't travel on stages by themselves," Matt said, with a snap.

"I said I'd go with her, didn't I?"

"I don't think I'd plan to be away from my, ah, post too long," his uncle reminded him.

190

"And I don't think I'd better try to leave right now," Anna said.

"There's not even a guarantee that she'd reach Augusta on the Georgia road," his uncle went on. "That particular road and the connection with Columbia. . . ."

"Oh for God's sake, just wait a minute. . . ."

"It ain't necessary to holler like that at the dinner table!" Matt cried.

Dammit, he thought, a regular family row, and getting no place!

"Now, when you have to contemplate leaving your property," his uncle said reasonably.

Something inside of him burned down on a short fuse and let go.

"Uncle," he cried, "are you going to talk to me now about looking after the damned property? I went off to war with people talking about their property, and it sounds like I'm going to wind up the war with them talking about the same thing. Only it was niggers before, and its houses and land now. I don't believe people give a damn how many boys get killed . . . yes, I mean their sons and relatives . . . what really shakes the starch out of them is to have something happen to their property. You let me talk a minute! A person can get over losing a son or two, it looks like, but damned if he can get over being burned out and ruined and set on the road to starve. But goddammit, I'm getting sick and tired of hearing about it!"

"Now, John," his uncle said.

"And when you come right down to it, the most damned fool thing that ever sent a nation to war was that property that started this one, and don't you believe it didn't . . . property that most of us never had any truck with! Niggers! A rich man's war and a poor man's fight! That's the gospel. Black property never meant a thing to most people in this state, only about a hundred or so that call themselves planters, aristocrats, what-have-you. But we got sold on it

191

one hundred percent. I mean we did, and that means me, too, because I went off same as the rest, I didn't have any niggers, didn't intend to have any, and wouldn't fool with them if I did, and yet I wasn't by God going to let some damned pinch-nosed Yankee come down here and throw things in an uproar over niggers. And now what have we got? Lord, a person can pick up more starving, clay-mouthed niggers between here and Atlanta than any man could want, or feed. You don't have to advertise, paper them, pay commission, none of that, all you got to do is take them up and promise to look after them and you've got a hundred quicker'n you can say scat. How about that? You don't have to fight over them, you can hide out and gather up niggers and be rich as Croesus! Now I ask you, why can't some enterprising soul see that and while the rest of us are fighting, gather up a whole city full of niggers and make himself a king? Because nobody believes in black property anymore, that's why. Nobody says anything about it, but they don't. And nobody believes that one southerner can whip ten Yankees anymore. I can't see why not," he said with fine sarcasm, "but they don't!"

It had all come bursting out of him, and now they sat silent, looking at him as if he had gone crazy. His aunt wasn't even angry anymore. She just looked a little surprised and determined, as if she had found him running a fever or broken out in spots or something that would account for all this.

He hadn't intended to make a speech. And it wasn't even what he had planned to say to them. He had gotten royally sidetracked.

"Well, we'll talk about it some other time," Matt said, standing up. "We'd better clean off the table."

He sat right where he was. He had only said the truth, he told himself, even if it was a little off to one side of what they had been discussing. But he guessed he had gone at it too hard for his first day at home.

192

"I think we're through in here," his uncle said to him, and cleared his throat.

But he didn't want to go sit out on the damned front porch. Instead, he let his uncle go on ahead and he hung around in the hallway waiting for Matt and Anna to get through with whatever it was they were doing back there in the kitchen.

Everywhere he turned he found marks of destruction; he had just noticed that all the pictures that used to hang in the long, dark hallway were missing. Not that he missed any of that clutter, but it didn't make him any happier to keep finding marks of where the Yanks had been. Right in his own house.

Matt came to the door of the dining room.

"You lookin' for something?"

"No."

"Well, don't stand there, go out on the front porch."

Hell, he wasn't going to spend the afternoon sitting out there rocking, waiting for somebody to go by on the road, and hashing over every detail of what had happened to him since January.

"I'm waiting for Anna. What'n the devil are y'all doing back there?"

His aunt didn't like that. Wanting to see your own wife in the middle of the afternoon suggested all sorts of things that people weren't even supposed to think about. He knew how that went.

"Go set on the front porch," Matt said.

"I'm not going to," he told her.

Anna came up behind his aunt, a pitcher in her hand. He thought she looked out at them nervously.

"Go on," Matt said, "and quit prowling around like a restless cat."

But he went between the two women and through the dining room and out into the kitchen passage and got his shirt off the back porch railing where it had been put out to dry in the sun. When he came back through Matt was standing in the kitchen, hands on hips, watching him. He passed her by without a word and went to where Anna was standing by the sideboard in the dining room.

He took her by the arm and pulled her along with him, and she stared at him but didn't say anything. He pulled her into the hall, and then into the stair well that led upstairs and then all the way upstairs until they got to the upper landing, where he opened one of the doors and pushed her inside.

It was the right bedroom, he knew at once, for he saw the old garden hat lying on the dresser. This was where she stayed. It was hot up there, just like an oven under the roof. Perspiration broke out all over him at once.

He still had his shirt in his hand and he needed a place to put it down. He put it on the dresser, beside the hat.

CHAPTER 14

A hundred months have passed, Lorena,
Since I felt that hand in mine,
And felt thy pulse beat fast, Lorena,
Though mine beat far faster than thine.

"I want to tell you something right off," he said, and his voice was too loud; he had to lower it some. "Because I can't stand up around here and pretend I've got all the fool time in the world when I haven't. You see, I came off without a pass, and I've got to get back in time to make morning muster."

It took a minute for that to sink in. She had gone to the far side of the room by the window and with the sunlight glaring there, he couldn't make out her face.

"You mean," he heard her say, "you left without telling anybody about it?"

"Yes."

"But wasn't that wrong?"

"You mean, will they catch up with me? Hell, I don't know. Not down here, probably. I don't know about going back. It all depends. But you didn't think I could stay up there without knowing what had happened to you, did you? I was half out of my head worrying about it."

Now that he was there with her in this familiar room, it was all as unreal as the rest of the day had been. She was standing over by the window, and it was quiet enough to hear the birds singing outside in the limbs of the oak tree which spread over that part of the roof. The room was filled with a warm, golden light that reflected somehow from the dresser mirror, throwing a white spot on the wall, pure light,

195

and another on the ceiling. There was not a breath of air now that the door to the stair well was closed. All was still and burningly hot. God, it was hot! He was suddenly so confounded hot and worn out he could hardly stand up, and he tried to shake it off.

"How could you get away like that?" she murmured. "Weren't they watching you?"

"They always watch you. But I just told the corporal that I was going to take some time to look for the Jonesboro company and Ed, down the line. I had just come in from scout duty, anyway, and was due for some sleep. Nobody cared. I just went up to the yards and when anybody stopped me I told them I was looking for the 79th Georgia, and why, and most of the time they would get so busy pointing it out that I didn't have to make excuses. I caught the first train that stopped at the water tower, and as luck would have it, uncle was on it. That's the first time in this whole war I've seen a train show up right when I needed it, and with uncle where he could do me some good for a change. He got me in the wood car so I could dodge the guards."

He expected her to comment on this, but she didn't, and he couldn't tell whether she was interested in how he managed to get out of East Point or not. Well, she had brought it up.

As for himself, he was nearly stifled by the heat and the sun pouring in at the window and the low, shut-in quiet of the room under the eaves..

"Well," he said, "I'm going back. That's what's important. Nobody makes a fuss if you get caught going back. There's too damned many slipping off to stay, these days."

There was another silence.

Whatever had passed between them in the yard, those first few happy moments were gone now. He might have known this was how it would be as soon as he was alone with her.

Irritably, he pushed his hair back with his hands. He

196

had forgotten, sure enough, how suffocating it could be upstairs in the summer. You couldn't take a nap up there for love or money, he remembered; you had to use the cooler downstairs bedroom.

But this was the only place in the house with a little privacy right now.

"I haven't had a chance to get two words with you," he muttered. "I don't even feel like I know you, or have got a right to be with you, the way everybody acts. You might as well be somebody that visits here or something."

There was still no answer.

"Anna?"

"Yes." It was so low he could hardly hear it.

"Well," he said. The excitement which had brought him all the way home was draining out of him now, thanks to the confounded stillness and heat. He had expected too much, that was the trouble. He had been willing to settle for pretty nearly anything coming down on the train, even just to find her alive. He would have settled for fifty years of married misery if need be, just to find her alive and unhurt. It should have been enough, to find that she was.

"I want to tell you something," he said. "Are you listening?"

If things had gone at all differently he would not have to speak now. He was the world's biggest fool to hope that things would be any different. Together with her in this room it was pretty clear. She had got into that spot over there by the window, as far away from him as she could.

"When I heard what happened down here," he said, "I knew it was all my damned fault. You wouldn't have gotten caught in that raid if it hadn't been for me writing you and telling you to stay and not go back to your pa in Augusta."

She didn't give him any encouragement. She just stood there in the yellow-flowered dress, looking at him.

"I knew there wasn't any reason for you to stay, I didn't much think you *would* stay to tell the truth—I just kept

197

hoping you would. But God, that was all I could think about
. . . that you were somewhere close by and that I might get
a leave somehow to come home and fix things up. When I
knew all the time all you wanted was to go home and get
out of it. You didn't have to say as much, I mean write it
down, but I could tell it in every damned letter I got. I
could tell."

"I'm not very good at letters," she said, opening her eyes
wide. "I. . . ."

"Oh, I don't mean there was anything wrong with the
letters," he said quickly. "They were first-rate. When I
didn't get any I . . . hell, it made me feel low. There was
nothing wrong with the letters. Except that you could tell
what was the matter, that was all."

He sat down on the bed and wished he knew what in the
hell he wanted to say, and how he could get it out. He was
almost too tired to think.

"I've been going over it," he said. "I mean, not going over
it, but damned well thinking about it day and night. You
don't know how a thing can stick in a person's mind and
just wear itself out running over and over. You keep trying
to find an answer somewhere, and there's answers, alright,
but not the ones you want. What I mean to say, dammit, is
that you can go home. I want you to go home. I'll write
your pa a letter and try to explain how things are."

He saw her move away from the window. She went to the
dresser and moved his shirt aside and picked up the garden
hat and put it over to the left a bit, and he saw that she was
watching him in the mirror, looking timid and, he thought,
frightened.

"No, don't do that," she whispered.

"Hell, God knows I'm not out to ruin any girl's life," he
told her. "It doesn't make me any happier to know that everytime I'm near you, you jump like a scared rabbit."

She kept staring at him in the mirror.

"I don't have any pay except army pay, and you know

198

even that's come and go . . . sometimes we get it, sometimes we don't. But I guess it will have to do. Your pa can make his peace with it anyway. I'll bet I know what he's going to say about it . . . damned near the same thing he said about it last Christmas, and I haven't forgotten it, either. But it's the best I can do. And the property, count that in—though not right away. Half the farm is mine."

"I can't go home," she cried. "What will I do at home?"

That took him off balance. It was the last thing he had expected her to say.

"Well, you mean, what happened to us? Well . . . tell every-body you're home on a visit. That goes on all the time, that sort of thing. Some women live more at home than they do with their husbands. You can tell . . . I mean, nobody knows the difference." Hell, what was he going to say to her—that nobody would suspect? At first they wouldn't. That was all he could offer.

"I can't," she whispered.

"God, I can't help that!" he cried. "You should have known this all along. When things don't work out, its one damned infernal mess. You can do what you want to do, any time you feel like doing it. I only ASKED you to stay, I didn't order you!"

"Do what?" she asked, baffled.

"Besides, its too damned dangerous here. You heard what I said downstairs. That ought to be a pretty good excuse to go home. The way things are going, with the war and all, nobody'll notice for two or three years, maybe. Then I might be dead. That's the only confounded way I can see out of this mess. If you want to hope for anything," he said bitterly, "hope that it won't be long before you're a pretty young widow. Just don't get married again."

"Don't," she said, and winced.

"Oh dammit, I'm not blaming you! It's my own damned fault. I ruined things. You don't have to tell me that."

"I'm not going home," she said.

199

"Oh, for Christ's sake, don't keep saying that!" he burst out. He had to make an effort to lower his voice again, as he was making too much racket. "Don't you know how I feel?"

His shouting at her had one effect, at least. Her mouth trembled, and she put her hands up to her face and began to weep.

"Oh, godalmighty," he said. "Don't do that, Anna. Please don't do that."

But she didn't pay any attention. She picked up the hem of the yellow-flowered dress and put it to her mouth and cried right out loud into it.

"What the devil have I done now? What's the matter for God's sake?"

"I'm not going home," she said, her voice smothered. "I won't."

Well, he was in the same boat. He had nothing to look forward to, either.

He could not stand to see her crying into the hem of her dress—it downright unnerved him, and all he could think of to do was go to the dresser and scratch around, eventually opening a drawer to find something, only to discover it was full of her things. Full of stockings, it looked like. He unrolled a pair before he knew what they were. He found a stack of letters, and marveled at his own handwriting on them. It was strange, to open a drawer full of her belongings and find his letters in a neat bundle, with a ribbon around them. He pulled up something white, too long to be a handkerchief.

"Never mind," she said quickly. She was only sniffling a bit now. She came at once and reached across him and opened a little fabric box with one hand and there were the handkerchiefs. She pulled one out.

He noticed that she had reached right across him purposefully, and her hand had touched the bare skin of his ribs.

She took a long time, wiping her eyes with the handkerchief and leaning over to look into the mirror to see if they

200

were turning red, he guessed. She dabbed at the tip of her nose with the cloth, too.

"Anna," he said huskily, "you could still write and I could still write. No need to shut things all the way down. I could still look for your letters. Lord, if I didn't have any letters to look forward to, I think I'd want to die, sure enough. It's too damned miserable in the army without any letters or anything."

He paused, but she was looking at herself in the mirror, in the same way.

"I'm not going home," she repeated, her lips quivering. "Oh, HELL," he groaned.

They were smack-up against a stone wall again, right, he reminded himself, where they usually were, only this time the confounded stone wall was really not a stone wall at all, but a mirror, with both of them standing side by side and looking into it. But it was a stone wall. He was so tired his thoughts kept circling around like curs with their tails in their mouths, round and round.

She leaned forward a little more and pushed the damp strands of her hair back from her forehead with the balled-up scrap of handkerchief.

That, he thought crazily, was a stupid looking sonofabitch standing there beside her in the mirror, alright; he didn't look like he had good sense . . . if he had ever had any to begin with. Lord, on close inspection, he was worse-looking than he had imagined. He hadn't taken a good look at himself in a mirror, . . . really looked, in such a long time, he half-scared himself. He didn't know that he had got so burned black in the sun. He looked almost like a mulatto, and he hardly ever sunburned that dark. His face was so dark the rest of him seemed extraordinarily light by contrast: his eyes were as bright blue and transparent as a match flame, . . . they reminded him of Ed Grimes' eyes in a way. And his hair was sun-bleached to the point of whiteness. He was thinner than ever. The veins on the muscles of his forearms stood out like

201

blue webs. Everytime he breathed the skin stretched tight across his rib cage and outlined his ribs. The skin there was a slightly lighter color than the rest of him from wearing a shirt, although he had a dark, tanned strip down his belly where the shirt usually hung open.

Talk about somebody being wild—a curly wolf . . . that didn't half cover what he looked like now! He looked, he told himself, more like a starved-out wildcat, one of those moth-eaten spotted kinds that took to chicken stealing sooner or later, all gone to eyes and hair and bone and frenzy.

Poor Anna. No wonder she stayed backed-off all the time!

But she hadn't changed, he thought, looking at her. In small ways, perhaps, and she was hot now, and upset, but she was still sweet and lovely and adorable. She couldn't help it.

On an impulse he reached up and touched her hair and first saw his hand suspended in the mirror, behind her head, and then his fingers as they touched and then the dark curls as they bent down with the weight of his hand.

She watched this, and for some reason she allowed it, and didn't move away.

It was as though they were looking at two other people.

He felt as though he couldn't go on with it any longer. The strain was wearing him out. The heat was bearing him down, pulling him down like a weight, and he had been without sleep for so long he knew he was going to keel over in the not-too-distant future.

He swayed.

"Listen, Anna," he heard himself say, "let's go lie down and talk this over. . . ."

He remembered bending over and picking her up, catching her right behind the knees with his hand, and the other supporting her shoulders, awkward enough, but it seemed the quickest and best way of getting her to do what he wanted her to do. Move her bodily. Just pick her up and go. The bed was right behind them, and he dropped her on it, and she curled up into a knot, braced, right away, looking up at him.

But he just piled right in after her and stretched out from toe to head and put his arms around her and pulled her head down against his shoulder and felt her hair brush his lips. It was hot, hot as hell, and her dress was damp against his skin.

"Let's just go to sleep," he mumbled. "I can't even stand up anymore."

And then he closed his eyes and let sleep drag him under.

He had no idea how long he slept; not long, anyway, it was too hot to sleep for very long. You woke up with rivers of perspiration running down your skin. Which was exactly what was happening to him. Great trickles of water ran down his neck into his collarbones and also down his sides where his arms touched his ribs, and more streams behind his knees.

But he felt better. A little sleep had taken all the ragged edginess out of him, that terrible feeling of walking over the other side into chaos if you weren't careful.

"Anna?" he said. He turned quickly, and she was sitting beside him, her knees drawn up on the bed, watching him. He was a little surprised to see her there. She had been fanning herself with the handkerchief, which didn't work too well, but the minute she saw him looking at her, she stopped. She stuck it into the front of the yellow-flowered dress, which, he noticed, she had unbuttoned two buttons.

"That's a good place to put a handkerchief," he said.

Her hand went to the top of the dress at once, to pull it together. She looked as hot as fire. Her face was pink and shiny and the heavy weight of her hair was drawn up in tight wet curls on her forehead.

"What'd you sit up here for," he said. "You didn't have to sit up here just to watch me sleep."

"But you wanted me to come up here with you," she said, puzzled.

203

"Well, not to boil to death, for God's sake. Aren't you hot? You look like you're going to blow up."

She nodded yes.

"I said everything I was going to say. It's all over."

"I thought you'd wake up, and wonder where I'd gone," she said, still sounding puzzled.

He couldn't make any sense out of that. He really couldn't figure why she hadn't gone downstairs.

"I went out like a light," he said. "I didn't," he explained carefully, "have anything to drink. That wasn't the reason. You knew that, didn't you?"

She nodded yes, again.

"I could tell you were awfully tired," she said. "I tried to move you, but you wouldn't budge."

"Why did you want to do that?"

"You were lying on my dress."

He looked, and saw she had the skirt of her dress tucked under her legs.

"I finally pulled it out from under you," she said. "I tried not to wake you up."

"I'm sorry," he said.

"Oh," she told him, "I didn't mind, really. I was just watching you sleep."

"That must have been pretty interesting," he said, meaning the opposite.

She gave him an odd, baffled look.

"It was. I've never watched you sleep before."

"The hell you haven't."

She turned a little pinker.

"Not . . . just like this. You were just lying there, as if nothing would . . . wake you up. You," she added, hesitating, "said something."

"Said what? In my sleep?"

"I don't know. I couldn't hear it. But you'd sleep for a while, and then you'd say something and almost wake up."

She hesitated again. "You grabbed my arm once, and I thought you really were awake, but you weren't."

"I was just tired," he muttered. "I missed a night's sleep somewhere. No, more'n that, I guess. I can't remember. I'll have to figure it out. This damned army duty runs around the clock so you forget when you're supposed to sleep, or how much you've had, that's the truth. Then, I was in such a damned tear to get home, and worried sick about things down here, it just wore me out. While we were arguing, I kept thinking I was going to fall flat on my face."

"Where, h-have you been fighting?" she said anxiously.

"Fighting what?"

"Before you came down."

"Oh, that. No, just running around in the woods, looking for Yankees that weren't there."

"Oh," she said.

He put his hand on her dress, at the shoulder, where it was tightly stuck, and pulled it away, just a fraction of an inch.

"Don't do that," she said.

"I just wanted to see if it was stuck to you, that's all," he said. "You need to wipe off your face. I never saw you look so hot and shiny."

"Well, it *is* hot," she said simply.

"I hope you blow up and bust, with all those clothes on. Don't you ever take them off? I mean, don't you ever take them off all by yourself, because you want to?"

"Of course I do," she said.

"When?"

"Sometimes."

"Sometimes when?"

"Sometimes when I take a nap, if that's what you mean."

"What, up here? It's too hot to sleep up here."

"Well, I do," she said, pushing out her mouth a little, petulantly. "It's not always this hot. And sometimes I like to be alone."

"I don't blame you." He could understand that. He knew

205

how it was to live in the same house with Matt. "What do you wear, a nightgown?"

"Well, yes. No," she said. "What are you asking me all this for?"

"What's yes, no?" he persisted.

"Well, no."

"No what? No nightgown?"

"Not in the daytime, for goodness sake!" She looked annoyed.

"Nothing?"

"In my . . . other things. The things I have on underneath."

"You mean you lay around in your underwear?"

"I don't see what's wrong with that," she said, turning pinker and pinker. "Nobody sees me."

"Oh, I'm not saying anything against it," he said quickly. "I'm all for it. I'm glad to hear you take your clothes off some-time." He felt like teasing her about it. He reached over and pulled the handkerchief out of the front of her dress.

"Don't do that," she told him. "Please."

"I'm not going to bother you. Here, you can have the damned thing back. You didn't have to sit up here all this time, you know. What do you want me to do, anyway?"

But he kept on teasing her. He raised up and blew into her cheek and into her neck, and she turned her face away.

"Don't she murmured.

"It's cool, isn't it?"

She shook her head.

"You can get up. I'm not holding you down."

But he pushed her hair away from her throat and held it up. She was soaking wet. Her hair was wet. He could see the pulse beating in her throat. And lower down, a drop of per-spiration was about to run into the cleft of her breasts.

"Where's the damned handkerchief?" he said. "You're sweating down there."

"I'll do it," she said, trying to pull back.

"Hell no," he said. "I'll do it."

206

"Don't."

She waited, her head turned, and then, slowly, she looked at him out of the corner of her eyes.

"What are you doing?" she asked him.

"Nothing." He was really doing nothing. He had stopped. He wasn't touching her. He was just lying there, looking at her sitting with the top of her dress partly unbuttoned and her breath making the V of the white exposed shift rise and fall slowly. "I was just looking at you."

"What was I doing?" she said.

"Nothing. Just nothing. You were just sitting there waiting for me to do something."

"No I wasn't," she denied.

"The hell you weren't. You were waiting for me to do something. Then you were going to try to make me stop it."

She shook her head, no, puzzled again.

But he knew better. He picked up a strand of her hair and wound it around his finger. He moved closer to her, sitting up, propped up on his elbow.

"I'm not going to get any closer," he told her.

"It's alright," she said.

"Dammit, don't say that," he muttered. He lifted the dark strand and put it to his mouth, and then rubbed it along his cheek, watching her.

"I'm sorry," she said, not knowing what to say.

"Sorry? What in the devil does that mean?"

"I don't know. I don't know."

He let the strand of her hair fall, and it lay lightly against her shoulder. He put the tip of his finger against her mouth, outlining her lips, and then slowly, again, across the top of her lip.

"You sure have got a pretty mouth," he said. "Did you know you've got a pretty mouth?"

He put his mouth where his finger had rested against hers and her lips were soft and baffled, her eyes wide open, watching him all the time.

207

He stopped.

"Will you quit looking at me?" he told her. He put his arms around her and held her gently. She had her hands on his shoulders, not pushing him, but cautious. "Now shut your eyes for a minute," he murmured. He kissed her again, and her eyes stayed shut and after a while her body seemed to move right into his arms without moving, just flowing against him and her head drooped back, her hair falling over his arms, and she let him kiss her on her throat and at the corner of her mouth and on her lips again, getting warmer and drowsier, her eyes not moving, not opening or even stirring, once. She put her hand against the back of his neck.

"Anna," he whispered, "I don't want to make you do anything you don't want to do."

"I know," she said, her eyes still closed. And she let him kiss her again.

A long time later he still could not shake off the strangeness of it, and he looked again to see her lying perfectly still beside him, the sheet drawn over them, covering them, but underneath he could feel the pressure of her knee, half-bent, against him and the weight of her head against his upper arm.

"You alright?"

"Yes," she said.

"I thought you were asleep."

"No," she whispered.

Lord, he thought, taking a long, slow breath, this was something now, wasn't it? Did she know? Did she realize? He expected she didn't.

He had tried to behave himself. But that wasn't the half of it.

Now she was opening her eyes, looking straight ahead, straight into the room without seeing it.

"What did I do?" she said.

He knew he wasn't going to be able to explain things right

208

then. He was just beginning to get some sense himself. He wanted to explain to himself first off, and try to figure it out. He knew damned well he couldn't give himself much credit. He had never been that well organized.

"Uh, don't worry about it," he told her. "Everything's fine. Don't you feel fine?"

He knew she ought to feel fine. It was just so damned amazing, that's all.

"What did I do?" she said, just a little bit louder. "Did I do anything wrong?"

There it was. How could you come right out and put it into bald, bare words? He didn't know any words that would fit. None that he could tell her, anyway.

"I don't exactly remember," he said. "I wasn't too damned clear and cool myself."

But he remembered, alright.

"Nothing bad?" She sounded a little anxious.

"Hell, no, nothing bad!"

She wasn't so sure.

What could you do, he told her silently, what could you do right here in my arms that would be bad? Tell me, what could you do that would be bad?

"I don't know," she said, looking straight ahead. "I feel . . . I guess. . . . The way, the way people do, I wouldn't want to do anything. I mean I wouldn't want to do anything I wasn't supposed to do. Ever. Ugh, it all makes you feel so horrible, anyway," she ended, with a little shiver.

"Horrible? Horrible, for God's sake?" he said.

"Well, I mean nice-horrible. You know what I mean. Like you don't know what you're doing. Like you ought not to think about what you're doing."

"That's right," he said agreeably.

"But," she said slowly, "something happened. I know something happened. Could you," she turned now, and looked at him, "did you know something happened?"

209

He couldn't lie to her with her looking him straight in the face.

"Yes," he said.

"Well, for goodness sake," she cried, "what was it?"

He started to laugh. He knew she was going to think him crazy, laughing like that, but he couldn't help it. He just hee-heed and haa-haaed right out loud.

"Oh, stop it," she said, frowning.

He couldn't help it.

"You," she said, "wouldn't care what I did."

He nodded yes, still holding her, still laughing.

"No," he said finally, half-choked, "I wouldn't. I wouldn't care."

"Well, tell me. Don't just keep laughing. Is it alright? Is it supposed to be alright? What did I do?"

"It's alright," he said. "But I wouldn't go around bragging about it, if I were you, . . ." and this set him off again, it was so damned funny.

"Johnny, please don't laugh!"

He stopped right there, because he didn't want her to get upset. They had had so much trouble the last thing in the world he wanted was to go back to the way things were before. But he was so damned happy he couldn't lie still, he was damned if he could! he told himself. He rolled over against her and tried to catch her and muss her up and love her some, but the sheet was all tangled around them and he couldn't get her to hold still long enough to kiss her. Which was all he wanted to do.

Great godalmighty, see her jump! He hadn't meant to scare her. He was just fooling around. To show her, he kissed her hair and blew along her eyelids, teasing, to make them blink.

"You're not afraid of me now, are you?" he asked her huskily.

"No. But let's not talk about it," she said quickly.

"About what?"

210

"Anything."

"Want me to tell you what you did?"

"No!"

"I will, if you want me to."

"No. No."

"Want me to tell you what you said?"

She shook her head violently, fascinated.

"You said," he told her drawing his words out to tease, "you said, 'Johnny,' just like that. Right at the end."

"Don't make fun of me," she whispered.

Make fun of her?

He grabbed her to him and held her tightly, his face buried in her neck and the sweet smell of the dampness of her hair.

God, he would never make fun of her. What gave her that idea? Because she was sweet, and adorable, and he loved her fit to bust?

Her legs were caught against his and her soft belly pressed against him. He could feel himself drawing and tightening. It didn't take long. Twenty seconds.

No, ten damned seconds. Ten seconds just for that. He knew that any time at all from now on, half-dead, half-starved, any lonesome night in a bedroll blanket it would be only ten seconds for that feeling, the quick remembering of the brush of her thigh against him. He hoped he would remember the exact feeling of it.

Lord, he told himself, it would be harder to try and forget it!

How long was she going to let him love and crush her like this, and kiss and muss her hair?

She tried to move her hand, the one caught in the sheet. "Ouch," she said.

"Wait," he told her. He tried to get her hand loose but it was wrapped up in it like a bandage. Damn the confounded sheet, it was too hot for such damned nonsense.

He sat up and tried to pull the sheet from them, but she

was a lot quicker that he was. Before he could do anything she had got the whole business wound around her and was moving away.

She took not only the top sheet, pulling it loose from the bottom of the bed where it had been tucked in, but also part of the bottom sheet as well. She just kept on going until she had got to the far side of the bed with the sheets wound nicely around her and only one arm sticking out which she used right off to lift her hair and fling it up off her neck, holding it there to get a little cooler.

He got out of the bed. She flashed him a look, quick, to see what he was doing, and found him buck naked, and the look went chasing off, quick.

"I wasn't going to do anything," he said.

Oh, that. Well, hell, he meant what he said.

But she stood up then, the sheet still wound around her, and moved to the dresser. She had the bottom sheet trailing behind her, caught up somewhere.

"Here, don't tear up the bed," he said. "What is it you want? Just tell me where it is, I'll get it for you."

She kept looking up into the air, not at him. Well, she would just have to get used to it. He couldn't jump into his clothes every moment she was around.

He opened a drawer in the dresser.

"What do you want? Nightgown?"

She looked surprised.

"A nightgown? It's daylight. I need to get dressed."

"Well, yes," he said. "Alright. You going to put all that junk on? I mean, are you going to get all the way dressed?"

"Why, yes."

"Well, I didn't know, that's all."

She got something out of the dresser drawer, and he found the yellow-flowered frock by the far side of the bed, and some of the underclothes she had worn, and looked for the forbidding object that should have been around, but wasn't.

"Where's the corset thing?"

212

"I didn't have one on," she said. She picked up the hair-brush from the dresser top.

"Why not?"

"I didn't have one on," she said, almost whispering, "that's all."

"Too hot?"

"Yes," she said, embarrassed. She picked up her things and moved to the bed and sat down on the edge. She looked at him, waiting.

He remembered.

"Alright," he said, and turned away and picked up his britches from the floor and sat down on the chair with his back turned to her and put them on. When he was through he just sat there looking out the window at the hot, listless tree leaves on the oak just outside, and hearing her rustling behind him.

Lord, it was hot! It was confoundedly, ever-presently hot, and it wouldn't let you forget it, not for a minute! He wiped the sweat from his mouth with his arm, absently.

"Yes," she said, after a while.

He turned, expecting to find her dressed, and she was kneeling in the middle of the bed with her arms held up, brushing her hair in a quick, nervous way, her body stretching slim and straight and her arms flashing against the dark brown shadow of her hair, her head bent forward a little. She had on a petticoat and the top of it clung to her and pulled tight against her fine, narrow waist. When she took her arms down a shoulder strap on the shift slipped down. She put it back, quickly.

What the devil was up, anyway? he wondered.

He went over to the bed and sat down as close to her as he could get and leaned to her. She got busy at once with the hairbrush, rubbing it against her palm.

"Anna, sugar."

"Yes." Her voice was so low he could hardly hear it.

"That thingamajig you've got on, . . . that's what I saw."

213

She still would not look right at him, but he saw her frown slightly.

"I thought it was a nightgown, but it was this thing, a petticoat, isn't it?"

"Yes," she said, and lifted her hand to put the strap back on her shoulder.

He told her of the sunstroke at Kennesaw and the pitcher of lemonade and the dream that was so real he could have sworn that it happened.

"That was what you were wearing. The very same."

"You haven't seen this before," she said, looking down at the hairbrush.

"Yes I have. Or one like it. That night in Atlanta."

She became silent and faraway, and he expected he had fixed things up good, harking back to all that. But it was the truth.

"What did you think," he asked her, "that I wouldn't remember anything about you, or that petticoat?"

She shook her head, this time neither yes nor no.

"Well, I remembered every damned thing. It may not have been so . . . may not have been . . . well, I remembered every damned thing, that's all. I used to—that's what I meant when I said you could think about something all the damned time. I used to think about you and that petticoat and how I'd give ten years of my life for a chance to get home and see you again. It's different now, isn't it?"

He was pretty sure it was, but he had to make certain. He could only be sure if she said so.

He couldn't keep his eyes off the top of that thing she was wearing. He could see right through it, right through the cloth straining over her breasts and the little dots of nipples showing through. She was so funny about such things she ought to know that this particular thing was like wearing next to nothing, sitting out in front of him like that.

She knew, alright, he realized suddenly.

She knew all about that little sticking, clinging nothing of a petticoat because she wouldn't look at him.

214

She could be so confoundedly strange and cool at times, he marveled, and then again, mysterious and jittery and shaky—all mixed in together. He could not figure it out. But if she wasn't careful, she was going to jerk all those bristles out of that brush, one by one.

He took the brush out of her hand and kissed her mouth and kissed her fine, downturned nose and then her forehead and pulled down both the shoulder straps just to see her yank them up.

"Lord, Anna," he whispered to her, "I love you so much. You're so pretty, so confoundedly sweet. I won't let anything happen to you, I swear. I'll kill the first son of . . . jasper that makes you miserable. Including me. I love you so much."

She caught at his arms to keep from falling because he was moving in on her, and he heard her laugh, a low, wobbly smothered laugh as though it still bothered her to have him so close and eager.

"What are you scared of? Are you scared of me? Listen, I was just frolicking back there on the bed. I didn't mean to scare you. I just wanted to muss you up and love you some. You didn't think I was going to hurt you, did you?"

"N-no," she said, and tried to laugh again. But he could tell she wanted him to clear off.

"Well, what are you excited about?"

"I-I'm not excited!"

"The devil you're not! You're jittering all over. Why didn't you get dressed?"

"Don't!"

"I'm not doing anything."

"Yes. Yes, you are! You're pushing me."

He leaned back, and to save her balance she had to hang onto him, which was what he expected.

But he did not expect that long moment when their eyes were close, her eyes looking into his as if trying to find out something she wished to know about him.

"What is it?" he asked her.

She held onto him, giving him that strange, thoughtful

215

look while he was all too aware of the soft petticoated flesh squeezed against his ribs. He felt her arms slide around his neck.

What was this?

He was almost afraid to think for fear it would jar them. How could she keep on looking and looking like that, right into the back of his head, into everything?

"Promise," she whispered.

"Yes." Hell, he'd promise anything, whatever it was. Forever.

Her arms slid like silk, and her mouth came up suddenly and touched his lips, pushing against them warm and wet and curious, and she breathed against his mouth and lifted her body closer. By God, he was a sainted angel, he didn't do a damned thing, he didn't move and all his weight drained into his hands to keep them down. There was silk skin of her arms against his ears and soft petticoat pushed against his breastbone and her legs slid against his and her mouth was damp and unsteady.

She took her arms away and it was all over. He was as good as his promise. He didn't move, even then.

She picked up her dress at the bottom of the bed and stood up and walked around and hitched it up to her waist and put her arms in the sleeves. In a few minutes she came around to his side of the bed looking for her shoes. They were by the chair. She slipped her feet into them.

When she stopped in front of him he reached up and took the back of her dress and started hooking it up, and she turned and smiled at him and then stood, waiting, her head bent down.

"Can you do it?" she said. "It's hooks and eyes, not buttons."

"Hell," he told her. "I can do anything."

CHAPTER *15*

Wake, dearest, wake! tis thy lover who calls,
  List, dearest, list! the dew gently falls,
Arise to thy lattice, the moon is asleep,
  The bright stars above us their bright vigils keep.

He had intended to wake at about one o'clock and for the first few minutes he was sure he had slept too long. But when he twisted his head to look, what sky there was showing was deep-dark, not a glimmer of light in it. Not more than one-thirty. The stirabout of the leaves at the window and the invisible, heavyweighted feel of green and damp corn in the field and high grass and open, plowed earth and heat and cloud and stars—all the taste, smell, and sense of summer filled up the room; it could have been any time in his life that he had waked too hot to sleep and found himself up there, at home.

Except that it was not. Not this time.

The heat overran everything. The rooms upstairs never cooled off even at night with doors wide and windows open to get the air; in spite of the work that his grandfather and his father had done the place was an attic and always would be, and certainly not fit for sleeping in summer. It was probably ten degrees cooler downstairs in the back bedroom where his aunt and uncle were.

He grinned.

Well, there was comfort and there was comfort.

He got out of bed, taking care not to wake Anna, and found his trousers and got them on and hunted around for his shirt in the dark. It had been somewhere on the dresser

217

when he had last seen it. He had to be easy, he didn't want to turn anything over and make a racket.

But he couldn't find the damned shirt. He went across the top of the dresser with his hands and then even felt the floor with his feet, sliding them around cautiously to see if he had dropped it somewhere.

Damn it. He couldn't go off without his shirt.

He went back to the dresser again because that was the only place for it to be. He touched something that felt like cloth but it couldn't be his shirt as it was all folded up, but it was, folded nicely and the collar buttoned and the sleeves tucked in. Anna had done it.

He took the shirt and went to the bed and stood there looking down at her as he unbuttoned it and shook it out and put his arms into the sleeves. He could just make out the dark spot of her hair flung across the pillow and then, his eyes straining, he could see that she was turned on one side with her arm up under the pillow and her body curved, one knee bent as though it reached out for his side of the bed.

He wanted to reach out and touch her, and it was all he could do to keep from it.

This one day, he told himself, this one day was like nothing he had ever been through before. He was still damned afraid it was going to turn out to be some dream and wake up and find himself back in the ditches at East Point to discover it hadn't happened at all.

He buttoned up his shirt and wondered if he leaned down to wake her, would she reach right up to him, put her arms around his neck and stir, half-asleep, to let him kiss her?

He bet she would.

It was a dream, alright, to be so confoundedly lucky. He shook his head and started to laugh, and it made a noise. He was going to wake her yet.

At night it was better. No clothes, no buttons, strings or

218

struggles, only darkness and their two bodies sliding together and her quick, quivering words, still frightened, in his ear: don't be rough. Please.

And afterward, still wanting him to hold her, when he could hardly lift his arms.

Johnny, you won't ever tell anybody?

Not a word. I swear.

Lord, he told himself, he couldn't begin to tell anybody. It would take a whole lifetime of telling and even then nobody would believe him.

If he was going to leave, he told himself, he was going to have to do it right off, for he couldn't stand there much longer. As God made trees he was going to bend over and wake her up, and then he would not give a damn after that. He'd never go back to East Point!

The door to the other room had swung shut and he pushed it back now to let the night air come through. There was no breeze, but a rush of air at the window ballooned out the curtains, carrying the draft. Already it was not so dark and thick as it had been a few minutes before. He was going to have to hurry.

He brushed the stair well with his hand going down because it was dark as a cave in there, and once he was in the hall downstairs it was a little better: there was sort of a night-shine from the inner part of the house. He got his gun and bedroll by the coat rack where he had left them. The house downstairs was cool and lonesome, and there should have been a clock ticking in the front room, but there was not. Not since the raid. It was the only thing which reminded him of why he had come home.

The noises he made at the front door and crossing the front porch sounded loud enough to wake the dead to him, but when he paused at the steps to listen, nothing stirred.

As he reached the last line of crepe myrtle bushes he turned to look back at the house with its hooding porch and close-standing yard trees and just out of habit, his hand gave a wave, as though there was someone looking on to demand a farewell. Then he turned and went down the road.

The night was one of those perfectly still summer nights as motionless and hot and unruffled as a bottle with the stopper on tight. After he had gone no more than a mile he was covered with sweat. The clay road reflected a faint sort of glow from the sky, and he knew his way well enough not to have to worry about the direction. He had only to make sure, now and then, since he was barefooted, that what seemed to be a stick was really that and not a snake lying out in the still-warm dust.

Gradually, ever so gradually, the light began to change, even as early as it was: the trees began to show as faint solid shapes and then the birds began, cardinals and orioles and thrashers and an early mockingbird and some delicate calls that he couldn't identify and that you didn't hear during the hot part of the day. Swamp birds, woodland birds, deeply hidden. Then a rooster crowed in a small hoarse voice off somewhere as if this was a signal.

The earth turned gray, layers of pearl mist were across the ground fading to the lightest, whitest of grays where it joined the sky and the fields were floating seas of Queen Anne's lace and bitterweed and morning glory vines like a late summer tide washed up in the clearings. The great grip of the morning was a vast silence, and he could hear even his feet shushing along in the dust. Lord, it was lonely and peaceful and fine!

When they had come down to supper, he remembered suddenly, his Aunt Matt's face was drawn up like a prune, full of outrage, and Anna in a dream, and conversation about as lively as a jug full of sorghum syrup in February, but it suited him fine.

Then for God's sake, his uncle had taken him aside and

had tried to give him what he judged to be the last of his money, five dollars Confederate, for no good reason that he could guess, than that his uncle wanted to do something for him and couldn't think of anything else. And this was even funnier than anything else that had happened because his uncle, of all people, was doing everything but clapping him on the back, just as though he knew what was up. He still wasn't sure whether he did or not, the whole thing was so confoundedly silly, but that was the only reason he could think of. His uncle was usually as tight as a new pair of shoes with his money.

Lord, the whole world was going crazy! But the right kind of crazy this time for a change.

A broad beam of the sun, rising over the trees, hit his face, as he came to the top of a rise that led into Morrow. The light was hot, hot as the devil, even before it cleared the horizon. Another hot day. He was somewhere south of Morrow sure enough. A train came rumbling and clicking by, buried out of sight in the trees.

The first house he came on as he approached Morrow was the Murphy place, and there was a troop of cavalry bivouacked in Mr. Murphy's front yard. The unsaddled horses were tied to all the bushes and part of the picket fence, and he could see the troopers inside, still asleep, rolled in their blankets, except for a couple, the night guards, moving around a fire making coffee.

He could smell the coffee.

They couldn't miss him as he came along the road. One of the cavalrymen stood up and strolled over to the picket gate.

"Heyooo," the cavalryman called lazily, when he was close enough.

"Hi," he said cautiously. No telling about cavalry. With just two of them awake he might be able to slip on by.

"Wheah you comin' from, sojer?" the cavalryman said,

leaning on the gate and letting his hand dangle carelessly over the post. He was a rakish-looking devil, red-haired and lank, wearing a checkered shirt and Federal blue trousers. Only his dust-covered hat with the cavalry insignia, pushed back on his head, showed what army he belonged to. The red hair was wet, plastered down from the morning wash.

"Been home," Johnny told him. He stood out in the road, trying not to look too anxious to get on. "What are y'all doing up here?"

"Oh," the cavalryman said, "we been on patrol. Come up to the railroad to make a report."

There was nothing else to say, but he had to say something, he guessed. "Y'all part of Jackson's cavalry?"

"Hell, yes. What's left. De-tached from Wheeler's. The rest of us is up in Tennessee somewheres. What's yore name?"

"MacLeod. Sharpshooter with the 1st Tennessee."

"You ain't no Tennesseean."

"No, I'm from around here. I just got attached to the Rock City guards in the spring."

"I know them. White's the captain, ain't he?"

It was just his luck to find somebody who knew White! "Yes."

"M'name's Cobb. Where do you live, around here?"

"Jonesboro."

The other thought this over and found it funny for some reason. He grinned.

"Just walked out, huh?"

The cavalryman opened the gate and stepped out into the road to look him up and down, grinning for all he was worth.

"Mornin' muster," he said slowly. "Gawd, that's the life! I chased mornin' muster aplenty in my day. Bet you got a sweetheart down here."

Damn, was it written all over him? he thought.

"Wife," he said.

He felt as though all his private business was being pulled out of him, but the cavalryman was being friendly as all get-out, grinning fair to split his head, and he didn't have any choice but to return in kind.

"You ain't been married long," the other said.

"Not long," he said, trying to keep his voice even.

Not a word, he had promised her, and yet here was this jasper looking him all over with stark envy in his eyes as if he knew just what had happened, and as though they were both enjoying the same thing.

How could this damned fool know anything about him?

"Is she yeller-headed, little bitty?" the cavalryman said softly.

"No, sort of tall. Dark hair."

They both sighed.

"I wish to hell I was close enough to home to slip off," the cavalryman said wistfully. "My wife's a little bitty thing, about so high." He held his hand across his chest to show him.

For a minute there they looked straight at each other, and then they burst out laughing.

"This war is hell, ain't it?" the cavalryman said.

It was peculiar as hell, he thought; he felt as though he knew this redheaded jasper inside and out. They were about the same age, twenty-one or twenty-two he guessed the other to be, and any other time he would have liked to stay a while to see what he was like.

"Where's your home?" Johnny asked him.

"Eufaula. Garden spot of the world, I mean to tell you. You want some coffee? You might as well rest yore feet, you got eight, nine miles to go and you ain't goin' to make it. Not for mornin' muster you ain't. You up at East Point with Hardee?"

"Yes." The offer of coffee sounded good, but he'd better

223

not. He had to get on. "I can't miss out. You know," he said pointedly.

"Aw hell, I knew THAT when I first saw you come stealin' up the road. You ain't the first one. And besides, you're goin' back, ain't you? Well, don't worry about it! There's plenty what ain't. We can pick up a bunch of flickers down here in the woods any time we've a mind to. Why, we'd shake a whole division out of that swamp along the river if we had time. And niggers 'n bluebellies, too."

The other trooper came up to the gate.

"Who's that?" he said, yawning and scratching.

"Aw, friend a mine. Boy lives around here goin' back for mornin' muster up at East Point. MacLeod, this is Calder Thompson. Say hello."

They made him come and squat by their fire and take a can of corn-meal coffee. They had got a kettle from the house and were cooking mush, Thompson stirring it with a stick.

He couldn't hang around their camp; it was getting later by the minute. He had his drink and although it tasted terrible, once he had got it down it felt pretty good. It was hot, anyway.

"You sit still," Cobb said. "There's a train comes through here anytime and you can hitch a ride."

"I can't hitch a ride," he told him. "Not unless there's somebody on board that knows me."

"Aw, yes you can. Yes you can. You just want to go up to the flagstop at Morrow and tell that old boy sittin' in the telegraph tent up there that Cobb said to put you on the train."

"That won't work."

"The HELL it won't. That's my brother, second lieutenant in the signal corps. Maurice Lucius Quintillius Cobb. Ain't that hell? Little bitty feller with red hair. Looks like a frawg. You tell him I said to put you on the train, and

224

send you up the line or I'll come up theah and beat the poop out of him."

It sounded like a farce, but when he went up the road toward Morrow sure enough, there was the signal tent, just as Cobb had said. The sentry challenged him, but he asked for Lieutenant Cobb and was passed. So there was a Lieutenant Cobb, too.

He did look like a frog, red hair and all, fat and surly, sitting in the signal tent reading a newspaper. This Cobb never said a word while he delivered his message, and he was sure he was going to be thrown out on the road and hauled up for the provost, but things went on as smooth as cream right up till the moment the train arrived. Then the frog broke his silence, jumped up, cried, "Well, c'mawn," ran outside, pushed him aboard the train, and stuck a paper into his hand.

"East Point," Cobb told the railroad guard. That was all.

When the train pulled out Johnny opened the paper and read it. It said, "PASS TO EAST POINT." It wasn't even signed.

By God, he knew that took gall! You could damn all Cobbs and the state of Alabama to hell and back as far as he was concerned. It was some kind of joke.

But it worked.

No one bothered him the whole trip, and the guards sat down at the end of the car where he was and discussed the news and then got into an argument over whether the Yankee General Black Jack Logan had ever been a corps commander or not and tried to drag him into it, which made him nervous. He told them he thought they had Logan mixed up with Hooker, which did not satisfy them, either. But by that time the train was coming into the army's lines around Atlanta, for there were troops camped all along the side of the railroad tracks and he could hear bugles blowing for morning muster.

225

He would never make roll call, he knew by then. Well, he was up for discipline, and God knows what it would be, it depended on how White was feeling. Stern, he guessed, and normal. Fair, stern, and the stockade for sure.

But he couldn't go to stockade and be shut up for a week, two weeks, . . . a month, all for nothing! Especially when he was so close to home he might have a chance to run down the line again after awhile. If he had to go to stockade it was going to be too much of a damned waste!

He got up and went to the train door as though to watch the East Point yards go by. When the train slowed he dropped off and went stumbling down the bank, nearly wrenching his legs off in the process, into a sutlers' camp, or a tent town of Negroes and laundresses; he didn't have time to look, he was too busy getting out of there. For a few hundred yards he kept parallel to the railroad track, bearing generally northward and then got tangled up in a muddy little stream through a field which led to the backs of some breastworks where digging was still going on.

He didn't know where he was. This might be some part of Steve Lee's corps for all he could tell, and he realized he was having more trouble up within the lines than he had had the whole way. And he was going to get caught, sure as Satan, if he didn't watch out. Of all the confounded luck.

The piece of paper in his pocket that said "PASS TO EAST POINT" he balled up and threw away. Get rid of all the evidence.

A pair of soldiers with a mule in tow passed him and stared at him, and he was tempted to ask for information but didn't. He kept walking.

"Johnny," somebody said, and it shook him so he jumped off and rammed the Whitworth in between before he could think.

"Hey, quit that!" It was a little dark fellow with a mustache. He peered at him for a moment without recogniz-

226

ing him, mostly because it was the last place on earth he would think to look for Byron NeSmith. "What're you trying to do, bust my ribs with that thing?" Byron said.

"What're you doing here?" he said stupidly. "I thought this was Lee's corps down here."

"Well, it ain't. Not now it ain't. What happened to you? You know that captain from the 1st Tennessee was up lookin' for you last night? That he thought you was over with us? He got all over Ed about it."

"What happened?" This was about as bad as anything he could have conjured up. He felt his stomach knot up with nerves, all at once.

"I don't know. At first I heard him say that you was down with us and then Ed said you wasn't, and then thought it over and said that you had been but that you had gone back, and the captain got as hot as pepper and said to Ed, 'You're some relation, ain't you?' and Ed said yes, and then that captain told Ed he was goin' to put you up for desertion. Then Ed tried to jolly him and said that you wouldn't desert and then he'd bet you just went home to see your wife what with the raid and all down there, and that really put it to that captain, I mean to tell you. As far as that man makes out, goin' home to see your wife is ten times worse than desertion."

Oh God.

"Where's Ed," he said. "I better see him."

"I guess you better had," Byron said.

He didn't particularly relish seeing his cousin but there wasn't much else he could do, especially if White had come all the way down to the 79th's lines to find him. The man wasn't going to let a damned thing get by, that much was clear. And now he, John Alford MacLeod was caught in between, neither in nor out, and no place to go without getting stuck. If he went into the 1st Tennessee he was up for discipline for going off without a pass, which he was sure meant stockade. And, since White was in a tear, it could mean his sharpshooter's badge and the Whitworth, too. Lord, the stockade was bad enough, but he had had the Whitworth long enough to know he couldn't go back to some broken-up Enfield or Springfield that nobody wanted. If he was lucky to get that much.

Well, come what may, he wasn't sorry that he had gone off. That was worth it and more. But he was going to be damned sorry if he got caught. He could see how things were going in that respect.

Ed was eating his breakfast out on a partly finished earthwork behind Company B's trenches, his knees folded up to make a table for his can of coffee, and his mouth full of corn bread. That was how he saw him first off: Ed's little round towheaded skull and stuck-out ears and his nose forever blistered by the sun, looking twice as large as life, and because of the heat, wearing his coat unbuttoned to show his naked, prow-shaped breastbone. The ugliest soldier in the army, officer or webfoot. Ed blinked at him.

"Whyn't you tell me you wanted to go home?" his cousin greeted him, as though he had expected to see him walk up like that, out of nowhere, and wasn't surprised a bit.

"Have you been home?" he said.

"No. How're things down there?"

"Alright." It took the wind out of his sails to see Ed so calm and nonchalant.

"The Dixons went off yesterday. They didn't say anything to me, but it don't make no difference. We all go but we don't go, if you know what I mean. The brigadier sort of keeps his eye on us lately. But nobody's been caught. Except you."

"I'm not caught. Yet," he added.

Byron was hanging around anxiously, waiting to ask.

"I didn't go anyplace but home, my house," he said, to get that cleared up. "Uncle . . . I mean, I got off the train and footed it into the creek and came out down in the back pasture. And came out the same way. Well, almost. But I didn't risk going into town. I heard the railroad was pulled up pretty bad until they got it fixed day before yesterday I guess it was, and the depot's burned. But my folks hadn't heard about anybody getting hurt. A lot of niggers went off, but that's usual." He could not think of any actual news that would be of any comfort.

"You didn't hear about my folks?" Byron said.

"No. Didn't ask. I didn't think I'd be seeing you."

"Well," Ed said, "if everything's all right at your place I guess its fair to middling over in town. No need to worry about it if you can't do anything about it. Pa would be up to see me by now if anything was wrong."

"It don't make me any hap . . . ," Byron said, and he was sorry, but he had to cut in, he didn't have all the time in the world and he had to get to his own affairs.

"Byron told me White was down here," he said to Ed.

"That's right. Said he was goin' to put you up for desertion if he ever caught you."

"Ever caught me! Dammit, he knows better than that. He knows I've been trying to get a pass ever since the first of July."

"Well, you go up there now and you'll get put under arrest. That's the way I understood it. That feller's a damned tin tyrant. I don't see how you stood it so long without putting up for transfer."

"Don't say that," he told him irritably. "You don't know anything about him."

"You just by God go up and see what happens then," Ed said blandly. "You just go ahead."

He wasn't going to defend White to anybody and yet there was more to it than that. It deserved some sort of explanation.

"He's hard," he admitted, "but the man's hard on himself, too. He's a pretty fair soldier. He's just down on me, that's all."

229

"What for?"

"Because of what I told you, dammit, don't you listen? He's down on me because I've been trying to get home ever since we left Kennesaw."

"Well, that ain't nothin'. That's natural, ain't it?"

"God almighty, Ed, not everybody runs things like you do . . . and a damned good thing, too! Why, . . ." he didn't know himself what he wanted to say. He wasn't on Ed's side, either. "White's just trying to do as he sees fit. He's just lost six out of his company since the fight at Ezra Church, that's all. He's got the jumps. I didn't expect anybody to hand me a bunch of flowers for going off."

"Make up your mind," his cousin said lazily. "I don't cotton to all that court-martial and stockade. It won't whip Yankees, not by a long shot. If you like it, that's your own business."

"I didn't say I LIKED it . . . ."

"The bombardment's stopped," Byron put in. "Didn't you notice?"

"No." It seemed to him that he had noticed, but a long time ago. In the first of the morning.

Tom Norse came down the hill toward them.

"What'n hell are you doin' here?" Tom cried. "Did you know that officer from the 1st Tennessee was down here last night lookin' for you?"

"I told him," Byron offered.

"You're supposed to go up to brigade headquarters." This was for Ed.

His cousin stood up, scratched, and buttoned up his coat.

"Well, what do you want to do? Do you want to wait and see if I can do anything for you? I could talk to old Rum Tom about it."

"No, don't do that."

"I could send Bobby over to the 1st Tennessee and see how the land lays this mornin'. He might have cooled off some."

"He won't cool off. Not White."

"We got to get you fixed up somehow. I could go up to brigade and see what the regulations say about takin' back prodigals today. Maybe you could transfer out."

"How can I transfer out when I haven't even gone back?"

"I could see about it. Lowrey knows you, don't he? Didn't he put you up for that sharpshooter battalion last winter? Well, lots worse things have happened in this army. It all depends."

"Just don't do anything. That's what'd help the most." But he knew he didn't mean that, and he could tell Ed didn't pay it any mind.

"You just sit back here," his cousin told him," and keep quiet and take that badge off your hat and if anybody comes along tell them you're diggin' necessaries and to see me about it if they don't like it."

Then Ed went off with Tom and Byron, and he was left alone.

The sun rose straight up, and the clay banks of the fortifications on that part of the East Point lines grew dry and hot as brick. It was quiet, almost earsplittingly quiet now after all the constant hammer of the artillery of the past few weeks. Some skirmishing in the picket area about a mile below sputtered on and off, but the heavy crump, crump of the siege guns was gone.

Something was up, there was no doubt about it.

He was hungry, and he had forgotten to bring any food from home and his rations had run out. The water in his canteen was more than two or three days old and stale. No one came down to him from B Company's position, and he sat without cover in the August sun for almost four or five hours (there was no way to tell exactly) with nothing to occupy his time but watching the flies work across the garbage which had been thrown down the hill and the puffs of smoke from the skirmish fire.

231

When he had just about given up and decided there was no reason for him to sit out there all day as it wasn't accomplishing a damned thing, he saw his cousin coming down the hill.

"Get up boy, and get a move on, "Ed hollered.

It was not what he wanted to hear at the moment and damned sure not the way he wanted to hear it.

"We're goin' to move," Ed informed him. "Lowrey's and Mercer's, anyway, so I guess that means all of Cleburne's division. General Hardee's gone up to Atlanta on a railroad engine to talk Hood into sendin' the whole corps down the line."

"What line? Where?"

"Jonesboro. Sherman's slipped down south of here and tore up the railroad at Fairburn."

He knew Ed had got things backward somehow, and was relieved. All that had happened days ago.

"You mean the cavalry."

"Hell no, I don't mean the cavalry, I mean the whole ruckus. The Orphan Brigade's down there, and Lewis says he's got about two thousand men and all they can see is bluebellies as thick as ants. Looks like Sherman is comin' to fix that railroad for good, same way as they went before. If we don't hop to it. I wish Hood was some sharper. He's got the slows, or somethin'. You got that sharpshooter badge off your hat?"

"Yes." That was all he could manage to say.

"You want to go, don't you?"

"Yes. Hell, yes."

"Then you come up with me and nobody's goin' to bother you, hear? When we fall into columns you go right in where you always was, between Byron and Tom." They started back up the hill to B Company. "You get enough time at home?" Ed asked him.

"Yes," he said, "enough."

"Well, how was everybody?"

"Fine," he said, "just fine."

CHAPTER 16

Oh! Dixie, dear land of King Cotton
   "The home of the brave and the free."
A nation by freedom begotten,
   The terror of despots to be.

It was the 30th of August. There had been no thunder-
shower to cool things off for over a week, and the tempera-
ture had lingered in the nineties the whole time. The ground
felt as though there was a fire in it; the earth was actually
hot underfoot long after dark and didn't begin to cool
until the dew fell, which was often past midnight. The
brigade commanders in Cleburne's division had given the
word to prepare to assemble as soon as orders came down
from Atlanta, and B Company had already moved from
their works to sit out where it was cooler, with only Babb
and Bob Cline left out on picket down in the empty woods.
There had not been an answering fire out there since noon.
Some of Granbury's men had pressed out for more than two
miles and found nothing, only the unoccupied ditches where
the enemy had been.

"What time is it?" Byron asked Peed.

"Past time." Peed was as restless as a bear with a belly-
ache. He kept lumbering up and down the litter of the
79th's dead mess fires, picking up trash and straightening
out. Peed's house and sawmilling sheds were over near
Shadnor between Jonesboro and Fairburn, right in the
way of any line of march between the two points.

Ed Grimes had been up to the railroad four or five times
since dark to get the news, but all that the left wing of
Hardee's corps knew was that General Hardee and Steve

Lee were still in Atlanta arguing their case with Hood. General Hood did not believe there was much reason for alarm down at Jonesboro—it was a cavalry feint or a trick of some sort, and Sherman had either withdrawn his army back up the railroad into north Georgia to get Wheeler and Forrest off his lines, or he was making another sweep across the railroads southward as a cover-up for a head-on attack at Atlanta. Hood had been sure for the past twenty-four hours that Sherman was probably set for an attack on the city.

Only what was left of Hood's cavalry, Jackson's brigade, and the Orphan Brigade down at Jonesboro could tell what was going on. And they kept telegraphing that there were more damned Yankees than you could shake a stick at down there, coming across on a six-mile front. Hardee believed them. So did Steve Lee. But not Hood.

As far as Company B was concerned, it was enough to drive a person crazy. Lord, think of Hardee and Lee up in Atlanta trying to reason with Hood! Especially Hardee. The old man has lost his temper by now, you can bet.

General Lowrey had gone up to General Maney's headquarters, and they were sitting together, waiting. Maney had bad nerves and thought Hood was a lunatic. Maney's adjutant was stiff as a poker; his wife had refugeed down to the hotel in Jonesboro a week ago.

Even Ed Grimes had the fidgets. When he wasn't up at the railroad he had Bobby Hart running back and forth to the 79th's HQ tent every half hour.

A wagon train came down from Atlanta along the main road with orders to get to Jonesboro with army records and valuables for safekeeping. Maney and Lowrey jumped up and sent the adjutant to find a courier to find Cleburne to countermand the wagon train's orders and get it the devil off the road. By whose orders had that damned thing come through? By orders of General Hood. Great jumping snakes! Carter's division said they could hear Maney howl down where they were.

It was along past midnight when they heard that Hardee's and maybe Steve Lee's corps were going to Jonesboro, and they had to be there by light to attack the enemy and drive him off. Part of the wagon train was still blocking the road. Steve Lee's corps had not got any orders to be on the ready, and some of the divisions were still out in the earthworks and most of those were asleep. Somebody found an engine to come down with the generals. Hardee was in command of the two corps; Pat Cleburne would command Hardee's corps, while Hardee himself went on to Jonesboro.

General Anderson didn't get any written orders. He had to send a courier over to Maney to find out what was going on.

Things were off to a good start!

When they did move it seemed to Johnny that the whole army had caught Hood's mysterious affliction: the columns stalled and the order of march was havoc—the 79th almost ended up outside the division—and when there was any movement it was of the most exasperating sort, stumbling, coiling, and backing over itself, and no one sure what was going on. From the brigadiers on down, everybody was mad and sweating. Hurry, hurry was the password. General Hood had finally acknowledged that Sherman was down on the railroads at Fairburn and menacing Jonesboro. Sweep forward then, Stonewall Jackson style, and crush them!

Cleburne did not have any maps, and one of his aides was out looking for some, only to find that there were none. Most of Lowrey's and Maney's divisions had not been issued their three-day rations and were carrying only water and meal. The artillery did not have orders to move anywhere. Coming out of the railroad yards at East Point Ed Grimes' horse stumbled on the tracks and threw him. It was too dark to tell what damage had been done to the horse, . . . he was not lame at any rate. But Ed was. He had hurt his knee.

"Aw to hell with it," Ed said. "It'll work out. It better. I'm not going to get left, that's for sure."

"Damn Hood anyway," Byron said.

A thunderstorm was flickering northward over Atlanta with red flashes of lightning outlining the high, towering clouds piled up in the sky, but where they were, it was smotheringly hot. Beyond the railroad yards where the countryside opened up in pine trees and fields the heat lay close to the ground, bitter with dust. Hardee's corps was to take the main road southward and Lee's the road which kept to the railroad tracks into Jonesboro, but Lee was not sure about anything. He kept his riders galloping back and forth between the fields to check the direction and the rate of travel, and once to report that the head of his corps was marching off without a body; a division that was supposed to be following had either got lost or had not yet left the yards back at East Point. Messengers went back to find out what had become of the rest of Lee's, and the messengers did not come back and more messengers were sent to find them.

There was never another night like it. There was an uproar in Hardee's corps that some Georgia and Alabama troops were straggling and would not come up as they ought. The 79th could not fall out to rest because of lack of orders, and Manson and Betts decided that they were going to give the whole thing up and go home on their own. They would make better time left to themselves.

"Ef I see you down there when we get there," Peed said, "I'll put a ball through your heads."

"This comes of sending the cavalry off," Tom Norse complained. "Nobody in this army can tell what they're doin'."

It came down to dogged, gasping runs, and then sudden stops when it seemed as though the whole division was going to pile up in the road, and then waits and more waits, and sometimes futile cutoffs that most of them knew were useless. They passed near Morrow Station and heard a train, the first of the night.

Then the whole sweating mass of Hardee's corps stopped, and they heard that somewhere in front they had come up

236

against a Federal picket at the mill. After an hour the columns began to bunch and back up and squeeze into a field road that was just a track between the trees, running east toward the railroad.

"I know where we are," Byron muttered. "We've just turned toward Muncus Creek. Don't you know where this is? I used to hunt rabbits down this damned road."

They were pretty close to home. Bob Cline knew where they were exactly because there were a lot of red foxes down along these bottoms. It was McPeak's field road. The house was over on the hill near the flagstop.

They filed down the narrow road at a snail's pace, sometimes standing in the dark for quarter-hours at a time, listening to the frogs and croakers in the swamp, and when they finally moved up the slope toward the railroad, they discovered Lee's corps in a shambles, right in their way, broken down and milling around with some of the troops resigned enough to their condition to lie down in the road and go to sleep.

A dark clump of horsemen that was Granbury and his staff rode up to see what the trouble was.

Company B began to shout.

"Look at those goddamned jaspers sleeping, mind you!"

"Where's that damned Lee? Don't he see his troops? Don't he have no force-march orders?"

"Get out of the way and let somebody through up there, you bastards!"

"Let somebody through what's got folks down here, for God's sake."

"Quit that," Ed told them, coming back. "Shut up that hell raisin'."

They stood and waited, and Colonel Blalock came back and rode around looking as though he was going to do something about it and had a conference with the colonel of the Alabama regiment behind them.

Still they waited.

"We won't get to see our folks," Tom muttered in the

darkness. "When we get to town, we can't go anywheres. We won't even know what's goin' on, most likely. That's the way it always is."

"Aw, shut up," Byron said.

"Wish the sun was up."

"No you don't."

"Yes I do. I could tell something then."

"You just said it won't do no good."

"Well, you can SEE then, can't you?"

"I'd like to see what the town looks like. I ain't been home since the raid."

"You can see town alright. That's all the good it's going to do."

"I wish I knew something," Johnny fretted. "I wish I knew where all those damned Yanks were—if they've got all the way into town." How could he be sure Matt and Anna were still out in the house on the side of the hill? Perhaps they had gone to Jonesboro. But he could not make himself believe that Matt would leave home, not even for the whole of Sherman's army. Matt would think she could hold the house against hell and the devil himself let loose.

"It'll be hot as hell-fire when the sun comes up," Peed said. "Y'can feel it now. We'll fry, guts and gizzard."

"You shut up, too, Peed," Tom Norse told him impartially, and for once Peed let it go.

The way they understood it, Hardee's and Steve Lee's corps were to entrench on the slopes outside of town facing the river and to hold the railroad at any cost.

"Drive them back," Byron said, morosely. "If we could just dig in and hold, that would be somethin' else again, but Hood won't let this army dig, not for hell he won't. Not dig'n stay, leastways. Go out and charge, that's all we've had since Joe Johnston left us."

"Johnston knew more about it."

"He wasn't dead set to kill off his troops, neither."

"Are those Yanks across the river?"

238

"Hell yes, they're across. Got their backs to it. Sherman ain't no fool."

"He ain't so damned smart, neither, or he'd have bottled up old Hood before now."

"Aw, confound it," Byron burst out. "Why can't we move! What's got into this division? Are we goin' to stand here all night?"

As it turned out, it was almost the rest of the night, at any rate. With the first dawnlight the wagon trains, or whatever it was that kept them there, began to be cleared up, to some extent. And when they did move, it was all at once, Ed Grimes coming back with his horse at a gallop, urging them up and double-quick.

"Tom, Johnny, get the hell out of there, y'hear? Up, up, jigtime!"

Ed was feeling better now, no strain showed in him, only the sheer glee of excitement. He kicked the old horse in a fancy pirouette along the stubble of the roadbank and galloped off.

But they did not go as fast as Ed would have had it. There was no order in even a simple thing such as filing down the road beside the railroad and as soon as there was enough light to get range, the Federal batteries opened up upon Jonesboro, shelling right along the tracks which ran through the middle of town. Shells and solid shot were dropping into the only right of way, and the troops coming in bunched up and ran and then stopped and bunched up again so that those following behind were kept at a ragged pace.

Byron started at a dead run, and Johnny kept behind him. Tom Norse was on his left, and he could see Bobby Hart's corn-silk hair ahead. Ed Grimes was making full sweep of their side of the column, the horse lathered and heaving. But Ed had his hat off and was whooping, urging them along, his big nose shining.

It was hot, as Peed had said. The oaks that lined Main Street did not move their leaves except for the gusts stirred up by artillery fire. The road was littered with broken twigs and limbs, and the dust was fine and floury underfoot, slow to settle once their feet had kicked it up.

It was the way the town looked that convinced them of disaster: the houses that lined Main Street were either shut up tightly or left standing open as though the people in them had bolted when the noise began, and there were people everywhere; Johnny saw people he recognized out in the streets running frantically as though they had somewhere to go, or standing at the gateposts of their houses with a stunned, absorbed look, as though they would not miss what was happening for the world. And children.

"Mr. Burnside," Byron shouted, but the man did not turn to look. It was the lawyer, standing out in his back garden with his hand to his eyes, looking up at the sky as though searching for the shells which were coming over. Burnside's garden, with its granite statue of Psyche, looked as though it had taken a hit of some sort, everything was knocked awry, and the Psyche was on her back, one leg broken off.

A drummer behind somewhere had started a roll and kept it going, Rrrrrrrrrrrrrrrrrr, rrrrrrrrrrrrrrrr. They pumped their legs with it. Bryon's face was beet red.

A shell fell across the railroad tracks and lay under a tree, still fizzing, and Clay Foster threw his arm up over his head as he ran.

"It ain't goin' to hit you, Clay," Tom Norse shouted.

"Git, git, git," Peed was grunting. "Want us to stomp you?"

They were running past his Aunt Mildred Grimes' house, and he searched the long porch with a sense of dread. If Matt or Anna had come to town they would be there. He saw two women on the porch, but it was Ed's mother and his Aunt Rose Nell.

"Johnny, . . ." his Aunt Mildred screamed. His Aunt Rose Nell looked as though she was trying to tell her that she was mistaken, but his Aunt Mill knew what she was doing. She started into the yard.

A hot wind was blowing now along the railroad, raising

the dust like a hurricane, and there were five thousand men scrambling along the street from one end to another trying to get through the town. And on the porch steps of the Grimes' house, his Aunt Mill and his Aunt Rose Nell were struggling with each other like maniacs, his Aunt Rose Nell trying to keep Ed's mother from running into the street.

Damn, he wanted to see his Aunt Mill about as bad as she wanted to see him! He jumped over the iron fence of the yard and heard Peed shout.

"Get back," Peed was hollering.

He met his Aunt Mill halfway.

"Where's Matt? Anna. . . ."

"Where's Ed?" She was screaming, not listening.

"Where's Matt?" he roared. He could feel the veins pop out at the side of his face, and he was shaking. "Where's Anna . . . you know, my wife. . . ."

But all his Aunt Mill would do was scream about Ed. Foster had jumped the fence behind him.

"You seen my folks? My ma, sisters?"

Peed was threatening to shoot both of them, trying to find a way to open the catch in the iron gate.

His Aunt Rose Nell grabbed the front of his jacket.

"We haven't seen anybody. Been in the house, all night, since yesterday, the firing started." And because Clay Foster was holding her arm and shaking it in a frenzy, she turned to him with, "Who are you, sir? Who? Foster?"

Peed got the gate open at about the same time Ed Grimes came trotting up on his horse. Ed threw him the reins to hold and loped through the gate. His mother flung herself upon him.

"Mama, will you listen a minute?" Ed began, grinning. "Aw, Mama, quit it, will you?"

Sick at heart, Johnny turned away and went back through the gate which Peed held open for him. Byron was waiting ⸱n the other side.

"You get your ass down toward town," Peed roared.

He started at a jog. From the porch, his Aunt Rose Nell

had a final word. She leaned over the railing, her hands around her mouth.

"They're still at home."

He turned, almost as if to go back, but a ball of solid shot hit the iron rails beside them and bounced into the air and rolled down into the street. Byron grabbed his arm.

"Watch out!"

And because Byron was half pushing him, they started, picking up to a run, going toward the stores.

"I can't run, got to get my breath . . . ." They had caught up with Ray Everett, hanging onto a tree, purple-faced and holding to his side.

"He's faking. He tried to run once," Bobby accused.

A window in Manson's house opened upstairs, and some woman screamed at them.

"Where's Manson?"

"God, I don't know, who's that, his mother?"

They did not have time for Manson. The colonel came along, trotting his horse, his whiskey-rose face as red in the sun as at any other time.

"Troops, move along," he told them, waving his hand.

They kept going, merging with a knot of Alabamians stopped down toward the business part of town. Under the tin sheds over the walkways there were a lot of old men and some boys, taking shelter to watch.

Ed Grimes came riding up, grinning.

"Get up, boys. These jaspers are holdin' us up. We got to get outside of town. Old Howard's out there they tell me, and waitin' for us to show."

All of Lowrey's were going out south and west of town, most of Lee's to the north and westward, pushing toward the creek called Flint River. The signal corps had already run up a station on the telegraph pole beside Connally's Saloon, and the signal officer up there, hanging on by his spurs, was having a rough time of it. Some sharpshooter close in was aiming for his flags. They could hear him cursing.

An engine came grinding up from the southward, and the artillery from across the river had seen its smoke; a sudden spurt of shells arched overhead and landed on the far side of the tracks. The ground shook underfoot, although the railroad embankment partly protected them, and a piece of metal came through the air and embedded itself in a large shade tree overhanging the walk. Some of the Alabamians on the other side of them crumpled over, and there was a stir as their friends rushed forward to help. Dust was whirling like a fog, with hot sunshine beating on its upper layers.

"Oh God, don't let us stand here and be bombarded," Byron groaned. "I'd rather go out anyday than stand reserve and just be cut down without even moving."

"We got to get out of this hoorah sometime," Tom Norse said, squinting. He was tallest, and could reach up on his toes and look over the heads of the Alabamians in front.

Johnny wiped his face against his sleeve. He was sweating, and the dust stuck to it, making a grimy layer on his skin.

They were standing at the intersection of Main Street and College, which became the Fayetteville road farther out of town. Mose Hansard's place was on the corner, a net hammock still strung between two chinaberry trees and an ammunition wagon drawn up in the yard, resting against the steps, blocking all entrance to the house. The place was closed up, deserted. Johnny noticed a big hole in the roof, right over the porch and knew a solid shot of some sort had gone through. The Alabamians were carrying their wounded up into the yard, the surgeon following with his case slung satchel-style from one shoulder.

He shook his head. He had seen other towns like this, under siege, but there was something dreamlike to be where he was, at home, and have it happening now. Across the river, God knows what was happening. He had to get out toward the slopes and see for himself, if they would ever move. His nerves were jumping, as though there was a wild man down inside of him, clamoring to be let go. He was like Byron, he could not stand and take punishment like this for long.

The close-packed mass, not even columns any more, began to shuffle forward agonizingly, at a caterpillar pace. Halfway down the first row of houses in town proper they passed the Methodist Church where Matt and Anna had heard the Atlanta preacher just a month ago, and Mr. Hanes, the Jonesboro pastor, was standing on the steps. He was in shirt sleeves rolled up to his elbows. He saw the Jonesboro company and came into the road.

"Boys, be careful. There's Yankee cavalry down the road. They came in trying for the railroad just an hour ago."

They hollered to him, but they had started on the run once more. There had been a lot of shelling here. The front of Cline's house was all but torn away. Mattie Cline was Bob Cline's wife. Johnny could not help it. In spite of the run, he looked at Bob and saw him stop. Then Bob was shoved from behind and started to run once more. His face was white.

"My God," Bob said, over and over. He was not even watching where he was going. Burnside took Cline's arm.

"They're gone," they told him. "There's nobody there. Can't you see? The house is empty."

"Mattie," Bob said. His lips were white as dough and wrinkled. He looked as though he could not stand up.

Johnny turned his face away. How would he take it now, when he got close enough to see across the river to his own house and what had happened there? If he *could* see. There was no telling where the 79th would light.

Ed Grimes dismounted and tied his exhausted horse to a tree.

"C'mon," he shouted. His long legs were carrying him up and down like a bounding bird. "There's a stretch that's hot, right behind Weir's . . . dammit, pick up your feet . . . ."

They followed him, running raggedly, their canteens banging, guns held out against their chests, cursing and panting.

244

CHAPTER 17

The country needs no ramparts,
   No batteries to shield!
   Your bosoms are her bulwarks strong,
   Breastworks that cannot yield!

The Kentucky Orphan Brigade, which had been sent to Jonesboro the day before to hold a delaying action against what Hood had been sure was only a cavalry raid, had dug some earthworks west of town during the night, but these were already filled. The company ran out into Tom Norse's father's cornfield under heavy fire and crouched there in the stalks, while Ed gave orders to dig like fury. All of Cleburne's division was doing the same, and the green flag of Irish Pat's troops was stuck in the corner of a field corncrib overlooking the slope. The burrowing along the lines stretched itself through Norse's field and Brockard's pasture and followed the river in a three-mile half-circle, roughly embracing the town and the railroad. The Federal lines were below them on the slope on that side of the river with the stream at their backs, and the fire was heavy. The Federal artillery had good range; when they had time to look they could plainly see the guns jumping and firing across the river like leashed dogs. Someone in the river trees was putting down a worrisome mortar barrage close to the rifle pits where Ed had sent Cleatus Mann and Dorsey Spears.

"Lord, let us do some good," somebody whispered. It was Ray Everett. "Let us do some confounded good out here, for a change."

Cleburne's lines were thin, and Lowrey's division was

245

wide-spaced; Johnny could not touch either Byron or Tom Norse, on his left, even with his arms outstretched. The breastworks they were working on looked too high against the slope of the hill; they were outlined against the sky with the slightest movement, and the Yanks down below them knew it. Buck LeHand lifted his head just a moment to call to Dorsey Spears out beyond them and took a spent ball in his forehead, right over his eye. Peed put a shirt around his head and sent him back toward town to look for a field hospital.

"Y'all keep your heads down," Peed told them. "Y'see what damned foolishness brings on?"

As soon as Johnny had dug a hole deep enough to lie down in he did so, and Byron crawled in beside him.

"Keep digging, it's not deep enough yet."

"I know that," Byron said crossly. "You lookin' for your house?"

He put his Whitworth along the top of the red dirt they had thrown up in front of them and carefully put his face against it as though he was going to sight a shot. He moved the barrel, searching. The cornstalks of Norse's field were in the way, and then, beyond, the thick trees of the river-bottom obscured his view, but some part of his house ought to be showing; it was tall enough to stand above the trees even in summer when they were leafed out.

He caught sight of the roof. God, that was his house alright! Brown shingles, and the top of the kitchen chimney. About a mile off.

He knew at once what Bob Cline had felt. His innards contracted, and he started to shake in nervous jerks that crept along his arms and shoulders and made his knees jump. That was no help. For some reason, he couldn't concentrate on what he saw. He told himself that it was his house over there behind the enemy lines, a mile or so behind. What in God's name would an army do to a house like that?

246

At the best some division staff would claim it for themselves, move in and take over. They would put a signal man up in the trees of the yard; on top of the hill like that, overlooking the river and the opposite slope, there was no better spot. Or perhaps fill up the porch with couriers, with some brigadier's adjutant setting up housekeeping on the dining room table. Or maybe they would even put a hospital in.

He put his head down against the stock of the Whitworth and shut his eyes. The shaking was just like some confounded chill, only it was nerves, all nerves.

Someone crawled up and got in beside them.

"Dig, boy, dig," Ed said. "You two are layin' out here with your asses in the air, don't you know that?"

"What the hell do you think I'm doin'?" Byron cried. His shovel was flinging a spatter of earth over them with every movement.

"That's your house," Ed pointed out.

He nodded.

"Johnny, you alright?"

He did not answer.

"Listen," Ed said, "Mamma told me she sent Pa out after them yesterday when the Kentucky boys was comin' back to town, but Matt wouldn't leave the house, and your wife wouldn't go without her."

It was just as he had expected. Damn Matt anyway, and her damned bullheadedness.

"You didn't know they was still out there," Ed said.

"I guessed as much," he muttered.

"Well, they're probably all right. Godalmighty, you've seen women out to themselves like that before. It's hard on the nerves but it usually ain't too bad. And shoot, they're better off inside a house than they are on a road goin' somewhere's where every loose jasper can . . . ." Ed swallowed. "Well," he said, "a big house like that ain't bad at all. Some general got his staff inside this mornin', you can bet your bottom dollar. I bet Old Howard has got his office up there.

It's the only house around on that side of the river for a mile or more. Two miles. Worse that could happen, some staffer put 'em in a wagon and sent them back off to Fairburn somewheres."

"Christ, will you shut your big mouth?" he shouted.

Ed subsided. Byron dug on grimly.

There was no shade in the cornfield. When the spattering of the rifle fire below them thinned at intervals, the sound of digging and the chink of metal spades against the stones of the furrows could be heard. It was ten o'clock. Neither side had moved, or given any sign of the fire which meant the beginning of the business. The Yankees seemed content enough to keep moving troops into the riverbottom, reinforcing their lines, until it looked as though they were trying to fill up a space of a half mile or more with solid troops. The trees shook with all the burrowing going on in the swamps.

"Why don't we start?" someone yelled down to the left.

"Can't start. Ain't up yet."

And anyone who cared to look could see behind them, in the streets coming out from town, a ragged straggle of troops doing the same things they had been doing an hour before, running the gauntlet of the shelling along College and Main Street. The army seemed to have a chronic case of disorder. At times there was no one in sight, and then a clump of running men would come into view, sprinting as though they were being chased, with some officer galloping along as though he was not certain, either, where they were headed.

The sun bored down. The day was bright and placid, and the leaves of the aging corn waved listlessly in the stirring air. A net of late-summer bindweed and morning glories had climbed the stalks in strangling profusion, and the goldenrod was blooming in the furrows. Small yellow butterflies drifted like tags of paper along the bindweed flowers. It looked like August; things were still green but not brightly so . . . a golden, faded cast was creeping into

248

earth and sky, and even the sunlight was bleached away to a hammering glare. Time was dying; the season was nearly gone.

Byron had linked his trench with Tom Norse's, and they threw fist-sized stones on top of the mound of earth in front, and patted it into place with their shovels.

"I ain't goin' to work anymore," Byron panted. "You know we ain't goin' to sit here behind any earthworks anyway."

"Hell, who wants to?" This time he did not want to sit behind breastworks and wait for them to come.

"Well, I don't want to neither," Byron answered. "I didn't say I wanted to, did I?"

"I want to roll them right back across the river," Tom turned his head to tell them. "Lord," he said, distracted by some thought. "Look at that damned corn. It's ruint."

The Texans from Granbury's brigade were finally coming up beside them.

"Hey boys," one of them yelled, "y'alls been granted leave. Go visit your folks whilst we take over!"

Johnny put a shot down into the woods where he thought he saw a speck of blue moving in the ditches. He had missed out going to the rifle pits in the first rush, and now Dorsey and Cleatus were pinned down and no one could relieve them.

It was getting late. What was keeping them? It was past time to do something, and yet College Street was jammed, only a few troops coming out at a time. Someone said some Louisianians had come up on the far side of town, on the wrong side of the railroad, like lost sheep.

General Cleburne came out on the slope for a while and sat his horse, looking across the river with his glasses. A gun had finally come up. It was rolled into Norse's back yard at the end of the street and for every crouped chorus of the enemy Parrotts across the river it would belch querulously and be still, and then belch again after a little while. It was the only artillery piece down on their end of the line. The artillerymen were running frantically around their gun, working it as fast as they could, the belches picking up a little speed, but not nearly enough.

A cracking volley of rifle fire opened on them suddenly, right in front and tore into the shade trees of Norse's yard high on the slope.

"Whup," Ed said, hunching along behind their ditches. "Watch out." He had a conference with Peed, and then Peed came down to them.

"You hear a fire up yonder," Peed dug his head northward, "over where Steve Lee's boys are at, that's the signal to go. Look sharp for the holler. Listen for the horn. We charge them bluebellies out yonder'n drive 'em across the river."

"I'm ready," Tom said. "You just get the burr under things, can't you? We can't wait much longer!"

"Who says we can't?" Peed grunted. "Half them damned troops ain't out of town yet. I heard they's some still backed up along the railroad for a long ways out of town."

"What's the matter with them?" Byron complained. He rolled on his back to ram his charge.

"Them boys is tired," Peed said. "They run all the way from East Point last night. They ain't been layin' out here like y'all, takin' a rest."

The rifle fire from below was cutting at the breastworks like sawdust bugs at work.

"When are we going to start . . . Christ, when are we going to start?" someone cried. "We ain't got all day!"

And still they waited, and the sun rose even higher and stood overhead, and some of the company got dry corn meal out of their haversacks and ate it out of their hands and washed it down with water. But Johnny was not hungry. His stomach was still jumping and fretting; yet he could not keep from searching out the corner of the roof and the piece of chimney that was his house and raging at it, which made him feel worse. He had occasional impossible visions of the army that lay partly hidden in the trees before him

250

and across the hill suddenly rooted out and blown away, blasted away and cleared out forever, gone miraculously from this one particular place which ought, somehow, to be left undisturbed . . . a house sitting on a hillside and a muddy stream that was called a river and a town sitting on a ridge with the railroad coming through it. There was nothing sensible in what was going on, not a bit of reality in all of this, lying out in Tom Norse's cornfield in the hot August sun, straining and raging for home with all the boys from Jonesboro lying down behind their earthworks doing the same thing. They had all gone mad, that was it, and all they had to do was stand up and go home, himself with them, stand up and walk down the slope and into the stream and make for home.

He put the Whitworth down against the ledge and rubbed his eyes with his knuckles. He was having nightmares.

The order came down to fix bayonets. It was two o'clock. If there was any hope for them, it had been eaten away by the hours. Two o'clock left almost nothing. The woods were full of the enemy, waiting for them.

"Hell, part of Lee's hasn't even got into the field," Tom Norse shouted to them.

A battery of Yankee horse artillery jerked up from nowhere right in front of them and came galloping hell for leather, bluecoats, brass buckles, dusty roan horses. The Texans down on Granbury's line whooped and screeched. Another horse gun came tearing after the first, and a third, the caisson bouncing off the cornfield hills three feet at the bounce. A blue hat flew off and landed in the corn.

WHUMP! WHUMP!

Tom Norse was hollering something incoherent about the god-damned corn, ramming charges home in a frenzy.

A messenger came up from behind, looking for Ed.

"General Weir wants to know if they're charging this position!"

251

"Can't he tell?" Ed shouted. "He can see a hell of a lot better'n I can!"

"Sir?"

"Tell him, yes, goddammit!"

Bobby Hart lay against the breastworks, the bugle expectantly to his mouth.

"You watch out," Peed growled. "You wait till you're told."

Bobby's eyes were on Ed.

"Now y'all," Ed shouted, "run 'em back to Hane's gin."

Byron pulled at Johnny's shirt.

"Look, look, can't you . . . there's a big hole between us and Maney's . . . we can't go yet . . . ."

"Listen, Lee is starting!"

"Logan's up in front of Lee . . . ."

"Who told you that?"

"Watch that gun, don't pay no atention to Lee . . . y'can't even see Lee for God's sake. . . ."

The horse guns were backing under their fire and trying to turn, and the blue troops which had come up with them were falling back down the slope and drawing off, some of them to the wooden bridge along the road.

Now the noise from Lee's out of sight northward was a warning roar. The signal.

Swords began to wave, and a bugle blew.

The Texans were up and out, caterwauling, starting down the slope. But a knot of staff officers were galloping up and down, shouting, as though something was wrong.

"Alright boy," Ed shouted. He scrambled up. Bobby put the bugle to his lips.

But Peed stood all the way up and put out his hand.

"Wait," he bellowed.

"Never mind wait," Tom shouted; he was out of his ditch.

The line started off with a rush, flags charging at an angle, the gun belching feebly behind them in Norse's yard.

What was there to wait for?

They came down from the trenches in a jostling spreading line which, after a few feet, bunched together to work its way through the last rows of Norse's cornfield. Ed Grimes was ahead, followed by the bugler, and Tom Norse in his own private frenzy close upon him, and the Dixon brothers after. The Texans had an open space before their works and they went out in style, standards whipping and half a dozen bugles blowing, full of shrieks and yips and catcalls, in a head-on dash against the thickets at the bottom of the hill.

Johnny plunged in, Byron with him, and the cornfield swallowed them. Byron knelt down to reload, holding his rifle against his stomach, the ram out, a cartridge stuck between his teeth.

"M-wait," he cried.

He knelt down beside him to load the Whitworth. Ahead of them in the cornfield, squatting down to reload also, were Ray Everett and Peed. The cornpatch was ruined, just as Tom Norse had complained. The horse batteries had cut a swath through it as wide as a locomotive's track, and the sweet, acrid, crushed smell of cornsap was everywhere. It was hot. The minute they stopped to kneel the air closed around them like fire, beating on the tops of their heads, their shoulders, and their baking backs.

A clump of Alabamians who had gotten out late came charging up on them and almost fell over them in the corn. As they passed, a load of canister came through the cornleaves like the sound of tearing bed sheets, and the Alabamians pitched over. So did Ray Everett, and Peed.

"Peed," Byron cried, "sergeant, . . ." but he did not move or answer.

They broke out of the corn and saw the rest ahead of them and Ed Grimes and Bobby, the bugler, still with the horn against his lips, blowing furiously.

Ed waved his arms.

"Come on, COME ON!"

253

A colonel from the Texas troops galloped up and hung from the saddle cowboy-style and urged him, "COME ON, COME ON!" . . . the very same words, unheeding, and rode on.

They had come down the slope far enough, stumbling and running, to be almost on the enemy in the woods. The Texans had reached the wooden bridge out to the left and were caught in hand-to-hand assault. Some of the blue wool suits, dismounted cavalry by the look, were running away, leaving the horse artillery, and making for the hill.

My God they were running, he thought exultantly. A ferocious satisfaction took hold of him to see them running. Nothing could stop them now, they were going to drive them after all, through the river and up the far sides of their hill over there and down the flats beyond . . . all the way to the Columbus rail line at Fairburn where they had come. And if so . . . then Hood would be right for once in his life.

Somebody ran past, going full blast, sprinting, no gun, no pistol, no hat, crying, "Oh God, Oh God," and then in broken, excited bursts, . . . "You were supposed to turn right, dammit . . . turn right! Turn right for God's sake!" He had caught up with Ed Grimes and was trying to hang onto Ed, catching him by the back of his belt frantically.

"Whoo," Ed cried, and turned, amazed, and tried to get him off, at least to get him to ungrab his pants.

Whoever he was, he kept hollering, "Oh God, oh God," over and over, and then, "Maney is having to close the gap behind you . . . can't you see it?"

It was a young officer from somewhere—none of them knew him—grabbing at Ed's shirt, trying to get a hold somewhere, as though to drag Ed back up the hill by sheer force. There was always some damned fool who lost his head at times like these, hollering and carrying on. The best thing to do was push him out of the way.

"Ahh," Ed cried, and swung him off. The minie bullets

254

were popping all around them. There was no time for foolishness.

Johnny got him by the shoulders and shoved, and the officer reeled off against a persimmon bush, clawing at the leaves. The boy had lost his hat somewhere, and he had long, curly blond hair which blew all about his face.

"Oh God, oh God," he began again, "I need General Lowrey . . . I need to find General Lowrey . . . ."

"C'mon," Byron grunted.

Just ahead, Ed Grimes and Bobby Hart had already charged into the canes and honeysuckle of the swamp.

"There they are!" Ed cried.

They were there all right, in the thickest part, hidden in the green wall. And all of the company that had come down the slope had kept together somehow in spite of everything —Tom Norse and Ed Grimes and Byron and himself and ahead, in a panting, stumbling bunch, Gillespie and the Dixon brothers and Cleatus Mann and Theo Pringle—Betts, Bud Fitzgerald, a couple of stray Texans. No Peed, no Clay Foster.

"Push them across, push them across," some one of them was shouting hoarsely.

They went into the thickets, beating the brush down with their feet, and there was a line of resistance here, rifles spitting yellow flames and bluecoats showing in the occasional break of underbrush.

Damn, he thought—it was so dark and green once you got under the big trees of the river that it half-blinded a person. It made you cautious in spite of the fact that every foot of the way was familiar. After the blasting open heat of the cornfield and the pasture slopes he couldn't see what he was doing at all, hardly, and couldn't even make out the bluebellies as they popped up. The whole blue sky and the white hole of the sun were suddenly masked by the arch of water oaks and swamp maples and gums and poplars and hickories, their roots in mud, their heads in sunshine, and a green limbo between. It was tough going: smilax and virginia creeper and other vines ran up the trees and laced back and forth, a whole maze of tangles and snarls that tried to trip them up as they came through. But cool . . . it was like stepping from furnace heat into the dark of a spring-house!

They were all crashing through in the green dark, staring their eyes out, trying to be quick and wary in spite of everything, for the place was full of Yankee skirmishers.

The slough of the river was about two hundred feet from one side to the other—you couldn't say banks, for there were none—all down here in the swamp and mud and trees the glittering cool light danced in their faces, tricking them, and underfoot puddles and grooves of brown water ran in a hundred dry midsummer channels.

Someone jumped up out of the canebrake and fired at him, just like a damned jack-in-the-box, and it did not hit him, it missed him somehow. He saw the whole thing in a wink of the eye: pistol barrel with the smoke curling out of it, black cavalry hat with one side turned up rakishly and a feather in it..

Johnny swung his bayonet sidewise—not enough room to lift it with all the vines around him—and the man caught hold of the barrel of the Whitworth. They struggled and strained, and he heard the other's breath queerly, oh, oh, as they wrestled.

In that one moment he was right into the other man's face, eye-to-eye, and he saw the bright blue eyes and white skin of the Yankee, a thin, graceful face, mouth open . . . .

He struck the butt of the gun at the man's chest, and the other tried to block him by hanging onto it. But he managed to get the point of the bayonet close enough to catch. It hit against the U.S. belt buckle, and he pressed, leaning onto it, his feet sliding in the mud.

There . . . push . . . damn you! He was frantic, sliding around, raging. He had to step back and jerk at it before he could get it loose, and the Yankee dropped forward, holding his belly, until he knelt in the mud.

Godalmighty, he wanted to get rid of a hundred of them just like that! Stick them on the point of the bayonet, drive his way through them back to Fairburn, back to the Chattahoochee, back to Tennessee, back the whole way they had come in the spring, just like a rug rolling up!

Byron came after him, struggling in the vines and almost fell over the Yankee still kneeling on the mudbar holding his innards, looking down vaguely.

"Watch it," he told Byron, "the sonofabitch's not dead!"

Ahead of them the Yankees had been rooted out by their charge and were wading across to the far side. They were driving them across!

"C'mon, God, it's working!" he yelled to Byron.

They plunged through the water after the retreating bluecoats, kicking up a spray.

"Yuh, yuh," Byron panted. It sounded funny. The whole think was funny, crazy funny . . . running and splashing and chasing the Yankees through the water. He started to yell. Yankees were running all along the river. If they didn't stop, if they didn't run into reserve lines or some fool with guts enough to rally and make a stand. . . .

He felt as though he could run, chasing them, for as far as was needed . . . three, four miles—hell, forever!

And on the other side was home.

Clear them out! Drive 'em across.

Eeeeeeeeeeeeeeeaaaaaaaaaaaaaaaaaahhhhhhhhhhhiiiiieeee!

It spun out of his mouth like a thread.

Hardly anybody was yelling like that, they didn't have breath to, as hard as they were running. Only a few Texans, farther off, down by the bridge.

Now they were in the river itself, between the ridges, hidden in the greenest, coolest part. The bluecoats had got across, a scattering line in the last of the swamp trees, hiking for higher ground. Some of them were already re-forming out on the first rise, among the pines. They could see them running and slipping and sliding on the brown pine-needle carpet. They were all the way across, on the far side of the river.

Johnny dropped to his knees in the last edges of the swamp, and Byron dropped down beside him, holding his gun in his lap.

"I saw a snake!" Byron was shaking all over with excitement. "Damned thing in a bush right in my face!" He dropped his cartridge into the mud and started to pick it up.

"Don't do that. It's wet!" He was not too calm himself, coughing and gasping for lack of breath.

Byron threw it away and got another.

Somebody came crashing upon them from behind. They put up their arms automatically, to ward him off.

"Aaaaaaaaaar," he yelled, passing them. A big Texan, hat pulled down to his nose.

They were late; everyone was getting ahead of them. They scrambled up and ran.

They could hardly find the rest of the company in the swamp trees, and some of them were already up the far slope into a pinewoods, making for higher ground. The ground sloped up sharply on the west side of the river, the edging of pinewoods and then grassy clear ground beyond that and right at the top, at the crest of the ridge, somebody's rail fence. There was another rise above this, the escarpment of the river gorge, but this was too far to see; all that was visible was this straight-up slope and the sky beyond it. There was a racket as though the first lines of the company had come upon entrenchments. They saw Company B, or a part of it, lying down in the edge of the pinewoods, firing. They ran up the last of the way and flopped down beside them, the hot, drier air of the woods enveloping them immediately.

"Where's Ed?" Johnny shouted.

"Up yar." It was one of the Dixon boys, pointing with his chin. "See him?"

Ed Grimes was lying in the open grass and weeds above them, near the corner of the fence.

He couldn't tell what they were firing at up there. Nothing to be seen.

It was useless for him to fire at nothing, unless he edged up on his belly closer to them, to get sight of whatever was holding them down up there.

"Whup!" Dixon said, slapping at his leg as though he had been stung.

"Aw c'mon up there," Byron shouted. "Let's pull up," he cried to Johnny, bending his face close.

Dixon was looking down at his leg.

"Where'd that come from?"

He had a hole in his leg, bluish, and slightly leaking blood.

They looked at each other. It wasn't a stray spent ball; it couldn't be. Dropping from the air it would not hit hard enough to make a hole in the calf of Dixon's leg.

They turned their heads cautiously. Someone was firing at them, fast, too, with none of the usual irregular pauses to reload. The dust was kicking up around them, across their legs.

"Sweet Jesus," Byron said, and squirmed to one side. "Where's it comin' from?"

Johnny ducked his head, and looked out across his forearm. To the right, that was where it was coming from. The woods had muzzle flames in a line of persimmon bushes and scrub pine trees slightly right and back of them. They were getting a cross fire. A restless hot wind was blowing across the tops of the pine trees over their heads, the needles soughing and whispering, branches cracking and groaning, breaking up the patches of sun which fell across their faces. And yet there was no real breeze. All was hot and still.

"Say," Byron shouted close to his face.

"I see it." The feeling of a few minutes before, the exhilara-

259

tion, leaked out of him and was replaced by the familiar flat, deadly caution of things gone wrong. The sputter of the bullets across the dirt had changed it.

"Don't pull back," Dixon begged, his eyes wide. "My brother's up with Ed."

Bobby Hart, lying near the fence, lifted his bugle to his lips and blew a rallying call.

"Hell, come off, Hart!"

"Captain, pull back, we're too far up!"

Some of the boys up near the fence turned their heads to look back. Down at the bridge on their left the Texans were still trying to drag the captured Yankee guns to the east bank. Shells from somewhere on the ridge had found them, and the range of the guns was lowering, chopping the thick heads of the trees in the swamps, trying to pin them down. The water splashed like geysers on both sides of the bridge, but the Texans were still working with the guns, shouting and yelling.

"What're we doing over here?"

"We ought to be back across the river."

More of them turned around to look. They were not high enough on that side to clear the trees of the riverbottom and look across to where they had started from, and the heavy gunpowder smoke, which had drained into the depression of the riverbed, was now rising like a cloud, drifting in between. There were some small fires already burning in the dry canes, and in the sky invisible flashes of cannon shook the air. There was a lot of smoke upstream, where Lee's charge should have been made.

They had charged straight across, diverted attack, and what the boy back on the field had said was right: the rest of the attack had closed the gap. They were stranded.

Oh Jesus Christ, he raged. Oh Jesus Christ!

Some of Granbury's officers had galloped onto the bridge down there, urging the Texans back across with them. Their bugles were blowing for a withdrawal. But it was not so simple up where they were; there was no bridge behind them, and Ed Grimes was still lying up near the rail fence, Bobby Hart with him, Bobby with his bugle to his lips. Couldn't even tell, in all the racket, what call he was blowing, but it was the wrong one, whatever it was. If they would only turn their heads up there and look back . . . .

And he knew his fool cousin would not look back, no matter what.

"Bobby!" Byron shouted. "Heeeeeooooo, dammit, up there!"

It was no use. But just a moment afterward they saw Bobby's head snap up and his body make a half-turn as though to roll over and look up at the sky. The bugle fell out of his hand up there and turned over twice and lay in the comfortless bosom of a clump of fennel and maypop weeds, glittering brightly. Bobby's knee was up, his arms flung out, his head arched back, and his tow hair like burst dandelion drift against the ground.

More than anything else, this was past belief. No one, not even Bobby Hart, had a right to have this happen to them when they were only fifteen years old. Nothing happened to anyone when they were fifteen years old.

They saw Ed move to Bobby and shake him, looking down into his face, not believing it, either. And then, head lifted, finally looking back down to them in the pinewoods. Dixon's brother was not far behind them, the rest of the company strung out on their stomachs, held down by the bullets.

Johnny saw Ed Grimes take Bobby under the arms and try to lift him, but the carbines in the trees had him in their sights; the dirt began to pop. He kept dragging Bobby, sliding back, trying not to lift up any more than was necessary. A bullet hit Bobby's face, and they all winced, watching it, another hit Ed, punching him in the back, under his arm.

Johnny got up on his hands and knees, the rifle dragging under him.

261

"Get up damn you," he yelled to Byron, and Byron got up, frightened, his face white, and followed after him. They scrambled up toward the fence, digging their hands and toes into the dirt, and when they got to them Ed had let Bobby go, lying with his face in the pine needles.

They were on enough of a slope to slide them; the pine carpet was slick. They took their feet and backed, crawling on their stomachs, pulling them after them: there was no time to get their rifles. Down the slope they went, feet first, with Bobby and Ed by their feet, heads bouncing.

The rest of the company was sliding back down too into the thicker woods, turning to fire and reload and fire as they went, rolling over to reload, their rifles held across their stomachs and chests.

You bastards. Dirty, stinging, chopping bastards from somewhere in the shining cover of persimmon leaves and rattling pine scrub.

They kept inching back, dragging Ed and Bobby with them down a gully and a slithering, draining gulch of a dry wash thick with brambles and fallen branches. There was not much cover in a pinewoods where the naked brown trunks rose about them like pillars. What they needed was the safety of the canes in the swamp. Around them a few strayed Texans and what was left of the original charge moved backward also, some crawling on their hands and knees to keep below the fire that popped away without stopping, a regular rat-a-tat that hit the tree trunks as though it was going to whittle them through. Tom Norse went down on his back and started jumping, snatching at his belt as though his belly was on fire.

Hains and Sharp fell before they got into the trees. Sharp was mad and scared, shouting at the top of his voice. He had dropped his gun. Cleatus Mann was dead, lying on the ground. They moved around him. Pringle and Fitzgerald were dead up by the fence. Manson McLendon was hit, dragging his leg. Asa Metts was wounded and somebody was

262

trying to help him crawl along. Peed had not even come across the river. And Ed Grimes was down and Bobby Hart was wounded.

God, no end to it. He didn't see how he had missed getting hit in that cross fire. And Byron, too. He looked for Dixon and could not find him. They had lost him somehow.

Dead were lying all over the woods, brought down by the damned repeating carbine fire. Dorsey Orr and Tom Norse were down here, lying together, both dead and bloody.

One of the lieutenants from the Texas company was standing in a brown, needle-carpeted gully.

"Back, back," he was saying to them. "Get across the river."

"Come on, Lieutenant, I'll help you."

He was wounded, using a pine branch as a crutch.

"No. No, go on. I'm coming in a minute."

Byron stopped and got to his knees.

"No use dragging Bobby," he cried. "He's dead. Look at his face."

He pulled Ed to a stop. They slid into the gully with the lieutenant, thankful for its cover. Ed's nose was bleeding.

He bent down over his cousin and looked into his face and put his hand around to the back of his head to see if he had a head wound to make his nose bleed like that.

"You busted my nose," Ed told him. "Draggin' me over a big old rock." He put his hand up to his nose and moved the tip of it in a circle. "Ouch. See there?"

"Oh hell, Ed," he said; any other time he would have laughed "Where're you hit?" He would not put it past him not to be hit at all, even though he thought he had seen the bullet strike him somewhere in the back.

"I don't know." Their faces were close enough so that they did not have to shout to be heard; Ed's voice was almost a whisper. "Wherever it is, it don't hurt none. Around in the back, I guess."

Johnny put his hand under him and pressed the middle of his back, between the shoulder blades. He hoped he was

263

wrong. But there was the hole, alright. His fingers felt it, soft and vacant, the stickiness spreading out. The hole was right under his shoulder blade. The shirt was wet below it, and a lot of wetness all the way down, on his belt, and the top of his trousers was slick.

"Poor old Bobby," he heard Byron say.

"Well, quit looking at him. You ain't going to raise the dead that way. Turn him over on his face."

He did not want to look at Bobby, either, not with his jaw all gone and his eye bored through.

The lieutenant in the gully suddenly eased himself down as though he was tired, pushing the pine branch crutch away from him, sighing. He half-slid against the side of the cut and then folded on his haunches, his eyes dull. He put his head back against the bank and closed his eyes. Johnny lifted his head to look at him. It was just as if he had gone to sleep, tired out.

He was dead, too.

"God," Byron shouted, looking white and strained. "We got to get out of here. Everybody's near gone."

"Help me carry Ed."

"Well alright." He sounded impatient, doubtful, and kept looking around as though the emptiness of the place bothered him more than the danger. "But let's hurry, hear?"

As still as it was where they were, in the patch of pine-woods through which the gully ran and disgorged its flow of dry needles downward toward the swamp, the air could have been noiseless. Nothing seemed to move except the soughing pine heads and the occasional whine and cut of the bullets. The gully itself was a vacuum of stillness.

On the other side of the river the roaring went on, creation tearing itself apart and shredding the day into strips, maddening and earsplitting, belching black powder which flowed into the riverbottom like spilled ink. They could barely see the bridge now; the guns were nearly all off it, and there were just a few skirmishers lying down in the vine-tangled flats on either side of the banks, firing away up the west slope, receding in the powder fog as though fading into night.

In the peculiar stillness they started down the open end of the gully toward the riverbed, holding up Ed between them, his arms thrown over their shoulders. They were not as tall as he, and he dragged his feet helplessly and kept them off balance. They stumbled and nearly fell, lurching through the narrow shoulders of the cut. Byron stepped into a hole covered with pine needles and lost his balance, letting Ed go and falling forward on his elbows, sliding into a tree, knocking his head against it. For a minute he was so hazy he could not get back up.

Johnny cursed him with everything he could think of. Byron seemed to be drifting away from him, and he could not make him listen or do what he wanted him to.

"I didn't know we had come up this far," Byron said stupidly. "Doesn't seem right. Where are we?"

"Almost to the river, dammit. Get up and help me!"

"Why is it so dark?"

"Smoke, damn you—you fool. Don't act like you don't know what you're doing. You want to kill us? I can't hold this fool jackass cousin of mine up forever waiting on you . . . ." He had had to catch Ed around the waist to keep him from falling, but it was like a woman grabbing at a big, helpless child which threatened to win out by sheer weight. He felt himself going down, still holding. I can't drop him, he thought desperately.

"Let's see if there's somebody down the river that can help us," Byron said feverishly. He started to scramble off on all fours.

"Goddamn you . . . don't you go off!" He knew how helpless he was without Byron and he wanted to kill him, if he could get his hands on him. He would kill him for sure if he went off and left him with Ed Grimes. "We can do it, if you'll just give me a hand."

Byron turned and put his hand up to his face. Johnny saw his mouth grimace, moving the beard and the thick line of his mustache. All the dapper, quick nonchalance was gone; Byron was scared and looked scared, and it did not flatter him any.

"Well . . . alright Johnny, . . ." he didn't look at him. "You stuck with me, I guess I ought to stick with you . . . ."

"You're goddamned right!" He did not have any sympathy for him.

If you fly off now, I'll kill you, he thought. I'll find you later and kill you, you slick, cowardly little devil.

But Byron was crawling back. He wouldn't look up at him but he was coming back.

"Don't hear so many balls hittin' trees," he said, half to himself. He tried to smile through the ragged black beard, his eyes still not looking at Johnny. "Ain't so thick down here . . . ."

And when he was almost up to them he seemed to catch in the midst of a step, still bent over cautiously, and something hit him with a crack like a board being split by an axe.

"Whoa, . . ." Byron said. He touched his chest.

"Byron." He couldn't do anything. He tried to hold Ed on his feet, staring at him.

Byron's eyes pushed out, his chin pointed forward, straining and pointing, and he slid forward on it, flat out on his belly all the way, his hand almost touching Johnny's foot as though reaching for something.

The fire was behind him, and above them, and he didn't stop to think more about it; he shook Ed off, fall or no fall, and heard him hit the ground hard and groan. He dived forward just as Byron had done and rolled out of the tail of the gully and down a little bit and kept rolling till he landed in a stand of blackberries and on until he was half under a holly bush.

Stopped, he lay dead still. He had his gun, thank God, he had not let go of it. But he did not move.

He was just as still and motionless as the leaf-shaped piece of sunshine falling beside him on the brown pine needles.

"Is that one over there dead?" a thin voice up high said.

The voice seemed to come from the tops of the trees, looking down.

"Don't know." Another voice just like it spoke, thin and resonant.

"Watch your step, Bill. I thought there was another one around here someplace."

The voices stopped and waited, and there was nothing for awhile but the roar on the far side of the river.

"Can you see?" the high-up voice said.

"Wait a minute."

They did not say anything for a good long while.

Johnny lay back as straight as he could, pressed against the earth and closed his eyes tight as though that would keep him from being seen. The last unbroken stalks of the blackberries under him snapped and jiggled, all the little hooks stabbing through his skin.

CHAPTER 18

❧❧ *Oh, band in the pinewood cease!*
Cease with your splendid call!
The living are brave and noble,
But the dead are the bravest of all.

He could not tell, lying there partly under the holly bush,
how early or late it might be, for the powder smoke had
crept not only into the riverbottom but now overflowed it
and lapped up the slope toward the pine trees. It might be
any time. God knows he had no way of estimating time on a
day like this.

The blasting and shrieking on the other side of the river
were still going on. The noise of battle waned at times and
then came back louder than ever, but it never stopped.

He looked up into the arms of the pine branches above
him, and the iron sky looked back with no clue as to how
things were going on over on the far slope.

They should have driven the Yanks back into the river by
now considering the way the first charge went off. If everybody all along the whole corps front had charged the way
Company B and those Texans had, the damned left wing of
the Federal army must be scampering back for Fairburn.
But he doubted it. A queer cautious dread like pine smoke
hung in that forest. Everything was empty.

The enemy could have been driven off northward in front
of Lee's corps. He wanted to believe that. He wanted to
believe something after the hoorah that had swept them all
across to land over there.

It was hot and empty as the devil now.

A cicada was scraping and whirring in the drowsiest, summeriest sort of way, enough to make a person sleepy, except for the sharpshooters. They were still somewhere about. He hadn't heard from them in a long time and it had been pretty quiet, but once he had heard some voices going along by the rail fence in Babb's pasture. There was the sound of firing down at the bridge, but he couldn't tell how the Texans were making out. He didn't dare move. He was lying flat on his back with no place to look but up, and the moving tops of the pine trees kept spilling bits of light and shadow into his eyes. He felt as though he had been lying out there long enough to put down roots into the ground.

After awhile he heard something rustling like a snake's dry belly over the pine needles. He hated snakes. Just the sound or thought of anything like a snake made him break out in a sweat. He kept himself rigid as a board.

Nine times out of ten, he told himself, it won't be a snake at all, but just a bird scratching around in the pine straw looking for grubs.

A whisper, "Is anybody there? Johnny?"

Oh for God's sake!

It was Ed. He couldn't answer him for he didn't know where those sharpshooters were and Ed ought to know it.

But the noise continued to rustle and scratch and in a few seconds his cousin's hand came crawling along by itself, right into his face.

"That you, Johnny?"

Damn him.

"Johnny?"

He had to answer him or the next thing, he'd be hollering out loud enough for the whole Union army to hear.

"WHAT?"

"They're gone off. Johnny, you hear me?"

"God, who can't! Be still, can't you?"

"I saw two of them get down out of the trees up there and go off. There was a bunch of bluebellies movin' along up there by the fence, and they got down and went off with them. I guess they thought we was all dead."

Ed was right. With the racket they had been making, they would have had some sort of answer by now.

He pulled up on one elbow, surprised at the pain. He was full of blackberry stickers, there must be a thousand hooks if there was a one, and blood through his shirt where the things had raked him.

There was Ed, lying on his belly where he had left him, his face thrust forward anxiously, looking. A lot of blood had formed in a puddle under him, and he looked pretty bad. His broken nose had swelled up like a doughball between his eyes.

"You hurt any?" Ed whispered.

Johnny was busy trying to pick some of the blackberry hooks out of his hide with his fingernails. The damned things hurt like the devil when he moved, a lot more than they ought, considering their size.

"No," he answered. "Just stickers. I dived for that patch like a jack rabbit. It must have hid me pretty fair."

"And I guess I looked pretty dead," Ed said, and grinned.

"You look alright," he told him.

"No I don't. You ain't beautified me in any way. Look what's happened to my nose."

"Listen," Johnny said, mostly to change the subject. "When dark comes I'll get you down to the river. We'll get back across tonight. I think the charge's swung off to the right somewhere, but we're not so far from town. There's a hospital back in town. Maybe two, by now. You know about where we are over here, so you know where we've got to go. If I can get you up on my back, it won't be so hard."

"Why, boy, you can't carry me. Stretched out, I'd make two of you."

"I'll carry you. You just wait and see."

"Well, you didn't do so good comin' down the slope. Knocked my nose half off and spoiled my good looks."

270

He wished there was some way to get Ed turned off the subject. It rubbed him raw.

"I can carry you now, if you want," he said stubbornly. "Right now. We don't have to wait for dark if you don't want to."

He leaned over and took Ed's arm to haul him up and show him, and in an instant Ed's mouth turned a somersault, upside down, and the cords stood out on his neck. But he didn't make a sound. A red, pear-shaped drop of blood appeared at one nostril and rolled down his lip.

"Lord," Ed said with an effort, "that hurts a mile."

He had never seen his cousin look like that in his life. He looked like a different person, quick and agonized, not like Ed at all.

"What's the matter with you?" he said.

"Nothin'." Ed tried to smile. "Just can't haul me around, I guess."

"It's just a graze," he said stiffly. "It's not much of anything."

"Yes, it is too," Ed said, still smiling. "You don't have to jolly me. I felt it when it hit. Must have come in under my shoulder blade. Its going to raise hell in there, too. I feel like I can't get any air into one side. Lord, wouldn't you know I'd get a hole bored through my back? Shot in the back! I swear, after all I been through, that's a mighty pee-poor way to end up. Think of what folks'll say."

In spite of Ed's words and the half-smile which, ghostlike, lingered between them, he had a perfect horror of what was coming. He had been through it all before with MacAllister and he couldn't go through it again. Not with Ed.

"Don't be a damned fool," he said, and had to turn his face partly away as it was crumpling up, ready to do strange things.

"You don't have to stay here," Ed said. "You can go. You can go back across the river and get somebody to come and get me with a litter. You can come right back with them, too, to show them the way. That's the smartest thing to do, bar none."

"No," he said, "I guess I'll stay. You'll feel better after a bit, and we'll try then."

The lie did no good. It was only embarrassing.

"You better go, sure enough," his cousin said urgently. "You better go."

"What's the matter?"

"Nothing . . . why, whups!" A burst of red blossomed from Ed's nose like a huge flower and rushed down his mouth and chin. Ed began to sputter and gag. Rivulets of blood ran down into the creases of his neck, and the main flow onto his jacket front. He looked as though he was drowning in a bright red river.

The sight of it sent Johnny to scratching about, opening Ed's jacket and trying to mop up the corners, but nothing helped. Blood was all over both of them, slippery and sticky. Ed coughed, and his hands grabbed Johnny's wrists to hang on.

"That's it," Johnny cried. "Hold on, hear?" He mopped around in the mess, doing nothing to help, working frantically. "Just keep your windpipe clear, can you?"

When all the time they both knew it was no use.

"Ah," Ed gurgled. He coughed, spraying blood through his nose. "Well, can't say I didn't . . . make a mess . . . whuf, Johnny, . . . help . . . ."

"Ed, stop it!" he cried.

" 'S alright, 'm alright," Ed said, and gave up. He tried to smile again.

Ed just gave a wheezing noise and lay back in his arms. One of his hands relaxed, let go, and fell to rest against Johnny's knee, and he was dead.

Johnny let go of him, let him fall back against the pine needles, and Ed's hand went with him, settling by Johnny's foot.

The only thing Johnny knew was that his mouth opened

as if to cry out in rage and horror and nothing happened. He could feel his neck muscles straining and his eyes staring but nothing came out and God knows there was some shriek of agony deep down inside that wanted to roar up and tear half his innards away with it.

He wanted to clear out of that place fast but he couldn't get away for the life of him, he was frozen fast. He was held down, nailed down right where he was, kneeling beside dead Ed Grimes when what he wanted most was to get up and go. He knew if he had the power in him right at that moment he would have been up, legs churning under him, to crash into the woods and persimmon bushes and blackberry briars to go roaring and yelling and howling away in the dark.

Help, Ed had said.

Poor old Ed Grimes, who would never say a thing like that, not at all.

But God, there was none of them now that could help each other. They were all gone.

His neck and back held him like iron rods, against his will, and for a long time he couldn't even draw a breath, gripped in that silent, frozen scream that would not come out. When the first air came into his lungs it wracked him enough to make him feel like he was going to split in two.

Bobby and Byron and Peed and Walt Ashford he could believe, but never Ed! Never Ed Grimes. The whole company had said that when the war was over Ed Grimes would still be there, still having one hell of a good time and twice as well off as anybody. It just wasn't so. But then it wasn't going to be so, any of it. It was all over, done with. Any fool could see that.

In spite of his terrible frozenness he found he could bend over and, by some sort of duty, look at his cousin and pull Ed's jacket together and make sure his eyes were shut. That much he could do for Ed, although he didn't know why he did it at all. He was dimly surprised that he had done it or felt that it needed doing.

273

He wiped his hands against his shirt afterward to get rid of the blood. Lord, it was awful—all that blood! It was the worst awful mess he had ever seen. Ed's blood was all over his pants and the front of his shirt and where his shirt hung open, buttonless, all over his skin.

He had blood all over him and couldn't get rid of it until he got to some water. He didn't know if he could stand it that long.

Oh Jesus, he was sick of it! He was mortally, mortally sick of it—he was about to bust with the misery and sickness inside of him. It was about to tear him apart.

He looked down at Ed and saw that his cousin's face did not look like Ed at all, the flesh was falling away and the brow was bare and the nose ugly and the teeth glistening through lis lips. Ed's face had the sharp, pale look of death like all the others he had seen. This was not Ed at all, just another damned corpse left out to rot in the sun.

He dusted his hands against his shirt trying to get rid of the feeling that the skin between his fingers was sticking together. He got to his knees and picked up his hat from the ground and got the Whitworth and once he found he was moving, he kept going.

He slid down the gully and scrambled along hoping to get up enough speed in his slow, paralyzed legs to break out and run. The pine trees thinned farther down the slope, and the swamp forest was ahead with the black gunpowder smoke like a veil. It was so dark and thick down there the place just swallowed him up.

CHAPTER 19

🙰🙰 *"Ah, I tell you brother, hell is a pit full of fire and lakes of steaming melted rock. Great pillars of fire are there brother, and souls in torment in the everlasting fire, and sinful flesh suffers in the flames and smoke, and there are red and yellow spouts of brimstone higher than the eye can see!"*

Johnny knew it now. He'd felt it, even at the time, the evening that the old Baptist preacher had hollered and blown, looking over the heads of most of the citizens of Jonesboro, that it wasn't true. He knew then it wasn't true. But now he knew what hell was. He had been there firsthand and he ought to know. Hell was not bright at all, but dark as sin and night and ankle-deep in water, and hot and stinking and what makes it hell is that you can't see a thing, not your hand before your face, and every now and then something goes plop, into the water, and you wonder what it is, is it a snake or some broken branch that's fallen or a man standing there you don't know about or a spent ball or the dead walking, and you keep moving and wading along because you ought to know where you're going but you don't and you keep twisting things off your face that have fallen against it and vines that have come up to catch you around the throat so that you have to back up and start off again and get turned around, wrong way, going nowhere.

Oh, there's fires all right, but the fires in hell are only campfires with strangers high up on the banks that don't see you, don't hold no good for you, don't know you are there, don't care whether you are alive or dead, it's nothing to them.

And dark things lying in the water that turn out to be a dead horse with its bowels torn out that you had to go and put your feet on before you knew it was there, slipping and sliding in all that coiling stuff and trying not to yell or scream, trying to get out of it quick, God, oh quick!

And turtles and snakes in the big swamp, the one that's backed up from the beaver dam, with trees standing in the water like columns and cool light showing down in streaks through the blackness of the smoke.

And dead men, why there's a perfect lake of dead men in hell if you know where to find them, lying out in the water farther up where the trees shut over . . . dead men floating about by themselves in water just deep enough to lift them, turning around and around in the dark until they catch up on some snag and hold. And big iron cannon balls lying there by themselves in the water and all sorts of things like canteens and rifles and hats and the big white crackers the Yankee army issues for bread.

And the watchman, he's the proprietor of hell, to come up on him sitting in a pool of muffled light that might be moonlight coming through the smoke and mixing with the mist that is rising from the water, sitting on a stump holding his gun across his knees, and say to him, MY GOD!

And then, quick out, Are you Reb?

And he doesn't answer back, because he's dead.

He must have cried out and struck out somehow or perhaps the dead man went over of his own accord, stiff as a stone, into the water. But it was as much as he could stand, and he heard his own voice keening out, hoarse and thin, and he went struggling away as fast as he could with the mud underfoot like deep silk, pulling and sucking at him and squirting between his toes. He was trying to get away so hard, he pumped his arms from side to side like pendulums

276

to help him go since his feet seemed to be doing the most they could to hold him back. When he had got out into the stream where it was deep he fell down and went under, and came up in a little while with his ribs fit to burst, and couldn't do more than just lay back against the dark water, holding onto his gun with both hands, letting the current pull him back downstream again.

When he had hit a shallow place he stopped and dragged up on one of the bars between the channels and crawled on all fours until he was out of water and threw the gun ahead of him, and then fell down in the mud and cold leaves that smelled of wet and dust and mold all together, and the frogs that had been wailing like banshees stopped dead, to have him right on top of them, sharing the same mudbar.

Then he started up in a fearful rage and flung himself against a tree and hit his shoulder, and it was so damned dark he couldn't tell which way he was going at all. He had to go back to the stream and wade out and put his hand in the water to feel which way the current was going. Upstream or downstream, black as night, everything under here.

Along the bank somebody said, "What was that?"

And he stopped.

"Hey, you out there, Reb or Union?"

And he tried to move himself along with only the slurring of the water against his body to make any sound.

"Can't see a damned thing. God, don't it stink out here with all this smoke?" the voice said.

He passed them.

He was in the clear for awhile and then he came up against some brush and logs caught in a big snag in midstream and when he tried to climb over instead of going around, he got his foot caught on the far side. He went up and down, and then into a mess of branches and twigs like a trap. He got his foot out, panting and cursing and fell over in the water again and went under, deep down under in a hole of some sort.

Why don't you drown and get it over with, he told himself.

Ah, do you think I'm crazy, he answered, this close to home?

Right in the trees, there was somebody frightened at the noise.

"Halt. Who goes there?"

And whurrang! came a shot without waiting for an answer.

"What's the trouble?" a voice called.

"Somebody out there, Lieutenant."

"Well, keep them on the other side."

"But it's over here, this side, wading along."

They brought a light down from the bank.

He kept wading away from them. After this, there was no one, and the noises groaned away until they either stopped or he did not notice them enough to make it matter. It was still, and he had a long, dark way to go and after a while he had gone so long a time without hearing something, he thought he might have dreamed away a part of it and be out beyond the town, just wandering through the creeks all by himself.

But then there was another, deeper, wider pool, bent trees dragging in the stream and dark along the banks. And suddenly the water gurgled up.

"Where you goin', boy?" it hissed.

"Who's that?" He could not see, it was all black and gleaming water and the trees.

"Secesh. You, secesh?"

He still could not find him. He sounded right in his face, and yet he wasn't.

"Lowrey's" he said, and his voice had gotten somewhat thicker and huskier, the way it ought to be, instead of fearful and high as before.

"Hmmm," the thing said. "Wal, that's good for you, I

278

guess. That's my gun pointed right at your belly button. Feel it?"

"Go to the devil," he told him.

There was a chuckle.

"Don't scare?"

"Don't care."

"You lost on purpose?"

"No, not on purpose. Not on purpose, I guess."

Their dark whispers struck the leaves and the smoking mist and whispered back.

"I'm going home," he said, and thought about it.

"Aw, you ain't neither!"

"The hell I ain't."

"You're crazy, that's what. Why, they's Yanks on both sides down here, ain't you seen them? You'un me's stuck in a big old swamp, Flint River they call it, with Yankees on both sides like biscuit around butter."

He did not want to stand there in the water, talking with somebody he could not see.

"How do you know they're on both sides?"

"I come down with Granbury's, got cut off in that charge. Been sittin' here in the mud waitin' for somebody to come chasin' off the Yanks and pick me back, been listenin' to those Yanks talk, and seein' them, while there was still light."

"You didn't try to get back?"

"Why, the whole damned 16th Corps of Howard's is in the way. Course's. You know old Course? Goddamned if they ain't played hell. But not like Lowrey did. When Lowrey's division charged, we went off and left Cleburne and the rest, chasin' that dismounted cavalry and split the field. And Lee got stuck up yonder and never did go. We ain't moved those Yanks one bit."

"Did they . . . did the Yanks get into town?"

"Don't know. Reckon not, or they'd be movin' over there tonight. But they will tomorrow. Hardee's only got twenty thousand men down here, and anybody that was out on that hill yesterday can see the whole Yankee army's piled up in this here river. We won't hold 'em long enought to do more'n let Sam Hood give up Atlanta and skedaddle. We're whipped. You stick right along the bank here, you can listen for them Yanks comin' down for water. They all talk about it. They say they got us now."

"No," he said. "Hardee won't pull off."

"I didn't say he'd pull off, did I? There'll be some fightin' tomorrow, but it won't be for no good use. You just wait'n see."

He knew the voice was right.

"Say, what's your name?"

"Whut's yours?"

There was a silence, filled with their mutual distrust.

"It don't matter none," the voice said blandly, after a while. "You ain't no Yank, leastways, not with that drawl."

"I got to go on," he said uneasily. They had made too much noise, even deserted and dark as this place was.

"Alright. Which way you goin'?"

He hoped it was in the opposite direction from the other.

"Upstream. My house's somewhere up here."

"Mmm," the voice said. "Well, I reckon I'll set here a spell. I ain't in no hurry. I ain't made up my mind yet."

So that was what was the matter. He wanted to get away from him.

"I'm going," he said, and moved upstream a little.

The voice did not answer, and after he had carefully gone a few yards he gave up all pretense of quiet and splashed away, as fast as he could go.

He thought he had gone a long way, but he hadn't; it was only time running itself out with incredible slowness, and the sucking, impeding pull of water and mud that made it seem like he was accomplishing something when he wasn't. Once, he sat down in the mud and held his head in his hands and thought despairingly of what the unknown voice had said about the battle, and knew it was true and yet could not bring himself to think of what would become of them now, the war and all the rest, the town and himself, and Anna and Matt beyond him on the hill. And right in the midst of it he interrupted his own thoughts with the sudden memory of Byron and Tom Norse lying out in the pinewoods in the dark at that very moment, and how he had not thought to cover them up or do anything for them to show that they had once been his friends, to help them, now that they were dead. And it affected him the same way as it had when he realized that Ed was dead; he put his hands across his face and felt it grimace, but nothing happened. He was drained dry.

Farther up, groping at the edge of the stream, he found a bridge where there had been no bridge before, a pontoon bridge. A great deal of fallen trash, timber, and logs lay on each side of it. He heard a wagon rumbling and, remembering sentries, crouched down in the water as the wheels passed him right at eye-level, and the bobbing lanterns spattered light into his face.

He could not chance going under the bridge. Talk about drowning, he told himself, that would be the best way to do it yet, to try and squeeze under the pontoons or between them, and get stuck, never to be found until somebody pulled up the whole contraption.

So he waited, and after awhile he worked around to the right and crept on his hands and knees along the mudbars and cane thickets until he was on higher ground, and then cut past a campfire, close enough to hear them talking, and then back again, feeling for the water. Then he was back into the canes. The stuff made an awful racket. The leaves were getting old and dry with late summer. He waited, inching along, sometimes on his knees. Once, he thought of throwing away the Whitworth, but could not bring himself to do it.

Then all of a sudden the place was alive and moving with enough noise to scare him silly. A crashing started up behind

281

him, and before he knew what was coming a drove of hunching, scurrying things came past going urgh! urgh! urgh! and bullets started flying through the trees. He could hear them ricochet and whang off into the dark.

He fell down and hugged the ground.

"Goddamn, did you hear that?" a voice cried shrilly.

"A whole bunch of them!"

"Sergeant, over here! This way!"

BAM, BAM, BAM!

"It's pigs, I swear it's pigs, a whole bunch of them!"

PIGS! Great God above!

He got up to scramble out of there but he could not get out of the pigs; they were all around him and under him and he was going to trip over them if he didn't get rid of them, or get shot. A big old sow took his bare heel in her mouth and rooted at it, and he nearly yelled. He rammed through a veil of honeysuckle and had his feet snatched out from under him and hung there as the pigs went by, leaving him swinging in a net of honeysuckle vines.

Right behind them, he could hear the shouters, their Yankee voices thin and oblivious.

"Pigs! Pigs! Pigs, Sergeant!"

"You pickets," a voice bellowed, "come back here!"

But the others were already far off. "Pigs, pigs," they were still shouting, and firing up toward the other side of the stream.

He lay back, shivering, in his honeysuckle hammock.

The whole pig business had scared him so badly it had torn his nerves clean out of him. Where he had been jittery and driven before, now he was slower, calmer, and could feel how tired he was. That's what he would have to keep in mind from now on: how to keep going without getting tired and careless. To make sure, he went over in his mind how to get close to home by coming up through the swamps and how to swing around so as to get in the back of the place, probably by Matt's cornfield.

He wiped his arm against his face and felt the mud, and discovered for the first time how muddy he was. He was a mud statue from head to toe, no skin showing, no gray shirt or pants, just mud. It was one help, anyway. It kept off all the bugs and gnats.

He lay a long time in the honeysuckle and there was no further sound, and he listened for the other voice which had shouted after the pig chasers, but nothing moved. After a while he slowly unhooked the creepers and half-fell out of them and began once more, on his hands and knees, to work back down toward the river.

But beyond the bridge there had been some heavy fighting. He was up near where Lee's corps had faced Logan's, he guessed, for the ground looked chewed over pretty badly and there were dead bodies lying piled up at every snag and tree stump. There were others like himself, wandering around, some of them groaning and muttering and some calling out, looking for their friends. He got into the river and waded out into deep water, and as long as the trees were joined overhead it was alright. But then the river opened into a clear spot, and there were people on both sides of the bank in a busy, murmurous darkness. He could not turn back. There was still a lot of powder smoke drifting on the water, but not enough to hide in, and there were the crowds lining both sides of the banks, not looking at each other or having much to do with each other, coming and going for water or sitting down on the banks groaning and trying to take care of their wounds. There was a perfect congregation of men, the right bank looking to be mostly the gray uniforms of Lee's corps and the left full of bluecoats, both careful not to look across or admit that anybody was on the far side. And of course he had to come wading along in the water right between them for them to stare at. Not at each other but at him. It was as though they couldn't see each other, only this

283

stray figure sloshing along, rifle held across his shoulders to give him balance.

He went right through them feeling that it was a dream. No one called to him, and there was no sound other than that melancholy soughing of the wounded and the muttering of men talking to themselves. It had been terrible down there. There were dead men thick as leaves all up in the mudbars and in the canes and high up in the banks, some even hanging and bobbing in the fallen tree trunks and branches in the stream, right where he had to pass.

No one called or asked him where he was going. He might have been a ghost.

Lord, he was glad to get out of there! That was the end of the world if he ever saw it. No one would ever have to paint a picture of it for him, ever again.

When at last he came out at the bridge below the house he just stood for a moment and made sure he knew it for what it was, that his eyes were not playing tricks on him. He was so tired, he had to be careful of what he was doing now, and not get careless or mistaken and see familiar things that weren't there. But it was the bridge all right. There was the road, and he had come out by it, almost on to it, without sense or strength enough to look for cover. He heard a troop of horses on the far side, and there were lights and lanterns and some Yankee officers reading something at the light, and pickets at each end of the bridge.

They didn't see him. But then no one that night was looking for a mud statue, come up out of four miles of river swamp.

A wagon load of wounded passed after the cavalry, and it stopped at the bridge and one of the pickets ran up to the horses and cried, "You can't stop here. You want the first house up there on your right. Just keep going."

And he did not realize it was his own house they were talking about.

The cargo of wounded was shrieking and crying, oh, oh, owww, oh God, and when the wagon started up again, the shrieking rose to a dreadful noise of pain. It set his teeth on edge. He stumbled across the road without caring and into the woods on the other side.

He was going home.

He was back of his house. The cleared slope of the corn-field went almost to the river on that side of the pasture and the field was fairly wide, narrowing at the top of the hill. The rows of corn were blasted and gouged. There were horses in it, he discovered . . . that was what the dark shapes were . . . horses walking and feeding in Matt's good corn.

The horses spooked and milled when he came up, but they were tied out, or hobbled, by the way they moved.

Any other time he would have been worried by the noise, but now he didn't care. He didn't care about one damned thing. His knees could just barely lift his feet clear of the furrows, pulling them up and down just enough to keep him from tripping and falling flat. If it hadn't been for the racket the horses were making, somebody surely would have heard him, crashing and sliding against the corn. As he came up the slope the smoke vanished; that damned clogging memory of guns and black powder and disaster just blew away, and the air was fresh and the stars were out in the dark sky. It was so clean and fresh so suddenly, the air so suddenly pure that everything was revealed in absolute clarity and sharpness. He saw the lights in the house, a light in every room, the place lit up like a fair, and lights in the yard, under the trees, and even lights and lanterns set out in the drive.

And campfires, there were dots of campfires all over the hill except in some parts of the corn, and all over the pasture in the grass, and in the pinewoods back of the house. There must have been hundreds of campfires. The cookfires of reserve troops, most probably, to be up here, camped around the house. There was a familiar noise mixed in—a hospital,

285

he recognized quickly, operating in the yard. There were a lot of people stirring, lights coming and going, noises and lights and people coming and going.

He didn't care. He was within sound and sight of home, all alone, coming up through the cornfield unseen. It was a damned good feeling, a wonderful feeling.

He just sprawled out in the dirt as he went, mashing the corn down with him as he fell, down in the warm, hard dirt which the heat of the sun had not yet left and which bulged up in rows and furrows, and the smell of dirt filled his nose and mouth, the holes and bumps of the earth not fitting his body at all, but he was so tired he did not care. He was there, pressing down close to the dirt, stretching out so tired and calm at last, dead calm, dead tired, stretched out, resting in his own cornfield, Matt's cornfield, home.

He flung one leg over, he felt Anna's body curled beside him and his arms, empty, around her, his legs and arms holding her, sliding off to sleep and feeling her, holding her in deep, sweet sleep.

CHAPTER 20

And when our fairhaired children
    Shall cluster round our knee
With wondering gaze, as we tell of the days
When we swore that we would be free.

It was a lost, maverick sort of day; touch of autumn was the way he had always heard it described. Right in the midst of the hottest, driest, longest part of fading summer it was not too unusual to have a cool wind blow in from the west, from somewhere in the grass-covered plains of Arkansas or Oklahoma or the Dakotas where summer was already gone, making the dawn over Georgia come in as absolutely fair and cloudless as a blue china dish with a fine crisp breeze that would make a person swear it was the middle of October or a warm, late-lingering November, when it wasn't. It was the first of September and that was all, with plenty of hot weather to come after.

The west wind scoured the sky clean and turned the white sides of the leaves up and hurried along in the dust of the roads. A pale golden shadow was in everything; the leaves of the trees were suddenly more yellow than green and the tall rank grass withered and sapless and the stems, bark, and limbs of the trees browner and older. And where there had been moths and bumblebees and butterflies in the sluggish warm air, the cool wind blew in a horde of black dusty crickets and grasshoppers the size of a man's thumb and mantis-like bugs and dirt daubers looking for a winter place to mud-in. In the still-tender shoots of Matt's elaeagnus bushes a crop of locusts were eating their fill, and the dry, businesslike breeze caught the curtains at the upstairs windows and sucked them out like white-winged birds.

From where he sat Johnny watched the curtains blowing, now and then catching in the twigs of the oak tree which spread its twigs so close to the window up there, and wondered why in the devil somebody didn't go upstairs and shut it up. But he already knew why. Matt and Anna were busy in the yard and didn't have time to attend to it, and the Yanks wouldn't let either one of them come close enough to let him tell them about it.

Right outside the back porch steps the Federal field hospital had set up its clutter, and everytime his Aunt Matt or Anna went in and out the back door they had to step over the Yankee wounded laid out, waiting their turn at the operating tables. It was getting pretty crowded toward the back of the house. A line of wagons from Course's division, which had its headquarters in the house, was parked all the way from the back porch to the barn, blocking the path, and Course's staff's mounts were tied to a line running under the old washline Matt used. Right in the middle of this a signal outpost had chosen the old pine tree, the tallest of all the trees on the hill, as their lookout post; a ladder had been nailed up the trunk leading to the highest branches which would support a man's weight, and a signal officer, somebody they called Fish, had gone up as soon as it was light enough to see across the river to the Yankee front lines. Every time a message was wigwagged from across the river Fish would write it down and drop the paper in a little sling basket and send it down to the Yankee corporal waiting at the bottom who would then deliver it to the adjutant of Course's division inside the house. Each time he got a message the corporal would have a devil of a time trying to pick his way through the hospital with its wounded lying all underfoot and then on to the porch where a bunch of regimental staffers had been standing since dawn and then inside, only to repeat the whole thing coming back. Johnny had watched him make a dozen trips.

"You feelin' alright now?" the Mississippian next to him asked.

"Fair," Johnny told him, feeling around with his fingers across his neck and the back of his head. "A little sore."

"I saw you come up," the Mississippian said, "I guess I was one of the first ones to notice, the rest of them all bein' so busy." They were sitting on the ground in the side yard opposite the dining room windows where the Confederate wounded had been told to stay, and when the Mississippian moved to make himself comfortable as he talked he moved carefully, for he had a ball in his leg and he had just managed to get the bleeding stopped. The bare leg with sprouts of wiry black hair against dead white skin rested between them like an object someone had put down for them to tend, and marvel over, the trouser rolled up past the knee.

"I said," the Mississippian continued, " 'Whut's that?' to George, here, right off, cause I couldn't make out no uniform nor color of gray or blue or nothin' like that, just mud. And I said to George, 'Whut's that?' cause I couldn't half make up my mind whether you was human or not. And you want to know somethin'? I guess everybody else was thinkin' the same thing cause I saw one of them Yankee surgeons that was still operatin' over there take one look at you and shake his head like he didn't know what it was neither, and let you pass right on. Well, damned if anybody could tell what you was, covered up with mud like that!"

George, the Kentuckian from the Orphan Brigade, who was sitting on the other side of them with one eye bandaged, leaned forward to get into the talk.

"That old dog robber that was helpin' out wasn't takin' no chances, though," he said. "He picked up a pot with that wire handle on it over yonder and hustled to you and hurled that thing smack into your neck. By the handle. I mean he hit and kept on swingin' right on past and never let go. I don't see how he held onto it, I swear I don't, for it bounced off a good bit after it struck."

He knew how hard he had been hit. They didn't have to

tell him. He knew he had been laid out like a piece of cold pork for several minutes, and it was a wonder the damned thing hadn't fractured his skull. His head still felt like it was fractured, whether it actually was or not. Whatever it had been, cookpot, boiler, what-have-you, it had come out of the sky like thunder when he wasn't even looking for any such thing. The quickness of it was just like being struck dead he guessed—one moment there and thinking and the next moment not. For some damned reason it hadn't crushed his skull or broken his neck, but that was just pure luck. He still didn't dare turn his head very far to either side, and he had a roaring bull of a headache. He even couldn't roll his eyes around too much; it hurt like the very devil. He had to keep looking more or less straight ahead and even that pretty carefully.

The wind was picking up, doing a fine imitation of November weather. A pile of bandages caught in a sudden gust came off one of the operating tables in a white flutter, and the attendant to one of the surgeons ran after them to gather them up from the ground. The old oak trees in the yard bent and soughed in their upper branches, making a noise like a great rustling bird hovering overhead.

Down the line of the drive, visible from the house, an endless column of blue-hatted troops marched by on the Fairburn–Jonesboro road, going west into town. Johnny could just see their hats and the tips of their guidons and the occasional face of a mounted officer.

"Your mamma's comin' back," the Mississippian said.

"That's not my mother, that's my aunt," he told him.

But, he told himself silently, that was not really Matt but some fat woman in a cotton dress and dirty apron with a rag tied around her head, that was all.

And this, he thought, looking about, wasn't his house, either. It ought to be, but it wasn't. It looked like it, but it wasn't. Woman and house were all someplace where the Yankee army had settled before moving on to some little town called Jonesboro which happened to be another town halfway between Atlanta and a slightly larger place called Griffin which was, in turn, a place halfway between Atlanta and Macon, the latter being quite a respectable-sized place on the railroad line that ran to Savannah and the sea.

It was all just part of another damned fight somewhere of the kind he had seen too many times, and there was the field hospital, and the house being used for staff head-quarters, and the couriers coming and going, tying their horses to the front yard trees, and the line officers con-gregated on the porch for the morning's orders, most of them red-eyed from lack of sleep and looking as though they had fortified themselves pretty heavily with oh-be-joyful before reporting in.

There he was, sitting with the Confederate wounded, a part of it all. There wasn't even a compound of unwounded prisoners anywhere about . . . a place where he rightfully belonged, only a sad clump of wounded waiting their turn, after the Yanks had taken care of their own.

The Yanks had, he guessed, just hauled him over and dumped him there because of the crack on the head. He felt it again. The skin wasn't broken, but there was a big goose egg there.

God, he hated to think what was coming! The whole thing had been a damnfool stunt, he was willing to recognize that much, but if he had it to do all over again, he didn't know that he would do it any differently. Yet he also knew he was going to pay for it. He didn't have the sort of luck that would pass this all off—encourage the whole of Course's division to just forget about it, let him go off with the wounded and not bring the subject up again.

He couldn't see Anna. She was somewhere in the house, and his Aunt Matt was at the end of the line of crepe myrtle bushes giving water to a couple of soldiers who looked pretty bad off. They couldn't even lift their heads to take the water Matt was giving them from a tin cup.

When Matt went back to the well to fill up her pitcher he saw a bluebelly guard posted there to see, most probably, that the Yanks didn't put too much of a strain on it while General Course was in the house. When Matt needed more water the guard turned the windlass for her obligingly. Once or twice, while Matt was waiting for the water to come up, she shot him a quick look to see what he was doing.

Well, he was sitting right where he had been told to sit, and he wasn't going to move. In fact, he counted himself sort of lucky to be there. There wasn't a thing wrong with him except a terrible headache from being knocked stupid a while ago and a scrape on his hand where some jasper had stepped on it out by the surgeons' tables.

What was you tryin' to do? they wanted to know the moment he had opened his eyes.

Trying to do? God knows!

He had just seen Anna standing out there in the yard, and all sense and reason had vanished. He had come crashing up from the cornfield with but one single-minded thought, and that was to put his arms around her and know she was all right.

Only before he could do it some jasper had flung a cookpot at him.

Over on the front porch of the house there was a little commotion and stir that caused some of the staffers to step back a little and one or two, sitting on the porch railing, pulled their legs out of the way. A Yankee lieutenant as natty and sharp as a jay bird came pushing his way down the front steps—somebody's aide-de-camp by the shoulder braid.

Oh God, Johnny thought, whoever he was, at that distance he looked just like Byron NeSmith! He would never see another one of those hairline mustaches again without thinking of Byron. It was still hard for him to realize Byron was dead. Byron had been alive yesterday, yesterday morning, this very time of day. Byron and he had been running on Main Street in Jonesboro.

It was just too damned soon to get used to a person being dead.

292

They were all dead, he reminded himself. Every last one of them. All the boys from Jonesboro.

Even Ed Grimes.

Somewhere over the hill in Jonesboro his Aunt Mildred was waiting for Ed to come see her as he had promised, and now somebody would have to tell her that Ed was dead. Except that there wasn't much of anybody left to carry the news. The boys from Jonesboro, most of them, were all up in the woods near Babb's pasture.

"You," a Yankee voice said.

He lifted his eyes painfully and he saw a pair of shiny new boots, black as sin, planted in front of him and there was the jaybird lieutenant all buttoned up to the chin and sparkling in the sunlight. The Yankee lieutenant's feet were braced and he was looking down his nose as if he had studied too damned many pictures of Napoleon Buonaparte.

"You reb," the lieutenant said, "stand up. You're not wounded. Are you?"

The Mississippian hurried to move his leg out of harm's way and Johnny looked around and saw he was the one being spoken to and, out of respect for the leg, got carefully to his feet. For some reason he felt awkward. The jaybird lieutenant was so confoundedly bright and shining, it made him want to pull his buttonless shirt over his belly and muster some particle of military snap from a long way back out of what he remembered it was like to have a whole suit of clothes.

"Sir," he said. He sure as hell wasn't going to salute.

"Speak up," the lieutenant told him. "I can't hear you."

"I didn't say anything," he said.

"Step out here."

He stepped out, away from the rest of the rebel wounded lying under the tree.

The lieutenant took a pencil out of his pocket and an envelope and wrote something down.

"Now I'm going to interrogate you," the lieutenant said. "You know what that means?"

"Yes," Johnny answered. Out of the corner of his eye he

293

could see a troop of Yankee cavalry cutting through Matt's field below the house, straight through the corn, looking for a ford higher up the river out of the traffic. The stalks came crashing down under the horses' hooves like falling bodies, the long leaves waving their green and yellow arms. Seeing the cavalry, he was as strangely far removed from it all and indifferent as if he had been Fish high up in the pine tree, just looking down over everything without being a part of it.

He even wondered if he was dead and if all this was a dream, if this was all a part of his last few moments on earth in which he was allowed to stay and go through a span of time in order to see Anna once more and sort of take his leave; so it wouldn't all be too sharp and severed.

The idea was so oddly appealing that he looked at the jay-bird lieutenant closely to see if he really *was* Byron NeSmith after all, for if he was, he knew damned well he was dead, they were all dead, for Byron was sure enough dead, he had seen him die.

But it wasn't Byron, it was some Yankee who looked enough like him to be his brother.

"What's your name?" the Yankee lieutenant asked him.

"John Alford MacLeod."

The lieutenant wrote this down.

"Rank? Private?"

"Private."

"Now. What division, what brigade, what regiment?"

"Cleburne's division, Lowrey's brigade . . ." here he had to stop. "Sharpshooter attached to the 1st Tennessee," he said finally. He didn't really feel as if he belonged to White's company anymore. That had all happened a hell of a long time ago.

"You're not from Tennessee," the lieutenant said. He flipped the envelope over, looked at the other side, then flipped it back again, satisfied.

"No," Johnny said.

The lieutenant looked up, impatient.

"Well, what about it?"

294

"What about what?"

"Where are you from? How'd you get into the 1st Tennessee?"

"I was attached to the 1st Tennessee," he said carefully. "I started out with the 79th Georgia. Company B, Clayton Volunteers."

"What?" the lieutenant said.

"What do you mean, what?"

"What was that about Clayton? You know what I'm talking about. Clayton County, is that it?"

"Yes."

"Well, isn't this Clayton County?" The lieutenant flung a thumb in the direction of the river.

"Yes."

"You mean you're from here. From RIGHT HERE."

"Yes."

"Speak up man, I can't hear you."

"I said yes," Johnny told him.

"That makes it very interesting," the little Yankee said. "What were you doing on this side of the river? What were you doing over here? What were you looking for?"

He had managed to pull his shirt over his bare belly and now he stood there, looking at the jaybird lieutenant who was bugging his eyes out at him as though he would bully him into saying whatever it was the lieutenant wanted to hear.

"Nothing," he told him, because he couldn't think of anything better to say.

The lieutenant made a noise of disgust.

"Corporal," the lieutenant barked without turning his head, "where's that gun?"

One of the Yankees nearby took off at a trot, returning in a matter of seconds with the Whitworth. A half dozen or so of the Yanks drew a little closer, hoping, it looked like, to see some excitement.

"It's a Whitworth," the Yankee corporal announced. "A reb sharpshooter's gun alright."

295

"I know that," the lieutenant said petulantly. The lieutenant took the gun and slapped the stock with the palm of his hand and fooled around with it, getting pretty well smeared with mud as he did so, bringing the rifle into all sorts of positions. When he tried to pull the trigger there was a small grinding noise. The chamber was full of sand and mud. The lieutenant was getting crisper and smarter; he seemed to swell about three sizes.

"You know this country around here pretty well, then," the lieutenant said.

"Yes," Johnny told him.

"Now suppose you tell me exactly where you came from."

"Here," Johnny said.

"No, no, I mean yesterday and this morning."

"The river."

"And when you came up here, what did you think you'd find?"

"Nothing."

"WHAT?"

"I didn't think about it," he muttered.

"Dammit," the lieutenant said to the corporal, "can you understand what he's saying?"

"What did you say?" the corporal asked Johnny.

"What did you ask me?"

The lieutenant handed the Whitworth back to the corporal and took out a handkerchief and wiped his hands on it and then stuck it back into his jacket and took out the pencil and the envelope and they went through every bit of it, where Johnny had been yesterday and when he had come up along the river and what time he estimated he had arrived at the cornfield and what time he estimated he had waked up in the cornfield and everything but the why of it which the lieutenant didn't seem to think was worth going over again.

"Then you were cut off and couldn't get back across," the lieutenant said, writing furiously.

"What?"

"Well, isn't that your excuse?"

"Sort of," he said cautiously.

"What do you mean, 'sort of'?"

"Well, I don't know. It was dark."

"It wasn't dark this morning. Did you desert? Or were you trying to give yourself up?"

"Hell no," Johnny said. "Not exactly."

" 'Sort of, not exactly'," the lieutenant mimicked him. He turned to the corporal. "They can't tell a straight story, not any of them, the hangdog bastards. Now then," he said to Johnny, "you ran up here into the yard and found your gun wouldn't fire, isn't that it?"

"I didn't try to fire it," Johnny said. "It was too full of mud."

"Listen here Reb, you don't deny you were carrying the gun, do you?"

"No," he said. "I don't deny I had it with me." He considered telling him, for a moment, that he didn't know why, but he did have it with him, and realized this did not make any sense.

"Corporal," the jaybird lieutenant said, positively snapping out his words, "you take charge of this prisoner. Keep him right out in the open. I want Major Fricker to hear this. And MacLaren," he said to another Yank, "you go get that medical orderly. I want Major Fricker to hear that, too."

The Yankee corporal trotted off to do as he was told and the lieutenant started for the house. The remaining Yankee stuck his hands in his belt and rocked back and forth on his heels as if expecting Johnny to do something.

Hell, he wasn't going to move. These damned reserve troops were jumpy as cats. They were always spoiling for a little action and he didn't intend to oblige.

One of the staffers from the front porch who had been leaning over the rail taking an interest in things, now disentangled himself from the crowd and came down to stroll around, a big cigar in his mouth and his hands stuck in his pockets, his jacket hiked up at the hips.

The colonel came and stood and looked them over for a

while in silence. Then he turned to the corporal.

"What's all the fuss about?" the colonel said.

"Reb sharpshooter sir," the corporal said. He snapped a salute which the other did not bother to acknowledge.

"How'd he get here?"

"Came up in the yard this morning," the corporal began. But the lieutenant was already returning with another staffer, a major. The lieutenant was talking all the way.

"Captain Coffin told him to sit with the wounded, sir, that's why he's been out here so long," the lieutenant was saying. "It seems he got knocked down and was slightly injured."

The major was buttoning up his coat against the breeze. He was tall and redheaded and not half so crisp and alert as the young jaybird lieutenant. He looked tired, and he had one of those craggy, freckled faces that sags with fatigue, and a two day beard. The envelope with the lieutenant's interrogation was in his hand.

"These things can deteriorate sir, if you'll pardon the expression," the lieutenant said, "when you have a surgeon who takes it on himself to put aside a prisoner . . ."

"Alright," the major told him. "Alright." And the lieutenant stopped short.

"Let me see the gun," the major said, and held out his hand. "Hello Charlie," the major said to the colonel. "You're up early."

"You're pretty damned funny," the colonel said around the cigar. "I heard we were going across the river this morning."

The major held up the Whitworth, squinted along the barrel and shook his head.

"Not that I've heard. We might. Colonel, this is Flinch, aide to the adjutant. Flinch is just out from Ohio."

"Sir," the lieutenant said, flinging a salute.

"Hmm," the Colonel said, not bothering. "What have you got there?"

"Whitworth. New. Year old, it looks like."

"Sharpshooter's gun. It's full of mud. Loaded?"

298

The major tried to pull the trigger and the gun made its grinding noise.

"Can't tell. Maybe a spoiled cartridge."

The colonel put the cigar firmly between his teeth and took the Whitworth and he held the gun up and squinted at it.

"Well why not?" the colonel said. "Always some kind of target around a house. Might get lucky."

"That's what I'm afraid of. What time," the major said to the lieutenant, "did General Howard leave with General Course?"

"They went up to army HQ at five thirty. But that was half an hour before this reb came in."

"What's your side of the story?" the major asked Johnny.

"What story?" They all talked so fast he could hardly make any sense out of it.

"What did you come up here for?" the major asked him, bringing his words out one by one carefully.

"I don't know," he said.

"You'd better try to remember," the major told him. "There's a lot of difference in being sent to the rear with the wounded and being made to account for this."

There was a fair-sized crowd around them now, and when Johnny looked over their heads he could see Matt at the well, looking as if she knew something was wrong.

He looked back at the major quickly. If Matt saw his face she would know something was up and God knows what she would do about it. Things were bad enough as they were.

"His story doesn't hold water," the major said. "He claims he was down on the edge of the river near the next bridge in the diverted attack, but if you know where that was you can see it would put him on this side of the river to begin with. It also puts us,—Course's,—right in the way, which means he would have had to come through reserve troops for almost two miles to get here. That doesn't make sense."

"No, you just don't wander through a whole enemy division," the colonel agreed.

299

"This is one for the books," the major said. "If you call it bushwhacking, the order on it is pretty clear. And these people will go to any lengths to ambush, I learned that in Tennessee. Pot shots, shots in the back."

"Mmmh. We took one at Ringgold," the colonel said through his cigar.

"Uniformed?"

"What do you call uniformed? Course thought he was uniformed."

"But he'd fired on you."

"That don't make any difference. The army's not a law court, Otto. If we argued whether every man carrying a gun actually intended to use it, we'd be dead ducks by now."

"I didn't say it was a law court," the major said irritably.

"Don't be so damned touchy," the colonel told him, grinning. "If you've got any doubts get a length of rope."

The two Yankee officers looked him over thoughtfully.

"These rebs know what they're doing when they give out Whitworths," the colonel said. "You've done special detail, haven't you?" he asked Johnny. "Ever fired on a special target?"

There was no way to answer that. And behind them Matt was crossing the yard swiftly. She came up right behind one of the corporals and stood there, her face worried.

"Come now, we see the sights on this thing," the colonel said. What did you come over here for?"

But the dogrobber from the medical corps came up just then.

"Did you send for me, sir?" A bandy legged little Irishman.

"Yes. Do you recognize this reb?"

"Yessir, he's the one what came into the yard this morning. Early."

"What was he doing?"

"Why, he came at a run, sir. He was carrying that gun, there. The one the colonel's holding."

"Then what happened?"

"I hit him, sir. Knocked him down. I saw he was armed."

300

"Did you know it was a Reb?"

"I guessed it sir. You cant tell by the clothes no more, and this one was all muddy. But since he came chargin' right in I wasn't takin' no chances. We had a man on the operating table just then."

Matt moved up slowly behind the dogrobber, her hand held up, her fist knotted tightly against her breast.

"It's alright," Johnny said to her quickly. "It's going to be alright. Just don't mix in."

The Yankees stopped talking and stared at him, not noticing Matt.

"What's going to happen?" Matt cried.

"Nothing, nothing I tell you." But just to make sure she would know something, anything, he blurted out, "Ed's dead. And Byron's dead. Poor old Byron NeSmith. And Bobby Hart and Peed the sergeant. You remember Peed, sawmiller from over near Shadnor Church. They're all dead. I'm the only one left."

Now the Yankees turned and saw Matt standing there with her fist pressed hard against her breast and her face white, her mouth turned down at the corners in fear, staring at him, every now and then lifting that hand and pounding it against herself as if she would beat the pain out of it by force.

"It's alright," he said in a rush, "for God's sake don't let them see you're scared, will you? Listen, if you want to do something, see that somebody carries a message to Aunt Mill about Ed. I'm glad I don't have to do it. All the boys, all the Jonesboro boys are piled up in the woods over at Babb's. I guess somebody will find them sooner or later."

It wasn't what he wanted to say, and he had the despairing feeling that he would never get the chance to say half of what he wanted to say to her, ever. It was no use. He was just bitter and angry that they had to spill it out in front of these sharp-talking strangers who had no damned business in on any part of it.

"If it wasn't for you and Anna I'd never have come back," he said. "I'd never want to see this place again."

301

"They ain't hurt us," she said finally.

The Yankees stood looking from one to the other, taking it all in.

"Mrs. MacLeod," the major said in a queer, patient voice, "do you know this young man?"

Matt nodded, not looking at him.

"Would you mind telling me who he is?"

"His name's MacLeod, too," the jaybird lieutenant put in. "He said his name was MacLeod. I put it on the interrogation report."

"Then this is his mother?" the major said.

"Aunt," Johnny told him. "This is my aunt."

The major turned and looked at him then.

"And you live here? That is, when you're not with the reb army?"

"Yes."

"So, being near your own home last night, you decided to come on in."

"No, not exactly."

"You came home to see your family."

"Sort of."

"Why did you run into the yard? Didn't you see the troops, the hospital, here?"

"Yes, I saw them."

"But you came up anyway."

"I guess so."

"Why?"

Johnny looked around at the circle of faces, beyond them the Confederate wounded under the tree, all watching, the guard at the well, out of earshot but straining to catch something. Just beyond the colonel's shoulder he saw Anna come out onto the backporch and stand with her hand on the railing post and her body leaning forward as though she had stopped in the moment of descending the three steps to the yard, her foot hesitating over air. She had seen him at once and he could tell her by her look that she couldn't understand what was going on and she was puzzled and a little afraid.

302

The whole length of the yard was between them—the whole earth and then some—and when their eyes met they were joined by that one look as though there was no space or barrier or trouble to interfere. The black curls of Anna's hair were lifting and falling in the touch of the cool wind and she was as sweet and beautiful and far away as ever.

"Can you tell me why?" the major was asking.

"Why what?" he said, looking back at the redheaded Yankee.

The man looked at him, baffled.

"Listen, major," Johnny said quickly. All else fell away because it wasn't important. "Listen major, would you do me a favor? Would you let my wife bring me a drink of water? They wouldn't let her come near me before and I'd surely like to have a drink of water and a word with my wife whatever y'all decide to do. I'd thank you very much."

For a moment the major looked at him as though he'd given sure proof that he was a stark, raving lunatic and then he turned and all the others turned and they looked behind them and saw Anna standing there on the steps and no one said a word.

"Major?" he asked him.

The redheaded Yankee turned back to him.

"Could you do that for me?"

The major looked down at the interrogation report on the envelope and then slowly folded it up and put it into his jacket and looked at the colonel who had taken the cigar out of his mouth to laugh.

"Damn," the major said.

This made the colonel laugh harder.

"Corporal Andersen," the colonel said, still laughing, "go bring Major Fricker's compliments and ask the young lady if she will be so kind as to fetch her husband a cup of water."

"Sit down," the major told Johnny irritably. "Go sit down with the reb wounded and meditate, damn you. And don't get up, whatever the reason."

"I want to thank you," he said to him, but the major turned

on his heel and walked off toward the front porch, leaning forward slightly with his hands behind his back, his friend the colonel with him, talking and laughing. The jaybird lieutenant trailed them, feathers drooping.

The Yankee corporal, Andersen, made him sit out to one-side of the Confederate wounded, away from the rest, so that, as he told him, he could keep an eye on him.

"You got off slick," the corporal said. "If it wasn't for the major you'd 've had your neck stretched by now."

He didn't bother to answer. He was damned glad to be where he was instead of hanging by the neck from one of the yard trees, and he knew it and he didn't have to have it pointed out.

Anna was coming from the well with a glass pitcher in her hands. She was wearing a big cotton apron like Matt's but underneath was the old yellowflowered dress he liked so much and she was carrying the pitcher ever-so-carefully, a little water sloshing over the top. She had a tin cup, an army cup, hooked in her little finger.

Oh my God, he thought, Anna, be careful. Where did that pitcher come from, and that tin cup?

The wind caught her skirts and lifted them out bell shaped and her hair blew to one side like a long dark scarf. She looked straight at him, coming quickly as she carried the pitcher, her eyes dark and anxious.

"You stay where you are," the corporal warned him. "You ain't got special leave, not by a long shot. Besides that, you got a long wait afterwards, til we make up a detail of prisoners."

He didn't mind. He had all the damned time in the world, he told himself. All the time in the world, no matter what happened.

Anna was close, so close he could almost reach out and touch her, and she lifted the pitcher so that he could see and know, and she smiled.

304

MUSTER ROLL OF COMPANY *I*

✪✪ *30th Regiment Georgia Volunteer Infantry*
Army of Tennessee C.S.A.
Clayton County, Ga. ("*Clayton Invincibles*")

Dollar, Chaney A., Captain, Sept. 25, 1861. Resigned Mar. 14, 1864.

Mann, John F., 1st Lieutenant, Sept. 25, 1861. On detached duty as Enrolling Officer Dec. 31, 1862. No later record.

McConnell, John L., 2nd Lieutenant, Sept. 25, 1861. Retired May 14, 1862.

Stewart, James H., Jr., 2nd Lt., Sept. 25, 1861. Retired May 14, 1862. Elected 2nd Lt. of Co. D, 44th Regt. Ga. Inf. June 15, 1862. Killed at Spotsylvania, Va. May 10, 1864.

Huie, Elijah, 1st Sergeant, Sept. 25, 1861. Elected Jr. 2nd Lt. June 1863; 2nd Lt. Mar. 14, 1864. Wounded, date and place not given. Admitted to Way Hospital at Meridian, Miss. with wound Jan. 12, 1865. No later record.

Tanner, George W., 2nd Sergeant Sept. 25, 1861. Private May 14, 1862. Roll for Dec. 31, 1862, last on file, shows him present. No later record.

Smith, John M., Appointed Musician of Co. I, 10th Regt. Ga., Inf. May 27, 1861. Transferred to Co. I, 30th Regt. Ga. Inf. and appointed 3rd Sergeant Sept. 25, 1861. Private May 14, 1862. Wounded at Chickamauga, Ga. Sept. 19, 1863. Captured near Nashville, Tenn. Dec. 16, 1864. Released at Camp Chase, O. June 11, 1865. (Born in Butts County, Ga. Sept. 18, 1836.)

Anthony, Jesse S., 4th Sergeant Sept. 25, 1861. Elected Jr. 2nd Lt. June 1864. Captured at Nashville, Tenn. Dec. 10, 1864. Released at Johnson's Island, O. June 16, 1865. (Born at Jonesboro, Ga. in 1839.)

Hamrick, Jackson H., 5th Sergeant Sept. 25, 1861. Private May 14, 1862. Roll for Dec. 31, 1862, last on file, shows him present. No later record.

Buchanan, Josiah H., 1st Corporal Sept. 25, 1861. Appointed 2nd Corporal May 14, 1862; 1st Sergeant June 1863. Wounded through left ankle and permanently disabled, at Chickamauga, Ga. Sept. 19, 1863. Examined by Medical Board, pronounced unfit for field duty be-

305

cause of gunshot wound, in left ankle and furlough extended, Mar. 30, 1865. (Born in Fayette County, Ga., Oct. 1, 1841.)

McKown, Elias H., 2nd Corporal Sept. 25, 1861. Private May 14, 1862. Captured at Atlanta, Ga. July 22, 1864. Sent to Nashville, Tenn., thence to Louisville, Ky., thence to Camp Chase, O., where he was paroled and transferred to City Point, Va. for exchange, Mar. 4, 1865. Received at Boulware & Cox's Wharves, James River, Va., Mar. 10, 1865. No later record.

Cook, Thomas G. L., 3rd Corporal Sept. 25, 1861. Appointed 4th Corporal May 14, 1862. Captured near Nashville, Tenn. Dec. 16, 1864. Released at Camp Chase, O. May 15, 1865.

Langston, Francis M., 4th Corporal Sept. 25, 1861. Private May 14, 1862. Captured in Clayton County, Ga. in 1864. Took oath of allegiance to U. S. Govt. at Louisville, Ky. and released to remain north of Ohio River during war. Oct. 14, 1864.

Abercrombie, Collville, Private Sept. 25, 1861. Admitted to 1st Mississippi C.S.A. Hospital at Jackson, Miss., with acute diarrhoea, in 1863. Returned to duty May 27, 1863. Died in 1863.

Abercrombie, Kellett H., Private May 13, 1862. Discharged, disability, May 18, 1862.

Adams, William T., Private Sept. 25, 1861. Died at Yazoo City, Miss. July 2, 1863.

Adamson, Augustus Pitt, Private Sept. 25, 1861. Appointed 3rd Corporal in 1862; 1st Corporal Aug. 1863. Wounded in left hip at Chickamauga, Ga. Sept. 19, 1863. Captured at Calhoun, Ga. May 17, 1864. Paroled at Rock Island, Ill. and transferred to Point Lookout, Md. for exchange Feb. 25, 1865. Received at Boulware & Cox's Wharves, James River, Va., Mar. 5, 1865. Admitted to Jackson Hospital at Richmond, Va. on account of debility, Mar. 7, 1865. Furloughed for 30 days Mar. 8, 1865. (Resident of Ga. since Mar. 20, 1844.)

Adamson, James R., Private Sept. 25, 1861. Captured at Nashville, Tenn. Dec. 16, 1864. Died of chronic diarrhoea at Camp Chase, O. Mar. 5, 1865.

Adamson, Samuel T., Private Sept. 25, 1861. Wounded and disabled at Atlanta, Ga. July 22, 1864. Captured at Jonesboro, Ga. Sept. 1, 1864. Released at Camp Douglas, Ill. June 13, 1865. (Resident of Ga. since 1847.)

Adamson, William J., Private May 1, 1862. Died in Newton, Miss. hospital July 1863.

Adamson, William R., Private Sept. 25, 1861. Captured at Nashville, Tenn. Dec. 16, 1864. Released at Camp Chase, O. June 12, 1865. (Born in Ga. in 1845.)

306

Allen, Benjamin Z., Private May 1, 1862. Wounded at Jonesboro, Ga. Aug. 31, 1864. Captured at Jonesboro, Ga. Sept. 6, 1864. Released at Camp Douglas, Ill. June 17, 1865. (Born in Heart County, Ga. Sept. 10, 1842.)

Allen, John Y., Private Sept. 25, 1861. Killed at Jonesboro, Ga. Aug. 31, 1864.

Allen, Joseph M., Private Aug. 1, 1862. Wounded at Pine Mountain, Ga. June 14, 1864; Jonesboro, Ga. Aug. 31, 1864. Pension records show he was wounded and permanently disabled at Franklin, Tenn. Nov. 30, 1864.

Allen, Morris H., Private Sept. 25, 1861. Transferred to Co. D, 1st Battn. Ga. Sharpshooters Aug. 1, 1862. Died in General Hospital in Mississippi Aug. 21, 1863.

Allen, Seaborn M., Private Sept. 25, 1861. Transferred to Co. D, 1st Battn. Ga. Sharpshooters Aug. 1, 1862. Roll dated Sept. 10, 1864, last on which borne, shows him absent without leave.

Allen, William S., Private May 1, 1862. Appointed Sergeant. Captured near Jonesboro, Ga. Sept. 2, 1864. Released at Camp Douglas, Ill., May 17, 1865.

Ansley, Joseph G., Private Sept. 25, 1861. Pension records show he was wounded and disabled at Chickamauga, Ga. Sept. 19, 1863.

Anthony, William Q., Private Sept. 25, 1861. Appointed 2nd Sergeant May 14, 1862. Captured near Atlanta, Ga. Sept. 8, 1864. Exchanged at Rough and Ready, Ga. Sept. 19-22, 1964. Killed at Franklin, Tenn. Nov. 30, 1864.

Askew, Thomas Jefferson, Private Sept. 25, 1861. Pension records show he was wounded at Nashville, Tenn, Dec. 15, 1864.

Barton, Robert M., Private Sept. 25, 1861. Captured and paroled at Yazoo City, Miss. July 13, 1863. Surrendered, Tallahassee, Fla., May 10, 1865, and paroled there May 18, 1865.

Barton, William D., Private May 1, 1862. Sick at Camp Young, Ga. Dec. 31, 1862. Pension records show he relapsed from measles May 1, 1863. (Born Sept. 9, 1834.)

Barton, Yancey M., Private May 1, 1862. Captured near Jonesboro, Ga. Sept. 1, 1864. Exchanged at Rough and Ready, Ga. Sept. 19-22, 1864. No later record.

Baxley, Joel, Private Sept. 25, 1861. Appointed 5th Sergeant in 1862. Admitted to 1st Mississippi C.S.A. Hospital at Jackson, Miss. with chronic diarrhoea, Aug. 25, 1863, and deserted from said hospital Sept. 3, 1863.

Baxley, Merriman, Private May 1, 1862. Roll for Dec. 31, 1862, last on file, shows him present. No later record.

Belcher, Henry C., Private Sept. 25, 1861. Roll for Dec. 31, 1862, last on file, shows him present. No later record.

Berry, John T., Private Sept. 25, 1861. Captured at Nashville, Tenn. Dec. 16, 1864. Sent to Louisville, Ky., thence to Camp Douglas, Ill. Received at Camp Chase, O. Jan. 4, 1865, where he died of chronic diarrhoea, Apr. 20, 1865. Grave #1898, Camp Chase Confederate Cemetery.

Betterton, Adolphus D., Private May 1, 1862. Captured at Nashville, Tenn. Dec. 16, 1864. Sent to Louisville, Ky., thence to Camp Chase, O., Jan. 6, 1865, where he was released May 16, 1865.

Boynton, Elijah Winston, Private Sept. 25, 1861. Roll for Dec. 31, 1862, last on file, shows him present. No later record. (Died in Campbell County, Ga. Feb. 6, 1906.)

Boynton, Moses Thomas, Private May 1, 1862. On detail duty as forage master at Camp Young, Ga. Dec. 31, 1862. No later record.

Bradberry, Francis E., Private Sept. 25, 1861. Roll for Dec. 31, 1862, last on file, shows him present. Pension records show he was at home, sick, close of war. (Born in Henry County, Ga., in 1833.)

Bray, Jesse N., Private May 1, 1862. Captured at Nashville, Tenn. Dec. 16, 1864. Sent to Louisville, Ky., thence to Camp Douglas, Ill. where he was released May 17, 1865.

Bray, William A., Private Sept. 25, 1861. Captured near Nashville, Tenn. Dec. 16, 1864. Released at Camp Chase, O. June 12, 1865. (Born in Ga.)

Brown, George W., Private Mar. 18, 1863. Died at Canton, Miss. June 3, 1863.

Camp, Andrew J., Private May 1, 1862. Wounded in right foot at Calhoun, Ga. May 16, 1864. Received pay at Columbus, Ga. Nov. 26, 1864, for services from July 1, 1863, to June 30, 1864. No later record.

Camp, Joseph S., Private Sept. 25, 1861. Wounded at Jonesboro, Ga. Aug. 31, 1864. Captured at Nashville, Tenn. Dec. 16, 1864. Released at Camp Chase, O. June 12, 1865. (Born in Clayton County, Ga. Aug. 13, 1845. Died at Confederate Soldiers' Home, Atlanta, Ga. Feb. 26, 1929. Buried at Orchard Hill, Ga.)

Campbell, Elijah D., Private Oct. 21, 1862. Wounded in right arm, necessitating amputation above elbow, and captured at Franklin, Tenn. Nov. 30, 1864. Paroled at Camp Chase, O. in 1865. Released at Fort McHenry, Md. May 9, 1865.

Carnes, James W., Private Sept. 25, 1861. Roll for Dec. 31, 1862, last on file, shows him present. Pension records show he was wounded at Chickamauga, Ga. Sept. 19, 1863, and was on detail duty on account of wounds from 1863, to close of war.

308

Carnes, John O., Private May 1, 1862. Furloughed for 60 days July 7, 1863. No later record.

Carnes, William E., Private Sept. 25, 1861. Disabled by disease. Surrendered, Tallahassee, Fla. May 10, 1865, and paroled there May 18, 1865.

Chriswell, Charles, Private Sept. 25, 1861. Discharged, overage, Aug. 21, 1862.

Conine, James W., Private Aug. 1, 1862. Captured near Nashville, Tenn. Dec. 16, 1864. Died from abscess at Camp Chase, O. Mar. 22, 1865. Grave #1733, Camp Chase Confederate Cemetery.

Conine, William P., Private Sept. 25, 1861. Wounded at Jackson, Miss. July 16, 1863. Captured at Calhoun, Ga., May 18, 1864. Transferred from New Orleans, La. for exchange May 23, 1865.

Cook, Ellsberry B. (or *Ellis B.*), Private May 1, 1862. Discharged, disability, Dec. 1, 1862. Died in 1863.

Cowan, Thomas F., Private May 1, 1862. On detached duty at Atlanta, Ga. June 4–Dec. 31, 1862. No later record.

Crow, Meredith (or *Merida*), Private Aug. 1862. Captured at Rough and Ready, Ga. Sept. 7, 1864. Released at Camp Douglas, Ill. June 17, 1865. (Resident of Ga. since May 15, 1826.)

Dailey, John F., Private Dec. 30, 1861. Admitted to French's Division Hospital at Lauderdale Springs, Miss. July 18, 1863, and was in said hospital Aug. 31, 1863. No later record.

Dailey, Philip J., Private Sept. 25, 1861. Wounded through left hand and arm and permanently disabled at Jackson, Miss. July 16, 1863. Died Nov. 20, 1900.

Dailey, William E., Private Sept. 25, 1861. Wounded at Chickamauga, Ga. Sept. 19, 1863. Captured at Rough and Ready, Ga. Sept. 9, 1864. Died of small-pox at Camp Douglas, Ill. Dec. 30, 1864.

Daniel, James C., Private Aug. 1, 1862. Captured near Nashville, Tenn. Dec. 16, 1864. Released at Camp Chase, O. June 12, 1865.

Davis, Elijah S., Private Sept. 25, 1861. Discharged, disability, May 17, 1862.

Dickson, Sherman G., Private Sept. 25, 1861. Wounded at Chickamauga, Ga. Sept. 19, 1863. Accidentally killed in Clayton County, Ga. in 1865.

Dickson, William W., Private Sept. 25, 1861. Appointed 3rd Sergeant May 14, 1862. Captured near Nashville, Tenn. Dec. 16, 1864. Released at Camp Chase, O. June 12, 1865. (Born in Ga.)

Dodson, John E., Private Sept. 25, 1861. Transferred to Co. D, 1st Battn. Ga. Sharpshooters Aug. 1, 1864. No later record.

Dollar, William H. See Private, Co. H.

Drewry, Nicholas B., Private Sept. 25, 1861. Appointed Assistant

Surgeon Nov. 7, 1861. Elected 2nd Lt. of this company May 14, 1862. Resigned Dec. 1862. Appointed Assistant Surgeon C.S.A. (to rank from Jan. 21, 1863), June 10, 1863. Assigned to duty at Atlanta, Ga. and was serving there Dec. 1863. Pension records show he was on detail in Medical College at Atlanta, Ga. June 1, 1865.

Duke, James W., Private Sept. 25, 1861. Discharged by civil authority Aug. 18, 1862. Died at Charleston, S. C. Apr. 1863.

Estes, Ira Allen, Private May 1, 1862. Sick at Camp Young, Ga. Dec. 31, 1862. Pension records show he was sent to hospital near Savannah, Ga., where he remained until Mar. 1863. Sent to Mississippi June 1863, where he contracted fever. Sent to Dalton, Ga. Mar. 1864, and from there to Atlanta, Ga. Overcome by heat at Peachtree Creek, Ga. July 1864, and was sent home. Unable to return. (Born in Ga. Apr. 22, 1833.)

Evans, James F., Private Oct. 1, 1861. Sick in Savannah, Ga. hospital Dec. 31, 1862. Killed at Chickamauga, Ga. Sept. 19, 1863.

Evans, John B. (or James B.), Private June 11, 1862. Sick in Savannah, Ga. Hospital Dec. 31, 1862. Furloughed for 30 days from C.S.A. General Military Hospital #4, at Wilmington, N. C. Jan. 30, 1863. No later record.

Farr, William B., Private Sept. 25, 1861. Pension records show he was wounded in arm at Jackson, Miss. July 16, 1863. Wounded in right thigh, permanently disabled and captured at Nashville, Tenn. Dec. 16, 1864. Sent to Louisville, Ky., from thence to Camp Douglas, Ill. where he was released June 12, 1865. (Born in Fayette County, Ga. Jan. 6, 1844.)

Fuller, Judge Warner, Private Sept. 25, 1861. Appointed 3rd Corporal May 14, 1862. Transferred to Co. A, 9th Battn. Ga. Light Artillery July 1, 1862. Captured at Cumberland Gap, Tenn. Nov. 9, 1864. Transferred from New Orleans, La. for exchange May 23, 1865. (Born in Ga.)

Gallman, George W., Private Sept. 25, 1861. Died at Savannah, Ga. May 6, 1862.

Gallman, John M., Private Sept. 25, 1861. Roll for Dec. 31, 1862, last on file, shows him absent, sick at Camp Young. Appointed 3rd Cpl. Aug. 1863.

Guice, Benton G., Private Sept. 25, 1861. Wounded at Chickamauga, Ga. Sept. 19, 1863. Paid on Apr. 23, 1864, for services from July 1, 1863, to Feb. 29, 1864. No later record.

Guice, John, Private Sept. 25, 1861. Wounded at Jackson, Miss. July 16, 1863. Received pay Oct. 31, 1863. No later record.

Guice, Thomas N., Private Feb. 7, 1864. Received pay at Atlanta, Ga. June 20, 1864.

Hamilton, Hezekiah L., Private May 1, 1862. Appointed 4th

Corporal in 1863. Admitted to General Hospital at Savannah, Ga. Apr. 25, 1863. Died at Atlanta, Ga. June 11, 1864.

Hamrick, Noah R., Private Sept. 25, 1861. Roll for Dec. 31, 1862, last on file, shows him at home, sick. Pension records show he was sick in hospital at close of war.

Hancock, Charles E., Private 1864. Wounded at Franklin, Tenn. Nov. 30, 1864, and captured there Dec. 18, 1864. Admitted to U.S.A. General Hospital at Nashville, Tenn. Dec. 25, 1864, and died there of wounds Apr. 6, 1865.

Hancock, Choiner T., Private Mar. 15, 1862. Discharged, overage, Aug. 1, 1862.

Harrison, Benjamin A., Private Sept. 25, 1861. Discharged, disability, Apr. 1, 1862.

Holbrook, Green B., Private May 1, 1862. Substitute for James G. McKown. Admitted to 1st Mississippi C.S.A. Hospital at Jackson, Miss. Aug. 27, 1863. Returned to duty Oct. 7, 1863. No later record.

Huie, Albert A., Private 1864. Captured at Nashville, Tenn. Dec. 16, 1864. Died of pneumonia at Camp Chase, O. Mar. 7, 1865. Grave #1583, Camp Chase Confederate Cemetery.

Huie, George W. Jr., Private Sept. 25, 1861. Roll for Dec. 31, 1862, last on file, shows him present. No later record.

Huie, George W. Sr., Private Sept. 30, 1861. Appointed 5th Sergeant May 14, 1862. Died in 1862.

Huie, James C., Private Sept. 25, 1861. Died at Savannah, Ga. Mar. 31, 1862.

Huie, Joseph H., Private Sept. 25, 1861. Elected Jr. 2nd Lt. May 14, 1862; 2nd Lt. in 1863. Wounded at Chickamauga, Ga. Sept. 19, 1863. Elected Captain Mar. 14, 1864. Wounded and captured at Atlanta, Ga. July 22, 1864. Released at Johnson's Island, O. June 16, 1865. (Born in Ga. 1837.)

Huie, Mathew H., Private May 1, 1862. Captured at Calhoun, Ga. Mar. 17, 1864. Took oath of allegiance to U. S. Govt. at Rock Island, Ill. and enlisted in U. S. service, but was rejected by mustering officer, Oct. 11, 1864. (Born in Ga.)

Huie, Robert L., Private 1864. Died in 1864.

Huie, Robert T. S., Private Sept. 25, 1861. Captured at Atlanta, Ga. July 22, 1864. Paroled at Camp Chase, O. and transferred to City Point, Va. for exchange Mar. 4, 1865. Received at Boulware & Cox's Wharves, James River, Va. Mar. 10–12, 1865. No later record.

Huie, William A., Private Mar. 13, 1862. Captured near Chickamauga, Ga. Sept. 19, 1863. Died, debility, at Camp Douglas, Ill. June 13, 1865.

Hurdle, William B., Private Sept. 25, 1861. Appointed 2nd Corporal Apr. 1862. Private Sept. 1863. Captured at Macon, Ga. Apr.

20–21, 1865. (Born in North Carolina in 1832.)

Idson, Thomas, Private Sept. 25, 1861. Died at Griswoldville, Ga. Jan. 2, 1862.

Johnson, Francis M., Private Sept. 25, 1861. Killed at Atlanta, Ga. July 22, 1864.

Johnson, John T., Private. Pension records show he was wounded in left leg four inches above ankle, resulting in partial paralysis to left side, at Jonesboro, Ga. Aug. 30, 1864. (Born in Ga. July 4, 1833.)

Kennedy, John B., Private, May 1, 1862. Died of disease at Newton, Miss. July 13, 1863.

Langston, William F., Private Sept. 25, 1861. Transferred to Co. D, 1st Battn. Ga. Sharpshooters Aug. 1, 1862. Captured at Yazoo City, Miss. July 13, 1863. Died of typhoid fever in General Hospital there July 26, 1863.

Lawrence, William N., Private Sept. 25, 1861. Died in Newnan, Ga. hospital in 1864.

Lawson, William A., Private Sept. 25, 1861. Appointed 4th Sergeant May 14, 1862. Wounded at Jackson, Miss. July 16, 1863. Admitted to French's Division Hospital at Lauderdale Springs, Miss. July 18, 1863. Wounded and disabled at Franklin, Tenn. Nov. 30, 1864. Admitted to St. Mary's Hospital at West Point, Miss., on account of wounds, Jan. 10, 1865. No later record.

Lites, Joseph E., Private Sept. 25, 1861. Appointed 1st Corporal May 14, 1862. Private Aug. 1863. Wounded through right leg and knee at Murfreesboro, Tenn. Dec. 7, 1864. Captured at Columbia, Tenn. Dec. 22, 1864. Released at Camp Chase, O. June 13, 1865. (Born in Henry County, Ga. Mar. 5, 1843. Died at Confederate Soldiers' Home in Atlanta, Ga. Sept. 13, 1925. Buried in Forest Park, Ga.)

Mayfield, John R., Private Nov. 1861. Died Nov. 1863.

McKown, James G., Private May 1, 1862. Roll for Dec. 31, 1862, last on file, shows him present. No later record.

McKown, Joseph W., Private May 1, 1862. Captured at Nashville, Tenn. Dec. 16, 1864. Died of pneumonia at Camp Chase, O. Mar. 20, 1865. Grave #1713, Camp Chase Confederate Cemetery.

Meeks, William W., Private July 1, 1862. Died in General Hospital at Augusta, Ga., May 24, 1863.

Niles, Henry T., Private May 1, 1862. Captured near Nashville, Tenn. Dec. 16, 1864. Released at Camp Chase, O. June 12, 1865.

Ozburn, Robert S., Private Sept. 25, 1861. Captured at Chickamauga, Ga. Sept. 19, 1863. Held prisoner at Nashville, Tenn., Louisville, Ky., Camp Douglas, Ill. and New Orleans, La., and exchanged at latter place May 23, 1865. (Born in Ga. in 1845.)

Peace, John W., Private Sept. 25, 1861. Transferred to Co. D, 1st

Battn. Ga. Sharpshooters Aug. 1, 1862. Captured near Nashville, Tenn. Dec. 16, 1864. Released at Camp Douglas, Ill. June 10, 1865.

Sanders, Henry M., Private Sept. 25, 1861. Died Nov. 6 or 10, 1861.

Sanders, Jesse T., Private Sept. 25, 1861. In Breckenridge's Division Hospital at Marion, Miss. Aug. 31, 1863. Died in Clayton Co., Ga. July 1864.

Simmons, Stephens S., Private May 1, 1862. On detached service at Atlanta, Ga. June 4–Dec. 31, 1862. No later record.

Smith, Allen C., Private Sept. 25, 1861. Pension records show he was wounded at Jackson, Miss. July 16, 1863, and, being unfit for further duty, was sent home. Reported to Gen. Wofford at Atlanta, Ga. (Born in Henry County, Ga. Mar. 20, 1846.)

Smith, Francis P., Private Sept. 25, 1861. Discharged, disability, at Thunderbolt, Ga. Apr. 1, 1862. (Born in Ga.)

Smith, Joseph B., Private May 1, 1862. Transferred to Co. D, 1st Battn. Ga. Sharpshooters as 1st Corporal Aug. 1, 1862. Killed by explosion of shell at Genesis Point, Fort McAllister, Ga., Feb. 12, 1863.

Stephens, Alexander A. (or *Stevens*), Private Sept. 25, 1861. Died of disease at Camp Hardee near Savannah, Ga. June 5, 1862.

Stephens, Curran P., Private Aug. 1, 1862. Discharged, furnished substitute.

Stephens, Green B., Private May 1, 1862. Captured near Nashville, Tenn. Dec. 16, 1864. Received at Camp Chase, O. Jan. 4, 1865, and released there June 12, 1865. (Born in Ga. May 9, 1838.)

Stephens, James Jackson, Private Sept. 30, 1861. Discharged, over-age, at Savannah, Ga. Aug. 1, 1862. (Born in Madison County, Ga. in 1820.)

Stephens, Joel M., Private Sept. 25, 1861. Captured at Rough and Ready, Ga. Sept. 4, 1864. Died of typhoid fever at Camp Douglas, Ill. Feb. 1, 1865.

Stephens, John W., Private Aug. 1, 1862. Wounded at Chickamauga, Ga. Sept. 19, 1863. Wounded in right leg and captured at Murfreesboro, Tenn. Dec. 7, 1864. Admitted to Division #4, U.S.A. General Hospital there Dec. 11, 1864. Released July 20, 1865. (Resident of Ga. since Dec. 9, 1843.)

Stephens, Leroy E., Private. Pension records show he was disabled by disease contracted in service at New Hope Church, Ga. May 25, 1864. (Born in Clayton County, Ga. Apr. 25, 1844. Died at Confederate Soldiers' Home in Atlanta, Ga. Feb. 8, 1929. Buried at Tanner's Church near Ellenwood, Ga.)

Stephens, Thomas J., Private Sept. 25, 1861. Pension records show he was wounded in right leg and permanently disabled at Jonesboro, Ga. Aug 31, 1864. (Born in Ga. Aug. 3, 1840.)

Stephens, William Martin, Jr., Private Sept. 25, 1861. Transferred from 1st Mississippi C.S.A. Hospital at Jackson, Miss. to General Hospital July 14, 1863. Pension records show he was wounded in left foot at Powder Spring, Ga. May 25, 1864, left arm was disabled, result of vaccination, in 1864, and he was at home, sick, close of war. (Born in Ga. Dec. 27, 1837.)

Stephens, William M., Sr., Private Sept. 25, 1861. Discharged, overage, Aug. 18, 1862.

Stephens, William P., Private Sept. 25, 1861. Discharged by civil authority Aug. 18, 1862.

Tanner, Branch B. See Private, Co. E.

Tanner, Joseph J. M., Private May 1, 1862. On detached duty at Atlanta, Ga. June 4–Dec. 31, 1862. No later record.

Thirlkill, George W., Private Sept. 25, 1861. Died at Savannah, Ga. Apr. 28, 1862.

Thomas, William L., Private Sept. 25, 1861. Transferred to Co. D, 1st Battn. Ga. Sharpshooters Aug. 1, 1862. Wounded at Jonesboro, Ga. Aug. 31, 1864. No later record.

Thomas, William R., Private Sept. 25, 1861. Transferred to Co. D, 1st Battn. Ga. Sharpshooters Aug. 1, 1862. Captured at Nashville, Tenn. Dec. 16, 1864. Took oath of allegiance to U. S. Govt. at Camp Douglas, Ill. and mustered into 6th Regt U. S. Vols. Mar. 25, 1865.

Toney, Seaborn E. (or *Sebron E.*) Private May 1, 1862. Captured at Nashville, Tenn. Dec. 16, 1864. Released at Camp Chase, O. June 12, 1865. (Born in DeKalb County, Ga. Nov. 30, 1835.)

Touchstone, William H., Private Nov. 28, 1862. Roll for Dec. 31, 1862, last on file, shows him present. No later record.

Trammell, Thomas J., Private May 1, 1862. Transferred to Co. E, in exchange for Branch B. Tanner, Mar. 20, 1862. Died in 1862.

This company was ordered to the relief of Gen. Finegan at East Florida Oct. 4, 1862, by order of Gen. Mercer. Arrived at Jacksonville, Fla. Oct. 6, 1862, and remained until Oct. 11th, when they returned to Camp Hardee, arriving there Oct. 15, 1862. Ordered by General Mercer to Coosawhatchie, S. C., where they remained one day, and returned to Camp Hardee Oct. 1862. Left Savannah on Dec. 14, 1862, and arrived at Wilmington, N. C. Dec. 19, 1862.

Further records of I Company are not available, but the company distinguished itself in the Atlanta campaign under Hood and fought at Jonesboro, August 31 and September 1, 1864. All personnel began service September 25, 1861, except as noted. The muster roll is reproduced here in the general interest and is not intended to bear any relation to the fictional characters in this novel.

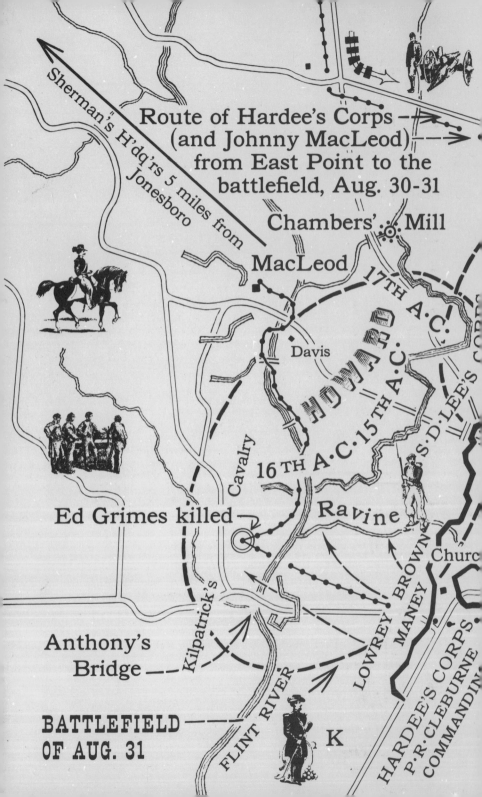

Route of Hardee's Corps — →
(and Johnny MacLeod) — →
from East Point to the
battlefield, Aug. 30-31

Sherman's H'dq'rs 5 miles from
Jonesboro

Chambers'. Mill

MacLeod

Davis

17TH A.C.

HOWARD

16TH A.C. 15TH A.C.

S. D. LEE'S CORPS

Cavalry

Ed Grimes killed

Ravine

Churc

Anthony's
Bridge

Kilpatrick's

LOWREY BROWN MANEY

HARDEE'S CORPS
P. R. CLEBURNE
COMMANDING

BATTLEFIELD
OF AUG. 31

FLINT RIVER

K